TREASURE COAST

GOLD

For Jodi

MAY you enjoy

HAppy Holidays

12-11-04

TREASURE COAST

GOLD

Paul E. McElroy

TREASURE COAST MYSTERIES, INC.
43 Kindred Street
Stuart, Florida 33494

www.TreasureCoastMysteries.com

Printed in United States of America

Publication date January 2004
1   3   5   7   9   1 0   8   6   4   2
Copyright © 2003 by Paul E. McElroy
All rights reserved.

Publisher
Treasure Coast Mysteries, Inc.
43 Kindred Street
Stuart, FL 34994
(772) 288-1066

LIBRARY OF CONGRESS CATALOGING-IN-PUBLICATION DATA:
McElroy, Paul E.

Treasure Coast GOLD by Paul E. McElroy
p.   cm.

ISBN 0-9715136-2-7

1. MacArthur, Phillip (McCray, James - Mack) Fictitious character – Fiction.
2. Undercover agents – Florida - Fiction
3. Florida – Fiction   I. Title.
PS-------   T --------------- ------------------

Books by Paul E. McElroy

Treasure Coast DECEIT

ISBN 0-9715136-0-0

January 2002

Treasure Coast ARCHIPELAGO

ISBN 0-9715136-1-9

March 2003

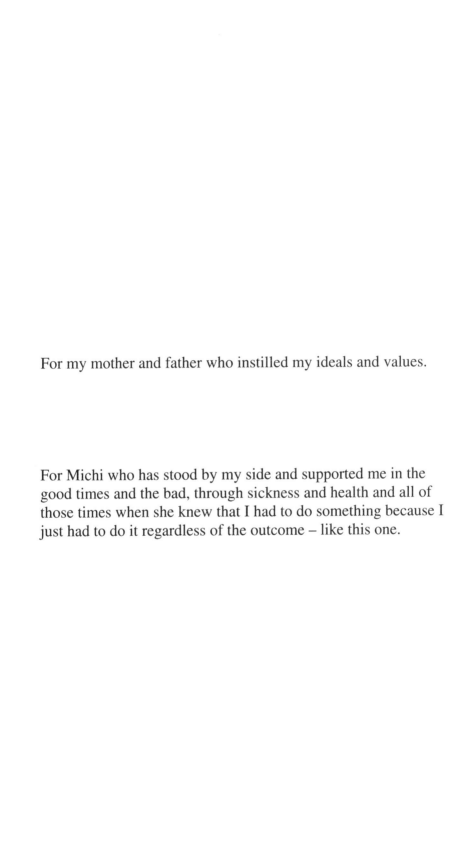

For my mother and father who instilled my ideals and values.

For Michi who has stood by my side and supported me in the good times and the bad, through sickness and health and all of those times when she knew that I had to do something because I just had to do it regardless of the outcome – like this one.

FLORIDA'S 'TREASURE COAST'

Appropriately named for the twelve ship *Spanish Plate Fleet* that sank along it's shores on July 30, 1715 Florida's *Treasure Coast* stretches along the Atlantic coast from Jupiter to Sebastian sixty miles to the north. Tucked in between Highway 1 and the Atlantic Ocean the *Treasure Coast* ambles along luring visitors to its Gulf Stream kissed beaches of fine sand.

Amateur treasure hunters strolling along the sandy beaches with metal detectors in hand attempt to appear disinterested in the trinkets that they scoop up from the sand in wire-meshed baskets.

The *Cartagena* and *Vera Cruz* Spanish treasure fleets arrived in Havana in May 1715 on their way back to Spain. They planned to replenish their meager stores and sail a few days later. The captain of the *Vera Cruz Fleet* had 1,000 chests of silver in the cabin beneath his own and had stuffed the holds of his other ships with gold bullion and silver ingots. The *Cartagena Fleet* was loaded with silver and gold coins from the mints in Columbia, gold jewelry from Peru and 166 chests of Columbian emeralds.

The combined ships, now named the *Plate Fleet* departed Havana the morning of July 24, 1715 to enter the Gulf Stream and proceed northward along the Florida coast. However, on July 30 a hurricane struck the fleet. All but one of the ships had its bottom ripped out on coral reefs and sank resulting in the death of more than 1,000 Spaniards and the scattering of treasure from *Sebastian* to *Stuart*. Historical records indicate that much of the treasure was salvaged, but the *Urca de Lima* has yet to be found.

Hopeful treasure hunters from around the world come to the *Treasure Coast* to try their luck. Why don't you visit us too? You might catch sight of Rat, Mack or Tina and can even wet a line in hopes of catching a record setting *'cat-snapper'*.

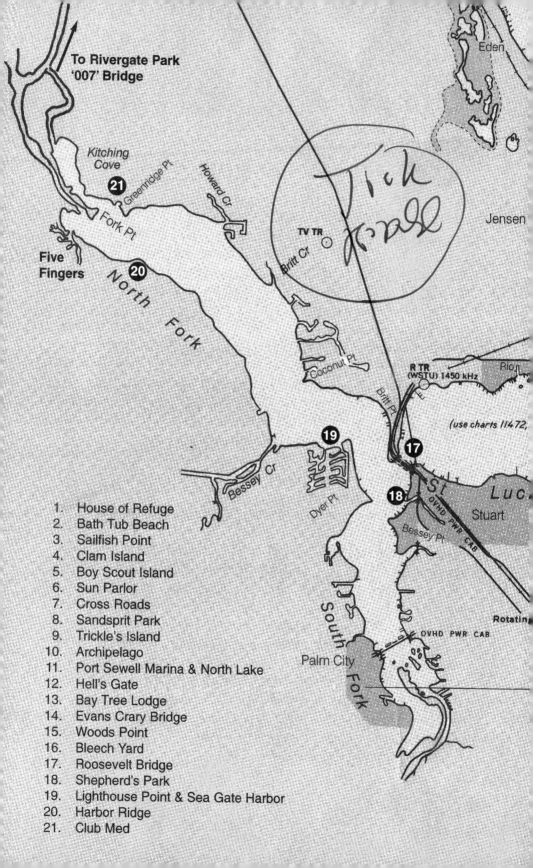

To Rivergate Park
'007' Bridge

Kitching Cove

Greenridge Pt

Howard Cr

21

Fork Pt

Five Fingers

20

North Fork

TV TR

Britt Cr

Jensen

Eden

Coconut Pt

R TR
(WSTU) 1450 kHz

Rio

(use charts 11472,

Britt Pt

19

17

St Luc.

18

Bessey Cr

Dyer Pt

Stuart

OVHD PWR CAB

Bessey Pt

Rotating

OVHD PWR CAB

South Fork

Palm City

1. House of Refuge
2. Bath Tub Beach
3. Sailfish Point
4. Clam Island
5. Boy Scout Island
6. Sun Parlor
7. Cross Roads
8. Sandsprit Park
9. Trickle's Island
10. Archipelago
11. Port Sewell Marina & North Lake
12. Hell's Gate
13. Bay Tree Lodge
14. Evans Crary Bridge
15. Woods Point
16. Bleech Yard
17. Roosevelt Bridge
18. Shepherd's Park
19. Lighthouse Point & Sea Gate Harbor
20. Harbor Ridge
21. Club Med

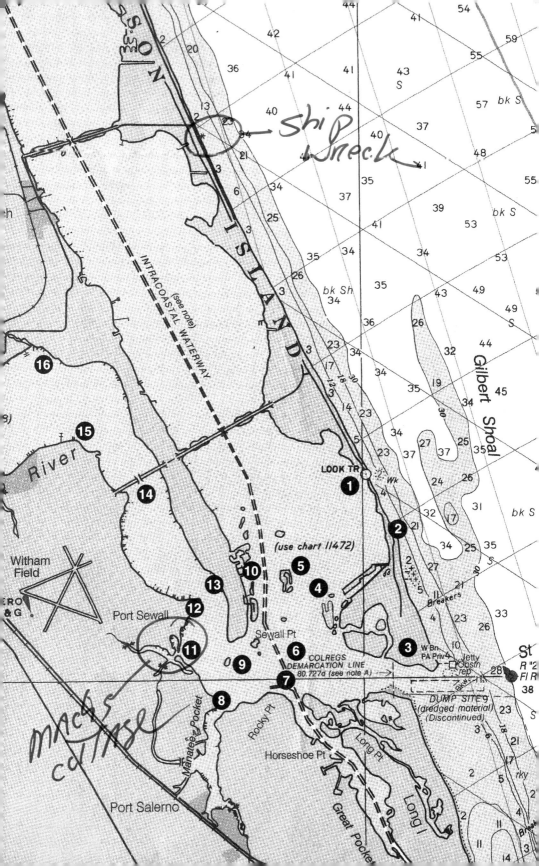

Prologue

Truth is indeed stranger than fiction. Wouldn't you agree?

There are many rumors about buried pirate treasure along the sandy coast of south Florida, but recorded history provides little documentation. Locals whisper among themselves about what their grandfather found years ago while walking along the beach after a storm or cached in a coral cave high on a ridge. However, they immediately become silent when a stranger approaches.

Several years ago I met a cultured lady at the Stuart Post Office. Her car battery had failed and needed a jump-start that I willingly provided. After that encounter whenever we met she never failed to share a tantalizing local historical tidbit with me.

During one of our innocuous conversations she mentioned that she knew the location of a shipwreck on the beach. She was working in a local inn, since long gone, in August of 1949 when a hurricane with winds exceeding 160 miles per hour dealt Stuart a violent blow. During the eye of the hurricane, roughly a period of twenty minutes, she left the safety of the inn and walked out onto the beach. Thirty feet of beach sand was cut away by the violent wind and the wreckage of a wooden ship was exposed. She never mentioned another word about that ship until recently when I had the opportunity to spend some time with her.

What follows is a work of fiction, embossed with historical facts and a sprinkle of imagination for flavor. How much of this tale is true and how much is not? I can't say, but I certainly enjoyed penning it for your enjoyment.

Epigraph

"The irrationality of a thing is no argument against its existence, rather a condition of it."

Nietzsche

Chapter
1

James 'Mack' McCray arrived in sleepy Stuart Florida from Chicago in March of 1995 and in four months became a solid, but often controversial, member of the local community. His temperament required a significant amount of re-adjustment.

Monday July 18, 1995 dawned as another sunny day in Paradise. It was 7:17 A.M. and sunshine streamed through the east windows of the cottage. Mack reluctantly crawled out of bed at the urgent urging of the black and white patches cat named 'Kitty' who insisted that it was time for him to go outside. After two cups of black coffee, three scrambled eggs and two strips of crisp bacon accompanied by whole-grain toast and a glass of orange juice Mack was ready to face the day. He strolled out onto the front porch with a cup of hot coffee in his hand and sat down in one of the two white wicker chairs. His 6' 4" height allowed him to easily raise his feet onto the wooden porch railing. He closed his eyes and drifted back to the day in March when he exited the Florida Turnpike onto Martin Downs Boulevard in search of Port Salerno and Port Sewall Marina.

It didn't take much searching to find Indian Street because it runs east and west off of U.S. 1. He crossed the Willoughby Creek Bridge, took a right turn onto Old St. Lucie Boulevard, passed Whiticar's Boat Works on his right, made a sharp bend to the left and one hundred yards past Whiticar's on the right side of road sat Port Sewall Marina. The gray heavily weathered Cape Cod style cottage perched atop a boathouse. A vacant lot in front of the private marina served as the parking lot. It was once heavily graveled, but the aggressive St. Augustine grass had taken its toll and only small areas of pea gravel peeked from among the patches of ragged grass. Mack's title was Port Sewall Marina Manager.

Tina Louise McShay, a feisty red headed Assistant State Attorney in the West Palm Beach office inherited the marina in 1982 after her parents were killed in an automobile accident. A suspicious fire burned down the main house in 1987 and she chose not to rebuild it. Tina utilizes the marina to store her classic fifty-four foot sailboat and treat her friends to weekend getaways. Thirteen wooden steps lead down the east side of the cottage to the boathouse. Twin finger piers extend out from each side of the boathouse. The east side piers are reserved for sailboats and those on the west side for powerboats.

The boathouse is exactly what a wooden boathouse should be. It smells of saltwater, tar, fish and musty cloth. The single boat slip provides enough room for Mack's 22-foot center console fishing boat matched with a 250-horsepower supercharged Yamaha outboard. The boathouse outside access door leading to North Lake operates via an electronic garage door opener. A master control unit is mounted on the left hand inside wall above the light switch.

Mack was nestled in the arms of *Morpheus* the ancient Greek God of Sleep. His deep slumber was interrupted by the bleating of a tinny horn echoing across the parking lot accompanied by screeching tires in the remaining pea gravel. Ralph's green pickup truck slid to a stop and Mack didn't move a muscle to acknowledge his arrival.

Ralph was a long time Port Salerno resident and made his living as a commercial fisherman netting mullet and other food fish in the St. Lucie and Indian Rivers. During the summer months when the weather was nice he ventured outside the St. Lucie Inlet into the Atlantic Ocean in search of fish that provide prime dollar at the Port Salerno fish house.

Ralph was almost six feet tall, middle-aged, redheaded and slightly balding. He preferred to wear well-worn blue jeans, white T-shirts and a pair of white rubber boots recognized as the trademark of commercial fishermen. Ralph is not easily riled, or confrontational, and often serves as a soft-spoken mediator. He provides a buffer between Mack and those in the community who want to pry into his background. Ralph didn't know much about Mack except that he grew up in Fort Myers on the west coast of Florida, attended Florida State University, spent four years in the United States Air Force and spent the last several years in Chicago.

Ralph strolled through the parking area and the sparse pea gravel crunched under the soles of his white rubber boots. He tromped down hard on the first wooden porch step in an attempt to get Mack's attention, paused for effect, and carefully watched Mack's face for any sign of recognition. He didn't move. Ralph tromped down hard with his right foot on the second step. Mack flinched in his chair and almost flipped over backwards. His eyes opened wide and he spilled the remaining tepid coffee into his crotch.

"Ralph! What the hell are you doing here so early in the morning? I thought I was going to have a peaceful day all to myself."

An ear-to-ear grin spread across Ralph's flushed face as he rested his left shoulder against the corner post of the porch. "You know better than that. There's some good news! Tina's back at work in West Palm Beach and you don't have to worry about her until Friday night when she comes up here for the weekend. Rat was out cat snapper fishing until almost daylight and he's hunkered down in the bowels of his broken down sailboat over at Shepherd's Park. You won't be hearing from him all day." Ralph smiled and sat down on the top porch step.

"If that's the good news what's the bad news?"

"I'm not sure," Ralph responded. "You've been home for four days and should know what's going on around here."

"I have to go back to the Veterans Administration Clinic on Willoughby Street for a check up. This letter came in while I was in Hawaii last week. I have to have another physical examination in order to keep my VA benefits current." Mack passed the letter to Ralph.

Ralph's quickly scanned the letter, folded it and handed it back to Mack. "Do you really want to go back to the VA Clinic after what happened to you the last time? You look perfectly healthy to me. They must have a good reason for having you come back."

"They want me to come back for an annual physical. If I don't they'll drop me from the program. I can't allow that to happen because I don't have any health insurance benefits here. My appointment is at three o'clock this afternoon."

"I saw something real strange yesterday afternoon and again this morning when I was fishing the outgoing tide for pompano with frozen sand fleas on the grass flat north of Trickle's Island. Two guys in an 18-foot Jon boat were taking some kind of readings between Hell's Gate and Sewall's Point. They were dragging something behind their boat and writing down things in a notebook. It looked fishy to me."

"I don't think it's anything sinister. They're most likely marine surveyors taking readings to update the maps and charts of this area."

"You could be right about that. One guy held something in his hand that looked like a surveyor's instrument. He'd look through it, put it down and write down something in his notebook. They'd make a run from Trickle's Island up to the Evans Crary Bridge and then back down again. They'd pull the thing they were towing behind the boat out of the water, open it up and make more notes."

"What did it look like?"

"It was shiny, I think it's made out of brass, and had a propeller on the back like a torpedo."

"It's most likely a patent log. Years ago, before the advent of electronic navigation equipment such as LORAN and GPS, navigators used patent logs to estimate distance based on the number of revolutions the propeller made in a given period of time. It's an old-fashioned method but it can be fairly accurate if used properly."

"What are you going to do to waste time before you go to the VA Clinic?" Ralph asked and looked at Mack as if he had a thought of his own as to what Mack should say.

"I read in today's paper that a guy who used to be a local treasure hunter is giving a talk and doing a book signing at the Blake Library at one o'clock. I'm going to stop by and check it out. He might be able to provide some interesting background about this area."

"If you want to get background about this area you should talk to the old man who spends all day fishing for pompano over by Boy Scout Island. He moves over to the Hell's Gate grass flats in the evening. His family came to this area in the late eighteen hundreds and he can probably tell you anything you want to know about rumors of buried pirate treasure."

"I'm sure he knows a lot about the history of this area, but I seriously doubt he did any serious investigation. I'm a history buff and I read about the famous Spanish treasure fleet that wrecked along the Treasure Coast in 1715 in a hurricane. I doubt there's much left of the treasure because of all the people who have been salvaging it over the years. I probably won't learn anything about any hidden pirate treasure, but it gives me something to do before I go to the VA Clinic. I might stop by Gordo's Tackle Shop on the way over and see what he's been up to."

"I saw Deputy Elmo at the Queen Conch for breakfast. I told him about those two guys I saw poking around Hell's Gate and Sewall's Point the last couple of days. He didn't seem to think too much of it either, but he said that he'll go by and check on them today."

"Ralph what are you doing for the rest of the day? Why don't go to the library with me? You might get some local history and a little culture under your belt. You could use a little culture."

"I think I'll go home and take a nap. I'm going over to the flats by Hell's Gate about an hour before dark to do a little pompano fishing on the outgoing tide. After that I'm running over to Sewall's Point and set a couple of gill nets for mullet. They were in there hot and heavy all day yesterday. They run in the channel between the oyster bar and Trickle's Island. I thought

I'd check out what those two guys were doing when I saw them walking in the water on the end of Sewall's Point. They tied little red and yellow ribbons on some of the trees," Ralph added.

"Don't mess around with those ribbons! They're surveyor's markers and they're going to use them for future reference. Don't get in their way! They're professionals and are paid a lot of money for what they do. They're probably checking out the old Spanish Land Grant markers."

"Don't worry. I'm not going to disturb their precious little plastic ribbons. I just want to get my gill net set and catch some mullet, but it doesn't hurt to look around a little bit. I thought I'd count how many red and how many yellow ribbons there are and make some notes like they did." Ralph's smiled and winked at Mack. "Somebody should check them out."

"You don't have the qualifications needed to evaluate how good a job they did at surveying that area. I advise you to stay well away from there until they're done with their work." Mack lifted his feet off the railing and placed them flat on the porch as he sat up straight in the chair. "If you're going home to take a nap you might as well get on your way. I've got a few things to straighten up around here before I leave for the library. It'll be just my luck that everybody in town shows up to ask where I was last week." Mack rose to his feet and gestured toward Ralph's truck. "I'll be back here about four o'clock. Call me if you want some company to go pompano fishing. Oops! I forgot. I have to take my boat over to Billy Bob's Marina this afternoon for a bottom job."

"No problem." Ralph stood up and held out his hand. "Give me your boat keys and I'll drop it off for you. I'll stop by here between five and five-thirty. Be sure you're ready." Ralph winked, turned and marched down the parking lot toward his pickup truck. "I'll see you then." He waved backward in Mack's general direction.

After Ralph pulled out of the parking lot and headed toward Old St. Lucie Boulevard Mack walked out into the parking lot and turned back toward the cottage to survey his surroundings.

The faded gray wooden Cape Cod structure was a far cry from his bachelor apartment on the forty-fifth floor of the John

Hancock Building in downtown Chicago. However, during the last four months the cozy structure became his home and he was satisfied with his simple life. He leaned against the trunk of an enormous banyan tree to rest his eyes from the bright sun and gazed south toward the cottage. The sides of the cottage and boathouse were constructed of native cypress and had weathered to a dull gray. The vertical four-paned windows were accented by white trim. The silver tin roof was slanted at a sharp pitch to reflect the sun's withering rays and deflect the heavy summer rains. The concrete walkway leading to the front porch was flanked on each side by a concrete, Greek classical style urn containing a flowering tropical plant. The roof was festooned with several antennas and satellite dishes. An eight-foot diameter parabolic antenna was enclosed by a woven wire fence closure. Local residents thought it was for a satellite television receiver. It was best that they didn't know it's true purpose.

Two large rhombic antennas suspended from giant, brown ceramic insulators attached to trees in each corner framed the parking lot. Rhombic antennas are directional and used for very long range, high frequency radio reception. These antennas faced both east-west and north-south.

As Mack walked back towards the cottage he glanced at the small television camera mounted under each corner of the roof. The cameras were mounted inside clear plastic housings and looked like giant upside down fishbowls. The wooden stairway of thirteen steps each led down to the twin wooden finger piers that extended from each side of the boathouse. The boathouse could only be accessed by the separate covered stairway that led down from the front porch. He stepped onto the porch and looked overhead at the two sets of halogen floodlights mounted under the eaves. "*It all looks secure,*" he muttered to himself as he opened the screen door.

Before Mack took the first step into the cottage a green and white Martin County Sheriff's patrol car sped in from Old St. Boulevard slid to a stop in the marina parking lot. The driver's side door opened and Deputy Elmo stepped out with a grin on his face that rivaled a Cheshire cat. He tipped his cowboy hat in

Mack's direction with his right hand and addressed him. "Mornin' Mack. How's this fine day finding you?"

"I guess I'll make it if people will just leave me alone. What can I do for you this morning?" Mack gestured toward the two white wicker chairs that sat side by side on the front porch.

Deputy Elmo paused with his right foot on the top stair leading to the porch. "I saw Ralph over at the Queen Conch this morning for breakfast. He's concerned about a couple guys he saw sneaking around Sewall's Point making some kind of measurements and writing stuff down in a notebook. Do you know anything about it?"

"I don't know any more than what he told you. He told me the same thing. My guess is that they are surveyors re-mapping the Sewall's Point area to update the local charts."

"He said that they tied yellow and red plastic ribbons on some trees at the end of Sewall's Point."

"That's a normal thing for surveyors to do. I don't think it's anything to be concerned about."

"Nobody ever saw those guys before except when they came into town a couple of days ago. Nobody knows where they are staying or what their names are. I thought I'd take a run over there in the boat this afternoon and ask them a few questions. What're your plans for today?"

"I'm going to stop by the Blake library at one o'clock to hear a guy give a talk about treasure hunting. Then I have to be at the VA Clinic at three o'clock for a physical. After that I'm going pompano fishing with Ralph over by Hell's Gate about five o'clock. If you're in the area stop over and we'll chat."

"It sounds like a good idea. I'll let you know what I find out about those two guys." Deputy Elmo tipped his hat, turned and walked back to his patrol car. He left the marina parking lot in a cloud of dust and a shower of loose pea gravel.

"I sure hope he's the last person who's going to come around here and bug me today," Mack muttered to himself as he opened the screen door and entered the cottage.

The cottage was a homey place and ideal for a single man. The front door opened directly into the small living room. The quaint cottage was about 800 square feet, more or less, in area. A stand-alone home entertainment center, with speakers at least four feet tall, and equipped with a television set and CD player dominated the northeast corner of the left wall. A fake brick fireplace, with a wooden mantle, was framed between two windows on each side. Above the mantle hung a painting of a gray haired man wearing a straw hat, and long-sleeved blue cotton shirt and khaki shorts. He was standing up in a green skiff and the open cast net leaving his outstretched arms arced in a perfect circle over a terrified school of silver mullet. The walls of the cottage were polished knotty pine.

The right side of the room featured a continuous bookcase constructed of polished dark wood, possibly mahogany, that ran from the southwest corner to the short hallway leading to the bathroom and the two bedrooms. The magnificent bookcase rose gallantly upward from the bare pine floor to the vaulted ceiling ten-feet above. A green throw rug formed the centerpiece of the floor. Two pea-green fabric-covered recliners and an oblong glass-topped coffee table mounted on a spindly-legged, gray driftwood base completed the living room's sparse furnishings. The pea-green recliners formed a divider between the living room and kitchenette.

There were no overhead air-conditioner ducts, or wall mounted air conditioning units in sight. A solitary ceiling–mounted, slow-moving, brass fan equipped with four wooden paddles stirred the stale, humid air around the room. An avocado-green refrigerator stood as a silent, tall sentinel on the corner next to the hallway. Next to it was an avocado-green electric range, followed by a short length, maybe three feet at most, of green plastic countertop leading to the corner and an avocado green ceramic sink. The white microwave oven stashed in the corner niche between the sink and electric range looked out of place.

The south side of the kitchenette featured a sliding glass door that opened onto a small deck overlooking North Lake. A 1950's vintage chrome-legged, plastic-topped, oblong dinette table and four matching chairs completed the furnishings.

Compared to his Chicago bachelors' pad the cottage's sparse surroundings seemed meager, but they were adequate for his needs. The crude wooden statue of *Kalai-pahoa*, the Hawaiian

Poison God, sat in a dark corner. Its yellow, clamshell eyes glowed and followed him as he walked across the kitchenette to deposit his coffee cup in the sink.

Mack had a lot to think about before he went to the VA Clinic. It was only 10:47 A.M. and he had time to take a short nap. Then he'd mosey over to Shrimper's in the Manatee Pocket for lunch before stopping by the Blake Library to hear the treasure hunter's lecture. He was mentally exhausted and needed time to think and gather his thoughts. He was concerned that someone would find out his true identity and he'd have to relocate once again.

Chapter 2

'*Brinng*!'

The sharp clattering of the obnoxious metallic telephone bell traveled across the room at the speed of sound, reverberated off the far wall of the living room entered through Mack's eardrums into the center of his brain. He tried to ignore the sound, but it was as piercing and obnoxious as the whine of a woman who wanted to go to Miami for the winter season.

'*Brinng*!'

Mack leaped out of the green recliner and made it across the kitchenette area in three long strides to reach the telephone before its obnoxious ringing began again in earnest. He jammed the plastic handset against the side of his head.

"Hello. Captain Mack here." He leaned back against the countertop and tried to regain his equilibrium as the blood rushed to his brain.

"Good morning Mack," whined the sultry female voice on the other end of the telephone line.

"Tina! What can I do for you this morning?" Mack grinned from ear to ear and began to closely examine his fingernails.

"I'll be tied up here in West Palm Beach all week with depositions and a felony trial. If I get out of court early on Friday afternoon I'll run-up there and we can go out to dinner at Indian River Plantation. How does that sound?"

"You're the boss. It sounds fine to me as long as you're going to pick up the check," Mack replied and continued to examine his fingernails.

"I'll pick up the check. You just make sure that everything in the marina is shipshape before I get there. Some friends of mine from the state attorney's office may come up Saturday and stay on their boat overnight. They want to meet the dolphins. Make room for their boat on the powerboat dock. They have a fifty-four foot Bertram and need lots of space."

"Yes ma'am. I'll see that they're well taken care of. Anything else?" Mack continued to study his fingernails and paused to burnish them against the side of his blue jeans.

"They'll want to fuel up when they get in and load on some block ice because they're going fishing Saturday afternoon. They want to go out to dinner at Shrimper's Saturday night. Sunday morning we're all going to brunch at Indian River Plantation. They'll leave about two o'clock and we'll have the rest of Sunday afternoon to ourselves."

"I'll make some notes on my calendar. Everything will be taken care of. Is there anything else?" Mack burnished the fingernails of his right hand against his blue jeans.

"Where are *Puka* and *Kea*? Do they miss me?"

"Those silly dolphins are in the river romping with their friends. I'm sure they miss you. Anything else?"

"No. That's it. I may not be able to call you for the rest of the week. I'm going to be working some late hours taking depositions and getting ready for a pre-trial run through."

"That's to bad."

"Don't get smart-mouthed. You do work for me, or did you forget that detail?"

"No ma'am. I didn't forget."

"If you need anything leave a message on my home voice mail."

'Click.' The telephone went dead and Mack realized the conversation had ended.

"Tina certainly has a way about her. She must have gotten some male chromosomes mixed up in the gene pool and doesn't realize that she's supposed to be female." Mack replaced the telephone handset on the switch hook and turned toward the living area. *"It's eleven-eighteen, I'd better grab some lunch at Shrimper's. Then I'll run down to the Blake Library and get a good seat for that guy's lecture."*

Mack pulled into the Blake Library parking lot at 12:47 P.M. figuring that he had enough time to look for a book on treasure hunting before the 1:00 P.M. lecture began. As he passed the check out counter the clerk waved at him and smiled. He waved back.

"I know who he is – he's an author," she remarked to a worker beside her. *"He's writing a book about Hawaii and was in here doing research a couple of weeks ago. I spotted him right away. I knew that he was an author and he pretended he was a regular patron, but I could tell. I can spot an author right away because of the way they talk and act – they are so cool."*

Mack decided to swing into the men's room before the start of the lecture. He drank several tall glasses of water at lunch because the crunchy grouper sandwich was very spicy. When he entered he heard a muffled voice from inside a toilet stall.

"Sssh! Be real quiet. Somebody just came in."

Mack thought he recognized the raspy voice. "Rat! Is that you?"

"Mack is that you?" Came back the whispered response.

"Yep. It's me. What are you doing in there and why are you whispering?"

"Black Jack and me are in here taking a bath. We gotta' be careful. Some guy wrote a book and told about us homeless guys cleaning up in here. We can't take a bath in the open anymore because of a new library policy about not taking baths in the bathroom. Isn't a bathroom a place to take a bath?"

"Rat it's difficult to explain, but this is a men's room not a bathroom. It's a technical point, but I won't tell on you. Have a good time." Mack rinsed his hands in the sink, dried them with a paper towel and left for the lecture hall.

The author was there to promote and sell his books. He vigorously delivered a dry narrative history of the 1715 Spanish Plate Fleet that he could probably recite in his sleep. He hinted that people walking along the beach after a bad storm often find gold and silver coins, but he didn't talk about pirates and their rumored treasure caches. After he had signed books for everyone in line and answered the most obvious questions several times the crowd disappeared. Mack stepped alongside him as he was packing his unsold books into a cardboard box.

"That was a great lecture. I'll bet that you know a lot more than you tell the general public."

Startled by Mack's less than subtle approach he stepped back from the table and took a deep breath before he responded. "Are you a treasure hunter?"

"No. I'm a fishing guide and have only lived in the area since March. I heard rumors about a pirate named Don Pedro Gilbert who apparently hung around Sewall's Point, lured ships onto Gilbert's Bar and plundered them after they went aground. I figured that just maybe he stashed some of his ill-gotten booty in the area. I thought I'd do a little snooping around here and there. Do you have any suggestions as to where I should begin?"

"You're really barking up the wrong tree. There wasn't any pirate treasure buried in this area. The local treasure hunters spend their time working the 1715 Spanish Plate Fleet wrecks that are spread between Fort Pierce and Sebastian. Wait a minute! I worked one lead several years ago that turned out to be a very expensive flop"

"Where was that?"

"About thirty years ago a woman out on Sewall's Point wanted to build a swimming pool behind her house and she called in a survey crew to make borings and check soil consistency. They broke through in several places less than five feet down and thought they'd found a tunnel. She called me and I went out there with a full crew. I offered to make a full survey of her property at my own expense and if I found anything we would split it. It cost me almost twenty-five hundred buck right out of my pocket! There was a tunnel there all right and it ran from her house in the direction of the bluff.

"What was in it?"

"We drilled a few test holes and dropped in some miniature cameras to take a peek. We found piles of leaves and the nicest otter den that you would ever imagine."

"What else did you find?"

"Nothing. It was a dry hole."

"Where's the property located?"

"I can't tell you exactly. The current owners wouldn't want half of Martin County digging up their back yard with picks and shovels. Just believe me that there's nothing there. I've been in the treasure hunting business a long time. If there was buried treasure there I'd have found it."

"You said the current owners. What happened to the woman who called you to check it out?"

"She changed her mind about a swimming pool and hired a black guy from Tick Ridge in Jensen Beach to dig a hole for a septic tank. Soon after that she sold the house and moved to New Orleans. She moved back here a few years later. Now she lives in Trailer Town."

"Where's that?"

"It's on Old Dixie Highway where it intersects with Martin Luther King Boulevard. She's not listed in the telephone book so you'll have to stop at the office and ask for directions."

"What's her name? Can you tell me that much?"

"Certainly. It's Lorna Belle Mobley."

"I've got a three o'clock appointment at the VA Clinic on Willoughby and it's two-seventeen now. I've got enough time to stop by and see her on the way. Thanks for your help."

"You're welcome. If you find anything keep in mind that I'm entitled to a five percent share."

Mack raced down East Ocean Boulevard, crossed the railroad tracks at Confusion Corner onto Colorado Avenue and turned left onto Martin Luther King Boulevard. Trailer Town was located on Old Dixie Highway at the intersection with Martin Luther King Boulevard. It had stood there for several decades and was the current hot topic of urban renewal for many people who considered it an eyesore.

Mack pulled his blue Ford F-150 pickup truck into the gravel, pothole pocked driveway of the trailer park and parked in front of a yellow, blue-trimmed trailer that sported a weather beaten sign labeled 'OFFICE'. A thin man was slopping blue paint onto a wooden porch railing with the finesse' of a street paving machine.

He was slight of build and perhaps six feet tall. His stiff blue jeans were held in place above his bony hips by a wide leather belt festooned with a brass belt buckle replica of a *Peter's* shotgun shell box. He wore a black and white checked long-sleeved cotton shirt that sported flashy, obviously very cheap imitation mother of pearl buttons. His weathered face was framed by large downward sloping 'mutton chop' sideburns and at least two days growth of black stubble intermixed with ragged swatches of white whiskers. His *Dallas Cowboys* baseball cap appeared to have gone through many a monsoon and dried off beside a smoky campfire. The right side of his jaw line bulged with a wad of chewing tobacco large enough to choke a steer.

Mack walked up to him and opened the conversation. "Excuse me. My name is Mack McCray and I'm looking for the manager."

"I'm the manager, at least I can say so on the days when my wife isn't here. My name's John Thomas. What can I do for you?"

"I'm looking for someone."

"Are you a cop or something? We can't give out information about our tenants to just anyone who walks up and asks."

The man frowned and spit a stream of black tobacco juice a good twenty feet toward a green chameleon perched on the side of a palm tree. The napping chameleon didn't see it coming and was obliterated by the black nastiness.

"He's going to learn not to sleep over there one of these days."

"No I'm not a cop. I'm a fishing guide and live in Port Salerno."

"I always wanted to be a fishing guide myself but I never figured that I had enough school learning to understand all the goobledy gook. I know how to get a boat around the water because I've done it all my life. I ain't never hit nothing in the river and I can find my way around Lake Okeechobee better than a bull gator in the middle of the night during mating season. I know every stump and rock in that lake like the back of my hand." His arms and hands flew in all directions like an animated puppet under the control of an unseen puppet master from above."

His vivid deep blue eyes snapped and flashed as his mouth ran at breakneck speed. Mack suspected he had swallowed a few too many cups of black coffee a few hours earlier.

"I'm fifth generation in this here town and my grandfather owned most of the land on John's Island that's now covered with million dollar homes. He sold it all off for about $250 during the depression." Never missing a beat he emphasized each point with his constantly darting hands the excited, overly exuberant cowpoke continued his egocentric rhetoric. "Up until a few years ago I was a hunting guide for a couple of the big ranches out by Lake Okeechobee. They raised pheasants, quail and ducks for their clients' entertainment. Rich folks came there from all over the world just to shoot birds.

I even guided once for a prince from Saudi Arabia. When we went out to the shooting blind to get set up for ducks he wouldn't sit down in the chair. I kept hearing him cough slightly under his breath like he was clearing his throat. I asked him if he was okay, but he never answered. He never made eye contact with me and held out a folded white handkerchief between his left thumb and forefinger and shook it in my face. He nodded with his head toward the aluminum-folding chair behind him and coughed like he was trying to clear a big goober out of his throat. Then I realized he was a clean freak and he expected me to dust off the chair before he would sit down.

He stood there with his arms folded and just stared out of the slit in the blind. I wiped off the back and seat real good and tried to hand the handkerchief back to him. He waved me away and pointed toward the legs of the chair. Then I realized he also expected me to clean off each of the legs. I dusted them off real good and gave him an 'okay' sign by making a circle of my thumb and forefinger and pointed at the chair. I even tried to give him back the handkerchief, but he waved it away. So, I stuffed it in my back pocket. I've still got it somewhere.

He brought four Italian-made shotguns with him and expected me to unpack, load and place each one out in front of him on the shooting bench. That was okay by me because I knew I would have to clean each one of them and put them back in the cases when we were done. Because he was some kind of prince in Saudi Arabia I expected to get at least a hundred buck tip for the day. When we got back to camp I made real sure that he could see me swabbing out each one of the barrels with lead solvent and cleaning each little nook and cranny with a clean rag. I used a brand new baby diaper for each shotgun. I packed the guns away real careful in their individual cases and returned them to the trunk of his Mercedes. When it came time for him to leave I opened the back door of the Mercedes for him and held out my hand for a tip. He waved me away and said something in a foreign language to the driver.

The driver unhappily got out and motioned me to follow him toward the rear of the car. He reached into his fancy chauffeur's britches' pocket and removed a wad of cabbage large enough to choke a manatee. He peeled right through the hundreds and fifties. When he reached the twenties he pulled one out and passed it over to me.

"The prince asked me to thank you for a very enjoyable outing. You were most courteous to his Highness and respected his special needs. He requested you for his guide when he returns to hunt again next week." The driver spun on his heel and returned to the vehicle.

"That was a real kick in the head. I spent all day dusting off the chair for his big behind and the best he could do was to tip me twenty bucks. I decided because he was a lousy tipper that I'd teach him a little lesson. All I had to lose was twenty bucks next week – if he booked me.

I walked around to the big shot's side of the car and made sure that he could see me through the window real good. I put my right finger next to my right nostril to block it off, tilted my head toward the ground and blew as hard as I could. Snot flew all over the place. The big shot stared out of the car window completely engrossed in what I did. Before he could say anything to the driver I closed off my left nostril and blew the snot out of the right side. I smiled, waved at him with my left hand and wiped my nose on my sleeve.

He didn't show up the following week. He returned a couple of weeks later and requested another guide for the day. That guide got a twenty dollar tip."

"What kind of place was that?" Mack raised his eyebrows and turned the palms of his hands upward in an inquisitive gesture.

"It was a private hunting club and used to entertain very special guests for very special reasons. There wasn't really much hunting because the birds were pen-raised and acted like barnyard chickens. The guides called it the 'dog and pony' show. While the guests ate breakfast in the clubhouse the guides were out in the dark planting pheasants and quail in the palmetto patches along well-worn Jeep trails through the piney woods.

The dogs were trained to act 'birdy' when they got close to those particular patches. The jeep driver pulled up right behind the dogs on point so our guests wouldn't have to walk more than ten feet. The birds were expecting to be fed and sometimes they ran out of the palmetto bushes right toward the hunters. We'd have to reach down and kick at 'em with our foot in order to get them to take off. There was many days that I waded through the palmetto bushes and chased the quail out the other side. I was always afraid a big rattlesnake might be curled up around one of the stumps. I was lucky." The exuberant hunting guide shifted his weight from one foot to the other in a feigned dance step utilizing the unspent adrenaline racing through his bloodstream.

"That must have been a very interesting job. Is the hunting club still open?"

"Nope. Florida Fish & Wildlife closed it down a couple of years ago because they caught a couple of state senators shooting mourning doves over a baited field. The birds are still there and turned wild because no one feeds them anymore. I slip in there with my pointer dogs a couple of times a year just to give the dogs some practice and keep the birds thinned out a little bit."

He locked his chubby thumbs into his belt loops and rocked back and forth on his heels. "Would you like to go out there and shoot a few birds with me tomorrow morning?"

"I can't. I have a fishing trip in the morning. I can't turn down three hundred bucks to go quail hunting. But I have a nice Ithaca twenty- gauge pump gun in my closet gathering dust."

"Do you want to sell it?"

"No. I don't. What are you doing now that you aren't guiding?"

"My wife and I manage this trailer park. We live here for free, except we have to pay our own utilities. Plus, a couple of years ago we started a cake business. We did thirty-six thousand in cakes last year. Plus, I pick up a few bucks guiding people on Lake Okeechobee during gator season. We do okay." He sat down on the porch steps to rest and looked up at Mack. "I ran my mouth so much that I forgot to ask you what I could do for you. Are you looking to rent a trailer? We've got some good ones open."

"No. I manage Port Sewall Marina and live on the premises."

"Isn't that the place that some hot shot female lawyer from West Palm Beach owns? I remember when her parents were killed in a car crash. The main house burned down a few years later and the local folks didn't think it was an accident. Somebody was trying to kill her. She was lucky that she was sleeping in the cottage over the boathouse."

"That's where I'm living for now. If she kicks me out I might have to come back and see you about one of those open trailers." Mack smiled. "I'm here to see Lorna Belle Mobley. Can you show me which trailer is hers?"

"She doesn't have a trailer here anymore."

"Where did she go?"

"She fell down, broke her hip and wasn't able to get up. She rolled around on the floor of her trailer for three days and almost died right there. She's lucky that my wife stopped by her trailer to collect the rent. She found her on the floor and called an ambulance. Lorna Belle was in really bad shape."

"What happened after that?"

"Her daughter came by to get her out of the hospital a week or so later. She's married to some big shot lawyer in Boston. She got Lorna Belle to sign a Durable Power of Attorney, moved her into a nursing home and sold her trailer. Nobody's seen her since. Lorna Belle's not coming out of there until the day she dies."

"Where's the nursing home?"

"Out in Palm City off Loop Road. Wait here and I'll get you the address."

Mack studied the ramshackle trailers and realized that if he hadn't gone to college on the GI Bill he might have wound up living here also.

The trailer park manager returned and handed Mack a folded slip of yellow tablet paper. "I wrote down the address. It's not hard to find. She's in room one twenty-six."

"Does she have any other relatives here?"

"Nope. She has one sister. The last I heard she was running a strip club in New Orleans. Don't tell anyone where you got the information. It wasn't from me."

"I never saw you before." Mack tipped his hat and headed for his truck. He pulled out of the Trailer Town at 2:47 P.M. and headed for the VA Clinic on Willoughby Boulevard.

The physical was fast, routine and uneventful. There was no pain except for the 'vampire test' blood sample required for a full blood scan. At the conclusion the doctor came into the examination room to give him the results.

"Mr. McCray you're in excellent physical health. Your total cholesterol is two hundred and twenty-five. It's a tad high. I want you to watch your diet and come back in six months for another evaluation. She clasped his medical records close to her chest, stood at least six feet away from him and stated, "You aren't going to get close to your medical file again. We both know what happened the last time you were here." The doctor spun around and silently fled the examination room.

Chapter 3

Mack arrived at the nursing home at the four o'clock shift change. Nurses and attendants flowed in and out of the main entrance without a glance at one another. He paused until there was a break in the foot traffic and approached the front door.

There was a sign mounted on the right side of the front door. *"For the safety of our guests please press the white button on the control box mounted alongside the door."*

Mack thought it strange for a door lock release button to be located on the outside of the door. There was a matching white button mounted on the inside door. Mack tested the alarm system by opening and closing the door without pushing the button. The alarm went off, but no one responded to it.

The door labeled *"Administrator's Office"* was closed. Mack turned the knob to open it so that he could check in and ask to see Ms. Mobley, but the door was securely locked. He walked to the end of the short hallway and stopped. A hand-printed sign posted on the wall indicated with a crude red arrow that rooms 100 to 140 were down the hallway to the left.

He opened the door and entered the dimly lit hallway. The putrid stench of stale urine permeated the air and overwhelmed Mack's senses. He gingerly touched the crotch of his pants to assure himself that he had not wet himself. Mack's nostrils cringed in terror and contorted in an effort to cut off the pungent odor, but he couldn't block out the horrific smell! It wouldn't go away. It sifted into his nostrils, clung to his nose hairs like beads of dew on the morning grass, enveloped his senses and drove itself into his brain.

A deep, probing, thrusting, sharp penetrating pain bored into his brain. It was as if the home was talking to him. *"You'll be here some day and we'll be waiting for you. We're very patient and we can outwait you. When it's time we'll welcome you and you'll embrace us. We'll take you away from your pain, remorse and sorrow and allow you to sit in silence and dream about the days gone by that can never be again. No one will care about you – except for us. We'll bathe, groom and feed you and see that you are adequately medicated. You'll not care about anything because no one will care about you. We'll care as long as you can continue to pay your monthly fees. In the end, when your funds run out, you will plead to stay with us, but we must cast you out. We will need your space for a patient that can pay. But don't worry about that day – at least not yet."*

An elderly woman seated in a wheel chair reached out for Mack with outstretched arms. He winced, closed his eyes and turned away. *"She's someone's daughter, perhaps someone's sister and perhaps even someone's mother. If she's a mother where are her sons and daughters? How could they permit their mother to live like this? Is there no memory in their souls for the many years that she tended to their needs? She nursed them when they were sick, fed them when they were hungry and changed their soiled diapers without complaint. Is there no room in their cozy home for her?"*

The crowded hallway reminded Mack of a cesspool of human waste cast off to waste away unseen until the cold uncaring fingers of Death reached out and freed their tormented souls from physical pain and mental anguish. Moaning men slumped over in wheel chairs stared ahead with unseeing eyes. Their heads lolled onto their necks as they urinated helplessly in their clothes. The odor of human waste permeated the stale air. Mack could not escape it. It clung to the fabric of his cotton shirt as a poignant reminder that he could do nothing for them. He continued down the dark, dank hallway of human misery, mental anguish and physical pain.

The nurse's station was in total disarray and there was no one there. Patients' manila file folders were scattered lying haphazardly on the counter. As he gingerly walked down the hallway he could see into the tiny rooms. Some patients were unclothed, or only half covered by a thin sheet, and the aroma of human excrement steamed out from every room. It was the epitome of *Dante's Inferno* without the flames. Human suffering was everywhere and Mack expected *Lucifer* himself, with pitchfork in hand, to leap from behind one of the open cell doors.

He continued down the hall toward Room 126 and tried to block out the moans and groans emanating from the darkened grottos. The ambiance was one of hopelessness, despair and frustration. Once in the home an inmate would not get out alive unless they ran out of funds for their care and were relegated to a state-run home for indigents. The other alternative was to waste away while draining whatever personal funds were available.

Mack thought to himself, *"When it comes my time will I become part of a storage facility filled with rotting human flotsam and jetsam?"* He reasoned that the Indian way of permitting the 'old ones' to walk alone into the forest with a small bag of pemmican to meet the Death Spirit on their own terms wasn't such a bad way. He pondered the Alaskan Aleut way of placing the 'old ones' on an ice floe and casting them adrift to face their fate. Either way seemed to be better than a slow death, extended by medication, in a nursing home.

When he reached Room 126 the door was wide open and an obese nurse was in the process of changing the urine-stained bed sheets. She paused and looked up at Mack as if to say, *"What the hell are you doing here?"* Mack beat her to it.

"Where can I find Lorna Belle Mobley?"

"Who wants to know?" She responded and stood up to face him with her hands on her hips.

"I'm her nephew. I was passing through town and wanted to stop and say hello."

"She's downstairs smoking in the lounge. She's been there for almost an hour and should be back up here any minute. You can wait for her here if you like."

"I think I will. Thank you. How come there aren't any family photos or mementos of any kind in sight?"

"She keeps knocking them off so we put them in a drawer. We took her cigarettes away because she almost burned the place down last month. If you need me call me by pushing that little white button alongside the door." The nurse sniffed and strode out of the room, paused in the hallway and stuck her head back in the doorway, "Here she comes now."

A white-haired woman spun into the tiny room in her battery-power wheelchair, stopped halfway through the doorway and looked up at Mack. "Who the hell are you and what do you want?" Her front teeth were rotten and her breath smelled like rotten tripe.

He bent down and smiled, "My name is Mack McCray. I stopped by to ask you a few questions for a book I'm writing about the area. The manager at Trailer Town told me how to find you. Will you please talk to me?"

"Don't push me young man! I'm like a badger. Don't corner me or you'll get hurt." They know me real good here. I like to smoke and when I want a cigarette I get one. They keep them at the nurse's station for me. They know they'd better watch me real good because I try to get away with anything I can. They know that." She chuckled through cracked lips and exposed her rotting teeth. "I'll try to help you if you help me into my rocking chair."

Mack lifted her out of the wheelchair and carefully guided her into the padded ladder-backed rocking chair.

"What do you want to know? I've lived here most of my life and I know most everything that's ever happened here." She rolled her eyes, crossed her arms over her chest and glared at Mack as if daring him to challenge her mental capacity.

"Lorna Belle I don't mean to be rude or obtrusive, but I understand that you lived here when some pirate gold was supposedly discovered on Sewall's Point. I'm going to tell you the story as I heard it." Mack flipped open a small spiral spring-backed notebook and pulled out a ballpoint pen to make notes.

"Chime in anytime that you want to make additions or corrections."

"A lot of things happened here years ago that people forgot about as time went by. Most of the old timers are gone now except for me and a few others."

"I'm going to tell you the story as I heard it." Mack snapped down the plunger of the ballpoint pen to expose the writing tip. "Are you ready?"

"I'm ready as I can be. Fire your best shot."

"I'm guessing that pirate treasure may have been buried on Sewall's Point. The pirate Don Pedro Gilbert spent a lot of time here, but there have been no reports of discovered pirate booty. I read that he made his headquarters in two places. One was at High Point on Sewall's Point and the other one was on a sandy ridge on Jensen Beach across the highway from where the Sand Club used to be years ago," Mack paused for effect.

"I don't know anything about pirates. They were here a long time before I got here."

"I also heard about a woman who lived on Sewall's Point and hired a black man from Tick Ridge to dig a hole for a septic tank shortly after a swimming pool company survey crew found a tunnel on her property."

"So what? There's no law against digging a hole for a septic tank is there?"

"There weren't many regulations for septic tanks back in 1965, but there are lots of them today. The story gets more interesting because shortly afterward the black man bought a large parcel of land on Tick Ridge and built a real nice house. He never worked again after that." Mack raised his pen from his pad and rubbed it alongside his nose. "Does this make any sense to you?"

"I never heard that story, but there were several wealthy black families living in Tick Ridge. I never got over there because we were told to stay away from that part of town."

"Do you think he found buried pirate treasure in that hole?"

"I remember hearing about somebody finding treasure behind their house on Sewall's Point. But I don't know who or where the house was."

"The woman who lived in that house moved away shortly afterward."

"So what?"

"I think that you were that woman."

"Maybe I was and maybe I wasn't. So what if I was?"

"Did he find any treasure when he was digging that hole?"

"Hell no! If he did I sure as hell wouldn't be rotting away in this dump!"

"Did a local treasure hunter come out and dig some test holes on your property?"

"Yeah! What a waste of time that was. He didn't know what he was doing. And didn't find a damn thing except an otter's den. He wanted to charge me for digging holes in my back yard."

"Who was the black man you hired to dig the hole for the septic tank?"

"His name is Frank Holmes. He was the maintenance man at the Sand Club when I worked there. The last I heard he was in a nursing home on Palm Beach Road. I haven't seen him in years." The frustrated woman rolled her eyes upward, tossed her arthritis-crippled hands into the air and allowed them to fall back in her lap. I wanted to go over to see him, but I can't drive anymore."

"If I took you over there would you ask him about the things we talked about?" Mack asked apprehensively.

"They won't let me leave this place without my daughter's okay and she a real bitch! Why don't you go over there yourself and talk to him? I'm sure he'd like to have a visitor."

"How do I find the place?" Mack responded.

"Go down East Ocean Boulevard until you hit Palm Beach Road. Make a right turn and go down about three-quarters of a mile. It's on the left-hand side of the road. Just walk in and tell them that you're there to see Frank. They'll probably bring him out in a wheelchair."

"Okay. I'll give it a shot. I'll let you know what I find out." Mack rose from his chair and tucked his pen back into his shirt pocket. "Is there anything you would like me to tell him for you?"

"Tell him I asked about him and I'll get over there to see him when I can." She rocked back and forth in her rocker and smiled. "I'll get out of here soon. My daughter put me in here after my hip surgery last month. She's going to get me out as soon as it's healed up and I can walk."

"I bet you will!"

Mack thought to himself. *"Little does she know that her daughter sold everything she owned, cleaned out her bank accounts and sold her trailer. She probably won't even come back for her mother's funeral. That would cost money."*

"I own a real nice house trailer in Trailer Town over by the Stuart Post Office. I've lived there for almost thirty years. Everybody in town knows me."

"Yes. I was by there today and I saw your trailer. It's real nice."

"I'm never going back there. My daughter took all of my stuff to the dump and sold my trailer."

"How did you know?"

"My neighbor Fannie Mae Bridges came by yesterday and told me. We went to high school together. If you get to see Frank ask him what we found on the beach in front of the Sand Club after the hurricane. If his mind's still working he'll remember. He'd better."

"What do you mean he'll remember what you found there?"

"In August of nineteen forty-nine a big hurricane ripped through here. The winds reached one hundred sixty miles per hour and ripped the wind gauge off the Stuart Feed Store. When the eye was going through it calmed down and we went out on the beach to see how much damage the wind and high waves had caused. Thirty feet of sand was gone from the beach and part of an old ship was sticking up out of the sand."

"How'd you know it was a ship?"

"There were several wooden ribs and part of a cabin sticking up. My sister Hattie Lou was visiting me from New Orleans and she'd seen a lot of shipwrecks along the Gulf Coast. She knew what it was right off."

"What did you do?"

"We poked around it for awhile and ran back inside the Sand Club when the backside of the hurricane started coming through and the wind kicked up again. My dumb ass sister hung around outside until the wind almost blew her butt away."

"Did you go back out and look for the ship after the hurricane went past?"

"Of course we did, but it was gone. The wind blew the sand back and covered it up."

"Thanks for your time. I'm on my way to see Frank and I'll tell him that you asked about him. I'll come by and see you again soon."

As Mack headed toward East Ocean Boulevard he mulled over the recent conversation. *"She just collaborated that someone found treasure on Sewall's Point. It's obvious that she found something because she moved away and the guy that dug the hole became rich overnight. I hope the old guy can shed some light on it for me."*

Many things swirled through Mack's mind as he headed down East Ocean Boulevard toward Palm Beach Road. *If the old man found gold in the hole I wonder how he explained it to his family? Do they know the details? I have to watch who is within earshot when I talk to him. The last thing I want to do is jeopardize the old guy's safety."*

Mack turned into the driveway of the nursing home at 4:47 P.M. The front door opened into a large foyer and hallway. Several ancient warriors and wrinkled queens confined to their wheelchairs waited patiently in various strategic locations of the sitting room area. Each of them gazed at him with a wistful far-a-way look in their cataract-clouded eyes as if they expected to see a concerned family member come through the door to rescue them from their living hell. Each of them smiled at Mack as though they recognized him. He realized that most of them wouldn't recognize themselves if they were looking into a mirror directly in front of them.

He crossed the sitting room area and headed toward the reception desk. A tall, well-dressed black woman in her mid-thirties clutched a black leather briefcase between her hands and rested it on top of the counter. She was obviously patiently waiting for someone in authority.

A receptionist gestured toward Mack and spoke out, "Yes sir. How may help you?"

Mack gestured toward the black woman and responded, "I believe she's ahead of me. Why don't you take care of her first? It appears she's been waiting for quite some time."

"She's been taken care of and you're next. What can I help you with?" The receptionist snottily retorted.

"I came here to see Mr. Frank Holmes. I'm a novelist and I'm trying to check out a few things that he may know about. I've collaborated with several sources already and he seems to be the key in solving the puzzle. Do you suppose I could see him for a few moments?"

"Mr. Holmes isn't allowed to see anyone except family members. I'll call the facility administrator. He might be able to help you." She lifted the telephone receiver, dialed a series of numbers and mumbled into the handset. "Mr. Smith. There's a man here at the reception desk to see Mr. Holmes. He says he wants to check on some facts for a book he's writing. He's very insistent. Would you please come up front and talk to him?" The receptionist looked at Mack and opened her eyes wide indicating she was doing her best to get him some assistance." Yes sir. I'll tell him." She hung up and turned to face Mack. "Mr. Smith will be right out to talk with you. Please have a seat over there." She gestured toward the sitting room flanked by a wheelchair-bound brigade of hopeful inmates.

"If you don't mind I'll wait for him right here at the counter. This woman appears to be here on important business and I certainly don't want to get ahead of her."

The black woman turned toward Mack and responded, "That's perfectly fine. I placed an employment application here two weeks ago and I've come back to follow up on it because I haven't heard from anyone. They can find no record of me placing an employment application with them. I work for the State of Florida and they may have a problem. Could it be that they discarded my application because of my skin color?" She smiled and glanced at the receptionist." I gave them five minutes to find it and if they don't someone has some explaining to do. Perhaps I can talk to the facility administrator when he comes down to see you?"

"It sounds like your situation is much more serious than mine."

"It is for them," she responded with a sly smile.

A tall, somewhat obese, balding middle-aged white man wearing a long sleeved white shirt and haphazardly tied green tie turned the corner walked briskly down the hallway in Mack's direction. He didn't have a smile on his face and seemed to be irritated at being disturbed from his lunch or afternoon nap. He approached Mack and the well-dressed black woman.

"I'm Mr. Smith the nursing home administrator. How may I help you?" He responded by looking directly at Mack and ignored the black woman.

"I believe this young woman has a situation of much higher priority than mine." Mack gestured toward the black woman. "I'm only here to speak to one of your residents to verify some facts for my novel."

"I can't allow you to speak to him without the written permission of his family. He isn't credible because over the last few months his dementia has gotten much worse. He constantly babbles about buried pirate treasure of all things. You might ask him a few questions, and he might agree with you, but I doubt that he would make a credible source for anything at this point. I'm sorry, but I can't help you." He rested his elbow on the counter, smiled in Mack's direction and ignored the black woman.

"I appreciate your time and candor. I won't bother his family because I already have two substantiations of the story. I hoped he could add the final key to the puzzle." Mack extended his hand to shake the man's hand, but he ignored Mack's gesture.

The black woman spoke up and addressed Mack," Sir. Would you please give me one of your business cards? I just returned to Stuart and I might want to write a book some day."

Mack reached into his shirt pocket for a Port Sewall Marina business card and passed it over to her. "You said that you just returned to Stuart. Where have you been?"

"I was born here and after I completed high school I went away to college in New York. I graduated from Cornell and took a job in New York City where I spent the last fifteen years."

"What did you do for a living up there?"

She whispered in Mack's right ear. "I worked in the State Attorney's office. I specialized in civil rights and job discrimination cases. Now I work for the State of Florida. If you'll excuse me I have some business to discuss with the facility administrator." She smiled and turned away to focus her undivided attention on the very nervous nursing home administrator.

Dejected Mack left the nursing living home and returned to Port Sewall Marina. He had some serious research to do if he was going to search for pirate treasure. It was 5:27 P.M.

Chapter 4

When Mack pulled into Port Sewall Marina at 5:46 P.M. a jet black Lincoln town car followed him and stopped alongside his pickup truck. The passenger's side window slid down and a silver-haired man in the driver's seat motioned to Mack with his right index finger.

"Get in! We have some things to talk about and you don't have much time."

The window quietly slid back up into position as Mack slipped out of his pickup truck. He opened the passenger side door and slid into the soft leather seat alongside the silver-haired man. This seemed to be a déjà vu' scenario. Mack took a quick backward glance into the back seat to make certain no one was lurking there to garrote him from behind.

"What do you want to talk about?" Mack leaned against the door and stared at the silver-haired man. "The last time you came down here to talk to me I wound up in a big mess."

"Something came up in the past few days I had to make a quick trip down here to brief you. Is there anybody inside the cottage?"

"No."

"The silver-haired man released the brake, tromped down hard on the accelerator and pointed the car toward Old St. Lucie

Boulevard. "We have to sit down and talk. I made a six o'clock reservation at Luna's Italian place downtown. After dinner we'll slip over to Howard Johnson's on U.S. 1 and have a private discussion. After that you're on your own. I have to catch a nine forty-seven flight out of West Palm Beach back to Chicago." The silver-haired man never glanced at Mack and looked straight ahead as he maneuvered the car down the gravel driveway toward Old St. Lucie Boulevard. He didn't utter a word during the ten-minute trip to downtown Stuart. He spoke again when he pulled the car into a parking space in front of the Lyric Theatre and shut off the engine.

"Here we are one more time. I don't know when we'll we have the opportunity to dine together in this restaurant again, but I enjoy their food. Let's go in and break some bread. I'll tell you what I can while we're in here."

After the pair was seated in a back booth next to the drink cooler the silver-haired man opened the conversation. "I understand you're into looking for buried pirate treasure. I doubt you'll find anything. However, the new assignment you're about to take on will allow you to rekindle some old memories from over thirty years ago."

"What do you mean rekindle some old memories?" Mack responded as he dipped a piece of soft Italian bread into a steaming bowl of minestrone soup.

"How long has it been since you were last in Biloxi and Gulfport, Mississippi? Your military records indicate that it was about thirty-four years ago. Your new assignment will take you back there for at least three days and in your spare time you can do some sightseeing."

"What type of assignment would take me back to Biloxi? The last time I was there I was in a riot. I didn't leave anything there and there's nothing there that I need to see again," Mack responded as he carefully maneuvered a soup-soaked piece of Italian bread into his mouth.

"We have some big problems in the witness protection program. Congress cut our funds and we've had to pull several people in Florida out of the program and cut them loose. You're one of those people."

"What! You told me that I'd be covered."

"Hold it down. Someone might hear you. Before we cut you loose we have one more very important assignment for you to undertake and you must go to Biloxi, Mississippi."

"Why should I take on a new assignment if you're cutting me loose? What's the incentive for me? Why don't you cut me loose right now and we'll be done with it?"

"It's not quite that easy. You have several things that belong to us and we must maintain complete secrecy of the project. I can't talk about it here. Certainly you can understand that. After dinner we'll wander over to the Howard Johnson's. I have a small conference room reserved and I'll be more specific."

"I suppose I can wait another hour."

The cautious pair finished dessert, left Luna's at 7:03 P.M. and headed for Howard Johnson's on U.S. 1. The silver-haired man maneuvered into a parking spot in front of the hotel, turned off the engine and opened his door. "Come on Mack. I don't have much time to get back to West Palm and catch my plane."

"Why we going in the front door? I thought this was supposed to be a secret meeting. I assumed that you have a room somewhere in the back of the hotel so people won't see us coming in together."

"If I was to get a room for only two hours wouldn't it seem suspicious to the people running the hotel? I told them I needed a small conference room until nine o'clock for the purpose of holding job reviews for door-to-door magazine sales people. There may already be a couple of other job candidates inside waiting for me to arrive." The silver-haired man closed the car door and briskly walked toward the front door of the hotel. Mack followed close behind. The silver-haired man mumbled something to the bored registration clerk who handed him a room key. Apparently satisfied he motioned for Mack to follow him down the hall. He paused in front of Room 125, slid the white plastic card key into the electronic door lock and a tiny green indicator light flashed on. He opened the door and gestured for Mack to follow him inside.

The hastily converted sleeping room contained a wooden desk positioned in front of the single window, a black leather executive chair sat behind it and a single straight-backed, armless chair sat in front of it. The silver-haired man slipped behind the desk and took his seat. He motioned for Mack to sit in the single chair strategically placed in front of the desk.

"Take a seat and we'll begin the interview. Are you ready to answer a few questions so I can evaluate your suitability for this new assignment?"

"Yes sir." Mack responded tersely.

"We are interviewing you for a very delicate assignment which requires a person of your specific physical, educational and psychological attributes. We scoured all of the available records and found that you are the only candidate who perfectly meets all of the requirements for this assignment. You have the necessary physical characteristics, education, overall experience, speak the appropriate languages and are in the correct age group. If you complete this assignment satisfactorily you will be cut loose from the witness protection program. Special numbered bank accounts will be established for you in Switzerland and the Bahamas. Only you can access them and you will have no worries for funds in the future." He placed his fingertips together and made a steeple with his hands. It was an obvious signal of superiority and confidence in his position of authority.

"If you decide to take this assignment you have three days to prepare for it. During that time you will be photographed wearing various types of clothing, walking and talking, sitting behind a desk, working under a car and perhaps even a farmer's fields. You will be provided with videotapes of each day's activities which you will playback to review your progress."

"Review my progress toward what? It sounds like you're looking at some kind of personnel switch and I'm not quite sure that I want to do this. What if I say no?"

"I'm afraid that you have no choice in the matter. Look behind you." The silver- haired man pointed over Mack's left shoulder with his right index finger.

Mack turned and looked over his shoulder. Sitting directly behind him on each side of the door was a man wearing a black suit, a long sleeve white shirt, a black tie and smoked sunglasses.

Their arms were folded across their chest and they slowly nodded their heads in acknowledgement to Mack that they were there.

The silver-haired man re-initiated the conversation. "So you see Mr McCray, you have no choice in the matter. If you choose not to accept the assignment I must turn you over to the two gentlemen behind you. I strongly suggest that you say 'yes'." He nodded his head up and down as if to encourage Mack to say 'yes'.

Mack realized that he was considered to be a disposable collateral loss and not expected to get out alive even if he completed the assignment. It was also very obvious that if he failed he would not get back alive. It was a 'no-win' situation for him in either case. He decided he would have the best shot at survival if he agreed to take it.

"What's your answer Mr. McCray?"

"You're an enthusiastic, but not very convincing salesman," Mack responded. "I'll accept the assignment with two provisions and I want both of them in writing. First: I want to be released from the agency's control once the assignment is satisfactorily completed. Second: If something happens to me those persons who have been personally involved with me over the past few months will be protected from any future harm."

"Mr. McCray the agency cannot put things like that in writing. However, I'll give you my personal assurance that your dog and your cat will be well taken care of for the rest of their lives and none of your friends will be harmed. We will take steps, if for some reason you do not return from this assignment, to add a layer of protection to Ms. McShay and those other fine people in Martin County that you call your friends. That's the best I can do." The silver-haired man clasped his hands together, put them behind his head and leaned backward. "Do we have an agreement?"

"Yes. We do. Where do we go from here?" Mack inquired and began to stand up.

"Don't stand up! Fast actions make the two men behind you nervous and they react to sudden movement in a very negative fashion. Please sit down and we will discuss the project in more detail. Please give me your wallet with your Social Security card, voter's registration card, credit cards and driver's license. You may remove any money that belongs to you."

"Why? They're all I have to identify myself!" Mack stammered as he reached for his wallet.

"That's exactly the point Mr. McCray. You must lose your present identity. Those things provide positive identification of your current persona and it must change. You'll take on a new identity and won't need your current forms of identification. You will be issued new identification papers that will prove to be quite adequate for this short-term assignment."

"Where am I going and why do I have to change my identity?"

"The details of the assignment are contained in a manila envelope taped to the back of a wooden plaque mounted on a piling alongside RAZE'S Restaurant at the foot of the Roosevelt Bridge. It's easy to find. The front of the plaque contains a plastic sign advertising 'Junkadoo' sailing charters. The envelope is taped to the back of the plaque. You're expected to report to Biloxi, Mississippi no later than fourteen hundred hours tomorrow afternoon. No one locally is to be told where you're going, or why. Do you understand?"

"Yes I understand, but I have to make arrangements for someone to take care of my dog and my cat," Mack responded.

"Call your buddy Ralph. I'm certain he'll watch them for a few days. If all goes according to plan you'll be back in your cozy cottage Saturday afternoon."

"How am I expected to get to Biloxi by noon tomorrow?"

"It's a very scenic ten hour drive. I've made it several times myself. You'll find a red Ford Mustang convertible waiting for you at the marina. Lock up your truck and leave the keys on the kitchen counter. You won't need them where you're going. It's only seven twenty-six. If you leave now you can be almost to Tallahassee by midnight. You can catch seven hours of sleep, start out at seven o'clock in the morning and make Biloxi by noon. Keep in mind that you gain an hour because of the change in time zones. I don't see any problem. Do you?"

"Not if I drive like a stock car racer at ninety miles an hour the entire way. I don't know if I can make it that soon," Mack retorted sharply.

"You don't have a choice. You must report to your new assignment by fourteen hundred hours tomorrow afternoon. I suggest that you hurry back to the marina, pack your bags and get on the road. Every minute counts." The silver-haired man rose from behind the desk and extended his right hand toward Mack. "Good luck. I'll see you again real soon."

Mack ignored the insincere gesture, turned and walked out of the hotel into the side parking lot. He didn't want the desk clerk to think that he was the only applicant for a door-to-door magazine salesman's position. Strangely enough his blue Ford F-150 pickup truck was parked directly outside the door and the engine was running. He didn't care how it got there.

He turned onto U.S. 1 and headed toward the Roosevelt Bridge and the empty site of what used to be RAZE's Restaurant. He turned left onto First Street, then right onto Atlanta Avenue, passed the Stuart Anchorage Marina and parked in front of the large concrete apron that formed the foundation of the restaurant. He got out of the truck and walked toward the row of creosoted, wooden posts that reared out of the concrete seawall like silent black sentinels. They witness everything and say nothing.

It was almost dark, but Mack made out a rectangular, glowing yellow sign mounted on top of the fourth piling north of the wooden dock. Apparently it had been there for many years because the thick plastic was chipped and cut away in several places. He looked around, saw no one and reached behind the piling with his right hand. There was no envelope there!

A nasal, squeaky voice rang out from under the wooden dock. "Hey Mack! What cha' doing down here this time of night? Don't you have better things to do?" It was Rat!

"Rat! What're you doing hiding under the dock?" Mack responded with a grin. "What're you afraid of?"

"I ain't afraid of nothing, I was over here cat snapper fishing and this old white-haired guy, we call 'em 'cue tips' you know, came racing up in a black Lincoln Town Car and stapled a big manila envelope to the back of that old charter sign. I recognized him right off because I saw him at your place before. I figured he was up to no good so after he pulled out I grabbed the envelope."

Rat held up a bulky, rectangular manila envelope in his dirty right hand. "Is it for you?"

"Why do you think I was down here groping around that piling? I wasn't looking for cat snappers. Yes. It's for me. You didn't open it did you?"

"Do you think that I'm as dumb as I look? It might have been a letter bomb. There's some people around here who don't like you very much." Rat offered a toothless grin through his tangled beard. "Hang on a minute and I'll bring it over there."

Rat gingerly placed the envelope in the bottom of his green rubber kayak and paddled toward the sea wall. Mack reached out his right arm to pull him alongside.

"There's no name written on the envelope. How do I know it's really for you?"

"It's for me. Now hand it over here before I pop that grungy kayak with an ice pick."

"Where are you going to get an ice pick out here?" Rat smugly replied and folded his arms across his chest.

"Right here," Mack replied as he lifted his right pant leg to display an ice pick nestled in a brown leather sheath strapped to his calf. "Would you like me to take it out and show you?"

"No thanks," Rat responded as he pushed away from the concrete sea wall after handing Mack the envelope. "I'll just wait out here for you."

"You don't have to wait for me because I'm leaving. I have to go out of town for a few days. I should be back Saturday afternoon."

"Should I ask where you're going?"

"No! Before I leave I'm going to call Ralph and ask him to keep an eye on the marina and to feed the dog and cat. And you stay away from them!"

"I won't bother 'em. Ralph hasn't been himself for the last few days. The VA put him on some new blood pressure medicine and he's been acting strange. Plus, he's all hyped up about them guys doing the survey work on Sewall's Point. You might ask his wife Joy to look after the animals because Ralph might forget."

"He stopped by the marina this morning and he seemed normal to me. When's the last time you saw him?"

"About four-thirty this afternoon around the tip of Sewall's Point. He was setting his gill net for mullet. I didn't have time to stop and chat so I waved at him and went on my way. Two surveyors were staking out some trees on the southeast side of Sewall's Point about twenty feet up the slope. I think he was watching them."

"If he's out fishing I'll call Joy and ask her to relay the message to Ralph when he finally gets in tonight. Rat, I've got to get going. I have a long way to drive tonight." Mack saluted Rat, turned and headed for his truck.

"You're driving? You can't be going very far away in that old truck."

"I've got a red Mustang convertible waiting for me a the marina."

Mack raced down U.S. 1 and made it back to Port Sewall Marina at 8:08 P.M. He fed the dog and cat before dialing Ralph's phone number. His wife Joy answered.

"Joy. It's Mack. I understand from Rat that Ralph's out mullet fishing tonight. I'm leaving town for a couple of days and need him to watch the marina and feed the dog and cat."

"I don't see any problem. I'll tell him when he gets home."

"Thanks. I should be home sometime Saturday afternoon."

"Did Rat tell you that Ralph hasn't been himself for the past few days? He went to the VA Clinic on Willoughby last week for a check up and they put him on some new blood pressure medication. I blame it on that. He couldn't even find his underwear drawer this morning."

"He stopped by the marina this morning and I didn't notice anything strange. But, he seems to be bent out of shape over the surveying work that's being done over by Sewall's Point."

"Maybe that's what causing it. His family has lived here for generations and they all get upset when somebody starts building something new. I won't say anymore about it to him."

"That's a good idea. I'll give him a call when I get back in town on Saturday."

"Where are you going?"

"I have to see a cousin in Tallahassee. He's in the hospital and not doing very well."

"My family is from Tallahassee. I grew up there. Maybe I know him! What's his name?"

"I don't think so. He moved there about five years ago from Pennsylvania."

"Oh well. I thought I might be able to help."

"Thank you for your concern. I'll see you and Ralph when I get back on Saturday."

"When're you leaving?"

"Right now. I'll stop somewhere around Lake City and spend the night."

"Drive carefully. Good night."

"I will. Good night."

Mack hung up, went into the bedroom and packed a suitcase with enough clothes, underwear and socks for a week and tossed in his shaving kit. He thought about taking the .25-caliber semi-automatic Berretta pistol, but decided to stash it in a kitchen drawer under a light green dishcloth. He dumped the contents of the manila envelope on the bed and made a quick inventory. There was a bundle of cash in ten and twenty dollar bills, a Biloxi street map, a Mississippi driver's license, a voter registration and Social Security card plus a VISA and Shell credit card. His new address was 121 Melody Lane, Bay St. Louis, Mississippi. The name on the documents was Paul McElroy! There was also a plain white legal inside envelope with instructions written across the flap with a black felt tip pen. *"Open this when you arrive at the Beau Rivage Resort and Casino in Biloxi. You are pre-registered. Do not attempt to check in at the front desk!"*

Mack realized that someone was being very certain to protect his true identity! After shooing the dog and cat back into the cottage for the night Mack threw his suitcase in the red Ford Mustang convertible, pulled out of the driveway and headed toward the I-95 ramp on Route 76.

"I'll take I-95 as far as Fort Pierce, exit and change over to the Florida Turnpike. It's only eight twenty-three. I can make it to Orlando by 10:30 and be in Gainesville about midnight. I'll pull off for the night after I reach I-10 and headed west toward Tallahassee."

At 12:47 A.M. Mack pulled off I-10 at the Madison Exit west of Lake City and headed for the Motel 6 sign. The bored clerk was more interested in watching the action on the porno channel than checking in customers. After three minutes of rummaging around he handed Mack a key.

"Room 106 is to your left and behind the main part of the motel." The clerk handed Mack the plastic-tagged key through the arc-shaped opening in the bulletproof plastic window and never took his eye off the television set. "Park in front of your room."

Mack accepted the key without an audible response. *"That dumb ass couldn't hear me anyway. Why should I waste time trying to talk to him?"*

Mack pulled around to the back of the motel and was amazed to find a literal junkyard of tireless cars resting on concrete blocks. *"It looks like somebody in town makes their spending money selling used tires."* He flipped on the car's alarm system and slipped into his room for the night. He was bushed!

"You dirty son-of-a-bitch! Get your ass out of here before somebody gets hurt!"

Mack thought he heard voices, rolled over and tried to ignore the tirade outside his window.

"You bastard! Leave her alone! She's my wife and I'm going to kill you! Get out here before I break the door down. I can do that you know. It's common law in this county and you can't do anything about it. I can shoot your ass too!"

The last comment rang in Mack's ears. His intuition told him to get out of bed and find out what was going on outside. *"I don't need a drunken husband crashing through the door with a loaded gun!"* His watch read 2:18 A.M. *"What the hell am I doing in the middle of a family spat in the middle of the night?"* Mack muttered as he looked through the door's security hole.

The drunken man stood across the black asphalt parking lot alongside a black 1984 Chevy Nova parked in front of Room 118. He wore only black jockey underwear and white socks and was desperately attempting to urinate. The intermittent yellow stream dribbled onto his white-socked feet and he didn't seem to notice. The Nova's driver's side window was covered with a sheet of clear plastic held in place with silver duct tape. The top right hand corner of the plastic sheet was flapping in the wind. The car's engine was running, but sputtering and coughing in protest. The steaming stream of hot water flowing from the car's tail pipe indicated a ruptured head gasket. The drunk opened the driver's side door and fell across the front seat apparently oblivious to the running engine and possible carbon monoxide poisoning.

The door of Room 118 cracked open and light streamed out. The door slowly opened and stopped at the limit of the brass safety chain. A woman's face peeked through the opening and a bearded man's face appeared above hers. When the pair realized that their verbal tormenter was incapacitated they pointed in unison and laughed at the inert driver slumped across the front seat of the Nova.

"Hey dumb ass!" The bearded man yelled in the man's direction. "Are you trying to kill your dumb ass self? Your car engine's still running."

The sleeping man stirred, sat up rubbed his eyes and shook his head. The motel room door slammed shut and the light went out. The only noise to be heard in the parking lot was the coughing and sputtering of the protesting car engine. The drunken occupant ripped the fluttering plastic sheet from the car window and tossed it to the ground. He gingerly reached out of the window with his left arm and opened the driver's side door from the outside.

"Obviously the door can't be opened from the inside," Mack muttered. *"Now what's he going to do? Maybe he's going to shoot both of them? I wouldn't blame him a bit. I'd do it myself."*

The drunk shoved the Nova's door open with his right foot and smashed it into the side of the red Ford Explorer parked beside it. He leaned forward and fell out of the car face first onto the black asphalt with an accompanying loud 'splat.' The rubber-backed window curtain of Room 118 lifted up at one corner and the two occupants cautiously peeked out.

The prone drunk was vainly attempting to get up. He managed to get his left knee under his chest and used it as a fulcrum to force his body off the asphalt. He reached for the door handle of the Ford Explorer with his right hand, found it and tried to pull his body erect. He lost his finger hold, fell, bounced off the side of the Explorer and the shock set off the Explorer's alarm system. The parking lot was suddenly filled with the raucous bawling of a siren, whooping horn and flashing lights.

The terrified drunk dove headfirst into the front seat of the crippled Nova, slammed the door shut and disappeared beneath the doorframe. The interior lights came on in Room 116 and the door flew open. A huge man, at least six feet tall and weighing at least three hundred pounds stood in the doorway clad only in white boxer shorts and black socks. A thick linked gold chain swung from his gigantic neck.

"What's going on out here? Who's messing with my SUV?"

There was no response and a purring female voice emanated from inside the room. "Frankie. Use your remote control button and turn off the alarm before somebody calls the cops. It was probably a raccoon! Come back in here and go to bed. I'm cold."

"It must have been that damn sneak ass private investigator that my wife hired to watch me. I caught him trying to install a satellite-tracking transmitter in my Explorer last week. I told him I'd break his legs with a tire iron if I caught him again. He told me that if I paid him ten grand in cash he'd tell my wife he didn't find any evidence of me messing around with you. I took a swing at him and caught him good right beside his left ear. He ran off before I could finish the job."

"It might have been a stray cat that jumped on the hood to keep warm."

"Yeah. Maybe it was a cat. Okay. I'm coming back in. Get ready for Freddy. He's ready!"

The motel room door slammed shut and the lights went out.

The dazed Nova occupant slowly rose up to eye level and peeked over the car door in the direction of the source of the verbal tirade. Mack returned to bed.

Chapter 5

It was 6:17 on Tuesday morning and Mack awoke to the sounds of an agitated, high-pitched woman's voice followed by the slamming of heavy vehicle doors.

"Frankie why don't you wake that guy up and tell him his car engine's still running? It was running all night long."

"Because it's none of my business! Shut your trap and get in the damn SUV before that private investigator across the parking lot wakes up and starts taking pictures. I'm sure that's the clown my wife hired to spy on us. I recognize the sorry fink's car."

Mack opened his eyes, rolled out of bed and headed for the bathroom. *"I've got to get on the road. It's still almost 400 hundred miles to Biloxi."* Fifteen minutes later when he opened the door to the parking lot the bright sunlight momentarily blinded him. Through squinted eyes he saw that the red Ford Explorer was gone. The Chevy Nova was there and it's engine was still running. He tossed his bag into the back seat of the Mustang and walked across the parking lot toward the Nova. The single male occupant was still clothed only in his black underwear and white socks. His face was beet red!

"You poor bastard! You fell asleep out here and the carbon monoxide from the car exhaust got you. I should've come out and checked on you. I apologize."

Mack turned off the ignition, tossed the key ring on the floor and walked back to his room. He returned with a white terry cloth bath towel and carefully spread it over the dead man's face and torso. His naked legs and white-socked feet protruded eerily from under the towel.

When Mack walked into the tiny lobby to check out the night clerk was sound asleep in front of the television set. The porno flick blasted across the television screen as whoops and giggles of feigned joy emanated from the speaker. Mack elected not to disturb the snoring clerk and tossed the plastic card key threw the window slot. He used the pay telephone on the lobby wall to call '911' and report the dead man in the rear parking area.

Mack pulled out of the Motel 6 driveway and turned into the Waffle House parking lot next door for breakfast. Just as the seedy waitress delivered a steaming cup of hot coffee to his table two Madison County Sheriff cruisers pulled into the motel driveway with their lights blazing and sirens howling like banshees.

The bored waitress offered an experienced observation of her own. "Somebody's always overdosing over there. I wonder who it was this time?"

"I pulled in there after midnight to sack out. About two o'clock this morning there was a lot of yelling going on in the parking lot outside my room. It sounded like a domestic dispute and I learned a long time ago not to get between an arguing husband and wife. They'll stop fighting with each other long enough to turn on you and kick your ass. Then they'll go right back to fighting with each other."

"It's most likely some horny housewife who got drunk in the Copper Penny bar down the street and got herself picked up last night. She probably woke up this morning and found out she was in bed with a smelly cross-country truck driver and didn't remember how good he looked to her last night when she was shit-faced on booze," she dryly replied and clucked her tongue.

"Maybe it was the truck driver who woke up this morning and realized that the woman next to him was 'coyote ugly' and chewed his arm off at the shoulder rather than risk waking her up."

"That's really good! Where'd you hear that one?" The waitress smiled as she took out her stained order pad to write down his order. "I gotta' write it down so I don't forget it. I've got a lousy short-term memory. What cha' want for breakfast honey bunch?"

"I'd like a western omelet with a side order of hash browns and a large glass of orange juice. Is the orange juice freshly squeezed?"

"I'll squeeze the can with both hands just for you."

"What's your name?" Mack asked.

"They call me Trouble. Want some?"

"What? Your name's Trouble?"

"That's right buster and don't wear it out." She leaned down. "Read my name tag."

"Why's your name Trouble? Was your mother playing a joke on you?"

"Nope. The manager here is a pain in the ass. He told me I'm always causing trouble for him so I went out and got a nametag that reads 'Trouble'. Now he's got Trouble." She turned and swished away in the direction of the short-order cook behind the counter.

Mack pulled out a well-worn road atlas and began to calculate the driving time to Biloxi. *"I'm about sixty-five miles from Tallahassee and it'll be seven o'clock by the time I get out of here. I should make Tallahassee about eight o'clock and might have enough time to pull off and run through town. It's about two hundred-fifty miles from Tallahassee to Biloxi and that'll take me four hours. I pick up an hour when I cross into the Central Time Zone at Chattahoochee and should hit Biloxi about noon unless I stop for lunch."*

Mack pulled out of the Waffle House parking lot onto the I-10 access road and was almost run over by the two Marion County Sheriff cars and ambulance that silently whipped out of the Motel 6 parking lot.

"No need for them to be in such a big hurry. Their passenger isn't going anywhere."

Mack got back on I-10 at 7:04 and settled down for the one-hour ride to Tallahassee. He set the cruise control for seventy-five miles an hour and slipped in a Jim Croce CD. The sounds of *'MISSISSIPPI LADY'* filled the car and he sang along although drastically out of tune.

> *"Mississippi Lady*
> *My lovin' Gulfport gal*
> *She taught me how to love*
> *And she really loved me well*
> *She took me up to heaven*
> *Then she brought me down*
> *That Mississippi Lady,*
> *Sweet Cordelia Brown*
> *Hot July in Gulfport*
> *And I was working in the bars*
> *And she was working on the street*
> *With the rest of the evening stars*
> *She said, I never met a guy*
> *Who could turn my head around*
> *And that's really sayin' something*
> *For sweet Cordelia Brown"*

At 7:48, just two miles before the Aucilla exit, the traffic came to a sudden halt. A tanker driver had fallen asleep and smashed his rig into the center divider. It took almost thirty minutes before the Florida Highway Patrol opened the westbound side of I-10 to through traffic. Mack glanced at his watch when the lane opened. It read 8:18.

"That trucker really screwed up my schedule. I was thinking about pulling off at Exit 30 and running down Capitol Circle to visit the old neighborhood. But, that would take at least a half hour and make me late for my Biloxi rendezvous. Maybe I'll try to stop on my way back."

Mack swung off I-10 at Exit I-110 at 12:15 P.M. and turned east onto Beach Boulevard. He spotted 'McElroy's Seafood Restaurant' and swung in the parking lot for lunch. He briefly thought about identifying himself as Paul McElroy to the waitress, but decided that might raise some unanswerable questions.

The restaurant sat far back from the main road and the parking lot was large enough to accommodate several hundred cars. The hostess seated him at a table next to a large bay window that overlooked the boat docks. A large brass ship's lantern festooned with red and green glass running lights hung next to the window.

Mack slowly scanned the dining room. A mounted Tripletail hung from the wall opposite his table, behind him a mounted flounder stared down with unseeing glass eyes, a wooden ship's wheel graced the natural wood lattice room divider and a montage of a flying sea gull, twisted banyan tree, the Biloxi lighthouse and Gulf of Mexico beachfront occupied the opposite wall. A three masted schooner model decorated the wall directly behind the cashier. A clear plastic overlay protected the nautical charts pasted to the tabletop and red plastic covers protected the fabric seats from the spills of sloppy customers.

"What cha' want for lunch?" The plump waitress had slipped alongside Mack's table without him noticing her. "Hey bud! I don't have all day. What cha' want for lunch?" She tapped the menu with the top of her ballpoint pen.

"I'm sorry," Mack responded. "I was daydreaming. What do you recommend?"

"Try the half and half. It's good. You'll like it." She began writing on her order pad. "What do you want to drink? How about a glass of sweet tea? That's what most people want."

"That'll be okay. What's a half and half?"

"It's half shrimp and half crab. You'll like it. Most Yankees do."

"What makes you think that I'm a Yankee?"

"You look like one and you don't have a southern accent." The waitress turned to leave and paused, "Okay. That's a half and half with sweet tea. Do you want anything else?"

"That's just fine thank you."

After lunch Mack slipped out of the parking lot, pulled into the entrance of the Beau Rivage Casino and Resort and parked in a space marked 'Guest'. He remembered the hand-written instructions on the front of the envelope. *"Open when you arrive at the Beau Rivage Casino and Resort in Biloxi. "You are pre-registered. Do not check in at the registration desk!"*

Mack reached into his briefcase, removed the envelope and opened it. It contained a plastic card key, but there was no room number on the key. He removed the triple-folded sheet of brown cotton stationary and carefully unfolded it. It contained a brief message.

"Remove your bags from the car, put the car keys in this envelope and drop them in the outgoing mail slot located next to the registration desk. Take the elevator to the ninth floor and go to Room 933. You are pre-registered. Do not check in at the front desk"

The room was a suite and it appeared normal except for the multiple television cameras, the overhead lights, the commercial photographer's backdrop and several racks of clothing. A deep male voice boomed out from behind a black lacquered Chinese screen decorated with Mother of Pearl pheasants and peacocks. It wasn't the voice of CNN!

"Come in. I've been expecting you. We have a lot to accomplish this afternoon. Make yourself comfortable and we'll proceed."

"Can't we start tomorrow morning?" Mack responded. I just drove five hundred miles and I'm pooped. I didn't get very much sleep last night."

"I know. Did you see that red Ford explorer across the parking lot from your room?"

"Yes I did. Why?"

"Those were two of our folks who were watching out for you. There was a trap set for you with a drunk as bait and you almost fell for it. Be thankful that you didn't leave your room to investigate the ruckus, or you may not have been here today. "

"They killed that guy!" Mack responded sharply. "They could've turned off the car's engine and saved his life!"

"No they didn't and they couldn't. There were two sets of shooters on the roof of the motel set up in a cross fire over that car last night. If Frankie had so much as reached out to touch the ignition key they would have blown him away without a thought. That would have brought you out in a flash and they wanted you dead. You were smart not to get involved in a domestic spat."

"Who wanted me dead?" Mack stammered. "Why didn't you do something?"

"It's not important who wanted you dead and we did do something. We sent Big Frankie outside to investigate and that blew the whole thing for them. They packed up and left."

"What about the guy in the car? He died!"

"But you didn't and that's what's important. The other was the bait for you and he didn't know that it was a setup. They got him drunk and told him where to find his wife. He couldn't leave because they took his clothes away from him."

"Why didn't he get away from the car or turn off the ignition?"

"He couldn't get away because there was a wire tether attached to his right ankle. He couldn't turn off the ignition because they had jammed it with a wedge!"

"But I turned it off this morning when I left the motel."

"Fat Frankie waited until the guy's wife and her boyfriend checked out and pulled out the wedge before he left this morning. That's why you could turn it off."

"Why didn't Fat Frankie turn it off?"

"It wouldn't have done any good. The guy'd been dead since about three o'clock. That's enough gabbing. It's a quarter after two. We don't have much time and we have a lot to do."

"Why can't we wait and start first thing in the morning?"

"Our analysts will compare your samples to someone else's who is under consideration for this assignment. They'll study them tonight and we'll let you know tomorrow morning if the sessions will proceed. Sit down at this desk and we'll begin with a handwriting sample."

Mack complied with all of his handler's requests. He provided a multitude of handwriting samples including signing and printing his own name plus ten names chosen at random out of the Biloxi telephone book. He wrote the numerals from 1 to 100 and also wrote them out in longhand as if they were intended for a check.

His congenial handler made a show out of comparing Mack's efforts to someone else's but would not permit Mack to see what he was doing.

"Mack I can't let you see the comparison because you might 'push' to match it and the result would be forced. We prefer a natural flow and suggest you use that white erasable board to practice your cursive writing style with lots of loops and hanging serifs, etc."

After the exhaustive writing exercise was over Mack's handler informed him it was time for a photo shoot. "Now we need some still photos of you with these various backdrops we borrowed from a commercial photo studio. "We'll use the clothes you brought with you for today's shoot."

Later that afternoon Mack was videotaped walking across the room and sitting in a chair reading a book in an easy chair. His handler showed him slides of New York City, various United Nations building offices, Washington, DC's Embassy row and Georgetown and asked him to identify them.

At 5:12 P.M. his jovial handler made a startling announcement. "Today's session is over. We'll pick up again tomorrow morning at eight o'clock sharp. I suggest you turn in early. You need a good night's sleep because you were up pretty late last night."

"How can I go anywhere? I turned in my car keys."

"A blue Trans Am is in the parking space. Here're the keys. Enjoy yourself this evening."

"Thanks. I'll keep your suggestion in mind. I thought I'd go looking for a good book."

"There's a Books A Million store down Beach Boulevard about a mile. Do you remember the Tiki Hut bar on Porter Avenue? It was right behind a gas station. The gas station is long gone. There's a pawnshop there now. You got yourself in big trouble in there when you were stationed at Keesler. The Tiki Hut's still there, but there's a new owner and the name's changed."

"That was a long time ago and I've grown up since then. I'd just like to relax after dinner with a good book. I'm here on business and don't have time for sightseeing."

"Have it your own way," Mack's tormenter responded as he slipped out the door into the hall.

Mack went into the bathroom, shaved, took a shower and put on a pair of tan polyester slacks and a light blue polo shirt. On his way out the door he muttered, *"I'll try to find that book store. I'd like to find a book on Biloxi history and maybe one on pirates."*

Mack got onto westbound Beach Boulevard and kept his eyes peeled for Books A Million. As he pulled between Cajun's Chicken and Wendy's into the Village Shopping Center parking lot he mumbled, *"I need to get my mind off of what happened today."*

Mack entered Books A Million and looked toward the Joe Mugg's café. Two gray fabric-covered easy chairs sat next to the window. He decided to sit down and relax and chose the chair that faced the bookstore entrance. Seconds after he sat down something caught his attention. An excessively obese woman was lumbering across the asphalt parking lot toward the front door.

She was aided by an aluminum walker equipped with wood-grained plastic imitation walnut handles and wore a formless blue denim sack dress and open-toed white plastic sandals. Her yellowed toenails curled inwards and she appeared to be in extreme pain. Her forward movement could not be called walking because she demonstrated no forward steps. Instead she utilized a rolling side-to-side motion similar to the gait of an aged elephant. Her ponderous body rolled awkwardly from side to side and used the walker to keep her balance. When she rolled to one side her weight shifted to that side and the foot on the other side of her immense bulk rose off the asphalt. Then, with a great heave of her hip she thrust that foot forward a few inches. When the foot made contact with the asphalt she tilted to that side, the other foot lifted off the ground and the ugly process began anew. Tilt, heave and thrust; tilt, heave and thrust; tilt, heave and thrust.

She eventually overcame the force of inertia and the massive body tilted, heaved and thrusted its way through the front door. Out of breath she gasped deeply as she rested her massive bulk on the handles of the walker with both hands. She panted like a beagle hound exhausted from chasing a terrified rabbit through thick briars and stopped directly in front of Mack.

"Hey Bub! Mind if I sit down in that chair and rest my bones?"

"No problem. No one's sitting there."

Mack scanned the face of his new companion. Her oval face was blessed with plump, ruddy cheeks, she wore no makeup and had an interesting twinkle in her blue eyes.

Mack decided to open the conversation. "What brings you in here today?"

"I came in to buy a couple books of crossword puzzles. I hate the damn things, but they keep my mind from turning into mush. The body's shot as you can see for yourself, but if I can keep my mind active I'll remain a human being at least for a while longer."

"You look fine to me," Mack responded. "How're you on roller blades?"

She ignored the question. "I'm physically ready for the scrap pile and would check myself out of this world if I could. Did you read *Soylent Green*? I thought the movie sucked, but I like the idea of recycling ourselves. If we can do it with paper, tin cans and plastic bottles why not ourselves?" She gasped, wheezed, took a deep breath, slumped forward and shoved her right hand into Mack's face. "I live with immense pain everyday of my life. I broke this pinky finger yesterday, but it doesn't bother me. I'm used to constant pain in my knees and hips. Somebody else would piss and moan if their pinky finger was bent and discolored like mine. But, for me it's no big deal. It's just a little more pain."

Mack nodded and grunted something unintelligible so that she would think he was attentive.

She had him cornered and decided to share her adventurous past with him whether he wanted to hear it or not. She came to Books A Million several evenings a week to share her ramblings with unwitting and uncaring strangers. It was a good catharsis for her.

"I believe that some of us are destined to live with chronic pain so we won't bitch when it comes time for us to die. If we can put our sick pets to sleep why can't we get enough guts to do it to ourselves? I believe it's because the doctors, hospitals and nursing homes have such a hold on the politicians. We, and our families, spend most of our savings on the final few years of our life. I'd prefer a credit card that I can take to a euthanasia center and just check myself out. I liked that scene in *Soylent Green* when the people went to the center and were entertained with screen images, smells and soft music as they just went to sleep."

"I agree with you. How long have you lived here?"

"Since before you were born! I worked as a stripper from the time I was fourteen years old. I was born in a cesspool in Helena, Montana and ran away from home at fourteen. I went to Seattle and began stripping. I made more money in one night than a waitress could make in a week. But, because I was under age I switched strip clubs and social security numbers every two weeks. If my family knew where I was they would force me back home. Once I turned eighteen I could tell them where they could go. And, I did!"

"That's interesting." Mack leaned forward in his chair and rested his chin in his hands.

"I wound up striping in New Orleans at the *Five-hundred Club* for two hundred bucks a night. I worked with Al Hirt and Louis Armstrong back in the late forties and early fifties. I was a 'tassel twirler' because I wasn't the thinnest or the prettiest girl who ever hit the stage. I was called a 'cow' by the strip club owners. Today the politically correct term is large boned. Because I wasn't beautiful I had to rely on my wit and ability to deliver comedy. I made my own costumes and had a good time on stage. I was known as a 'tassel twirler." I can still get 'em going in opposite directions. Look here!"

She reared back and began to slowly gyrate her upper torso. Her massive, limp breasts attempted to move in opposite directions under the coarse blue fabric. "Back in my prime those babies stood out straight as arrows and my nipples would poke your eyes out if you got to close. Today I can throw 'em both over my shoulder and they'll touch the crack in my butt. But, there was a day when they stood at attention like the Washington Monument. I used to wear a thirty-eight D bra, but now I wear a thirty-eight long." She paused and rolled her eyes toward the ceiling.

"Those were the days. One day I was on stage with Al Hirt and I was wearing a tiger costume that was missing the front of the top half. I was twirling my tassels in opposite directions and twitching my tail all over the stage; tiger suit tail that is. The damn tail got caught in a fan sitting in front of the drummer and it just about jerked me off the stage. Pieces of that damn tiger tail flew all over the stage. I ignored it and strutted away twirling my tassels. When I got to the microphone I held up a piece of the shredded tail and said, "Anybody want a good piece of tail? I'll make you a good deal on this one. The audience roared. The next day I made up a whole bunch of tiger tails and added them to the act."

Mack smiled and nodded his head.

"People should understand that strippers aren't hookers. For the most part they're just regular girls that need to make a living and support their kids. I know girls who worked their way through college by stripping. We have one girl at the club right now who is working on her Masters degree in Business Administration at Clemson."

"What do you mean the club?" Mack interjected.

"I manage a little strip club on Porter Avenue behind the pawn shop. It's not much, but it keeps me off the street. Where're you from bud?"

"I live in south Florida."

"I worked a few clubs on Miami Beach over the years. I'm seventy-two now so that should give you an idea as to how long ago it was. Where 'bouts in Florida do you hang out?"

"Stuart. It's about thirty miles north of West Palm Beach. It's a quiet place."

"I came in here to buy a book called *Treasure Coast Deceit*. A customer was reading it at the bar and he showed it to me. It's a mystery novel set right there in Stuart and there's a picture in it of a character named Rat. He looks like a guy named Bruce who washes dishes in my club. His head's messed up a little, but deep down inside he's a real person like the rest of us.

"I know a guy named Rat."

"I was staying with my sister and went through a big-ass hurricane in nineteen forty-nine in Stuart. I learned the hard way about a hurricane. When the eye went through the wind stopped and the sky turned clear blue. I was out walking on the beach in front of the Sand Club on Jensen Beach when the opposite side came through. One minute I was walking around proud as a peacock and the next minute I was hanging onto a tree for dear life. My arms were wrapped around the tree and I was hanging out straight as a board. My boobs slipped out of my bra and flew up around my ears. I thought that they were going to beat me to death. I never want to see a hurricane ever again."

"Don't a lot of hurricanes come through this area?"

"Nothing serious since Camille. I live in a trailer and four steel cables run across the top to hold it down. If another hurricane comes I am not going to wimp out and evacuate. I'm going to sit tight and ride it out come hell or high water. If it's my time to go I'm not afraid to die. When I do, then all of this pain that I am going through now will be gone and I'll be able to finally rest."

"I hope that's not for a long time."

"How long are you going to be in town?"

"I think I'm leaving Friday, but I'm not certain. I might leave tomorrow."

"If you have some free time while you're here come by the club and ask for me. My name's Hattie Lou. The club's right down the road on Porter Avenue about a mile on the left hand side. Just look for the pawn shop on the corner."

"I might just do that. When I was in the Air Force and stationed here in nineteen sixty-one me and several friends got into a fight in a seedy bar called the Tiki Hut. We got our butts kicked by about a dozen local boys from Point Cadet. They shoved us out of a pickup truck right in front of the main gate about three o'clock in the morning. We're lucky they didn't beat us to death. They stopped half way through and told us they were giving us a break."

"I remember that night! I'd just moved here from New Orleans and was stripping there. You guys got your butts kicked real good. I bought the place and I renamed it 'Lorna Belle's' after my sister in Stuart. Although she hit the jackpot in nineteen forty-nine she came back here and stripped with me for a few years after that. Come by the place if you get a chance."

Before Mack could utter a reply she lumbered to her feet and headed for the door. "Wait a minute!" He shouted after her. He couldn't stand up to follow her because his legs had gone numb from lack of blood circulation. By the time he regained circulation in his legs it was a quarter after seven. Mack decided to stop by McElroy's Sea Food Restaurant for dinner before returning to the hotel. During his dinner of deep-fried grouper, hush puppies fresh coleslaw and three draft beers he mulled over his recent experiences.

"Who tracked me from Stuart to that Motel 6 outside of Lake City and why? Who wanted to whack me in the motel parking lot? Who was the drunk that they sacrificed?" Why don't the pieces fit together? Why did they photograph me in so many types of clothing?"

Mack suspected an identity switch for someone who looked like him. The last time he had been involved in a switch was in Vienna in 1964. It was relatively simple. A Russian envoy arrived at his office building every morning at exactly 8:45 A.M. with his black suede leather briefcase in his right hand and pushed through the revolving door. Once inside the lobby he took the first elevator on the left up to the 33rd floor, exited to the right and turned into the men's room to check his hair before entering his office. His vanity and daily routine were his downfall. Mack waited for him inside the door, slipped the spring steel garrote over his head and dragged him into a toilet stall. He lost consciousness in eight seconds. Mack pulled his pants down to his ankles and left him propped up on the toilet seat.

The clothing switch was simple. The back of Mack's business suit was held closed by three strips of Velcro and a quick jerk stripped it off his body. He stuffed it into a black plastic bag and stashed it in the trash container for the cleaning crew. His new identity as a wire service delivery agent fit him well except when he got onto the bicycle waiting at the curb. The downward curved handlebars were set to low. He managed to pedal off down the street and up an inclined ramp into the waiting truck without falling off or destroying his manhood on the cross bar. The flight back to Geneva was routine.

"Maybe I'm going back to Vienna," Mack thought. *"But he only showed me photographs of the United Nations building in New York and embassy row in Washington, DC."*

He had his suspicions, but wasn't certain. Thirty years had passed and he wasn't as fast or agile as he was then. But it didn't appear that he had any choice in the matter. It had been a long day and he was bushed.

Mack returned to the Beau Rivage at 8:47 P.M., parked the car and entered the lobby. The front desk clerk looked away as if Mack was non-existent. Mack glanced around the lobby, saw no one and headed for the elevator. The door slid open. Mack paused and looked inside before entering. It was empty

On the ninth floor, outside of his room, Mack slipped the white plastic card key into the automatic door lock, the tiny green indicator light came on and he slowly pushed the door open. The room's interior lights were on and classical music drifted across the room. Mack cautiously entered and noted that the overhead studio lights, commercial photo backdrop and television cameras were gone. The red 'message waiting' lamp mounted on the top of the beige telephone eerily flashed on and off. Mack lifted the telephone handset and dialed '0' for the operator. Just as the return ring echoed in his ear he noticed the folded over white piece of paper under the telephone base.

"Front Desk. How may I help you sir?"

"My message waiting lamp is flashing. Do you have a message for me?"

"Yes sir. It says to look under the telephone for a note."

"Thank you."

Mack replaced the telephone handset on its cradle, pulled out the slip of paper and unfolded it. The hand-written message read, *"There has been a change in plans. Meet me in front of the hotel at 0730. Wear something casual because we are going fishing."* There was no name or signature.

"Going fishing? What change in plans? What the hell is going on? They dragged me all the way over here, photographed me, videotaped me and made me feel like a kid who had to stay after school and practice his handwriting. Now they want to take me fishing?"

He wadded up the slip of paper and tossed it in the trashcan alongside the television set. Tired and thoroughly disgusted with the day's events Mack decided to call it a night.

Chapter
6

It was early Wednesday morning. The screaming alarm clock wasn't Mack's friend. It chattered incessantly as a signal that it was time for him to get up. Mack lazily rolled over onto his left shoulder and glanced at the glowing red dial of the digital clock sitting on the nightstand. It read: 6:30 A.M.

"I'd better get my butt out of bed and get cleaned up," Mack muttered as he heaved his long legs over the side of the bed. *"They're supposed to pick me up at seven-thirty and if I know them they'll be sitting down there at seven o'clock."* He stood up and headed toward the bathroom.

Mack walked out onto the gabled front porch of the hotel and wasn't surprised to see a black Chevrolet Suburban with heavily tinted windows parked in front of the hotel. There were several short beeps on the horn and the rear door facing the hotel opened. A deep male voice called out to him from inside. "You're right on time. Slide on in and have a seat. We're going to stop and have breakfast before we tackle the water." A hand beckoned Mack toward the interior.

When Mack slipped into the back seat his handler sat on his left and two unidentified men sat in the front seat. The man in the passenger seat was extremely large and Mack felt he had seen him somewhere before. The obviously tall driver scrunched down in the seat to blunt his height and wore a black ski mask over his face. It looked out of place with his suit jacket, white shirt and tie. Mack assumed he was bashful. His handler wore an open necked blue knit polo shirt.

"Let me introduce you to your companions for this morning's activities," offered his handler. "Up here in the passenger's seat we have Fat Frankie. I believe you may have seen him on your drive over here Monday evening. Our driver had a bad car accident. His face is severely disfigured and he prefers to remain anonymous."

"I thought we were going fishing? How come I'm the only one wearing fishing clothes?" Mack asked. "You guys are wearing slacks and dress shirts. I look out of place."

"You're the only one going fishing and we're going to watch you. We're going to shoot some video of you and our analysts will review it this afternoon to determine if you fit the needs of this assignment," retorted his handler. "First we'll have some breakfast over at McElroy's Restaurant and then we'll pick up the boats at the Biloxi Small Craft Harbor."

"What do you mean boats? I thought that I was the only one going fishing."

"We're taking two boats. We'll be in a camera boat and you'll be in a boat by yourself. But, don't worry about catching any fish and getting yourself all smelly. You won't have any bait."

"No bait! I'm going to look pretty damn silly sitting out there dangling my bare noodle in the water." Mack retorted.

"There's a large lead sinker attached to the line. You can use it for casting practice while we're shooting video of you. If by chance you happen to find a fish stupid enough to chomp down on the lead weight we'll have some action footage. The key factor is that we are going to observe you on the water so that our analysts can evaluate how you handle yourself in a boat."

After a hearty breakfast laced with idle chitchat at McElroy's Restaurant the group headed for the Biloxi City Marina. His handler pointed at a center console boat tied to a nearby slip.

"That looks exactly like my boat," Mack remarked.

"It is," replied his handler. "We want you to feel and act just as if you were at home."

After the uneventful fishing trip they pulled into the Bea Rivage driveway at 11:47 A.M.

"I suggest that you have lunch in the hotel dining room and charge it to your room I'll meet you at one o'clock," stated Mack's handler as he opened the vehicle door.

"Where?"

"The note under your telephone contains instructions."

Mack headed for his room with thoughts of a hot shower. He did his best thinking in the shower because he could talk to himself. Upon entering his room he saw the folded slip of white paper under the telephone. He pulled it out and opened it. A hand-written note read: *"Room 447."* Mack wadded the paper into a tight ball and arced a high lob into the corner trashcan.

"They've done everything except strip me naked and check for scars and marks to see if I'm perfectly matched with whoever else is involved in this project. Maybe the next step is to X-ray me from top to bottom to be sure I have the right number of bones in the proper places," he smirked as he lathered himself with soap. *"One thing's for sure, whomever I am studying to replace sure likes to do a lot of the same things I do,"* he mused and grinned as he dried off with a white, fluffy terry cloth bath towel.

Mack had a lunch of Cajun chicken and a big bowl of seafood gumbo accompanied by three glasses of sweet ice tea. At one o'clock sharp he knocked on the door of Room 447. The door softly opened and his handler beckoned him to enter. "Sit down and make yourself comfortable.

We have a lot to do. While you and I are working this afternoon the analysts are reviewing the videotape we made this morning. We'll have a decision tomorrow morning."

The first part of the afternoon regimen included watching video tapes of people going in and out of the United Nations building in New York City, the U.S. Capitol Building, the White House Executive Office Building, several restaurants in Georgetown and three embassies. Mack was shown still photos of several people, listened to their conversations through earphones and asked if he knew or recognized any of them. He didn't.

The image of himself fishing the grass flats east of Boy Scout Island appeared on the television monitor. "That's me! What's that doing there?" Mack sputtered.

"It's been a long couple of days and I wanted to know if you recognized yourself." His handler smiled. "Mack, it's just a joke. Lighten up a little."

Mack was understandably confused.

The afternoon agenda switched from people recognition to videos of several airport terminals including; Mobile, Pensacola, LaGuardia, Kennedy, Washington National, Dulles outside of Washington, DC and Atlanta. They included shots of concourses, gates, outside parking places, taxi and limousine stands. He was also shown the interior of men's rooms, elevator banks, entrance and exit doors in several office buildings including the United Nations and the U.S. Capitol. Mack ordered to put on a United Parcel Service deliveryman's uniform and a plumber's shirt complete with denim bib overalls.

After a short break his handler handed him a strange knife. It had a solid steel handle, the back of the blade was serrated halfway down its length and there was a small hole only large enough for his little finger in the end of the handle.

"Can you identify the source and intended purpose of this knife?"

"Of course. It's an Indian Gurka's assassination knife. The end of the handle is used like brass knuckles to stun the victim and with one swipe cut their carotid artery or jugular vein. The assassin's little finger slips through this hole so the knife won't slip in his hand."

The exhausting session ended at 5:17 P.M.

"We'll meet again tomorrow morning at eight o'clock. You know where to find the instructions as to where we'll meet. I'll advise you then if you were selected for the assignment. Our analysts' results are inconclusive, but I can tell you that it looks good at this point."

"Is that good or bad?" Mack inquired and smiled.

"It all depends on how you want to look at it. Is the glass half full or half empty?"

"Do I have any choice?"

"No. But I can assure you that if you are selected, and you succeed, you will never be asked to take on another assignment anywhere. There will be adequate funds credited to your account to enable you to live quite comfortably. In a way I envy you."

"Why don't you go in my place?"

"I don't fit the profile they want and you do. Have you found the old Tiki Hut bar yet?"

"No. I haven't had any spare time since I got here. What day is it anyway?"

"It's Wednesday. You have the rest of the day off and the bar's not that far away. It's right off Beach Boulevard behind the pawnshop on Porter Avenue. It's about three blocks from here and you can walk there in five minutes. It's now called 'Lorna Belle's' and it's run by an ex-stripper from New Orleans. The lunchtime entertainment is great! They do a fashion lingerie' show every day from eleven-thirty to one-thirty. From the outside it doesn't look like it did when you were there, but they serve a mean hamburger and call it a Bionic Burger."

"What do you mean it doesn't look like it did?"

"They rebuilt it after Hurricane Camille. But they managed to save the bar and most of the interior. It's almost five-thirty and I still have to stop by the shop to find out what the boys decided after reviewing the videotape. I'll see you tomorrow morning."

Mack's handler stood up and motioned for him to leave the room.

Mack went back to his room and decided to lie down for a few minutes. It was 5:37 P.M. and there was lots of daylight left. He woke up at 6:23 P.M., washed his face and decided to take a walk. *"Maybe I can find the old place. I don't know what a Bionic Burger is but it might be okay."*

Mack crossed Beach Boulevard and walked west towards Porter Avenue. The rush hour traffic had died down and the tourists were heading for the restaurants and casinos. Mack paused at the intersection with Porter Avenue and spotted 'Lorna Belle's' across the street behind a pawn shop. The dancing neon hula girl was still in the front window.

"The last time I was here was in 1961. Three buddies and me were beat up by a group of rednecks from Point Cadet and

dumped out of a pickup at the main gate. A riot ensued which shut down Keesler for two days until things calmed down. I sure hope nobody recognizes me."

When he walked in the front door Mack noticed several framed pictures of Jim Croce on each side of the entranceway. Croce was one of his favorite singers. He sidled up to the bar and ordered a Budweiser in a bottle with an accompanying frosted mug. He preferred warm Merlot after dinner, but drank beer when he was thirsty. It was a hot three-block walk from the hotel.

He cautiously looked around the darken room. A tall, perhaps five foot eight or better, skinny, buxom and topless, longhaired, brunette in her early twenties was sliding up and down a brass pole mounted in the center of the seedy stage to the slow pulse of Jim Croce singing *Mississippi Lady*. A hard slap between the shoulder blades got his attention.

"It's about time that you got here!" Bellowed a raspy female voice from behind him. "I figured that you'd drag your sorry butt over here last night just for a taste of the memories."

Mack turned to face his assailant. It was Hattie Lou the woman from the bookstore! She held onto her walker with her left hand as she extended her right hand toward him in greeting.

"I've been waiting for you since five o'clock. Isn't that when most people get out of work?"

"I got hung up in traffic."

"No you didn't. I watched you walk right down Beach Boulevard. Where did you come from?

"I'm staying at the Beau Rivage.

"Are you in town for a little gambling? Want some companionship?"

"I'm here on a job interview and I don't need any companionship."

"What kind of work do you do?"

"You could call me a repairman. I fix things that are broken. Nothing special."

"Do you see that young girl up there on stage dancing her little heart out for you?"

"Yes. So what?"

"She's my grandniece Polly Jo. She goes to Tulane University and dances here in the summer to pick up money to pay her tuition. She's been dancing here since she was sixteen years old. I'd rather have her dancing in here than in a dive on Bourbon Street in New Orleans like I did. I tried to talk her out of dancing, but she won't pay me any mind. She's hardheaded just like my sister."

Mack decided to change the subject before she tried to pimp her grandniece or one of the waitresses to him. "What's with the autographed Jim Croce photos on the wall?"

"He got his start right here in this bar. He wrote *Mississippi Lady* on that table over there." She waved toward a table in a back corner. "The girl he wrote about in *Sweet Cordelia Brown* lived in an apartment over the bar. It broke her heart when he left for New York."

"Why did you call that girl on stage your grandniece?"

"Because she is. She ran away from home when she was sixteen. Her mother didn't want her back and decided to let her live here with me. I have her guardianship papers."

"Where's her mother?"

"Her mother is my sister Lorna Belle's daughter. She's a snooty, high-society broad up in Boston. She married some rich attorney and is living high on the old hog. She wants nothing to do with her mother, her daughter or me. Awhile back she went down to Stuart, cleaned out everything Lorna Belle owned and put her in a nursing home. Lorna Belle's all crippled up just like me and she'll most likely die there. I don't know which one of us is the lucky one."

"I think I met your sister."

"How could you meet my sister? She's in a nursing home. She doesn't know you!"

"It's a long story, but I visited her in the nursing home. You're much better off than she is. At least you can walk around. She can't."

"You saw her in the nursing home? When?"

"Monday afternoon. I was running down a rumor about buried pirate treasure and a retired treasure hunter told me to go see her. The trailer park manager told me she broke her hip and that her daughter put her in a nursing home. She thinks she's getting out when her hip heals up."

"She knows better than that! She won't get out of there until the day they carry her out feet first. But it makes her feel better to talk that way. What did she tell you?"

"She said that she found the ribs of an old wooden ship on the beach during the eye of a hurricane. She said thirty feet of the beach had disappeared. When the backside of the hurricane passed through the sand washed back up on the beach and covered the wreck up again."

"I remember that hurricane. I was there visiting her in August of nineteen forty-nine. Right after that she got real snooty and took to hanging around with a black guy from Tick Ridge. Before that she used to come over to New Orleans and dance with me once in awhile. She stopped dancing after that hurricane came through."

"What happened to cause that change in her behavior?"

"About six months after the hurricane went through she married some old rich guy and moved into a big house on Sewall's Point. He died of a heart attack two months later. She never had to work again and even sent her daughter to a private school in Boston. I kept dancing in the topless clubs on Bourbon Street in New Orleans until my body wore out."

"Why did you come to Biloxi? Why don't you live closer to New Orleans?"

"Our parents were cotton sharecroppers on a fifty acre farm ten miles north of Biloxi. We lived in a two room wooden shack that looked like a barn and my momma used old newspapers for wallpaper. Kids called us white trash to our faces. I dropped out of school in the ninth grade and ran away from home when I was fourteen. Lorna Belle made it through eleventh grade."

"How did she wind up in Stuart?"

"She met an Air Force guy who was stationed at Keesler. When he got discharged she went with him to Stuart because she was four months pregnant."

"Did they get married?"

"Nope. His family didn't like her one bit. They rented an apartment an apartment at a little inn in Stuart. He opened a bait shop at the north side of the Roosevelt Bridge and was stabbed to death one night when a couple of drunks broke in looking for money."

"What happened to her and the baby?"

"She had the baby. It was a girl. She took a job cleaning rooms and waiting tables at the Sand Club on Jensen Beach. The owners felt sorry for her and let her and the baby live in a spare room in the back of the place. I think she was fooling around with the black guy that did the yard work at the hotel, but she'd never admit it. That's where she met the rich guy she married."

"What was his name?"

"Darned if I can remember. It's not important because he died about two months after they got married. She got everything and became a real do-gooder after that. She even marched in the Freedom Marches in Selma, Alabama and almost got killed."

"How did her husband die?"

"She tells everybody that he died of a heart attack, but I know better. He was out back watching a guy digging a hole for a septic tank. He fell in the hole, hit his head on something and died of a brain concussion. The black guy dragged him out of the hole."

"What black guy?"

"The same one who was working as the yard man over at the hotel on the beach. Doesn't that sound a little strange to you?"

"No. It would be normal for her to hire someone she knew to help her husband dig a hole. She knew that she could trust him."

"That's the point. Trust him to do what? Hit her husband over the head with a shovel? Right after that the black guy came into a lot of money and built a big house on Tick Ridge."

"Maybe that's the guy that she told me to see at another nursing home. Does the name Frank Holmes sound familiar?"

"That's him! What did you find out? Did you talk to him?"

"No. The nursing home administrator told me that he was suffering from severe dementia. He wouldn't allow me to talk with him without written permission from his immediate family."

"When you get back to Stuart you need to find out who can give you that permission. When are you going back?"

"I'll be done with the interviews on Friday and should be home by Saturday. I'll run over to see Lorna Belle first. She might be able to fill in some blanks."

"Let me know what you find out. Now kick back and relax. I'm going to call my dishwasher out here so you can meet him. He favors that guy Rat in the book I told you about."

"I don't think that there is anyone else on this earth like Rat! He's one of a kind." Mack smiled and took a long draw on his frosted mug of cold beer. "Didn't you tell me last night that you were from Helena, Montana?"

"Might have. I forget. I tell a lot of people different things. They can't keep track of me that way. Bruce! Get your skinny ass out here. Somebody wants to meet you! Hurry up!"

The skinny, bearded derelict slowly shuffled out of the swinging kitchen door, paused for a second to allow his eyes to become accustomed to the darkened room and stopped at the end of the bar. "Yes ma'am. Who wants to meet me? Do I owe somebody money?"

"You owe everybody in the next three counties, but that's not why I called you out here. I wanted this guy to take a look at you. He knows a guy in Stuart, Florida who looks like you."

The dishwasher squinted, stroked his greasy black beard with both hands and looked at Mack. "Who do you know that looks like me? I ain't never been to Florida!"

"Doesn't he look like the guy in the book they call Rat?" She opened the book and pointed at the illustration of Rat in the back. "They both have the same squinty eyes and beard."

"He does resemble Rat a little," Mack responded as he leaned forward to get closer to the nervous dishwasher. "Where are you from?"

"I was born in Turkey Foot, Kentucky right next to the Daniel Boone National Forest."

"Do you have any brothers?" Mack asked and drained the last drop of Budweiser out of the mug and signaled to the bar tender to set up another fresh one.

"I had an older brother named Rodney. He was drafted in sixty-three and killed in the Viet Nam war. The Army reported him as Missing in Action and never found his body."

"What's your name?"

"Richard Mathers."

"He may look a little like Rat, but they have nothing in common," Mack directed his comments at the trembling man. "I'm sorry that we took you away from your work." Mack nodded toward the kitchen door.

"Yes sir. I have a lot of dishes to wash and put up before the late dinner crowd gets here."

Mack turned toward the disappointed woman, "Every town has its own version of Rat and he's yours. Somewhere out there he has a mother, a father and perhaps even brothers or sisters, who worry about him, wonder where he is and if he's okay. There's no doubt he also worries about them, but he's happy here. Just allow him to live in his world as he sees it." Mack took a long draw from the frosted beer mug. "He'll be just fine just like Rat."

"I worry about him and take care of him as best I can, but he won't allow me to get close to him. He's very secretive about his past. Some people think he's nuts!"

"Aren't we all just a little nuts?" Mack reached for his mug. "Who defines sanity? Perhaps it's better for people to think he's a little nuts, that way they'll leave him alone."

"I understand." She maneuvered her walker close to the mahogany bar and looked Mack in the eye. "When I met you last night you told me that you were stationed at Keesler in nineteen-sixty one and got in that big brawl right here when it was called the Tiki Hut. Now what's the real reason for you being in town?"

"I'm writing a book about my life and came back to do some research," Mack winked and reached for the frosted mug. "I want to be accurate and the memory has faded over the years."

"Would you like to meet a couple of the Point Cadet boys who kicked your ass? I watched the whole thing because Lorna Belle and me were dancing that night. My ex-husband was one of the guys and the bartender was another. My husband's sitting over there at the end of the bar nursing a beer. He's crippled up with arthritis and can't talk to good because he had a stroke last year."

"I'd rather pass at this point. I still have nightmares about it."

"Do you remember what started it?"

"I think so. I was flirting with one of the dancers and her boyfriend got pissed."

"That was me you were flirting with and my husband is the guy who was pissed at you."

"I remember that it was real late. The Air Force guys were gone except for my two friends and me and there was a bunch of drunked up rednecks over by the pool table. One big guy went over and locked the front door and stood in front of it with a baseball bat in his hand. Another guy pulled down the bamboo window shades and then all hell broke loose. I don't remember anything else except being shoved out of the back of a pickup truck in front of the main gate. I crawled up to the sentry and passed out. That's it." Mack reached for his beer mug.

"That was it exactly. My husband hit you over the back of the head with a bar stool. That's why you don't remember anything. They wanted to castrate all of you, take you out in the bay in a shrimp boat and throw you overboard. Lorna Belle and me talked them out of it. We probably saved your lives." She rubbed his forearm and tears ran down her cheeks.

"Thank you, but those are memories that I really don't want to remember. I still have dreams about it." Mack drained the mug and motioned for another beer. "Didn't the base erupt in a riot the next day?"

"It was a big mess. Airmen came off base into town with metal bunk dividers and beat the hell out of any guys they could find. It took several years before it cooled down around here. I always wondered what happened to you guys. Are you going to write about this in your book?"

"I don't know yet. It wasn't a good thing and I was only eighteen years old at the time. I got into a lot of other similar scrapes after that and some of them still haunt me. It would be boring to someone who wasn't there." Mack drained the mug and looked at the fuzzy clock mounted over the bar. It read 9:56 P.M.

The skinny girl had quit dancing and sidled toward Mack and her aunt. It was time for the ten o'clock show. The bar had filled up with young airmen from Keesler and an equal number of locals. "*Some things never change*," Mack thought. A young, chubby very drunk man, obviously an airman from Keesler, slipped off his bar stool and hit the wooden floor with a loud, meaty 'thump.' A tall, big-boned local tough grabbed the young man by the shoulder, dragged him up off the floor and held him at eye level against the bar.

"You spilled my beer," he shouted as he shook his fist in the young man's face. "I should bust your ass right here. I don't think that anyone here will disagree with me. What do you think?"

The terrified young man frantically looked around the bar for an ally. His Air Force buddies had abandoned him. He was surrounded by seven local toughs from Point Cadet and realized that his fate was almost sealed. He looked toward Mack and pitifully pleaded.

"This guy's going to beat me up because I spilled his beer. He says that everyone here agrees with him about beating me up. Do you?"

Put on the spot and outnumbered by many younger men Mack had little choice.

"I don't." Mack lifted his empty beer mug, held it over the edge of the bar and looked the young tough in the eye. "Put him down."

"What if I don't?" The young tough drew back his fist to hit the terrified young man. "Are you going to kill me if I don't?" He shook his cocked fist at Mack and grinned.

"If I have to I will," Mack coolly responded and took a step back from the bar. "Let him go."

"You never killed nobody," the tough responded and grinned. "I'll kick your ass."

Mack set the beer mug on the bar, reached over with his right hand, removed his watch from his left wrist and slipped it into his pants pocket. When Mack turned to face the young tough a strange emotionless look came over his face. He didn't say a word, but the crowd around the bar disappeared and left the tough guy standing alone with his terrified victim in his grasp. Tears ran down the young man's face and he sobbed with accompanying wheezing gasps.

"I was just fooling with him," stammered the town tough as he released his victim. "I wouldn't have hurt him. I just wanted to see him cry a little." He smoothed out his victim's shirt.

"Abner! Get your sorry ass out of here before you make this man mad!" Bellowed the gravely female voice from behind Mack. "You're damn lucky that you can still walk. Get going!"

"Yes ma'am I'm leaving," he stammered out. "I was just fooling around with him." As he went out the front door he shot Mack a 'bird' and grinned.

"Don't let him bother you none. He's nobody unless he has a dozen of his pals around to support him," remarked Hattie Lou. "I'll send the airman back to base in a cab so they can't bother him any more. He's drunk as a skunk and can't defend himself"

"I might just take a cab back to the hotel myself," Mack responded. "I'm about half in the bag and I don't need to get in a street brawl with a dozen guys twenty years younger than me."

"Why don't you let Polly Jo walk you back? She's done dancing for the night and she lives over that way. They won't mess with you because they know that I'll find out."

"It's getting late and I wouldn't want to put her out. I'll just take a cab back to the hotel."

"It's okay," responded a soft southern drawl from behind him. "I'm going that way anyway and I'll walk with you. The fresh salt air blowing off the bay will help sober you up."

The young dancer had changed to tight jeans with a low cut top that exposed most of her midriff and breasts. She squeezed Mack's right arm and pulled him toward the front door.

"Auntie, I'll give you a call when I get home. I'll take good care of him. He'll be okay."

The couple strolled down Beach Boulevard toward the Beau Rivage and the young girl squeezed Mack's arm to get his attention. When he looked down at her she smiled up at him.

"There's a lot that my auntie doesn't know about me. I make my spending money working stag parties at college and I love having sex with older men."

"What!"

"I'm young. I want to have fun before I get old and wrinkled."

"You're to young to worry about wrinkles."

"No I'm not. I've already got one."

"I can't see any wrinkle. Where is it?"

"I'm sitting on it."

Chapter 7

Mack awoke to the sound of running water emanating from the bathroom shower and a female voice humming *Mississippi Lady* in a key far above Jim Croce's original recording. He rolled over and glanced at the red glowing numerals of the digital clock nestled on the bedside table. It read 8:23 A.M.

"I'm late. I was supposed to meet him at eight o'clock," Mack mumbled to himself as he swung his legs over the side of the bed and suddenly realized he was buck naked.

A lilting female voice wafted from the bathroom, "Your shower is ready." Then the meadow sweet voice changed to a sultry 'come hither' tone. "Are you?"

"That little hooker must've slipped me something in the bar. I don't remember I damn thing. I'll wring her scrawny neck when I get my hands on her," Mack muttered under his breath as he stood up, jerked the top sheet off the bed, slung it around his waist and headed for the bathroom.

"Stop right there!" Boomed out a deep, resonant male voice. It wasn't CNN. "Do you see how easy it is to be taken advantage of in a strange city?"

Mack paused to get a bearing on the direction the sultry voice came from and homed in on the black Chinese screen festooned with Mother of Pearl peacocks and Chinese pheasants.

"If this were New York, Washington or Vienna you may not have woken up. Let this be a lesson to you. Go take your shower. My assistant is running the water for you and we have many things to accomplish today. You were selected for the assignment and you leave tomorrow morning. Please hurry!"

The faint scent of *White Diamonds* suddenly filled the room. Mack felt a puff of air as someone slipped out of the bathroom, passed behind him and out the door into the hotel hallway. "*Guess I'll never know*," Mack mumbled to himself as he entered the steamy bathroom.

Breakfast was served by room service and immediately after the waiter left the room Mack's handler got down to business. "Our analysts stayed up all night reviewing your video tapes. You match the profile and at five-thirty this morning we made the decision that you're the man for the project. Now we have to review your language skills. What languages do you speak?"

"English, Spanish and Japanese. I can generally understand Italian and German, but can speak very little of it. I know enough to get by in a pinch."

"How about Russian?"

"*Nyet!*"

"That's what I thought. Let's get down to business and begin by reviewing several video tapes. You're going to watch the tapes that we made of you yesterday and some tapes of someone that looks very much like you. It's important that you get his mannerisms down perfectly because you will only have one opportunity and you can blow this assignment by missing one small detail."

Mack spent the morning in the darkened room staring at two television monitors. His handler paused and re-started the tapes to make a point here and there. "Look how he tends to drag his right foot when he carries his briefcase in his right hand. When he carries it in his left hand there's no drag. When he stops at a corner he looks to the left first, then to the right and touches his nose before he starts across the street."

"Is he right handed or left handed?"

"Right handed and he is left brain dominant. There's a simple test for brain dominance and you can't afford to fail it if someone tests you."

"What is it?"

"Clasp your hands together and interlace your fingers. Good! Now fold one thumb over the other and tilt your hands toward me so I can see your thumbs."

"Like this?"

"Exactly! You're left brained just like him. That's perfect!"

"How can you tell that I'm left brained?" Mack quizzically looked at his folded thumbs.

"Your left thumb is folded over the top of your right thumb. Now try to fold your right thumb over your left thumb."

"That doesn't feel natural," Mack responded and switched his thumbs back so that his left thumb folded over the right one.

"That's because it's not natural for you."

During the afternoon session Mack watched video tapes of people entering and leaving the United Nations in New York, the United States Capitol and what appeared to be an embassy on Washington's elite Embassy Row. He was given samples of handwriting to duplicate over and over again. At 5:17 P.M. his handler tapped him on the right shoulder.

"Okay. That's it. You're as ready for this assignment as I can get you in three days.

"What do I do now?"

"You're flying out of Pensacola on Delta Flight 2154 tomorrow morning at six-thirty. Here's your ticket. Leave your car in the short-term parking lot because you're coming back Friday afternoon. Leave your suitcase in the car as well. You won't be needing it."

"Where am I going?"

"First to Atlanta then most likely to New York." His handler handed Mack a brown envelope. "There's a tourist map of New York City and a United Nations building interior office floor plan in here. Study it tonight! There's also a pager in there. If it goes off catch the first flight back to Atlanta or Pensacola depending on where you are at the time."

"What did you mean when you said most likely New York? Don't you know for sure?"

"I'm not at liberty to discuss your assignment with you. Just be on that plane to Atlanta in the morning."

"What do I do when I get back to Pensacola? Do I come back here?"

"I can't discuss any portion of your assignment with you. Oh, I overlooked telling you one little detail."

"What's that?"

A contact will be waiting for you in Atlanta to pass on additional instructions. If your contact doesn't show call this number immediately and leave a message." Mack's handler passed over a white slip of paper. "Memorize the number and give the paper back to me."

"Come on. You know what's going on. Tell me something. Anything!"

"Okay. Your target is scheduled to give a speech at the United Nations at two o'clock tomorrow afternoon. He'll be arriving via private car about one-thirty. If he cancels the speech you will be diverted to Washington, DC via Dulles International."

"Why Dulles?"

"Because if he doesn't show up in New York you'll have to look for him in Washington."

"Why can't I fly into Washington National? It's thirty miles closer to downtown DC."

"They'll have it locked down tighter than a drum fifteen minutes after you make the switch."

"Won't they lock down Dulles?"

"Most likely, but you stand a better chance of getting out of there."

"Why do I have to fly to Pensacola? Why can't I fly directly back to West Palm Beach?"

"They'll have the West Palm airport staked out. Get rid of your Pensacola to Atlanta ticket when you get inside the Atlanta terminal. We can't afford to have you tied to us if something happens to you."

"When will I know where I'm going for certain?"

"Someone will meet you in Atlanta and give you a packet containing your instructions."

"How will I know who it is?"

"Don't worry. He'll recognize you. Don't attempt to engage him in idle conversation. Just take the packet and be on your way. Don't forget to destroy the Pensacola to Atlanta ticket stub. Don't throw it in a trashcan! Someone will be watching you."

"What do you mean someone may be watching me? Does someone know that I'm here?"

"I have to go. It's almost five-thirty and my wife will have dinner on the table by the time I get home. I suggest that you go out for a good meal at a fine restaurant tonight." Mack's deep-voiced handler smiled, rose up from his chair and headed toward the door.

"Do you have any suggestions where I should go for my last meal?"

"Try Mary Mahoney's 'Old French House' on Beach Boulevard."

"I'll give it a shot. How far is it from Biloxi to Pensacola and how do I find the airport?"

"It's a two-hour drive. Allow some time for traffic because you have to go through town to Airport Boulevard." He smiled, gave Mack a wave of his right hand and left the room.

Mack looked at his ticket and slowly reviewed it. *"Delta Flight 2154 to Atlanta leaves Pensacola at 6:30 A.M. and arrives in Atlanta at 8:42 A.M. I return from Atlanta back to Pensacola on Delta Flight 2289 at 10:05 P.M. It arrives at 10:13 P.M. Central Time. If the flight's on time I might try to drive straight through back to Stuart. It's only a nine hour drive."*

Mack elected to go next door to McElroy's Seafood Restaurant for dinner. He felt uneasy all during dinner because a single male diner directly across the dining room seemed to be watching him. After dinner Mack returned to 'Lorna Belle's' and found the front door locked.

"May I help you sir?" The deep baritone male voice came from directly behind Mack. "May I help you sir?" The tone of the man's voice clearly indicated authority and he expected a reply.

Mack turned and found himself face to face with a middle-aged Biloxi City cop.

"May I help you sir?" The cop asked again. His tone of voice showed his obvious irritation.

"I thought I'd stop in here for a beer before I went back to my hotel and turned in for the night."

"Can't you see that the place is closed?"

"What time do they open? It's six forty-five and they were open at this time last night."

"We closed her down last night for hiring under-age strippers and running a string of street girls. Were you propositioned last night by one of the strippers?"

"No."

"I think you were because I saw you leave with one right after the fight broke up. Her name is Polly and she's only twenty years old. You were damn lucky that she didn't slip you a Mickey Finn and roll you for your cash."

"Were you here last night?"

"Yes. I saw the whole thing. I was working undercover vice on the inside and I couldn't blow my cover. You were damn lucky that punk kid from Point Cadet didn't pull a gun on you. He was waiting for you outside and we picked him up before you came out. We charged him with carrying a concealed weapon because he had a .38 Police Special tucked in his waistband under his shirt. He was going to kill you."

"Who do I thank? You?"

"Nah. It's no big deal. You were just another dumb Yankee tourist in a place where you had no business being. That's why me and my cousins from Point Cadet kicked your ass thirty-five years ago."

"What do you mean?"

"I was one of the guys in the bar that night. My brother is the guy who hit you over the head with a bar stool."

"Hattie Lou said that was her ex-husband!"

"He is! They got divorced over thirty years ago. He still comes around for old time's sake and she keeps an open tab for him at the bar."

"Why didn't he recognize you and tell her that you were there?"

"He's almost blind and I was wearing so much makeup and crap that my own mother wouldn't recognize me. I left right after you did and followed you back to the Beau Rivage. I wanted to be sure that the stripper's biker boyfriend and his friends didn't smack you over the head for kicks."

"I didn't see you."

"Of course not. You were smashed. You drank seven beers that I counted and you got there about an hour before I did. Do you remember anything?"

"Nope. I don't remember leaving the place. I woke up this morning in bed by myself."

"Of course you did. She got you upstairs, tossed you on the bed when you passed out, went through your pockets and split. Her trademark is *White Diamonds* perfume."

"I wasn't missing anything this morning. My money was all there."

"We were waiting for her outside your room and grabbed her when she came out. We got everything back and replaced it. She's in jail right now if you want to go down and see her. She doesn't have any money to bond herself out and her biker boyfriend is pissed that she got picked up because her tip money was impounded as evidence."

"I'll pass. I have to get up early in the morning and drive to Pensacola."

"Okay. Come back and see us when you have more time. Biloxi's a very friendly town."

"Thank you. I just might and I won't wait thirty years to come back again."

Mack decided to drive down Beach Boulevard to Books A Million and catch up on the news via the local newspaper. Shortly after he settled down in an easy chair and started to scan the newspaper Mack a scruffy-looking male approached his chair. He was unshaven, his blood-shot eyes as wide open as dinner plates and his clothing looked like it came from a dumpster. He wore ragged blue jeans, mud-dappled brown leather boots and a red/black checkered, Buffalo plaid hunting shirt over a ragged, coffee-stained white tee shirt. He even smelled like a dumpster. He slowly approached Mack, paused and carefully looked around before speaking.

"Are you a finder?"

"What do you mean a finder?" Mack cautiously responded.

"I'm a finder. I find things out in the woods. Just this morning I found some fresh mammoth poop."

"Don't you mean fossilized dinosaur poop?"

"Nope! It's fresh, real soft too, and still warm. There was steam coming off it when I found it. I've got a piece of it in a cooler in the back of my pickup truck. Do you want to see it? It'll just take me a minute to get it."

"No thanks. I'll take a pass. How do you know that it's mammoth poop?"

"I was tracking them through the woods in the dark. They're night feeders you know."

"How do you know you were tracking mammoths if it was dark?"

"I've had the herd staked out for about a month. I dig vegetables out of the dumpsters behind grocery stores and take them up to them in my pickup. I know where they bed down during the day. Nobody ever goes up there because of the snakes."

"What kind of snakes?"

"Rattlers! There's some real big ones up there. The local folks know better than to go up there."

"Where's up there?"

"If'n I told you you'd go there and tell everybody about them. I can't tell you exactly where, but it's just across the Alabama line. It's not safe. It used to be an Air Force bombing range and there's still a lot of unexploded bombs up there."

"Will you take me up there this afternoon?"

"No. You have to go there at night so nobody sees you going in the gate and you have to know exactly where you're going or you'll get lost. Wait here! I'm going out to my truck and I'll bring in some real fresh mammoth poop for you to look at."

"That's okay. I'll pass on the poop."

"What would you say if'n I told you that I was really hungry and hadn't eaten for two days because I don't have any money?"

"I'd tell you to find a job and make some money. That's what most of us do."

"Are you going to tell the store manager that I asked you for money?"

"Yes."

"I'll get in trouble and she'll throw me out."

"That's fine with me."

The dumpster diver didn't offer an audible response, frowned, spun on his heels and headed for the door. Before exiting he paused, looked back at Mack with a grin and gave him a 'thumbs up.' He lingered around the front of the store and waited for Mack to come out. When Mack exited the front door the man approached him from his left. Mack tried to ignore him, but he reached out and tapped Mack on the left arm.

"Hey there bud! Wanna' hear another true story?"

"No." Mack continued walking toward his car as the babbling man trailed behind him,

"Did you know about the Declaration of Armaments that Jefferson Davis sent to Abraham Lincoln? The Civil War started two days later because the North didn't respond in time."

"No I didn't hear about it and I really don't care."

"The South sent a Declaration of Armaments to President Lincoln by horseback courier describing the South's manpower, equipment, cannons, guns, amount of ammunition, etc. The North supposedly sent their Declaration of Armaments to Jefferson Davis the same day – but the courier never arrived. Thus, the South never knew the advantage held by the North. If they had known of the North's military superiority they would have capitulated and the Civil War would have never begun. The North claimed that their courier was killed, but the South knew better. The North's Declaration of Armaments was never sent because the North wanted the war. The South declared seven hundred-fifty thousand men and the North had two million plus."

"So? That was a long time ago and it's ancient history."

"Hang on! You haven't heard the best part yet. It's current all right! The people of the South prayed that the holder of the North's Declaration of Armaments, or their heir, would be killed and eaten by an alligator in Biloxi, Mississippi." The enthusiastic man continued. "Have you seen George Bush Senior lately? No one's seen him for two weeks."

"No. I haven't and I doubt that he was eaten by an alligator in Biloxi."

"The newspaper people kept it quiet because they don't want to upset the tourists."

Mack shrugged off his new admirer and returned to the Beau Rivage to pack his suitcase. He wouldn't be in the mood to do it in the morning after a three o'clock wake up call. When he opened the door to his room the musty-sweet aroma of *White Diamonds* drifted out of the room into the humid night air.

Chapter 8

Mack tossed and turned waiting for the three o'clock wakeup call that just wouldn't come. It seemed like he had just dozed off when the telephone chattered. He sat up and looked at the digital clock on the nightstand. It read 3:00 A.M. He lifted the telephone handset off its cradle and placed it beside his right ear.

"Hello," he answered in a groggy voice.

"It is now three o'clock." The monotone computerized voice seemed surreal. *"This is your requested wakeup call. Have a nice day."*

Mack paused at the stop sign at the junction of the Beau Rivage parking lot and Beach Boulevard. He was still confused. *"Where am I going after I get to Atlanta?"* A car pulled out of the parking lot, pulled in behind him and flashed its lights. It was a signal for Mack to hurry up and pull out onto the highway. The car followed him as he turned onto Beach Boulevard, swung onto the north I-110 ramp and headed for I-10 and the Pensacola airport some two hours away. Something didn't seem right, but Mack couldn't put his finger on it. *"Why did he drop the hint about New York and in the same thought include Washington, DC? Who is going to meet me? I'm dead meat when I touch down in either place. I'm considered to be disposable and not expected to come back. I'll be written off as a minor collateral loss and included as a footnote in the Executive Summary of the project."*

Mack exited I-10 south in Pensacola onto I-110 at 5:45 A.M. *"Not bad time even if I say so myself."* He passed the Steak & Ale and resisted the temptation to pull into the Waffle House next door for a cup of coffee. He turned left onto Airport Boulevard and caught the traffic light just as it turned from green to yellow. He pulled the blue Trans Am into the short-term parking lot at the airport and parked in space C-4. He had thirty- five minutes before his flight left for Atlanta.

Delta Flight 2154 arrived at Gate 18 in Atlanta on time at 8:42 A.M. Eastern Daylight Savings Time. Mack walked off the boarding ramp into the gate waiting area, looked around hoping to catch a glimpse of a familiar face, but there was no one there to meet him.

"That's really nice. Now what am I expected to do?"

He walked onto the concourse and looked up at the flight status board mounted on the wall. There were four Delta flights to New York City that left within the next hour. Only one of them left from this particular concourse and it was scheduled to depart from Gate 24 at 9:37 A.M. Mack headed for the gate figuring that his handler mentioned New York City as a deliberate hint.

At Gate 24 Mack walked up to the check-in counter and addressed the blonde female ticket agent. "Excuse me. I'm supposed to be on this flight and someone was supposed to meet me at my arrival gate with my ticket, but he didn't show up. He must be stuck in traffic. Would you please check the passenger manifest for my name?" Mack slid his driver's license over to her.

"I'm sorry Mr. McElroy, but you're not on this flight. You're on flight twelve eighty-six to Washington's Dulles International Airport. It leaves from gate twenty-eight, that's four gates down that way, at nine forty-five. You may pick up your ticket at the gate when you check in for the flight. It's waiting for you" She smiled and winked.

"Thank you very much." Mack turned away from the counter and headed toward gate twenty-eight. He had almost an hour to kill *"Why would he say New York when he meant Washington?"*

Mack wondered. *"Maybe he got me mixed up with someone else?"*

Mack arrived at Gate 28. A middle-aged, obese, balding white man manned the check-in counter and he was obviously not overjoyed. "May I help you sir? The bored ticket agent asked as he reached across the counter with his right hand. "Do you have your ticket envelope with you?"

"No. My ticket is supposed to waiting for me here at the gate."

"You are who?" The cautious ticket agent frowned and looked at his glowing green computer screen.

"Paul McElroy. Do you have my ticket?"

"Yes sir. It's right here and the aircraft will be ready for boarding in about twenty minutes." The agent passed the ticket folder across the counter to Mack.

"Thank you."

Mack took the folder, turned and walked toward the waiting area. He felt strange and knew that something was missing. *"I thought I was going to New York and now it turns out that I'm going to Washington and landing at Dulles. What a rip off,"* he muttered his displeasure to himself. *"Why didn't they book me into Washington National? It's a ten-minute cab ride from the airport. Dulles is thirty miles out of town and it takes almost an hour to get downtown."*

Mack took an empty seat in the waiting area facing the gift shop. He spotted a discarded copy of *USA TODAY* on an open seat and decided to catch up on the news. He hadn't seen a newspaper since he left Stuart on Monday. He looked over the top of the open newspaper and saw a white man dressed in a black suit, white shirt and sunglasses standing directly across the concourse. Next to him stood a black female wearing the uniform of a cleaning person. She leaned against her cart, her eyes were closed and she seemed to be sleeping. About fifty feet down the concourse on the same side of the concourse stood a clone of the first guy.

"Now isn't that a trio to draw to?" Mack thought. *"The Blues Brothers theme died out a long time ago. That guy and his clone look like a pair of heavies in a B-grade spy movie. She isn't any Mata Hari, but is obviously connected to them. They're waiting*

for someone to throw something away. I wonder who it could be? I'll give them a thrill to write home about."

Mack removed his ticket folder from his jacket pocket, took out the Pensacola to Atlanta ticket stub and scribbled 'Got 'cha! on the inside flap of the folder. He stuffed the ticket stub in his shirt pocket, stood up and walked toward the gift shop. When he passed the trashcan he tossed the ticket folder so that it landed about three feet away from the trashcan opening. The cleaning lady dove onto the ticket folder like a defensive back covering a fumble.

"I got it!" She yelled. "You dropped this ticket folder on the floor. Do you want it back?" She growled as she clasped the folder to her breast.

"No. I meant to throw it in the trashcan. Thank you for picking it up." Mack continued walking into the gift shop toward the magazine rack. He watched the pair in the round, overhead mirror that was strategically positioned so that the cashier could observe potential shoplifters. The first man talked into the sleeve of his suit jacket as he motioned to his clone some fifty feet down the concourse. The trio briefly assembled in front of the gift shop and disappeared down the concourse together.

Mack chuckled, *"I'm glad that they didn't open that folder while they were there. I'd better head for the gate before they come back."*

Delta Flight 1286 arrived at Dulles five minutes late at 12:28 A.M. Mack strode off the aircraft fully confident that his contact would meet him with a full set of instructions. But, there was no one waiting for him. Mack hung around the gate waiting area until 12:52 hoping against hope that his contact was delayed in traffic. After all, it was Friday afternoon and many politicians and their staff members would be heading out of town for the weekend. A lot of Congressional staffers lived in the Reston area and Dulles was close to their homes.

At 12:57 P.M. the beeper on Mack's belt vibrated signaling a page. He glanced at the digital readout panel and it listed an 800 number. Mack raced to the pay telephone bank and dialed it. The telephone rang seven times and was answered by a computer with a digitized voice message. *"You've been compromised. The mission has been aborted. Get out of there now! Catch the next flight back to Atlanta. When you get back to Pensacola, get in your car and drive back to Stuart. That is all.*"

'Click.' The telephone went dead.

Mack imagined a miniature tape recorder bursting into flame on the other end of the line. It was bizarre! His flight back to Atlanta wouldn't depart for almost five hours! He glanced up at the flight status board and noted that Flight 1697 was scheduled to depart for Atlanta at 2:45 P.M. "*If I can make it to Atlanta I should be able to get a seat on a flight to Pensacola,*" Mack thought as he headed for the Delta ticket counter.

The four giggling young female interns in front of him were attempting to book a flight to Atlanta for a wild weekend in 'Underground Atlanta'. After considerable haggling with the flustered, middle-aged male ticket agent the girls got their tickets and at last it was Mack's turn. He placed his ticket envelope onto the counter and slid it toward the red-faced agent.

"If those girls were my daughters I'd ground them for a month of Sundays," the ticket agent offered as he opened Mack's ticket folder. "How may I help you sir?"

"I'd like to have a seat on the next available flight to Atlanta and a connection to Pensacola, Florida," Mack responded as he glanced over his right shoulder. "My meeting was canceled and I want to get back home as soon as I can. If I get home early enough I might have time to take the boat out and catch a few fish for dinner."

"Sir, you have a very big problem."

"What kind of problem?"

"This is a non-changeable, non-refundable ticket. It's only good on flight eight twenty-three that is scheduled to depart at five thirty-five this afternoon and arrives in Atlanta at seven thirty-three this evening. You then connect to flight twenty-two eight-five which departs Atlanta for Pensacola at 10:05 P.M. and arrives in Pensacola at 10:13 P.M. Central Time."

"Can't I get on flight sixteen ninety-seven? It leaves at two forty-five!"

"That would be nice if you could because it connects to flight sixteen ninety-three that departs Atlanta for Pensacola at five-thirty-five and arrives in Pensacola at five forty-seven Central Time. That would be ideal for you, but you can't do it!"

"What do you mean I can't do it? Is the flight full?"

"Oh no. There're plenty of seats, but you have a non-changeable, non-refundable ticket. You are locked into flight eight twenty-three at five thirty-five this afternoon. But, there is an option."

"What's that?"

"If you're willing to pay the spot ticket price of seven hundred and fifty-three dollars I can book you on the flights you want right now."

"What! That's highway robbery!"

"It certainly is, but that's the rate. Do you want the ticket or not?" The ticket agent yawned.

"I don't have that kind of cash on me."

"How about a credit card?" The agent tried to appear concerned about Mack's dilemma and then his desk phone rang. "Excuse me sir. My supervisor is calling me on the intercom line." The agent turned away so that his broad, sweaty back faced Mack and the counter. He hung up the telephone and turned to face Mack. "I have some good news for you. Delta is willing to exchange your tickets for the flights you requested. Give me just a few minutes and I'll print out your tickets and boarding passes." The agent returned to punching keys on his computer terminal.

The flight to Atlanta was uneventful except that the ticket agent had assigned Mack a seat directly between the four giggling interns. Two of them were seated ahead of him, two of them were seated behind him and all four of them seemed oblivious of his discomfort. They exchanged jokes back and forth across the seats as they drank beer after beer.

"Hey mister," yelled back the pony-tailed blonde directly in front of Mack's aisle seat. She might have been all of nineteen years old. 'Wanna' go to Underground Atlanta with us for the weekend? We'll show you a real good time if you buy us some booze. We're all over eighteen. We're not jail bait! We're legal." All four girls giggled profusely.

"No thank you. I think I know your parents."

The girls were very quiet for the remainder of the flight to Atlanta. The flight arrived on time at 4:40 P.M. at Gate 28. It was the same gate that Mack's flight to Dulles had departed from only seven hours earlier. When Mack walked into the main concourse he saw the same trio in front of the gift shop that was there earlier and they didn't appear to be happy campers. Mack smiled and nodded when he walked past them.

"You're a real smart ass aren't you?" Spoke up one of the Blues Brothers. "We've got your number and we'll meet again real soon."

Mack ignored the comment and looked for a flight status board to check the departure gate for Flight 1693 to Pensacola. It was scheduled to leave at 5:35 P.M. from Gate 18 and he had to hustle.

During the one-hour flight Mack mentally reviewed his situation. *"If the mission was aborted because I was compromised then someone knows who I am. There might be someone on this flight looking to pop me in the airport parking garage. Wait a minute! A car followed me out of the of the hotel parking lot when I pulled out. Who else would have been up at three-thirty in the morning?"*

Things didn't make sense to him, but he was too tired to spend time worrying about it. He looked forward to getting back on the ground and on his way back to Stuart. Tina would be wondering where he was and no doubt she had something planned because it was Friday night.

"If the plane arrives in Pensacola at five forty-seven it's six forty-seven in Stuart. If I drive straight through it will take me about nine hours if I average sixty miles an hour. That would put me in Stuart about three or four o'clock in the morning. That wouldn't be bad. Tina will be smashed and in bed on her boat. She won't know or care what time I come home."

The plane arrived at the gate at 4:43. When Mack arrived at parking space C-4 he was shocked. The blue Trans Am was gone and a shiny red Mustang convertible sat in its place. *"What the hell is going on? This looks just like the car that I drove from Tallahassee to Biloxi."*

Mack saw a folded white piece of paper stuck between the window and the doorframe on the driver's side. He gingerly pulled it out and unfolded it. The note, crudely written in penciled block letters, read, *"Try your key!"*

Mack slipped the Trans Am key into the lock turned it to the right and he inside door lock popped up.

"They switched cars," he muttered under his breath.

Chapter 9

Saturday morning opened softly as a July day should. Enormous sow snook were spawning in the St. Lucie Inlet and the hot summer sun rose in the eastern sky. Dozens of nook fishermen, exhausted from fishing through the night, dozed in their campers to build up enough energy so they could get back on the water at dusk to repeat the process.

Sewall's Point Marina's parking lot was serene. Tina's silver-blue BMW Z3 convertible sat at an awkward angle atop the telephone pole that served as a divider between the parking lot and red hibiscus bushes bordering the property. Mack's blue pickup truck hunkered in a corner and a blue Trans Am with Mississippi plates sat in front of the walkway leading to the front porch, The black and white cat was enjoying the sun from his roost on the front porch and slowly licked his butt savoring every loose hair. All seemed serene until 10:47 A.M. when Tina crawled out from the cabin of her sailboat on her hands and knees to face another weekend hangover.

"Help! Someone help! Call 911! He's dead! Help!" Tina screamed as she ran out into the bright sunlight from inside the dark boathouse. "Mack's been killed! Somebody call 911!" She ran from the boat dock into the boathouse and back out again. "Help! Somebody please help! Mack's been shot! Help!"

Sewall's Point Marina was well out of earshot of the campers at Sandsprit Park almost a mile away, but someone close by heard her screams for help. Rat was just across the St. Lucie River on Trickle's Island where he spent the night sleeping in his kayak. He cranked up the ancient outboard motor and sped as fast as he could over to the mouth of Willoughby Creek, turned right into North Lake and headed for Port Sewall Marina. When Rat reached the boat dock Tina was racing around and screaming at the top of her lungs. The two dolphins *Puka* and *Kea* raced around North Lake in a panic. They knew that something was wrong with their pal Tina, but they didn't know what it was.

Rat pulled alongside the dock, slipped a couple of half hitches over a piling and slithered onto the splintered wooden timbers. "Tina! What's going on? What are you screaming about?"

Tina grabbed Rat's scruffy sleeve. "Mack's dead. He's inside the boathouse. Somebody shot him! There's blood all over him. Call 911 and get an ambulance over here."

"If he's dead he doesn't need an ambulance. Let me look inside." Rat gently pulled her hand loose from his sleeve. "Go upstairs, call Elmo on his cell phone and get him down here right away. He'll know what to do."

Tina ran up the wooden stairway to the cottage above as Rat cautiously slipped inside the darkened boathouse to check on his friend. He had seen a lot of dead men during his tour of duty in Southeast Asia and most of them died from gunshot wounds. He turned on the overhead lights to get a better look. The body was face down. The legs and torso were on the boathouse floor, but the head, shoulders and outstretched arms hung over the water.

"*It looks like whoever killed him tried to dump his body into the water,*" Rat muttered softly to himself as he reached into Mack's hip pocket, pulled out his wallet, opened it and removed his Florida driver's license.

"*It's you alright my friend. Somebody wanted you dead bad enough to follow you home from where ever you went Monday night. I hope you had some fun while you were gone because you won't be having any more.*" Rat stood up, turned to leave the boathouse and met Deputy Elmo standing in the doorway.

"Is it Mack?" Elmo asked hesitantly. "If it is I'm worried about Ralph too."

"Why?"

"Ralph's been acting strange for the past few days. His wife Joy told me that he forgets where he leaves things and gets lost driving around town. He went mullet fishing last night and hasn't come home yet." Elmo removed his 'Smokey Bear' hat as he knelt down beside the body. "I'm not so sure that Ralph is the Ralph we know."

"What do you mean not the Ralph we know?"

"I think that Ralph was either done in and replaced by a body double that looks like him or he was drugged so he didn't know what he was doing and set up to kill Mack."

"What? Why Ralph?"

"They were good friends and Ralph could get close to Mack without arousing suspicion."

"Ralph couldn't kill Mack or anyone else in a million years."

"Don't be so sure about it. I've seen a lot of strange things over the last twenty years. This guy looks like Mack. Have you checked his identification?"

"Here's his wallet. I pulled it out of his pants pocket. It's Mack all right. He was gone for a few days. Where'd he go?"

"He told Joy that he went to visit a sick cousin in Tallahassee and she's been watching the dog. I wonder when he got back? He wasn't here when I drove by about midnight. Come to think about it Tina's car wasn't here either. Neither was that blue Trans Am with Mississippi plates in the parking lot. Do you know anything about it?"

"Nope. Maybe Tina does."

"Let's go upstairs and ask her."

"You don't have to go upstairs. I'm standing right behind you. Is it Mack?"

"Yes," responded Elmo. "It's him. When did he get back from his trip?"

"I'm not certain about the exact time. I got here about six-thirty last night and expected him to be here. I waited until nine o'clock and when he didn't show I went over to Indian River Plantation for dinner and a few drinks. He wasn't here when I got back and I decided to wait up for him. I fell asleep in the recliner upstairs and he woke me up when he came in."

"What time did you get back from Indian River Plantation?"

"About ten o'clock."

"No it wasn't. I drove by the marina about midnight and your car wasn't in the parking lot. Based on the way you parked it on top of that telephone pole you had a good time last night. What do you know about the blue Trans Am in the parking lot? It has Mississippi plates."

"Nothing. I saw it for the first time when I went upstairs to call you. Whose is it?"

"I don't know yet," Elmo responded. "I'll go up to my patrol car and run the plate after I finish up here."

"What do you mean finish up? He's dead. Can't you leave him alone?"

"Tina, this is a crime scene and it must be preserved. I'll have to call in the homicide detectives and the county coroner."

"Why? Can't we just give him a peaceful burial at sea? That's what he would want."

"No. It's obviously a homicide and as you well know that's a felony. You're a material witness and possibly even a suspect. I have a few questions to ask you." Elmo reached for his notebook and took a pen out of his shirt pocket.

"What do you mean possibly a suspect? I didn't shoot him!"

"How do you know he was shot?" Elmo clicked his pen and began to take notes.

"Look at the bullet holes in the back of his shirt! There are six of them in a circle."

"I see them. How did you know there are exactly six bullet holes in his shirt?"

"I can count all the way up to ten. I went to college. The murder weapon was most likely a German or Italian-made .25 caliber, seven round magazine semi-automatic pistol."

'What makes you think that?" Elmo furiously scribbled in his notebook.

"The entrance holes are to large for a .22 and to small for a .32 caliber. Plus, they were fired rapidly at close range."

"How do you know it was at close range?" Elmo asked as he continued scribbling.

"Look at the powder burns on the cloth."

"How do you know it was an semi-automatic pistol and had a seven round magazine?"

"The shots were fired quickly and Mack didn't have a chance to move. That's why they're so close together. Most German and Italian-made .25 caliber pistols have a seven shot magazine."

"If it had a seven shot magazine where's the seventh bullet hole?" Elmo puffed out his chest and stopped his furious note taking." "I got you on that question didn't I?"

"I guess you did. Maybe there was a misfire. Can I go now?"

"No!" yelled Elmo. "You might just know too much for your own good. How did you know he was in the boathouse? How did you happen to find the body?"

"He got up about eight thirty and told me he was going upstairs and make coffee."

"What do you mean he got up about eight thirty? Where was he and where were you?"

"We were in my bed. We spent the night together on my boat."

"Wait a minute. Just a few minutes ago you told me that you waited for him in the cottage and fell asleep in the recliner."

"That's true. I did wait up for him and I fell asleep in that big fluffy chair. He came in very late in the morning and woke me up."

"Is that when you killed him?"

"No! I just told you we were in bed together in my sailboat."

"So, you killed him downstairs!"

"No! Why would I kill him? I finally got to have sex with him after all these months."

"Female black widow spiders kill the males after they mate," Elmo responded and continued taking notes. "Maybe you're a black widow!"

"Are you nuts? I told you that I finally got to have sex with him. Why would I kill him?"

"Black widow spiders do."

"Why don't you call in someone from the Sheriff's Office who knows what they're doing?"

"I was here first! It's my case and he was my friend."

"He was my friend too, but that doesn't make me a homicide investigator."

"I understand. Rat, stay here with her and watch him. I'll go up to my car and make the call."

When Elmo reached the top of the stairs he saw a tall man rummaging through the cab of Mack's truck. He drew his pistol with his right hand, held his baton in his left hand and quietly approached the man from behind.

"Stop what you're doing and raise your hands above your head where I can see them," Elmo ordered. "Don't turn around or I'll fire my weapon into your sorry ass. You killed my friend."

"Elmo is that you?" The man responded as he dropped his hands and began to turn around.

"I told you not to move," responded Elmo and smacked the man over the head with his baton. The man groaned and slumped to the ground. Elmo pulled the unconscious man's limp hands behind his back, securely handcuffed him and rolled him over so that he could see his face.

"What! It's another Mack! It's a body double!"

"Elmo! What are you doing to Mack?" Screamed a high-pitched female voice from behind him. "You've killed him!"

Elmo turned to face his accuser. It was Joy.

"I didn't kill him and this isn't Mack. It's a body double. This guy was waiting for Mack when he came out of Tina's sailboat this morning and shot him in the boathouse."

"He shot Mack? Is Mack okay?"

"Mack's dead and his body's in the boathouse. Rat and Tina are down there with him. I came up here to make a radio call to get some homicide detectives out here and caught this guy going through Mack's truck. I guess we don't need any detectives now. I'll throw this guy into the back of my patrol car and strap him down. Why don't you go downstairs and help Tina? She need's another female's companionship really bad right now."

"This sounds really bad," she responded. "I'm real worried about Ralph. He's been acting real strange all week. He went mullet fishing last night and hasn't come home. Do you think that this guy might have done something bad to my Ralph?"

"I don't know, but from what I saw downstairs this guy's capable of cold-blooded murder."

"Oh no! Maybe he killed Ralph too!"

"I hope not. I'll take this guy for a little ride so we can talk alone before I take him to jail. He just might have something to say to me." Elmo nodded toward the boathouse. "Joy, please go down stairs and check on Tina. She needs someone to hang onto right now."

"Okay. I will. Let me know if that guy has anything to say about Ralph. Can I go along with you on that little ride you were talking about?"

"No! Civilians aren't allowed to ride in our vehicles unless they're in the back seat behind the wire cage and wearing handcuffs."

"Okay. I'm on my way down to the boathouse."

After Elmo saw that Joy was on her way down the wooden stairs leading to the boathouse he waved an ammonia stick below his prisoner's flared nostrils. The man's head snapped back, his eyes opened, he looked up at Elmo through a mental haze and questioned his actions.

"Elmo, why did you hit me over the head? It's me Mack!"

"You're not Mack. You're a body double and you shot Mack in the back six times this morning in the boathouse. You're lucky that I didn't shoot you."

"Elmo, will you listen to me? It's me Mack. Ask me anything and I'll prove it to you."

"Who's identification are you carrying?"

"It's a long story, but I left my personal identification here when I left Monday night."

"That's an interesting story. Is that why the real Mack had your driver's license and wallet in his hip pocket? Let's take a look at yours." Elmo rolled his prisoner over, removed his wallet and spread the contents out on the ground in the bright sunlight. "From what I can see here, and keep in mind that I'm no expert, you're nobody. Your driver's license is blank and so is your Social Security card. It must be disappearing ink. I've seen this kind of stuff in spy movies. You had fake identification papers and the ink faded out when it was exposed to sunlight so that no one could identify you.

"Elmo, please believe me. I'm Mack. I can prove it."

"How can you prove it? You don't have any identification with you except those blanks."

"I can prove it. Where's Tina? She'll tell you that I'm Mack."

"She's downstairs in the boathouse crying her eyes out over the real Mack's body. I wouldn't want the responsibility of seeing what she might do to you."

"Call her up here."

"I don't have to call her. Here she comes. She looks furious and Joy's right behind her."

"Tina! It's Mack. Tell Elmo that I'm Mack before he takes me to jail."

"You're not Mack. You're an imposter. The real Mack is down in the boathouse with six bullet holes in his back. You hid in the boathouse, lured him in there and shot him in the back when you saw him come out of my sailboat this morning."

"No I didn't. I just drove in here five minutes ago. I've been on the road since seven o'clock this morning. You have to believe me!"

"I don't! What do you mean you've been on the road?"

"I spent the night in a Motel 6 outside of Lake City and left about seven o'clock this morning. I have the receipt in my briefcase."

"That doesn't prove anything."

"Yes it does. It has the checkout time printed on it."

"Whose name is on the bill?" Elmo pitched in. "Did it fade out too?"

"What were you doing in Lake City?" Tina interjected before the man could answer.

"I spent the week visiting a sick cousin in Tallahassee. I left the hospital about ten o'clock last night and decided to spend the night in Lake City because it was after midnight."

"Tell me something that only Mack would know."

"You drink Absolut' vodka gimlets and have a panda tattoo on your left thigh."

"Everybody in town knows what I drink and anyone who has seen me in shorts or a bathing suit knows about the panda tattoo. What else do you know about me?"

"Your parents were killed in a car accident."

"You did your homework before you came here to kill Mack. He told me that someone was after him. He staked out the marina until almost four o'clock this morning and waited for you to show up. But you snuck around in the dark and bushwhacked him in the boathouse."

"I didn't kill anyone. I'm telling you that I drove in here about five minutes ago."

"That's probably true because you weren't here when I drove in ten minutes ago," interjected Elmo. "That doesn't prove anything. You could've been waiting for her to find Mack's body and timed your arrival to match. But it didn't work. You killed Mack and you're going to jail." Elmo jerked roughly on the handcuffs to make his point.

"Wait! I can prove that I'm really Mack! I left my truck keys on the kitchen counter when I left town Monday night."

"Mack's truck keys were in his pocket! Spread out flat on the ground. You're not Mack. He's dead. You're an imposter and a darn poor one at that!"

"Here comes Joy! She and Ralph were watching my dog for me."

"She won't be very happy with you either," Elmo added. "Ralph went fishing last night and didn't come home. Did you kill him too because he could identify you as an imposter?"

"Ralph's missing?"

"That's right. After I get you down to the jail I'm going out looking for him. Did you stash his body in a boathouse too? Why don't you save me some time and tell me where it is?"

"I don't know. I told you that I just drove in, saw your car and wondered what was going on."

"What were you doing rooting through Mack's truck?"

"I was looking for my spare key to the cottage door. I keep one in a magnetic key holder under the dash seat. My key to the cottage is on the key ring with my truck key."

"Elmo! Show Tina who you got there," Joy hollered as she walked behind Tina toward Elmo and the prostrate form on the ground.

"It's the guy who killed Mack! He's a body double and he looks just like Mack. I caught him going through Mack's truck."

When Tina and Joy reached Elmo and his captive Tina paused and squinted at the prostrate form. "He looks like Mack. If I hadn't seen Mack's body in the boathouse I'd think he was Mack."

"I am Mack! Joy! Tell Elmo what I told you before I left town Monday night. Where did I tell you I was going and why?"

"You told me that you were going to visit a sick cousin in Tallahassee and that you'd be back sometime Saturday afternoon. That's today"

"That's exactly where I was and I've been trying to explain that to Elmo. But he won't believe me because I don't have any identification with me to prove that I'm Mack. But I am."

"Then how come all of Mack's personal identification was on the body in the boathouse?" Elmo retorted with a smug grin.

"I can explain that to you in confidence. Elmo, you know how those things go down. I was told to leave my wallet and identification here."

"Sure you can. But things don't add up with Ralph missing and your body in the boathouse."

"It's not my body. I'm right here. That must be a double! Someone pulled a switch and used a body double of me to get to Ralph. You've got to get me out of these cuffs! We have to find Ralph before something bad happens to him."

"I could swear that I saw Mack driving around in that blue Trans Am about two o'clock this morning down town by Confusion Corner," Elmo tossed in. "I didn't pay it any mind because I knew Mack was out of town and even if he was here he wouldn't be driving a Trans Am. I sure was surprised when I saw it sitting in the parking lot when I drove in."

"That guy in the boathouse was driving the Trans Am. Not me!"

"Tina, what time do you figure Mack slipped in this morning?" Elmo asked.

"I don't know. I told you I fell asleep in the recliner. You told me that you drove by here about midnight and didn't see my car. So it had to be after that."

"I'd guess it had to be after two this morning because that's when I saw Mack downtown. What did he say when he came in? Did he wake you up?"

"He acted real surprised to see me and tried his best to ignore me, but I wouldn't let him. He'd been gone for a week and I needed to be laid! I grabbed him in the crotch."

"What'd he do then?"

"He whimpered a little because I've got a strong grip. Then he started smiling."

"Tina! You hussy," Joy remarked and blushed as she gave Tina a 'high five'. "Tell us more."

"There isn't much to tell except that he spent the night on my sailboat. I'm sure that he had a good time, but I feel a little guilty now."

"Why's that?"

"He's dead and it wasn't as good as I thought it was going to be!"

"That's because it wasn't me," spoke up the handcuffed man.

"You'd better shut your mouth before she gets mad," chimed in Elmo. "She knows that you're the one who killed him."

"I didn't kill anybody. I told you that I just pulled in here ten minutes ago. I've been on the road since seven o'clock this morning."

"You'd better stop your lying and shut your mouth before I gag you," Elmo retorted. "I'm going to run you down to jail for protection before one of us does something that we shouldn't."

"Elmo, why don't you go in the cottage for a few minutes and leave him with me and Joy? I'll bet that we can convince him to tell us where he came from and what he did with Ralph."

"Tina, you know I can't turn a prisoner over to a civilian."

"Did you tell him that he's under arrest and read him his Miranda Rights?"

"Not yet. Why?"

"Then he's technically not under arrest and not a prisoner. Come back in five minutes."

"But."

"No more buts, or I'll have yours on a platter. Get going! I'll call you if I need you."

"You're an officer of the court and you could get in trouble if you injure him."

"Go!" Tina pointed toward the front porch of the cottage with her right index finger.

Elmo raised his hands in a mute feeble protest, shrugged his shoulders and walked toward the cottage. "Just don't leave any marks on his face," he quipped over his shoulder. "I can explain bruises on his body because he resisted arrest and I had to take him down to the ground."

Tina ignored Elmo's comment and prepared to work on her captive. "Joy do you have any clear fingernail polish with you?"

"No. I left my purse in the house. Why do you want fingernail polish? This isn't any time or place to do your nails?"

"Did you ever get fingernail polish in your eyes?"

"Of course not! It would burn."

"That's right. Now run over to your place and bring me back some clear fingernail polish, a roll of duct tape and one sock."

"Why duct tape and only one sock?"

"Use your imagination." Tina smiled and pointed at her shocked prisoner's mouth. "He might drool on himself and I want to protect his shirt."

"I think I understand." Joy shrugged, turned and headed toward her house on the other side of Whiticar's Boatyard.

"Hurry up! Elmo's going to get nervous." Tina smiled, gave Joy a 'thumbs up' and put her right knee in the middle of her captive's back. "Now I'm going to find out who you really are."

Chapter 10

"What do you think you're going to do with nail polish and duct tape?" Asked the prone prisoner as he twisted to relieve the pain in the small of his back caused by her knee. "You know I'm Mack. Stop playing games and get me out of these handcuffs."

"I don't know any such thing. As far as I know Mack's body is stone cold in the boathouse and you killed him. Why don't you tell me who you really are before I get real nasty?"

"You're already nasty and you can't get much worse." Mack twisted to the left in an attempt to make eye contact. "Get your knee out of my back and let me get up!"

"No way bubba! You're the bad guy and I've got you exactly where I want you."

"I answered all of your questions. I told you what you wanted to know about yourself."

"No you didn't. You missed something very important."

"What did I miss?"

"If I told you what you missed then you'd know and you're the bad guy. Shut up and wait for Joy to come back with the fingernail polish and duct tape! Then you'll have your chance to talk. You'll be singing like a canary within two minutes."

"What are you going to do with duct tape?"

"That's not nearly as important as what I'm going to do with the fingernail polish."

"What are you going to do with it?"

"There's an old trick to successful interrogation that only experienced interrogators know. I learned it from the Chinese."

"Pulling out a person's fingernails with pliers isn't new."

"I tried that once. I don't like it. It's gross and very messy."

"Stop playing games. You know that I'm Mack."

"No I don't."

"Yes you do!"

"You failed your test."

"What test? That silly word game?"

"That's correct."

"Let me try again. I'll figure out what you want."

"No you won't. It's to late. Here comes Joy. Now we'll find out who you are and why you killed Mack."

Joy came around the corner into the Port Sewall Marina parking lot towed by an anxious six- month old Brittany spaniel puppy. She held a brown paper bag in her left hand and ran as fast as she could in her yellow flip-flops, but she couldn't keep up with the anxious dog.

"Tina! I've got it and I found a note from Ralph in the kitchen. He's okay! He went fishing."

The excited dog gave a jerk on his leash and pulled it out of Joy's hand. She tumbled ass over teakettle into the gravel parking lot, but maintained her grip on the brown paper bag. The dog ran directly to Tina and gave the prone man a wet lick across the face.

"See! Rocky knows who I am. Now let me up," the tethered man pleaded.

The excited dog feverishly wagged its tail and licked the man across the face.

"Tina. He knows that it's me!" He managed to sputter between dog kisses. "Now let me up."

Joy arrived on the scene completely out of breath with bloody scrapes on both knees.

"Here's the clear fingernail polish, a bottle of polish remover and a roll of duct tape," she gushed between deep breaths. "That dog sure seems excited to see that guy. Are you sure he's not Mack?"

"Of course it's Mack," Tina responded. "I knew it all the time. I just wanted some verification and Rocky provided it."

"What did you want the fingernail polish and polish remover for?" Joy asked.

"I wanted to do my nails before Mack and I go out to dinner tonight. I left mine in West Palm Beach."

"How about the roll of duct tape?"

"I don't know why I asked for it, but it sounded good at the time." Tina shrugged and stood up. "Maybe I had a fetish in mind for later."

"If you knew that I was me why did you put me through all of this?" Mack asked as he rolled over on the pea gravel to look her in the eye. "Call Elmo out here and get me out of these handcuffs!" Mack yelled as best he could in the direction of the open cottage door.

"Not quite so fast big boy. You still have a few questions to answer."

"Like what?"

"Where were you since Monday?"

"I already told you. I was in Tallahassee visiting a sick cousin in the hospital."

"Then why is there a car with Mississippi license plates in the marina parking lot?"

"I don't know. I didn't drive it here."

"Then who did and how did you get here?"

"I'd guess that the dead guy in the boathouse drove it. I drove a red Mustang."

"Where is it?"

"I left it in Whiticar's parking lot."

"Why did you leave it there?"

"I saw Elmo's car with the blue lights flashing and figured that something serious happened here. I wanted to check things out before I drove in. I also saw that blue Trans Am with Mississippi plates in the marina parking lot when I drove by earlier. It looked suspicious."

"I saw the red Mustang when I walked past Whiticar's on the way to my house," Joy offered. "The dog went nuts when he passed it. I thought he'd pull my arm off trying to get to it."

"Why were you rooting through the truck?"

"I was looking for my spare cottage key. I leave it under the dash on a magnetic key holder."

"Tina what makes you so certain that that guy you spent the night with on your boat wasn't really Mack?" Joy gasped. "You really seemed excited about it."

"Mack wouldn't have taken advantage of me when I was bombed out of my gourd like I was last night. He's a gentleman," Tina offered with a grin. "Besides that guy wasn't that good. I knew that something was wrong when he was on top of me."

"What made you think that something was wrong?"

"Mack wouldn't howl and pant like a hyena in heat."

"I'm certainly glad that you have those positive thoughts about me," Mack responded with a smile. "Now get Elmo out here and get these handcuffs off me! We have to find out whose body is in the boathouse. Who's watching the body?"

"Rat. Do you think he might try to eat parts of it?"

"He eats road kill, but I don't think he's a cannibal. Get Elmo out here!"

At that instant Deputy Elmo strolled out onto the front porch with a coffee cup in his left hand and cautiously looked toward Tina and her prone captive. "Did you find out what you wanted to know about that guy? Who is he?"

"It's Mack!" Tina shouted back. "Get your butt over here and get him out of these handcuffs before they cut off the circulation in his hands."

"Elmo! Ralph's okay," Joy shouted in Elmo's direction. "He left a note for me in the kitchen." She waved a sheet of yellow tablet paper in the air. "He went fishing in the Keys for a few days just to get away because his medication wasn't sitting right with him."

"I'll take a look at it after I get Mack out of the cuffs," replied Elmo as he brushed past Joy. "Mack I sure am sorry that I didn't believe you. I was shook up real bad over the body in the boathouse. I thought for sure it was you."

"Don't worry about it. You're trained to be cautious. That's part of your job. Now get these things off of me. We have to find out who the guy is in the boathouse." After the handcuffs were removed Mack stood up and rubbed his sore wrists. "Let's get down to the boathouse."

"Wait just a minute," responded Elmo. "I want to take a look at the note that Ralph left. Joy pass it over here." He reached for the sheet of yellow tablet paper, took it from her hand and read the handwritten note aloud. *"Dear Joy. I know that I haven't been myself for a few days because of the new medication. I'm going fishing in the Keys to sort it out and will be back on Friday. Love Ralph."*

"Are you certain that this is Ralph's handwriting?" Mack inquired.

"Yes! Why do you ask?"

"Does he always draw a smiley face on the bottom of his letters?" He pointed at it.

"Yes. He thinks it's cute. Why?"

"Take a close look at the smiley face. It's upside down."

"Maybe he was just feeling bad when he wrote the note," Joy responded.

"Maybe and maybe not. Where did you find it?"

"It was on the kitchen counter right beside the microwave oven. Why?"

"Was it there last night after he left to go fishing?"

"It must have been. I didn't use the microwave last night so I wouldn't have seen it."

"Why did you happen to see it this morning?"

"I left my fingernail polish on the kitchen counter Friday afternoon after I did my nails. When I got home I went straight to the kitchen counter because Tina asked for fingernail polish."

"It doesn't sound very suspicious to me," Elmo offered.

"Nothing ever seems suspicious to you until it bites you in the ass," Mack replied. "Let's get down to the boathouse and find out who that guy is before Rat does something that we'll regret later."

The anxious foursome headed for the flight of wooden stairs that led down to the boathouse below the cottage and the dog led the way. When it reached the boathouse dock the dog stopped and stood as stiff as a board, the hair on it's back raised into a crest and an ominous growl emanated from deep within its throat.

"I don't think he likes Rat," Elmo offered as he paused in mid-stride.

"That's not what's bothering him," Mack countered. "He likes Rat because he brings him snacks once in awhile. You wait here while I go inside." Mack entered the darkened boathouse and found Rat kneeling beside the body. Tears ran down the sides of Rat's bearded face and pooled on the wooden dock.

"Hey Rat! What's going on?"

Rat screamed, jumped off the dock, turned around in mid-flight and saw Mack's grinning face just before he hit the dark water. He bobbed up, spat out a mouthful of tepid salt water and stammered out a stuttered response. "Mack! Is that really you or a ghost?"

"It's me alright." Mack reached out his right hand to assist Rat out of the water.

"You scared the hell out of me! Who's that guy?" Rat sputtered and pointed toward the body on the dock. "That's supposed to be you!"

"It's a body double. Get out of the water before something tries to eat you."

Rat slithered onto the splintered wooden dock. "He had your driver's license, your wallet and all of your identification papers in his pocket. Did you give it to him?"

No! I left it here when I left Monday night. He must broken into the cottage and found it."

"Where'd you go?"

"Let's just say that I had to visit a sick cousin in Tallahassee."

"When did you get back here?"

"About twenty minutes ago. Elmo thought I was the double when he saw me looking for the spare key to the cottage I keep in my truck. He whacked me over the head with his baton, put me in handcuffs and turned me over to Tina for interrogation."

"That must've been pure hell!"

"You don't know the half of it. Did you go through all of his pockets?"

"Nope. I just sat here watching the body so it wouldn't go anywhere."

"Those six bullet holes in his back are a good indication that he wasn't going anywhere. I'm going to get rid of Elmo and Tina. Then you have to tow the body offshore and let it go. It'll head for the Gulf Stream."

"What? Get rid of the body? That's a crime. I could go to jail."

"Only if you get caught. It's a better option than leaving it here in the boathouse."

"I can't tow a body out the inlet in broad daylight. Somebody will see me!"

"The tide will be high about eight o'clock tonight and will start going out about eight-thirty. It'll be dark about nine o'clock so wait until then before you pull out. That way you'll catch the outgoing tide and it'll be dark"

"What will Elmo say about it?"

"Nothing if we don't tell him anything."

"He knows the body is here. He already saw it."

"Let me worry about Elmo. Just keep quiet and follow my lead." Mack turned toward the open boathouse door and cupped his hands around his mouth. "Okay Elmo. You can let them in. Everything is under control in here."

"I'm coming in, but the girls want to stay out here." Elmo muttered as he slipped through the door. "I have to call this in right way. It's a homicide."

"No you don't. If there's no body there's no crime."

"I see a body."

"No you don't."

"Yes I do! I have to call this in and get the crime scene investigation unit out here."

"Listen to reason. Who is this guy?"

"It's you. Isn't it?"

"How can it be me? I'm right here. You must be mistaken."

"His driver's license says that he's you. Look." Elmo handed the wallet to Mack.

"This driver's license certainly does say that I'm me. So, I guess if that isn't me on the dock then I'm not dead and there's no body. Right?"

"I see a dead body."

"Come back tomorrow and there won't be a body."

"I see a body. I have to call this in to dispatch and get the crime scene people out here."

"Listen carefully. This guy was a 'Judas Goat' body double sent here to kill and replace me. Someone killed him because they thought he was me. Someone wants me out of the picture."

"What do you mean body double? This guy could be your twin brother."

"Doubles are used quite often in covert operations. This was a professional job and there's no reason to call in the crime scene investigators. It'll never be solved because the shooter is long gone and out of the country."

"He won't know that he killed you for certain unless he reads about your murder in the newspaper. Won't he read the obituaries to verify it?"

"He's not here to read the newspaper. He's on the way to the French Riviera, the British Virgin Islands or Aruba. He knows I'm dead. Can you see the bullet hole behind the right ear? The shot was at close range and the flesh is blown open. It was the coup de grace."

"That's what puzzled Tina," interjected Rat."

"What do you mean?" Mack responded.

"Tina said the murder weapon was an semi-automatic pistol because all six shots were in a circle in his back. She said there should be a seventh bullet because German and Italian-made semi-automatic pistols have seven shot magazines. The seventh bullet was behind his right ear."

"It looks like she had it almost all figured out. Did you go through his pockets?"

"No. I only pulled out your wallet to check your driver's license."

"We've been over that several times. That's not me! I'm right here."

Mack turned his attention to the dead man's body and emptied his pants pockets. Mack's key ring was in his right front pocket and he palmed it so that Elmo could not see it.

"Elmo there's nothing else here. His fingertips were cut off because someone didn't want him identified. I could use a pheromone sample to identify him if I had the equipment and access to the National pheromone database. But I don't. We'll just have to dump him offshore tonight."

"What's a pheromone?"

"It's a chemical secretion from the sweat glands that's particular to each human being. It can be detected with a special chemical sniffer and compared to millions of samples."

"Wow! That must be why some people smell when they sweat. I can tell when my brother-in-law is coming when he turns down my street. He stinks to high heaven in the summer."

"Elmo go up to the parking lot and check out that blue Trans Am. There might be something in it to identify him. Don't call this in to your dispatcher because the newspaper people have police frequency scanners. If they pick it up and print the story I won't be able to operate in town as a dead man."

"Okay." Elmo turned and left the boathouse.

Mack turned toward Rat. "I'm going to get rid of Elmo and Joy as soon as I can. I'll take Tina to lunch at Shrimper's and then up to Fort Pierce so she can rummage around her favorite antique shop all afternoon. I'll take her to dinner and get her so smashed that she won't remember anything. When we get back to the marina tonight you'll be long gone."

"Are you going to jump her bones like he did?"

"Of course not! That's no challenge. While we're gone you have to get rid of the body."

"How do I disguise a dead body and where am I supposed to take it? This is Saturday and the inlet will be chock full of snook fishermen tonight. Plus, I can't go offshore in my kayak!"

"Use that truck inner tube over there. Weight the body down by its feet with a concrete block, suspend it under the inner tube with a cast net and throw a canvas tarp over the top. Nobody is going to stop and ask you what you have under the tarp."

"Where am I supposed to find a concrete block?"

"There's a couple of them beside the storage shed."

"This is the middle of summer. How do I keep it from rotting? I have to wait almost nine hours before I can get rid of it tonight."

"I'll run down to the fish house and get a pickup truck load of chipped ice. I've got an old nylon sleeping bag upstairs. We'll put the body inside the sleeping bag, ice it down and wrap it in an aluminum insulated space blanket. It'll keep just fine until you tow it away tonight."

"Where do you want me to take it? I can't take my kayak outside the inlet. It's not safe."

"Tow it out to the north jetty and cut it loose after dark. The tide will be ebbing at about eight knot and it'll take the body northeast at seventy-four degrees. When it reaches the Gulf Stream it'll set off to the north at three knots an hour. By daylight it'll be twenty miles offshore of Vero Beach and long gone."

"How do I get the body out of the inner tube?"

"Purse the net weights together at the bottom and fasten it closed with a slipknot. When you're ready to let him go pull on the slipknot. The body will slip out of the bottom of the net and be carried away with the tide. End of story and he's history."

"Won't he float?"

"No. A drowned body will sink and stay down for two days or more depending on the water temperature. It doesn't float until the abdominal gases build up."

"But he didn't drown. He was shot in the back!"

"It's basically the same thing. The bullets went through his lungs and they filled up with blood. He won't float."

"If he stays here he'll warm up and the river water temperature is about eighty degrees!"

"That's why we're going to ice him down in the sleeping bag and wrap him in a space blanket. Once the body reaches a temperature below the ambient temperature of the water it becomes denser than the water and will sink. We should be able to cool it down to about seventy degrees in eight hours. The body temperature drops about two degrees an hour after death and this guy's been dead for at least three hours so we've picked up six degrees already."

"How do you know he's been dead for at least three hours?"

"Look at his facial muscles. They've already tightened up. Rigor mortis starts to set up in the face between two and four hours after death. We've got to get this guy laid out straight before he gets stiff as a board." Mack pulled the corpse's shoulders onto the dock and placed the arms straight down along the sides of the body. "You get his legs straightened out and get him ready to go. I have to go upstairs and check on Elmo and the girls."

"What about the inner tube? What should I do with it after I'm done with it?"

"You can cut it loose, tow it back here or take it with you."

"I just might take it back to Shepherd's Park with me."

"That's fine with me. I'm going up to the parking lot to see what Elmo's doing. While I keep him busy you get working on the net and getting this guy rigged up."

Mack turned, left the boathouse and closed the door behind him. Elmo, Tina, Joy and the dog were not in sight. He headed for the wooden steps that led up to the parking lot.

Elmo met him at the top of the stairs. "Mack you won't believe what I found in his car!"

"At this point I'd believe almost anything. Shoot!"

"I went through his car and found a manila file with all kinds of stuff in it."

"What kind of stuff?"

"Look!" Elmo handed Mack a manila folder and took a step backward.

Mack took the folder, sat down on the top step and opened it.

"Mack I think that guy killed Ralph!"

"What guy?"

"The dead guy in the boathouse!"

"There's no one in the boathouse except Rat and he's mending an old cast net for me."

"I saw a dead body in there with six bullet holes in its back!"

"We've already been over that. You didn't see any such thing. Don't you remember?"

"That's right. I saw nothing. There's no dead body in the boathouse."

"Where did Tina and Joy go?"

"They walked over to Joy's house to have a cup of tea and they took the dog with them."

"Why don't you go over there and see what you can find out from Tina? I'll go through this stuff and let you know what I find."

"I'm sure that guy killed Ralph. Read the note."

"What note?"

"The one in the file. It says for him to watch out for Ralph because he could blow his cover and that he should neutralize Ralph to keep him quiet. What does that mean?"

"I'm not certain. Let me study this stuff and I'll let you know what I find. Go check on Tina and Joy. They may need some protection. Check on the red Mustang in Whiticar's parking lot on your way over to Joy's."

"Okay. What do you want me to do with it?"

"Write down the license number and run the plate for me."

"Why?"

"I misplaced the rental contract and have to call it in to the agency."

"How about that blue Trans Am with the Mississippi plate?"

"What about it?"

"I ran the plate and came up with nothing. It's one in a series of ten plate numbers that was reserved and never issued by the state. I double checked with the Mississippi Highway Patrol."

"It must be a mistake. I'll call the Mississippi Secretary of State's office on Monday and run it down for you. Get over to Joy's and watch out for the girls."

After Elmo left Mack turned his attention to the contents of the file folder. The top sheet was a Stuart street map with a written description of how to locate Sewall's Point Marina. The second sheet contained a passport size photo and one sentence bio of Tina, Elmo, Joy and Ralph. Rat was not on the list. Beside Ralph's photo was a scrawled handwritten note. It read; *"This guy can be trouble. He is a close friend of Mack McCray and you are authorized to neutralize him if he gets in the way."* Mack silently mulled over the situation. *"Why was a body double of me here and who killed him? He was obviously after me and someone got to him first. Why? This guy must have killed Ralph to get him out of the way and was coming after me next. But who killed him? I can't tell the others where I was for the past week and they think I did it."*

Mack closed the file folder, slipped it under his arm and headed down the stairs to the boathouse to check on Rat's progress. When he opened the boathouse door Rat jumped half out of his skin.

"Holy crap! You scared the hell out of me. Why didn't you knock first?"

"Why? Were you doing something to him that you shouldn't be doing?" Mack grinned.

"No! But I'm not used to being left alone with a dead body. Did you get the ice? I've got this guy trussed up like a Thanksgiving turkey."

"He wasn't going anywhere anyway."

"How about the ice?"

"I'll run over to the fish house and get it in a few minutes. While I'm gone you go upstairs and drag out the brown nylon sleeping bag and aluminum space blanket in the bedroom closet. Roll him into the sleeping bag and we'll fill it with crushed ice when I get back."

"Where are Elmo and Tina? I don't want them walking in on me and this stiff."

"They're over at Joy's house. I told Elmo to keep an eye on them for protection."

"Protection from who? This guy isn't going to hurt anybody."

"The guy who whacked him might still be around. I'm the one he's looking for."

"You told Elmo that this was a professional job and that the guy who did it was on the way to the British Virgin Islands, the French Riviera or maybe Aruba."

"That sounded good at the time and it satisfied him. But I'm not certain about anything. Right now I'm worried about Ralph. Have you seen him anywhere?"

"The last time I saw him was about one o'clock this morning at the end of Sewall's Point. He had his gill net set and was waiting for the outgoing tide to slack off so he could pull it in."

"Did he say anything to you?"

"Nope. He just waved at me. I pulled in at Trickle's Island to set up for cat snappers and fell asleep. I heard Tina screaming to high heaven this morning and came right over."

"Did you see any sign of Ralph?"

"No! I wasn't looking in that direction."

"I'm really worried about him. He might be in big trouble."

"Why?"

"This guy was carrying a bio and photo of everyone in this folder. There was a handwritten note beside Ralph's picture that said he should neutralize him if he got in the way."

"Wow! That's heavy stuff. First you and now Ralph."

"Don't worry about me. I'm okay. Who ever whacked this guy thought he was me. I'm safe – I think. There was an odd thing about it though."

"What's that?"

"Your photo and bio weren't included. Do you have any idea why?"

"Who ever set this up doesn't know who I am?"

"That's doubtful. Everyone in town knows who you are."

"Maybe whoever wrote it was from out of town?"

"That's the most likely explanation. It looks like you have him ready to go. Run up and get the sleeping bag while I run down to the fish house for ice. We have to get him packed up and ready to go before Elmo comes nosing around again. I won't be here to help you later tonight."

"Why not?"

"I'm taking Tina out to get her smashed so that she doesn't remember anything about this."

"How am I supposed to get this guy off the dock and into the inner tube all by myself? He must weigh two hundred pounds."

"He's probably closer to two-thirty. He's supposed to be me."

"You didn't answer my question! How am I supposed to get him into the inner tube all by myself?"

"Tie a rope around his neck, walk around to the other side of the boathouse and pull him off the dock. He'll tip head first into the center of the inner tube"

"How do I get the body out of the net?"

"When you pull the slipknot the net will open and the body will slide out. It won't float because it'll be colder than the water temperature. The water temperature in the river is eighty-two degrees and we should be able to get the body temperature down to about seventy degrees after we pack the sleeping bag with ice. It'll only take you fifteen minutes to tow it to the inlet if you take the short cut between Sewall's Point and Trickle's Island. The body won't warm up enough to float."

"What if I don't make it in time and he starts to float?"

"You won't have any problem because the tide will start running out about eight-thirty. Plan to leave here about nine o'clock. It'll be dark then. If you travel at idle speed it'll only take you fifteen minutes to get to the inlet."

"You didn't answer my question. What if I don't make it to the inlet before the body defrosts and begins to float?"

"If you leave after it gets dark it won't make any difference if it begins to float because it'll be inside the netting and the concrete block will hold it down."

"How's a stupid hunk of concrete going to hold the body down? It's going to be standing head down in the net! If it defrosts it'll rise up out of the inner tube like a stalk of asparagus. People will see his feet sticking straight up out of the inner tube."

"Tie a board or piece of plywood over the top of the inner tube to hold his feet down. There's some scrap wood out in the shed with the lawn mower."

"What if I can't get him in the inner tube?"

"You don't have any choice because I won't be around."

"Where're you going?"

"I'm taking Tina to her favorite antique store in Fort Piece to take her mind off what happened today. Then I'm taking her out to dinner at Mangrove Mattie's and get her smashed on vodka gimlets. We'll be back late tonight."

"Okay. I'll do the best I can."

"That's all I can ask." Mack tapped Rat on the shoulder as he left the boathouse.

Chapter 11

Mack filled up two twenty-five quart coolers with chipped ice at the fish house. He tipped the fish house manager ten bucks because several commercial fishermen grumbled under their breath. He lugged the coolers down the steps to the boathouse and when he opened the door he found Rat huddled in a corner of the boathouse as far away as he could get from the dead body.

"Mack do you think that two coolers of ice are enough to cool this guy down and keep him fresh? Turkey buzzards can smell something dead from ten miles away and they wouldn't add much to the décor of the marina if they perch on the roof."

"I had to beg to get this much. Several commercial fishermen were filling up their boat holds for a three-day trip to the Bahamas and they pitched a fit. They didn't like the idea of a sport fisherman using their ice. If you think we need more run upstairs and empty out the ice cube trays in the freezer."

"A lot of good that'll do."

"Every little bit helps."

"After you leave I'll go down there and talk Fred out of more ice. I'll tell him that I need to keep a load of cat snappers fresh."

"That won't work. He knows that you never keep anything fresh. You might be better off refilling the ice cube trays a couple of times."

"I'll figure something out. Okay. The ice is packed all around him. Now what?"

"I'll spread the space blanket out on the dock and we'll roll him into it. Be careful that he doesn't burp and harf on you when we roll him over."

"What?"

"The stomach often regurgitates its contents when a dead body's rolled over. Be ready to jump if you hear a noise."

"Yuk. You roll him over. I'll watch."

"Okay have it your way." Mack proceeded to roll the sleeping bag clad corpse into the space blanket. "See he didn't barf."

"Now what?"

"I'm going to take a shower, change clothes and pick up Tina over at Joy's. We'll be back here about eleven o'clock tonight. Don't wait up for us."

"Don't worry. After I dump this guy I'm heading for Shepherd's Park. What if Elmo comes sneaking around after you leave?"

"I'll tell him to stay away. Elmo has to start looking for Ralph. This guy might have done something to Ralph last night to keep him quiet."

"I don't see how. I saw him fishing for mullet at Sewall's Point about one o'clock."

"Maybe he popped Ralph after you saw him."

"If he had someone would've found his body. I think Ralph slipped away for a couple of days to get his act together. That new medicine from the VA really has him upset. He hasn't been himself for the past week."

"Are you sure you know what to do after I leave?"

"Of course. I'm going to baby-sit him until about eight-thirty tonight. Then I'm going to plop him in that inner tube, tow him out to the inlet and let him go."

"You don't have to stay here and baby-sit him. He's not going anywhere. Go and do what you have to do today, but keep the boathouse door locked while you're gone. Use the electronic garage door opener to open the outside door that leads to North Lake when you're ready to pull out tonight." Mack tossed Rat a shiny brass key attached to a white foam rubber float. Rat stuffed it in his right shirt pocket. "Leave the key in the mailbox."

"How can I reach you if something goes wrong?"

"It won't and you can't. I'll be in Fort Pierce with Tina. Everything should go smoothly. Before you leave lace that cast net to the sides of the inner tube and rig up a slipknot to release it when you reach the inlet. Don't forget to drop a concrete block in the bottom to hold it down and tie a piece of wood over the top to keep his feet from popping out."

"You seem to have everything covered. Have you done this before?"

"Have I done what before?"

"Ditched a dead body at sea."

"Of course not. What kind of person do you think I am?"

"Resourceful?"

"That's an excellent choice of words. You get this guy ready while I get cleaned up and pick up Tina. I've got to get her away from here."

"What if she wants to take a shower and clean up too?"

"She looked okay to me and she didn't smell. I don't think she wants to come back down here." Mack turned, exited the boathouse, closed the door and left Rat to his own devices.

"I'd better get started. I don't have all day," Rat muttered under his breath as he turned his attention to attaching the nylon cast net to the inner tube. He laced the net around the inner tube with white nylon cord and cut a hole in the top to form an opening. The lead weights hung down seven feet below the inner tube and Rat closed off the bottom of the net with a simple slipknot at the end of a ten-foot length of nylon cord. *"When I jerk on this end the knot will pull out, the bottom of the net will open up and out he'll go straight down to Davy Jones's locker End of story."*

Satisfied with his clumsy handiwork Rat tossed the inner tube into the water and secured it to the dock with a round turn around the cleat, three figure eights and a half hitch. "That'll keep it in place 'till I come back tonight." He slipped out of the darkened boathouse, closed and locked the door and slithered into the inflatable green kayak moored to the boathouse dock.

Mack had his own problems and discussed them aloud with himself in the shower. *"I knew that I should've driven straight through last night. I could've been here by three or four o'clock this morning. I might've saved that guy's life and on the other hand I might be the one laying on the boathouse floor. Whoever whacked him was after me. Fortunately he was here already. Where did he come from and why was he here? Who is he? Was he driving that blue Trans Am or was the guy that whacked him driving it? If he was driving it then what did the hit man drive? Who wants me out of the picture and why? Maybe the two guys in the Atlanta airport terminal followed me back here. But why?"*

Mack rinsed himself off, parted the pale green plastic shower curtain with his right hand and reached for the fluffy white bath towel hanging on the wooden towel bar. A man's hand shot out of nowhere and grasped Mack's right wrist in a vice-like grip.

"We've gotta' talk! You have got a big problem," rumbled the deep baritone male voice from behind the shower curtain. It wasn't CNN!

"What the hell!" Mack bellowed in response and attempted to pull his wrist out of the tight grip. "Let go of my wrist!"

"Hold it down. Someone might hear you," responded the deep baritone voice. "Everything's going to be okay. Here's your towel. Stay behind the shower curtain and I'll fill you in as best I can."

"Aren't you the guy I met in Biloxi?"

"No! He's my brother. You've never met me. Just hold tight for a few minutes and listen to what I have to say. I don't have much time to spare. I have to catch a plane out of West Palm for Aruba in a little more than an hour."

"Aruba! Why Aruba?"

"Because it's a nice place. I've been under a lot of stress lately and I need a break. Shut up and listen to me before I have to whack you too!"

"Whack me too! Did you whack the guy in the boathouse?"

"Maybe and maybe not. It depends on what boathouse."

"What! You whacked someone else too?"

"Maybe and maybe not. Now are you going to shut up and listen?"

"Did you whack the guy downstairs in the boathouse? This boathouse!"

"I'll take the fifth on that. Now are you going to listen to me or what?"

"I'm listening."

"Someone was sent here to whack you and he got the wrong guy. That's the only reason you're still breathing."

"Why?"

"Why what?"

'Why did someone want me dead?"

"You got fingered by a snitch in Chicago. We sent you to Biloxi to get you out of here before they got to you. They had a tail on you when you left town and set you up in that Motel 6."

"Your brother already told me about that."

"You're lucky that Fat Frankie was watching your back. He was in the room right across the parking lot from yours. He was driving the red Ford Explorer and the drunk in the Chevy Nova was the bait. They tethered him out there like an Indian guide ties out a goat for tiger bait. Fortunately you didn't take the bait and made it to Biloxi. But you aren't in the clear yet."

"What do you mean I'm not in the clear yet?"

"It won't take long for them to figure out that the guy they whacked in the boathouse wasn't you and they'll be back to finish the job."

"How did he get my wallet?"

"We gave it to him."

"Why?"

"He was your body double. We sent him here to find the guy who was out to whack you, but the guy got to him first. By now they know he was a double."

"How?"

"Did you look at his fingers?"

"Yes! His fingertips were cut off!"

"They're soaking in a bottle of alcohol somewhere."

"Why?"

"They want to check his fingerprints against yours to verify it was you."

"Where did he come from?"

"Biloxi. We sent him down here Friday morning. He was right behind you when you pulled out of the Beau Rivage and headed for Pensacola. Didn't you see the headlights behind you?"

"Yes, but I didn't think anything about it."

"He followed you to the airport."

"Who was he?"

"He was one of our best agents. He was in training with you in Biloxi."

"What!"

"I was supposed to watch his back and I screwed up. He was a 'Judas Goat' decoy for you and he didn't know it. He thought he was filling in for you while you were on assignment and I blew it!"

"Where were you?"

"I was in the cottage waiting for him to arrive from Pensacola so I could brief him. But I didn't get a chance to talk with him because that redheaded bimbo waited for him to arrive. She was as drunk as a skunk. Did you see how far she ran her car up on that telephone pole in the parking lot? She fell on her ass three times just trying to get on the front porch."

"What time did all this happen?"

"About two o'clock this morning."

"What else did she do?"

"When she finally made into the cottage she plunked her fat ass down in one of the recliners and passed out. She snores like a Tibetan goat."

"Where were you?"

"I was hiding out in the bathtub. I couldn't get past her to get out the front door."

"Then what happened?"

"She has the predatory senses of a female fox! When he pulled in the driveway those little stones popped and cracked like cereal. She jumped out of that recliner like she'd been poked in the ass with an electric cattle prod!"

"What did she do?"

"She looked out the window to make sure it was him. Of course she thought he was you. She wobbled out the front door like she was about to pass out any second and he ran up to her to keep her from falling on her ass. She fell into his arms and started cooing and purring in his ear like a Peruvian llama in heat. The next thing I knew he was dragging her inside the cottage like a bear with a side of beef."

"If you were in the cottage why didn't they see you?"

"She was so drunk she couldn't see anything and he was busy trying to get her dress off. I ducked down behind one of the recliners and after they went into the bedroom I took off out the front door."

"Where did you go?"

"I figured that he was safe with her until morning. I still needed to talk to him so I slipped into the storage shed and sacked out. I woke up when I heard her screaming bloody murder about eleven o'clock this morning. She can really raise a ruckus."

"Did you go down to the boathouse and check on her?"

"How could I? I'm not supposed to be here. I stayed in the shed and listened through the door. When you showed up I figured that stupid deputy would shoot you on the spot."

"Why didn't you come out and tell him who I was?"

"I'm not supposed to be here. I figured that you'd talk your way out of it before that nutty broad stuck duct tape over your mouth and you did."

"I didn't talk my way out of it. I was damn lucky that my dog came by and saved my bacon. What're you going to do with the body? He's your man."

"That's your problem. I'm not supposed to be here."

"Did he have a wife and family?"

"I don't know. Don't let the media get wind of this. They'd have a field day figuring out why there're two of you! Why don't you tow him out into the ocean and let the fish eat him?"

"Rat's going to do just that after dark. The tide will be going out then."

"Who's Rat?"

"He's a friend of mine and I can trust him. What are you going to do now?"

"If you would get out of here and take that broad with you I'll be gone when you get back."

"Why the airport musical chairs between Pensacola, Atlanta and Dulles?"

"We figured you'd be followed to Pensacola and somebody would be waiting for you in Atlanta. They expected you to fly to New York and had two guys waiting for you on the plane."

"Who's the they?" I saw two guys in the Atlanta terminal who looked like they just came out of a Blues Brothers commercial."

"They were ours. They were making sure that you didn't throw away your ticket stub. If the wrong people got hold of it they could research the record number and retrieve your complete itinerary. The boys had a ticket for you for both New York and Dulles."

"Why didn't they just hand it to me?"

"We weren't certain where we were going to send you until the last minute. Once the bad guys boarded the plane headed for LaGuardia we sent you to Dulles. By the time they got to LaGuardia and caught a flight to Dulles you were already on your way back to Atlanta."

"What happened to my car at the Pensacola airport? I left the Trans Am in the parking place when I got back the red Mustang was there."

"The ignition key fit didn't it?"

"Yes. But GM and Ford have different ignition switches and the keys aren't interchangeable."

"They are if both cars are equipped with the same ignition switch."

"How did you pull that off?"

"It wasn't difficult. We have excellent mechanics. They changed out the ignition switch and door locks in the Mustang in about half an hour. Now both cars are equipped with a standard GM ignition switch and are even keyed the same."

"Is the Trans Am in the parking lot the same one I was driving in Biloxi?"

"Yes."

"Who drove it here?"

"He did."

"Do you mean the dead guy in the boathouse?"

"Yes."

"Why did he switch cars with me in Pensacola?"

"You were followed to Biloxi and he was waiting in the Beau Rivage lobby for you to arrive. After you parked the Mustang he switched it for the Trans Am. You were followed everywhere you went in Biloxi. That's why we switched cars in Pensacola and put you back in the Mustang. Whoever was following you in Biloxi figured that you might try to ditch them at the airport. You drove a blue Trans Am went into the parking garage and the same Trans Am came out a few minutes later. They followed it all the way to Stuart."

"Who drove the Mustang to Pensacola and made the switch?"

"That's not important."

"It was the dead guy in the boathouse wasn't it? They didn't know which one was actually me!"

"You got it bubba! They figured that you were the decoy and that he was you. That's why he's dead in the boathouse and you're still alive."

"You used him as bait!"

"I suppose you could say that, but we kept you alive. You should appreciate our efforts."

"The trip to Biloxi was a ruse to throw them off wasn't it? I thought I was being given a new assignment!"

"That's correct and you were given a new assignment. It was to get out of town and save your skin."

"Why did I have to go through those interviews, watch those tapes, dress up like a jerk and almost get killed in a bar fight?"

"The bar fight was your own doing. Our guy was there to study you and he watched you day and night. He did an excellent job and was almost perfect. Perhaps he was just a little bit too convincing and maybe that's why he's dead."

"What! He was studying me? Where was he when I was in Biloxi?"

"He drove the SUV the day our guys took you fishing. He was guy in the ski mask"

"Your brother said that he'd been in a car accident and his face was badly disfigured!"

"I guess he told you a little white lie."

"How did you get here? I didn't see a car outside except for the blue Trans Am!"

"Maybe I drove here, but then again maybe I didn't. If I left a car in the marina parking lot someone would've figured out that there was someone else here beside the guy the boathouse."

"Where's your car? How'd you get here?"

"Don't worry about it. After I leave get dressed, pick up the broad and get her out of here before she starts getting nosey. I'll find my way out. After you hear me leave count from one hundred to one backward before you open the shower curtain."

Mack heard the bathroom door 'click' and threw back the green shower curtain. The wet spray in his eyes stung and blinded him.

"I told you to count from one hundred to one backward after you heard me leave. Now be a good boy, sit down in the bathtub and count from one hundred to one backward like I told you to do. You're not blind. I sprayed you with a simple optic nerve paralyzing agent. It'll wear off in about five minutes, but don't rub your eyes or the blindness may become permanent. Do you understand me?"

"I understand perfectly. One hundred, ninety-nine, ninety-eight, ninety-seven."

"That's much better, but you are counting way too fast. Start over and count slowly."

"Yes sir. One hundred, ninety-nine, ninety-eight, ninety-seven."

The bathroom door shut with a soft 'thud' and Mack heard the soft 'squeak' of the door handle as it forced the brass striker into the doorframe.

"One hundred, ninety-nine, ninety-eight, ninety-seven."

Chapter 12

Mack staggered down the cottage steps and squinted to block out the fierce noonday sun. Even though he wore heavily smoked sunglasses the sun shot through his corneas, stabbed at his retinas and tore at his optic nerves. He stepped back under the shaded porch to allow his eyes time to adjust to the searing sunlight. He glanced at his watch. It read: 12:18. He shaded his burning eyes with his open palms and scanned the marina parking lot. The blue Trans Am was gone, Tina's silver-blue BMW Z3 convertible still sat astride the telephone pole dividing the parking lot from the flower garden and his blue pickup truck nestled alongside the utility shed.

"I don't have much choice of vehicles," he thought as he shook his head. *"I hope Tina likes to ride in a Mustang."* He loped across the parking lot and turned left toward Whiticar's Boatyard. *"I still have the ignition key,"* he muttered and tapped his right front pants pocket with the palm of his right hand. He got a shock when he turned the corner. The red Mustang was gone!

"What the hell? What kind of game are they trying to play?" He sputtered aloud. *"He didn't say anything about taking both cars! I hope Tina can stand riding in my pickup truck all the way to Fort Pierce. It's slightly below her standard."*

Mack turned back toward the marina and spotted Elmo's patrol car in the parking lot. Elmo rolled down the driver's side window and motioned for him to come alongside.

"Hey Mack, what did you do with the blue Trans Am? I need to check it for evidence."

"It was gone when I left for Ralph's. What did you do with the red Mustang convertible?

"What red Mustang convertible?"

"The one I drove here this morning. I left it in Whiticar's parking lot. I told you to stop by there on your way to Ralph's house, take down the license number and run it."

"There wasn't any red Mustang convertible parked at Whiticar's when I went by there. I figured you were joking."

"I wasn't joking. That's how I got here."

"How about the dead body in the boathouse? I need to look at it again."

"How many times do I have to tell you that there isn't a body in the boathouse?"

"Yes there is! I saw it with my own eyes." Elmo started to open the door of his patrol car. "I'd better double check."

"No! There isn't!" Mack shoved the car door shut. "It's been taken care of. Don't go near the boathouse until Monday. I'm fumigating it for rats and the fumes are very toxic."

"Come on Mack. Let me look."

"No! Why didn't you stay with Tina and Joy? They might be in danger."

"They're just fine. When I left Joy was showing Tina her wedding pictures."

"I'm going to take Tina to lunch at Shrimper's and after that I'm carting her up to an antique shop in Fort Pierce. I'm going to keep her away from here until Rat takes care of what isn't in the boathouse. We'll be back about midnight. You should you go looking for Ralph's boat and check on Joy every hour or so in case she hears from him."

"Okay. Now I understand. Rat's taking care of what isn't in the boathouse and you're leaving town until the coast is clear. Not a bad gig. And you're leaving me here to do your dirty work."

"Scat!"

"I'm leaving. Check in with me when you get back tonight."

"I'll give you a call when we get back. Keep your eyes peeled for the blue Trans Am and the red Mustang convertible."

"Should I put out an All Points Bulletin for them?"

"Hell no! Those cars weren't really here. Don't you understand? You didn't see them here, but keep your eyes open for them in case you do see them again."

"I guess I understand. I should be watching for two cars that aren't really here. I've got it." Elmo closed the car window and peeled out of the driveway in a cloud of dust.

Mack pulled into Ralph's driveway and beeped the truck's tinny horn twice to get Tina's attention. She purposely ignored him and he beeped the horn again. There was no response from inside the house. He realized that Tina would win no matter what he did. He slid out of the truck walked up to the front porch and cautiously knocked on the door.

"Who's there? If you're selling something we don't want any," echoed Joy's broken voice from inside the house. "Go away!"

"It's Mack. Can I come in?"

"The door's open. Help yourself."

Mack swung the screen door open and paused in the doorway.

"Come on Tina. Let's go," Mack barked and motioned to her with a wave of his right arm.

"Go where and why?"

"We have to get out of here before that guy comes back."

"Before what guy comes back?"

"The guy who thinks he whacked me in the boathouse.

"What makes you think he'll come back?"

"As soon as he runs the fingerprints he'll know it wasn't me."

"How can he do that? The body didn't have any fingertips!"

"That's exactly the point. He sliced them off and stored them in preservative. By now he's scanned them into a laptop computer and run them through a computer database. He knows he screwed up and didn't get me. If he doesn't come back and finish the job someone else will. Now let's get going."

"Where are we going? I've had a rough night and a terrible morning."

"I thought we'd drop over to Shrimper's for lunch and then run up to your favorite antique store north of Fort Pierce. We can kick around there for a while. When you get bored we'll go over to the Fort Pierce City Marina, hang around the Tiki Hut and listen to reggae' music. Then we'll go over to Mangrove Mattie's for dinner and a few drinks."

"It sounds like you've planned my whole day. Do I have any say in this?"

"Not this time. Let's get going. It'll be a lot safer somewhere else."

"What about Joy? She's worried sick over Ralph."

"Joy needs to stay here and sit by the phone. Elmo's on the way out to look for Ralph's boat. After what you said about his reaction to his new medicine I'd agree that he just wanted to get away for a few days. I'm certain that he'll call soon. Joy you need to stay by the phone."

"What about your dog?" Joy responded and pointed at the snoring pup. "He missed you."

"It looks like he's perfectly happy here with you. He'll raise a ruckus if someone comes sneaking around and I'd feel better if you kept him with you for a few more days."

"Okay. What time should I expect the two of you to be back?"

"We'll be back long after you've gone to bed. We're going to have a late night. Was there a red Mustang parked in Whiticar's parking lot when the two of you walked by on your way over here?"

"Yes there was. Why?"

"It's not there now."

"What do you think happened to it?" Tina asked. "Who took it?"

"The rightful owner I suppose," Mack responded. "My suitcase was in the trunk."

"No it wasn't," Joy remarked. "It was sitting on my front porch when we got here. I thought you took it out and left it here because you were coming back for your dog."

"Maybe I did and just forgot about it. I was very tired and half asleep when I pulled in."

"How are we getting to Fort Pierce?" Tina inquired, "My Beamer's riding a telephone pole like a horny dog humping somebody's leg. How about the Trans Am?"

"It's gone too. We'll take my truck. The engine needs a good run to clear out the carbon."

"That ratty old truck! I wouldn't be seen dead in that thing."

"If you don't get out of here and that guy comes back looking for the only witness you might find the alternative not to your liking."

"Does your truck have air conditioning?"

"Yep. It's got the best sixty-two air conditioning you ever saw."

"What do you mean sixty-two air conditioning? I never heard of that."

"It's very common in older vehicles."

"Tina he's messing with you," Joy piped in. "His truck doesn't have real air conditioning. It's just like Ralph's old green truck sitting out there in the driveway. He puts both windows down and drives at sixty miles an hour."

"Mack is that true?"

"Of course. It's standard for old pickup trucks. You'll like the feeling of the wind blowing through your hair. It's refreshing."

"Along with the road dirt, exhaust fumes, bugs and Lord knows what else," Joy interjected.

"Joy you're real smart. Where did you go to school?" Mack asked.

"I graduated from Wellesley with a Masters degree in Liberal Arts," Joy responded with a coy smile as she smoothed back her shoulder length coal black hair. No one except Ralph knew of her Cherokee Indian heritage and that she had dyed her hair for the past three years to hide the intermittent streaks of white interlaced among the black strands. "Library Science was my love and true passion."

"I should've known. No wonder you and Ralph make such a good match."

"What do you mean by that smart remark?" Joy retorted. Her Gulf Stream blue eyes snapped.

"I meant that opposites attract one another. Ralph is a commercial fisherman and you are a very cultured woman. You're good for each other and I was trying to be complimentary."

"You were putting Ralph down because he doesn't have a college education like you do."

"No I wasn't. Ralph's my friend and I respect him. Education isn't everything."

"Ralph feels bad that he didn't go to college after he got out of the military. He could've gone to college on the GI Bill, but he had to come home and work to take care of his family. His father got hurt real bad in a roller net accident and lost the use of his right arm."

"I understand. Ralph and I've talked about it many times. But he's very smart."

"Street smarts! That's all he's got to work with. I take care of the business end."

"Okay you two," Tina chimed in and raised her hands in the air. "Knock it off!"

"Ralph's okay," Joy responded. "That new medicine from the VA clinic knocked him off his feed and he's gone down to the Keys to do a little fishing for a few days. I showed you the note."

"Aren't you worried that he hasn't called you?"

"Why should he call me? He told me where he was going in the note. He went fishing in the Keys and will be back Friday. I'm not worried."

"Why didn't he put his boat on the trailer and tow it down there behind his truck?" Mack asked. "It's a long run to the Keys by water."

"Ask him when he gets back Friday," Joy responded. "Now the two of you get out of here and on about your business. I've got things to do."

"Why don't you go with us?" Tina asked. "We can make room in that ratty truck."

"No. I want to be here in case Ralph calls me. I'll be fine."

"What if the guy who shot the guy in the boathouse comes back?"

"He won't be looking for me. He'll be looking for Mack at the marina."

"Don't go anywhere near the marina until tomorrow," Mack offered. "Rat's in the boathouse taking care of business and he won't be done until well after dark. Tina and I'll be back about midnight."

"How do you know what time we're coming back?" Tina inquired. "Do you have a schedule worked out?"

"In a way I do. The tide will start ebbing about eight-thirty and Rat will be pulling out of the boathouse with our guest right after that. He should be done and gone by ten o'clock."

"Then why are we coming back about midnight?"

"I want to give him a little slack in case something goes wrong."

"What could go wrong? What's he going to do?"

"He taking our guest for a one way boat trip out to the mouth of the inlet."

"He's dumping the body in the inlet?"

"No. He's towing it out the mouth of the inlet and the tide will take it from there. It'll be well off of Vero Beach and in the Gulf Stream by the time the tide slacks off."

"Then what?"

"Then nothing. It'll be gone and no one will know anything about it. Case closed."

"What about Elmo? Is he going to file a report?"

"No. He understands completely that there is nothing in the boathouse to file a report about."

"What if the guy figures out that it wasn't you and comes back tonight."

"In his mind he knows it was me. By now he's on an airplane, sipping French wine and on the way to the French Riviera, British Virgin Islands or Aruba. I'm history to him. It's over."

"Okay you two," Joy interjected. "Go have a good lunch and try to forget everything. I'll see both of you tomorrow. Enjoy yourselves in Fort Pierce. Tina, if you see a Duncan-Miller green glass swan bowl at the antique shop ask them to hold it for me.

Okay? One of the dealers specializes in Duncan-Miller swans and has a display case right next to the staircase leading to the second floor."

"No problem. I'll even put down a deposit on it for you."

"That's not necessary. They know me. Just tell them that it's for me."

"Okay. Mack I want to stop by the marina and change clothes."

"I wouldn't recommend it right now. Rat's kind of busy in the boathouse. You look fine to me. Let's be impromptu and go just as we are."

"But . . ."

"Tina I agree with Mack. You look just fine." Joy offered. "Get on your way and don't forget to take advantage of the sixty-two air conditioning. The fresh air's good for your hair." Joy rose from her chair and gestured toward the front door. The sleeping dog didn't stir.

Tina and Mack were on their way to Shrimper's in the Manatee Pocket for lunch while Rat took care of business in the boathouse. Mack knew that Rat would take care of everything while he was showing Tina a good time in Fort Pierce later that evening.

Chapter 13

Against his better judgment Rat returned to the Port Sewell Marina boathouse in his green inflatable rubber kayak at 8:34 P.M. The tide had just turned from high slack to outgoing. It was twilight and the remaining daylight was fading fast.

"The tide should be moving out pretty good by the time I get that stiff loaded up in the inner tube and on the way to the inlet. Why do I always get the dirty jobs?" Rat muttered to himself while half-expecting a reply.

A harsh 'screech' from the roof of the boathouse caught his attention and he looked up. Six black turkey buzzards were perched on the back deck railing and four others claimed the peak of the tin roof. They carefully eyed him as if they were wondering if he was after their meal or if he was their meal.

"You slimy bastards! I knew you'd be here! There's nothing here for you. Get lost!" Rat waved his paddle in the buzzards' general direction.

A large male buzzard perched on the corner of the deck railing arched his back, spread his wings, screeched and regurgitated his most recent meal in Rat's direction. Green vomit filled the air and furry chunks of putrid brownish meat spattered the boat dock. Rat ducked and spread his arms over his head in a defensive posture, but it was a useless effort. He was drenched from head to foot in the foul liquid. Left with no choice Rat dove over the side of his kayak into the tepid water of North Lake.

He bobbed up, shook his right fist in the direction of his feathered adversary and blustered, "Napoleon! I know that was you. The next time we meet it'll be my turn to puke on you. Did I ever tell you that you'd look real good skewered on a spit slowly turning over a bed of mangrove coals?"

The agitated turkey buzzard responded with another screech and shower of green vomit. Rat dove under the boathouse door and emerged inside the dark boathouse. He wasn't alone. The dead body was still where he left it almost nine hours before, but there had been a change in it's appearance. The chipped ice had long since melted, the temperature inside the boathouse had risen to ninety-eight degrees and Mother Nature had taken her toll. The body was bloated and hundreds of buzzing bluebottle flies filled the air. Rat clasped his right hand over his nose and mouth.

"Holy crap! Mack told me this guy would keep 'til I got here. He's in worse shape than most of the things I pick up on the road. He's really ripe! If I stuck a fork in him he'd pop. He's well done!" Rat crawled up onto the wooden dock and pondered his situation. *"How the hell am I going to sink this guy? He'll float like a balloon!"*

Rat reached for the floating inner tube, pulled it close to the dock and tied it off to a pair of cleats. *"Mack said that I should tie a rope around his neck and pull him off the dock. What if his head pulls off? I'm sure glad I hauled two of those concrete blocks down here from the storage shed before I left. I'm going to need all the weight I can get to hold this stiff down."* Rat formed a noose in a piece of quarter-inch nylon rope, slipped it over the corpse's head and pulled it tight. *"He smells bad! I have to get to the other side of the boathouse. If he falls on me I'll die myself. How the hell am I supposed to get him out of the sleeping bag? He's bloated up so bad that it's bulging at the seams."*

Rat delicately unwrapped the space blanket away from the sleeping bag and exposed the zipper. He pulled the zipper down the full length of the sleeping bag, flipped the top over to expose the fully clothed body and fell back onto the dock as a cloud of dank green mist drifted upward from the body. *"This guy really stinks! I think he crapped in his pants!"*

The cloud of buzzing blue bottle flies descended on the exposed body and Rat made a futile one-handed attempt to wave them off. *"I'm outnumbered. If I make 'em mad they might go after me."*

Rat crept on his hands and knees around the dock until he was on the other side of the boathouse and directly opposite the body. *"Mack said that I should be able to pull him straight off the dock into the inner tube. That's easy for him to say. He's as big as that guy and I only weigh one hundred and fifty seven pounds soaking wet. I'll give it my best shot."*

Rat took the slack and pulled gingerly on the rope. *"Please God. Don't let his head come off. Please."* To Rat's amazement the stiff body slowly slid forward. He pulled gently until the head, shoulders and half the man's chest stood straight out from the dock directly above the floating inner tube. Rat dropped the rope, walked around to the other side of the boathouse to survey the position of the body in relation to the inner tube below it.

"Let's see." Rat rubbed his chin with his right palm and squatted on his heels in order to gain a better perspective of the relative position of the body to the inner tube. *"It looks like he'll make a straight drop into the inner tube. When he hits the bottom the net will catch him and hold him up. I'm ready to give it a shot."*

Rat returned to his vantage spot on the dock directly across the boat slip from the prone body. He tugged on the rope. The stiff unyielding body didn't budge. He tugged again a little bit harder and it still didn't move. *"What the hell's going on? Maybe he's afraid of the water?"*

Rat closed his eyes and gave a hearty two-handed jerk on the rope. The body shot forward out of the sleeping bag, paused slightly in mid-air before it slipped head first off the dock. It all seemed to be in slow motion and Rat could do nothing except watch as the events unfolded in front of him. The man's head hit the outer edge of the inner tube, bounced off and the body continued its downward plunge at a forty-five degree angle. When the green mist finally cleared Rat peered into the boat slip.

The body's bare feet and lower legs protruded from the dark water. The water in the boathouse slip was only four feet deep and the man's head, neck and upper torso were deeply embedded in the muck of the bottom.

"On my Lord! What the hell am I supposed to do now? I can't pull that guy out of the mud by myself and I sure as hell can't get him into the inner tube." Rat looked up at the ceiling of the boathouse in search of divine guidance and saw his salvation hanging above him. An electric boat hoist was mounted to the main truss and a pair stainless steel cables, each equipped with a stainless steel eyehook, dangled in the air over the boat slip.

"That's it! I'll hoist his ass up with the boatlift and drop him head first into the inner tube. That'll do it." Rat limped around to the opposite side of the boathouse and reached for the control box hanging on a cable from the ceiling. He pushed the green 'down' button, the low-geared electric motor whined and the pair of plastic-coated cables began their slow descent toward the water. *"Now his ass is mine."* Rat muttered though an opening in his greasy beard.

The excited turkey buzzards scratched and pecked at the boathouse roof. The movement of the body had released what could be best described as an aroma pleasant only to Napoleon and his band of black-feathered followers.

The electric motor whined to a stop when the cables reached their full length about eighteen inches above the water. The stainless steel eyehooks dangled about eight inches above the dead man's exposed socked feet. *"Now what the hell am I going to do?"* The rope's tied around his neck and if I try to pull him out of the muck his head might come off. But, I don't have any choice."* Rat formed a noose in the bitter end of the rope, tossed it over the exposed feet, and pulled it tight and grinned. *"Now he's attached at each end. All I have to do is loop the rope over the eye hooks and pull him out."*

Rat pushed in the red 'up' button with his right thumb, the electric motor whined and the steel cables slowly wound onto the reel above. Rat watched as the slack came out of the nylon rope and thought aloud, *"When I pull him up he'll be hanging straight across the boat slip by his neck and feet. He's stiff as a board and*

I can't stuff him head first into the inner tube. I'm gonna' have to stuff him under the inner tube and weight him down with something. Wait! Mack told me that he had some concrete blocks up in the shed. That'll work."

Rat pushed in the 'up' button and the body began to ascend from the dark water. A flurry of gas bubbles erupted from the water accompanied by a foul smell.

"My God! Now he's farting at me. I'm going to leave him hanging there while he airs out. I need to run upstairs and get those concrete blocks."

Rat released the electric boatlift control and headed for the boathouse door. He couldn't open the door because it was padlocked from the outside. *"Mack told me to keep it locked. Now I've got a problem. I don't have any choice 'cept to swim back out and open the door."*

Rat looked at the half-submerged body out of the corner of his right eye and slipped off the dock into the tepid water. *"I hope that guy hasn't attracted any sharks."* He ducked under the boathouse door and emerged on the other side into North Lake.

The turkey buzzards were waiting for him. They knew he had to come out sooner or later. The Alpha male, appropriately named Napoleon by Rat, still perched on the deck railing screeched and cleared his bowels directly over Rat's head. The foul material plunged straight down in a shapeless mass and plopped in the water directly beside Rat's exposed face.

"Oh shit!" Rat screamed and shook his closed right fist in the direction of the apparently smiling bird. *"Napoleon! When I get out of here I'm going to come up there, wring your scrawny neck and barbeque your black ass for dinner!"*

The agitated turkey buzzard set its wings, plunged off the deck toward Rat in a steep dive similar to a Navy torpedo dive-bomber, regurgitated the foul-smelling contents of his stomach directly on Rat's head and swooped away to the safety of an Australian pine tree. Shocked at the speed of the attack Rat froze and took the full impact of the foul mixture in the face. He ducked under the water and vainly attempted to rinse the greasy, foul-smelling mixture of putrid flesh and stomach acids from his beard. It was hopeless.

"Napoleon! It's over between us!" Rat sputtered in the direction of the Australian pine tree as he bobbed to the surface. "Your ass is grass and I'm the lawnmower. *You'd better sleep with one eye open tonight because I'm coming to get ya'. I know where you roost."*

The nonchalant turkey buzzard responded with a loud screech and began preening its tail feathers. Napoleon knew Rat was bluffing. He had changed roosts a week before.

Rat dog paddled over to the boat dock and pulled himself up the oyster-encrusted ladder. When he stood up the turkey buzzards took off. They had to get to their roost on the small island south of the Palm City Bridge before it was to dark for them to see. They wouldn't become active again until about eight-thirty the next morning when the air currents began to drift upward from the warm river water. Napoleon loudly voided his bowels just so Rat could see his displeasure.

Rat clambered up the wooden stairs to the marina parking lot and headed for the storage shed on the west side of the cottage. It was dark inside the shed and he groped around for two concrete blocks. *"Mack said that there were a couple of concrete blocks in here. It would help a blind man to find something if he spent a few bucks and installed a light in here."*

Rat slipped on something, fell against the riding lawnmower and smacked his head on a metal stanchion. The sharp blow hurt like hell, but it didn't cause him to lose consciousness. He used his hands to break his fall and felt around the sides of the shed in the darkness. *"Here they are!"* Rat hoisted a white block in each hand and headed for the boathouse.

"It'll be my luck that Napoleon has a horned owl for a cousin," Rat muttered. *"I'll never get the smell out of my hair and beard. I'm going to invite him to a special luncheon down at Shepherd's Park. He'll be the guest of honor,"* Rat snickered and tried to hold back his glee. *"Oops. I forgot. This is a solemn moment. I'd better respect the dead."*

Rat walked the ten feet to the boathouse door, sat the two white blocks on the wooden dock and groped for the padlock key in his right front pants pocket. It wasn't there. *"Maybe Mack forgot to give me the key. I always stick keys in my right front pocket.*" He thrust a furry paw into his left front pocket. It was also empty. *"Where the hell did I put the damn key?"* Rat mumbled and slapped his chest with his right hand.

The white foam float popped out of his shirt pocket and shot straight up in the air like a hunk of steak forced out of a choking fat man's esophagus by the Heimlich maneuver. It paused at the peak of its flight three feet over Rat's outstretched right hand, found new life and shot horizontally toward the boathouse. It smacked against the wooden wall, careened off at a forty-five degree angle toward North Lake and landed in the water. The outgoing tide grabbed the tiny float and hauled it toward the entrance to Willoughby Creek at about five knots an hour.

"Now what the hell am I going to do? I can't swim after it!"

A giant sow snook rose up off her nest on the bottom of North Lake, didn't pause in her attack and smacked the intrusive brass key with all the force she could muster. The torque of the fierce attack snapped the lightweight beaded chain and tore the brass key loose from the foam rubber float. The float flew in one direction and the key in another.

Rat watched the key splash into the murky water, shrugged his shoulders and turned his attention toward the padlocked boathouse door. The brass padlock was securely closed and Rat knew that he had to break it loose from the hasp. He looked around the dock for a suitable lever to use as a pry bar and spotted a steel boat trailer winch handle conveniently leaning against the boathouse. *"That's strange. I didn't see that before. Nobody in this marina has a boat trailer."* Rat wedged the flat end of the winch handle between the hasp and the padlock and heaved. The eye of the hasp obediently snapped off and dangled from the winch handle. Rat flipped it over his shoulder and heard a soft metallic 'ding' as it landed on the deck of Tina's sailboat. *"I'll pick that up later. I gotta' take care of this guy before he blows up and floats away."*

When Rat opened the boathouse door the foul order flushed out and drove him back several steps. He pinched his nose closed with his fingers and gingerly stepped inside. The body was exactly where he had left it ten minutes earlier. It hung by its feet and neck by the thin piece of white nylon rope that was looped over the steel eyehooks. The weight of the body had forced it into a slight backward arch and it appeared to be floating on top of the brown water.

"Now that I've got these concrete blocks I'm gonna' use 'em to weight him down. I'll tie 'em to his feet and neck. That'll keep him down until I get him to the inlet. When I get him outside the inlet I'll cut 'em loose and he'll float away on the tide."

Rat cut a three-foot piece of nylon line off the spool, passed one end through the center of the hollow block and tied it off with a bowline. *"These sure are light concrete blocks. I wonder where Mack got 'em. They musta' blown air bubbles into the concrete before it set up and hardened."*

Rat tied an overhand knot to form a loop in the other end of the rope, passed it over the body's feet and ankles, pulled it tight and dropped the block into the water. *"That takes care of that end. I sure wish he'd stop farting. It smells like something crawled up inside his butt hole and died."*

Rat duplicated his efforts with another piece of nylon rope and secured the loop around the man's neck. *"I hope that concrete block don't pull his head off."*

Satisfied with his handiwork he stepped back and paused while he contemplated his next move. *"Guess I'd better lower him down and slide the inner tube over him. The blocks will hold him down on each end, but I gotta' lash him up to the inner tube so he doesn't sink."* Rat pressed the green 'down' button on the boatlift winch control box and the geared-down electric motor whined as the body slowly sank beneath the dark water. *"Them concrete blocks sank him like a box of rocks,"* Rat muttered under his breath. *"Now he won't be a bit of trouble, but I wish he'd stop farting. He sure musta' eaten something really bad for dinner last night. Hope it was good because it was his last meal."*

Once the body was totally submerged Rat used an oar to slide the inner tube over the string of bubbles marking its position. The netting lashed to the bottom of the inner tube draped harmlessly along the body's right side. But, now Rat had an even bigger problem! He had to find a way to secure the body to the inner tube that could be quickly released once he got outside the St. Lucie Inlet. Then the idea hit him in the face!

"It's no big deal! I already got the cast net lashed to the inner tube and it's hanging over his right side. All I gotta' do is pull the weighted end of the net up under his left side, flip it over the top of the inner tube and drop the lead weights in the center. The weight of the leads will keep it in place. When I get outside the inlet all I gotta' do is reach over, pull the weighted end out of the inner tube and drop 'em in the water. The net will fall loose and he'll float free."

After he secured the body to the inner tube with the lead weights and cut the ropes looped over the steel boatlift hooks Rat used the electronic garage door opener to raise the boathouse door. He gave the inner tube a light shove and it slowly drifted out of the boathouse into North Lake. The inner tube floated serenely on the dark water and there was no sign of the stiff body hidden underneath it.

Rat tied a yellow polypropylene line to the inner tube and looped the other end around a hardened rubber cleat on the stern of his kayak. The kayak had seen better days, but it was Army surplus and Rat knew that it could take a beating. He put the ancient outboard motor into gear, idled out of North Lake into the St. Lucie River and aimed the bow at Trickle's Island.

The tide was running out at about five knots per hour. *"I sure hope those bull sharks don't catch a whiff of this guy before I make it to the inlet. They'd tear that inner tube to pieces in five seconds flat. They're probably waiting at the mouth of the inlet for their dinner to float to them. Maybe a dead goat will float past before I get there."*

As Rat expected the Crossroads, the Hole in the Wall and the mouth of the inlet swarmed with boats filled with half-drunk snook fishermen. They'd had all afternoon to get soused on beer and now it was time to go snook fishing! July is peak spawning time for snook and they congregate at the mouth of the inlet for a few weeks. Although the snook season is officially closed to protect the spawning fish it's a 'catch and release' fishery.

Rat didn't understand why someone would want to go fishing for something they couldn't keep. Often the over-played fish died from a build up of lactic acid and floated belly-up just outside the inlet. Because he didn't recognize any state regulations regarding size, bag limits or seasons Rat often spent many late hours gaffing dead snook outside the riprap that formed the St. Lucie Inlet. He had to be careful because his ancient outboard motor was no match for an eight-knot outgoing ebb tide. If he got pulled offshore by the swift current and into the Gulf Stream there would be no return. That was his concern tonight.

"I'm gonna' have to cut this guy loose before I get outside the inlet. The tide's running out at about five knots. If I'm out there when it hits eight knots I'm gone for good!"

Rat passed north of Trickle's Island and aimed for the flashing green light of Marker 239 marking the east side of the Intracoastal Waterway. It was one long mile to the inlet.

A boat was anchored at the edge of the deep cut at the Sun Parlor fifty yards east of Marker 239. The outgoing tidal currents from the Indian and St. Lucie Rivers converge here and cause a series of swirling eddies. Baitfish caught in the outgoing tide find themselves swirling in the current and unable to escape from voracious predators such as monstrous snook and rampaging jack crevalles. The boat's occupants were fishing with drop-back bottom rigs rigged with live mullet and four sets of lines streamed back in the swift current. Rat made a sharp turn to the right and narrowly missed one of the lines.

"Hey Rat! Are you trolling feet for bait?" Roared out the husky voice of an obviously intoxicated snook fisherman. "What do you expect to catch with those? Big soles?" Loud guffaws and belly laughs emanated from the boat's occupants. "The flounder and soles don't start runnin' again until spring." More loud roars of drunken laughter followed.

Rat spun around and looked behind at the inner tube bouncing about twenty feet behind in the wake. A pair of bare feet and shins stuck straight up in the air behind the inner tube! They alternately bounced in and out of the water in rhythm with the waves. A single strand of white nylon rope trailed behind the bound ankles. *"The concrete block must've dropped off! This guy's floating like a cork,"* Rat muttered to himself. *"I've gotta' slow down or he'll pull out of the net."* He pulled the throttle back to idle and the feet sank down even with the water, but they refused to sink.

"Hey Rat! Got any extra soles that we can borrow for bait? The snook ain't hittin' our mullet. Maybe they want stinky feet." Loud belly laughs and guffaws followed.

Rat wanted to respond to the catcalls, but didn't know what to say. Obviously the fishermen saw the feet bouncing in the wake. Then he had an idea right out of left field and responded.

"I'm doing some research for the Coast Guard. This here's a department store dummy," Rat responded through cupped hands. "I'm gonna' cut it loose outside the inlet and they're gonna' track it with radar. They're studying the tidal currents between here and Fort Pierce."

"That makes sense," came back the sober reply. "If one of us breaks loose in this current we'd wind up off of North Carolina by Monday. I'd want the Coast Guard to know how to track us. It's a good idea." The speaker popped another can of beer and returned to watching his lines.

"What was I thinking?" Rat muttered under his breath. *"They'll run their big mouths to everyone in town. If the Coast Guard gets wind of it they'll start asking questions. I'd better dump this guy as far off shore as I dare go. Maybe I'll run him to the red buoy."*

Rat pulled on the painter line connecting the kayak to the inner tube and it obliged by drawing closer. When it got within five feet Rat saw the problem! The piece of white nylon rope that tethered the concrete block to the man's wrists floated free in the tepid salt water. The man's upper torso, head and shoulders floated on the surface and his stiff arms projected straight ahead.

"The knot musta' come undone," Rat muttered. *"I never did learn how to tie a bowline when I was in the Boy Scouts. I remember something about the rabbit coming out of its hole, runnin' around the tree and popping back in his hole. Oh well. I'm almost to the inlet and he'll travel better this way anyway."*

Rat released the painter line and allowed the bobbing inner tube and its vile cargo to drift behind in the current. He nudged the throttle ahead, the ancient outboard increased in rpm and the kayak lurched ahead. There were at least a dozen small boats anchored along the riprap groins on each side of the inlet. A floating gauntlet! Rat swallowed hard, looked straight ahead and hoped for the best. He decided to ignore any catcalls because the word of his legitimate project would soon spread and his secret would be safe!

When Rat reached the mouth of the inlet the outgoing tide was ripping out at eight knots and tore around the ends of the riprap groins with a vengeance. The current caught the inner tube, swung it sharply to the right and brought it parallel to the kayak. Before Rat could react and counter with the outboard engine the inner tube sped ahead and swung the kayak around stern-first toward the open ocean. Rat panicked, shoved the throttle forward and the kayak reacted by lurching ahead.

"I saved my ass that time," Rat muttered as he attempted to maintain a stable position against the swift current. *"That wave could've flipped me ass over tea kettle into the water."*

The tiny motor, bogged down by the drag of the inner tube and its unwieldy cargo struggled to hold its own against the current, but couldn't. The kayak began to drift toward the open ocean. Rat had to do something and fast! He shoved the throttle as far forward as it would go, the motor coughed, sputtered and finally revved up to its maximum rpm. Suddenly, it lurched forward toward the inlet as if there was nothing holding it back. Rat swung his head around and saw the empty inner tube skipping across the cresting waves in his wake.

"What the hell!" He responded. "Where'd he go?"

The unfettered cast net waved in the wind. Rat saw a white object floating about 100 yards behind the inner tube. It rose and fell on the crest of the waves as it drifted northeast.

"He pulled loose," Rat screamed into the wind. *"There ain't nothing more I can do for him now. Mack told me to let him go outside the inlet and I did. He's on his way to North Carolina."*

Rat turned his attention toward navigating around the jagged rocks at the north end of the inlet. If he snagged the rubber kayak on a rock it would explode and he would be in trouble.

"It's about ten o'clock. I still have time to catch a few cat snappers at the end of Sewall's Point and maybe catch up with Ralph. Mack and Tina should be back at the marina by now."

Chapter 14

It was 12:15 A.M. Sunday when Mack pulled the blue Ford F-150 pickup truck into Port Sewall Marina. He flipped off the headlights, turned off the ignition key and scanned the area. Tina's Beamer was still perched on top of the telephone pole and there were no other vehicles in the marina parking lot. He noted when he passed Whiticar's boatyard there were no vehicles in the parking lot. If someone was waiting at the marina they had to come in by foot or by boat.

Tina had a fun evening at Mangrove Mattie's during dinner and afterward the couple went to the Tiki Hut at the Fort Pierce City Marina for a few drinks and to listen to *reggae* music. Tina half in the bag, was giggling and wiggling like a nervous cocker spaniel. She tickled Mack in the ribs with the fingers of her left hand as she stuck her tongue into his right ear and stroked the inside of his right thigh with her right hand. He did his best to ignore her, but her urgency made it extremely difficult. He rolled up the driver's side window and reached across Tina's pulsating body to roll up the window on the passenger's side.

"Why are you turning off the air conditioning? I was like it." Tina giggled and stuck her tongue deeply into his right ear.

Mack jumped and attempted to push her back with his right hand. "You had enough fun tonight and it's time to go to bed."

"That's exactly what I was thinking. Are you going to tuck me in?" She shoved her tongue deeper into his ear to the point that it caused excruciating pain and made Mack flinch.

"I don't need to tuck you in. You're a big girl and you can find your way into bed by yourself. Let me help you out of the truck and across the parking lot. Be careful when you go down the stairs to the boat dock. It's dark and you might trip."

Tina shoved Mack away, grabbed him by the shoulders and looked directly into his eyes. "I don't intend to spend the night on my boat. I remember what happened this morning and I don't feel like becoming a target in case that guy comes back. I'm going to spend the night in the cottage with you whether you like it or not." She took a step forward toward him and collapsed into his arms like a bag of turnips.

"I don't have much choice now and I can't carry you down those wooden steps in the dark." Mack put his left arm under her shoulders and his right arm under her thighs and lifted her limp body off the ground. Her head rolled against his left shoulder and she began to snore. "I'd better get you to bed because you've started counting sheep already."

Lights on each side of the walkway and triggered by motion detectors lit up progressively ahead of Mack as he made his way toward the cottage. He lugged Tina's inert form over the three steps of the front porch, pulled open the screen door with his left hand, twisted the front door knob and pushed the door open. The inside of the small cottage was dark.

He tripped the light switch up with his left elbow. The matching table lamps on each side of the green recliners flashed on and flooded the tiny room with light. He strode across the living area in three steps, slipped down the tiny hallway and entered the bedroom. He flipped on the light switch with his elbow and the bedside lamp came on. Mack placed Tina on the bed, carefully brushed the hair out of her eyes and kissed her lightly on the forehead. She moaned softly and turned over onto her right side.

"Sweet dreams. You'll wake up to a better day tomorrow." Mack pulled the light bed cover over her prone body and gently tucked it in around her shoulders. As he slipped out of the room, he tripped off the light switch and gently closed the door. He paused in the living room and carefully scanned the cottage interior. The bathroom door was open and electronics room door was securely locked. Nothing seemed out of place.

"I wonder if Rat got rid of our friend downstairs?" He thought to himself. *"I'd better go down and find out."*

Mack pulled out a kitchen drawer and removed the .25 caliber Berretta semi-automatic pistol from its cozy nesting place. He pulled out the clip. It was full. He racked a round into the chamber, slipped the pistol into his waistband and slid the drawer closed. *"If we have a visitor downstairs I want to take care of him before he zings me."* As he slipped out the front door Mack flipped off the light switch and plunged the cottage into darkness. *"I don't need to provide a silhouette to anyone who might be hiding in the bushes."*

He descended the steps to the boathouse carefully to avoid creaks and forewarning anybody lurking below. At the bottom step he paused to allow his eyes to adjust to the darkness. The lights of the Manatee Pocket sparkled across the water and reflected like the tiny mirrors mounted on a rotating ball in a disco. Mack carefully eased forward toward the boathouse.

"I hope Rat didn't lock the boathouse door. I gave him the only key and if he snapped the padlock closed when he left I won't be able to get in."

Mack grasped the padlock with his right hand and it fell into his hand. The hasp was gone! He turned the door handle to the right and gingerly pushed the door open. The strong odor burst through the open door like the ground wave from an atomic blast and forced him outside. He gagged and fought for breath in the thick putrid air. His eyes watered and he felt the urge to vomit.

"Good evening," boomed a deep bass voice from the shadows below the stairway." I've been waiting for you and was just about to give up when I saw your truck pull into the parking lot."

Mack swung around and slipped into a low fighting crouch as he simultaneously tore the semi-automatic pistol from his waistband. He stared at the stairwell and could make out nothing but darkness.

"What the hell are you doing here? I though you were going to leave me alone after our conversation in the bathroom. You almost killed me."

The booming baritone voice echoed back from the deep shadows slightly to the right of the stairwell. "It I had wanted to kill you I could have easily done so and there was little you could have done about it. You need me and I need you to solve this problem. Put that silly little gun away before you hurt yourself. I'm on your side."

Mack realized that his adversary had the better of him because he was standing on the boat dock and his body made a perfect silhouette against the lights of the Manatee Pocket.

"Okay. I put it away. How about coming out here in the light so I can see your face?"

"I don't think so. It's much better if I stay back here and you stay out there. It's not necessary for you to see my face because I know who you are. You have a big problem on your hands and I'm here to help you solve it."

"What do you mean I have a big problem on my hands? I didn't whack that guy in the boathouse! You had me running circles all over Biloxi, Pensacola, Atlanta and Dulles. I should come back there and teach you some manners." Mack took a step forward with his right foot and a razor-thin red laser beam emanated from beneath the steps and hit him squarely in the forehead.

"Don't take another step! I'm certain that you detect the laser sight focused directly between your eyebrows. One more step and you'll be history."

"What're you doing here?"

"You have some big problems that we must discuss."

"What kind of problems besides a dead body in the boathouse?"

"There's no dead body in the boathouse and it was never there in the first place."

"Were you here when Rat towed it away?"

"Whether I was here or not is unimportant. The guy that got whacked was your body double. He was trained to replace you because there was a hit out on you. It was his job to get the guy who was sent here to get you."

"You already told me that. That's old news. What did you do with Ralph?"

"We didn't do anything to him. We figure that somebody whacked him Friday night and dumped him offshore to get him out of the way. The same guy who whacked him came over here Saturday morning and whacked the guy he thought was you."

"What happened to the guy who killed Ralph and my double?"

"He's long gone and probably sunning himself on the French Riviera, in the British Virgin Islands or Aruba."

"Why do you keep mentioning Aruba?"

"It's a nice place. I flew there this afternoon after our little talk in the shower. I caught a late flight back tonight when I found out that we had this emergency situation.

"What happened to the blue Trans Am and the red Mustang convertible?"

"They were ours. We took them back."

"Elmo ran the Trans Am's license plate and it came back as non-issued."

"That's true. That license plate was never issued by the State of Mississippi. We have blocks of ten plates assigned to us in every state. It works out quite well for us."

"Why didn't the guy with the contract follow me on the plane to Atlanta?"

"He expected us to put your double on the plane and that you would double back out of the airport. It's an old counter-intelligence trick and he waited at the airport exit for you to come out. When the blue Trans Am came out he figured it was you and that your double was on the plane."

"Then I'm in the clear?"

"Not completely. When he finds out that he made a mistake he'll be back."

"You said he would be on the French Riviera, in the British Virgin Islands or Aruba."

"He's not in Aruba. I was there this afternoon and somebody else checked out St. Martin and St. John. He's not there either. We feel that he didn't fly to the French Riviera because his handlers want verification that he accomplished his mission. They want him to stay close by in case he has to come back. He's coming back because you're still breathing."

"Why don't you get him before he gets me?"

"Budget constraints and lack of manpower. I'm here and that's all you've got for right now. Keep watching over your shoulder and be careful when you waltz down those steps and head for the boathouse. I could have zapped you and you would never have known that I was here."

"Where are you going to be? Are you going to stay in the cottage?"

"Of course not. That would be too obvious."

"What if I need help and have to call for you?"

"Trust me. I'll be around and I'll be able to tell if you need me. It's almost one o'clock in the morning and I'm pooped. I had a very busy day. I'm going back over to Pirate's Cove and catch some shuteye."

"What if the guy shows up tonight?"

"He won't be around tonight. He didn't get much sleep last night because he was camped out in the boathouse from about four o'clock Friday afternoon until he made the hit this morning. We won't see any action out of him until sometime tomorrow night. Go back upstairs, jump on that redhead's bones like she's expecting you to do and then get some sleep."

"I can't do that! She's whacked out of her mind. It would be unfair to take advantage of her in her condition."

"It didn't bother your body double. It must've been a fatal attraction for him because he's not with us any more."

"You're leaving it wide-open for me to get whacked. It looks like I have to take care myself!"

"You and I share the responsibility for your sorry butt. You watch out for yourself half of the time and I'll watch out for you the other half."

"When are you going to start?"

"The first thing in the morning. Would you mind turning around and going into the boathouse while I leave?"

"Why?"

"Because if you don't I'll have to do something like I did this afternoon when I left you in the bathtub. I don't think that you'll like it."

"Okay. I'll go in the boathouse. Do you want me to count backward from one-hundred?"

"No, from ten to one will be just fine. My Jet Ski is parked at the end of the dock. By the time you count from ten to one I'll be long gone. What are those animals swimming around there in the water? They look like sharks!"

"They're a couple of dolphins from Hawaii that were used in special Navy experiments. They're harmless and won't hurt you unless you fall into water. They were trained to attack swimmers attempting to plant mines on the bottom of Navy ships."

"Okay. March into the boathouse, close the door and count from ten to one backwards. Then you can come out. I hope that you can last ten seconds in there. It really stinks!"

"I'll do my best. Don't fall into the water and get the dolphins excited. They might eat you!"

Mack took a deep breath, slipped inside the boathouse and closed the door. He reached for the light switch, flipped it up with his left hand, heard it 'click' but no light came on.

"I should've known better. It really stinks in here. I sure hope Rat got that guy out of here."

Mack heard the soft, deep-throated rumble of the Jet Ski's engine as it gained momentum on it's way out of North Lake and headed toward Willoughby Creek. He hadn't started to count backward from ten to one and decided, based on the high-pitched whine of the Jet Ski's engine, that his nemesis was far enough away. Mack pushed hard on the boathouse door. It didn't budge.

"What the hell?" He muttered under his breath. *"The hasp was broken off the door. There's no way that he could have locked the door."*

There was significant solid resistance. Mack shoved hard at the bottom of the door and it begrudgingly slid open a couple of inches. Through the narrow crack Mack saw that several concrete blocks were stacked against the bottom of the door.

"He must've rummaged around the storage shed to come up with those concrete blocks. Maybe Rat forgot to use the concrete

blocks when he towed the dead guy out and let him go offshore."
Mack spoke out loud to himself and didn't expect a reply.

"I didn't forget the concrete blocks and I towed him out just like you told me to do," rang out a raspy nasal voice from deep in the shadows of the dark boathouse.

"Rat! How long have you been there?"

"Since about eleven o'clock. I was sitting back here when that guy showed up on his fancy black Jet Ski. I need to talk to you."

"First come over here and help me to shove this door open. This place stinks."

Rat slithered across the boathouse floor to Mack's side and placed his shoulder against the bottom of the door. "Okay. I'm ready. Let's shove together on the count of three. You count."

"Okay. One, two, three and shove hard."

The door shuttered and begrudgingly slid open enough to permit Rat to slide his skinny body through the narrow opening.

"Okay Mack. I'm out. Give me a minute to move these concrete blocks so you can open the door and get out of there yourself." Rat lifted a concrete block and moved it to the side.

Mack couldn't wait any longer, shoved the door open and collapsed on the dock.

"Did you get rid of the body?" He gasped from his prone position.

"Yep. Just like you told me to do.

"What time did you cut it loose?

"I had a few problems with him and got hung up here. I let him go about ten-thirty."

"The tide started going out about eight-thirty, reached maximum ebb current about eleven o'clock and slacks about two-thirty. At a speed of three knots he should be twelve miles away and somewhere south of Fort Pierce when the tide stops running out at two-thirty this morning."

"Did you get him out to the sea buoy before you cut him loose?"

"No. The tide was running out hard to the northeast and I couldn't hold him back."

"What do you mean you couldn't hold him back? Back from where?"

"The waves were really kicking up and he floated right on past me. I let him go outside the north jetty. The last time I saw him he was headin' northeast at about eight knots."

"What do you mean he floated past you?"

"He was a floater. He didn't sink."

"Didn't you weight him down with the concrete blocks?"

"That's the problem that I forgot to tell you about."

"What do you mean the problem you forgot to tell me about?"

"I used the blocks I found inside the shed."

"I told you that they were outside of the shed beside the woodpile. You couldn't miss them."

"I guess I didn't hear you right. When I went inside the shed, I bumped my head on somethin' and fell down. I felt around in the dark and found a couple of blocks and dragged them out. I thought they seemed to be a little light for concrete."

"Did they have a hole through the middle of them?"

"Yep. I thought it was odd and it was hard to tie them down."

"You dummy! Those weren't concrete blocks! Those were salt blocks used as salt licks for the cattle on Tina's uncle's ranch. No wonder he floated! They would've melted down to nothing in the warm water in a few minutes!"

"Oh. That must be what happened. His feet started sticking out of the water before I got past the Sun Parlor. A couple of drunk snook fishermen saw me and asked if I was trolling feet for soles."

"What did you tell them? Were they suspicious?"

"I fooled 'em good."

"Now you really have me worried. How did you fool them?"

"I told 'em I was helping the Coast Guard with a research project to find out what direction a body would travel on the outgoing tide. They bought it hook, line and sinker."

"Did they know you were towing a dead body?"

"No. I told 'em that it was a store dummy."

The soft night air went quiet as Rat slunk off into the darkness. He realized that he had made a terrible error.

Mack shrugged his shoulders, turned toward the wooden stairs and headed for the cottage above. Maybe Tina wasn't sleeping after all.

Chapter 15

It was 7:14 A.M. and it appeared to be the beginning of a normal Sunday morning at Port Sewall Marina. Brown pelicans dove into a school of glass minnows cowering in the riprap along the tip of Hell's Gate. A flock of sea gulls screamed overhead and swooped down to pick up the injured and dazed fish. Mack dozed peacefully in a green recliner and Tina cuddled up to a pillow in the bedroom.

The day's litany of somber events began with Rat's frenzied knocking on the front door.

"Mack! Wake up! We've got a big problem! He came back!"

Mack shook his head in an attempt to dash the sleepiness out of his brain. "Who came back?"

"The guy in the boathouse that I dumped last night. He washed up in front of the lifeguard station on the public beach."

"Which one?"

"Which one what?"

"Which public beach?"

"The one at the end of the Jensen Beach Causeway road. A bunch of Baptists were down there dunking people in the water and they found him. He came floating in on a wave like a surfer dude. They thought he was one of their flock till they pulled his head out of the water and saw he was dead."

"How do you know?"

"I was down there rummaging through the dumpster when I heard a lady screaming like a banshee. I'd parked my kayak over on the Indian River side of the road."

"Damn! The incoming tide must've pushed it back to shore. That's why I wanted you to get it out to the red sea buoy before you let it go."

"I already told you that my rubber kayak couldn't make it that far. It was really rough!"

"Who else is there?"

"Elmo's up there checking everything out. He told me to come over and tell you about it."

"Anyone else?"

"There's a whole herd of reporters there with television cameras. It's a big deal. Elmo told me to tell you to keep a low profile because the media people think the body is you."

"What about the guy's hands? Did they see that his fingertips were cut off?"

"I don't think so. He's laying face down in the sand and Elmo put paper bags over his hands."

"What does Elmo want me to do?"

"He said to stay in the cottage and not to answer the door for anyone. He's going to come by later and put crime scene tape all around the marina to keep the media and nosey people out."

"What! I told him to forget about the body in the boathouse."

"He said that the game's over and he has to report it. He said that it's his duty as an officer of the law to report all crimes he sees. I think he likes the media attention."

"Go back over and tell him to shut up."

"I can't get near him. When I left he had a dozen microphones shoved in front of his face and was making a speech like he knew what he was talking about."

"What was he saying? Did he say anything about what he saw in the boathouse?"

"He was mumbling something about a hit man from New York being in town and that he couldn't talk about it because it could damage the case."

"Damn Elmo! We've got to shut him up."

"You could kill him."

"No! He's a good man and my friend. He's just a little dumb and needs some guidance before he does something real stupid and gets himself in over his head. He could get hurt."

"How could he get hurt? Who would hurt Elmo?"

"Do you remember that manila file that I showed you yesterday?"

"Of course I do. Why?"

"The hit man was carrying it around. Elmo's picture and bio was on one of the pages."

"Wow! How about me? Was I there too?"

"That's what was strange about it. You weren't on his list. I wonder why?"

"Maybe he doesn't know who I am."

"That's very doubtful. Whoever put together the dossier on me knows exactly who my friends are and where they live. It's complete except for you."

"Maybe you'll figure it out."

"First I have to figure out what I'm going to do about Elmo and his big mouth. He might be able to block off the marina with crime scene tape but those damn reporters will stake it out with cameras. We've got to get the boathouse cleaned up and fast. It stinks to high heaven."

"What do you suggest?"

"There's a gas-powered pressure washer in the shed. Fill up the tank with bleach and spray the boathouse down from top to bottom. Open up the door to North Lake and air it out."

"What're you going to do?"

"I'm not sure."

"What are you going to do about what?" Tina asked between yawns as she emerged from the bedroom. "What did you do this time?"

"I didn't do anything," Mack replied. "The body washed up on Jensen Beach this morning because Rat blew it last night."

"What do you mean Rat blew it? I thought he was going to tow it to the inlet and let it go out to sea with the tide."

"That's exactly what I did. But it washed back in with the incoming tide this morning."

"That's because you didn't take it far enough off shore before you let it go."

"I already told you why. What do you expect me to do?"

"Okay boys, stop your squabbling. What's the status?"

"Elmo's over on Jensen Beach talking to the media. He told them there's a hit man in town and he's going to block off the marina with crime scene tape. The media people think the dead body is me and in ten minutes the marina will be swarming with reporters and news cameras."

"I might be able to take care of that with a telephone call to my uncle. He's a judge you know. He wouldn't want me to be embarrassed with such a scandal. He's very protective of me."

"What are you going to tell him? You can't tell him about the dead body in the boathouse!"

"What body in what boathouse? I've been here all weekend and haven't seen any such thing. If Elmo says that he saw something in the boathouse then he's suffering from severe delusions and needs help. He's been working much to hard and needs some time off. I'm an officer of the court and I've seen this type of thing happen to cops many times."

"Mack! Turn on your television set and put it on Channel Twelve right now!" screamed Joy from the front porch of the cottage. "Elmo's on television and running his mouth. Hurry up! Turn on your television set!" Joy burst through the front door clad in a pink terry cloth bathrobe and blue flip-flops. Her hair was in huge rollers and she looked like a porcupine in reverse.

"What are you screaming about?" Mack responded.

"Elmo's on Channel Twelve! He's over on Jensen Beach running his mouth off about the possibility of a hit man being in town. You'd better turn it on and watch what he has to say before the marina parking lot gets filled up with television cameras and reporters." Joy nodded toward the television remote and made a clicking motion with her tongue.

Mack snatched the television remote off the top of the glass coffee table, pressed the 'on' button and clicked to Channel Twelve the CBS affiliate in West Palm Beach. The camera was focused on Elmo and he was standing alongside a lifeguard station with at least a dozen microphones crammed in his face.

The incessant 'click' of single lens reflex camera shutters was audible. Elmo was enjoying the media attention. Mack turned up the volume.

"That's all I can say about this murder investigation at this time," blurted Elmo as he tipped his cowboy hat to the media. "Ya'll have to address your questions to the Sheriff's public relations office and the homicide detectives who will be here shortly to investigate the case." Elmo glanced at his watch, eyed his enthralled group of admirers and elected to continue his dissertation. "I'll wait here for just a few more minutes until the Sheriff's helicopter arrives. I'll try to answer any questions that you have." Elmo gestured toward a middle-aged male reporter in the front row with his hand up. "Young man do you want permission to go the bathroom or do you have a question?" Elmo grinned at his own wit.

"Deputy Elmo this appears to be the body of Mack McCray the fishing guide who lives over the Port Sewall Marina boathouse in North Lake. You stated that it is not Mr. McCray. But it certainly looks like him. Can you qualify specifically how you know it is not Mack McCray's body?" The reporter smiled smugly. He had made his point.

Elmo glared at the reporter, clucked his tongue several times and began his ad-libbed response. "I've been in law-enforcement in Martin County for almost twenty years and I've known Mack McCray since the day he showed up in Stuart. I can assure you that this body is not Mack McCray. May I have the next question please? How about the young blonde lady in the back row wearing the pretty blue dress?"

"Deputy Elmo what makes you so certain that this is not Mack McCray and why did you put the body's hands inside paper bags?" The young blonde stood with her pen poised over her notebook in her hand as if she expected a detailed response that would require a set of copious notes for her editor.

"I already answered the first part of your question. This is not Mack McCray. The second part of your question dealt with the paper bags I placed over the victim's hands. A first year criminology student learns that the hands and fingers of a homicide victim must be bagged to protect any possible bits of evidence embedded under the fingernails or on the palms of the hands. I have time for one more question. How about the lady in the back row with the gray hair wearing blue jeans and checkered shirt?"

"Deputy Elmo I was one of the first reporters on the scene this morning. I had an opportunity to walk around the body before you got here and I noticed that the ends of the fingers were missing. Did you notice that and can you explain it please?" A smug 'got ya' smiled crossed her face. She wanted to watch him wiggle.

"I didn't pay any attention to the victim's hands when I arrived. My first instinct was to cover them in paper bags to protect any possible evidence. Questions about the condition of the body should be addressed to the coroner's office."

"I have a follow up question," the female reported quipped. "Will you take it please?"

"Certainly." Elmo's confidence grew by leaps and bounds. "What is it?"

"You referred to the body as a homicide victim. What makes you think that this was not an accidental drowning?" She smiled because she knew that she had him boxed in a corner.

Elmo's mouth fell open and he paled. He felt extremely nervous because no one from the corner's office or homicide unit had shown up to take over the responsibility of the investigation.

"Folks the interview's over. That's all the questions I can answer this morning. Please make room for the two gentlemen coming down the stairs to remove the body."

The crowd of reporters and spectators dutifully split as two grim-faced men wearing white long sleeve shirts, black neckties and black suits carefully maneuvered a gurney down the wooden steps leading to beach. They seemed oblivious to their task. It was their job. The men approached the body, immediately covered it with a blue blanket, rolled it into a black rubber body bag and lifted it onto the gurney for transport. As the two men departed up the wooden steps with the body a Martin County Sheriff's Department helicopter sat down on the beach. Four men in suits disembarked from the helicopter and headed at a trot toward the lifeguard station where Elmo was holding court for the media.

Elmo sensed an opportunity to get out of the spotlight, grabbed the closest microphone and began. "Ladies and gentlemen. These gentlemen are detectives from the Martin County Sheriff's Department. They'll take over the investigation and answer your questions from this point. Thank you." Elmo replaced the microphone in its stainless-steel holder, turned and hightailed it over a sand dune to his patrol car. He had to get to Port Sewall Marina before the members of the media did. He and Mack had to have a long talk.

Mack, Tina, Joy and Rat observed Elmo's television antics in shock. Mack knew that Elmo would lead the whole crowd to the Port Sewall Marina like the Pied Piper leading a pack of rats and they'd be there within fifteen minutes. He had to act fast.

"Rat. Get down to the boathouse and wash it out from top to bottom with the pressure washer and bleach. Open the door to North Lake and let the boathouse air out good. Joy you go back to your house and keep your eyes glued to the television set. Make notes of anything that I should know about and don't come back over here unless I call you. Do you understand?"

Joy trembled from head to toe. It was all she could do to speak without stuttering. "Yes. I understand completely. I'll go back to my house, shut the door and watch the television set to see what else happens. If it's anything important I'll give you a call and I won't come over here unless you call me." She rose and walked toward the front door.

"Keep my dog at your house. I don't need for him come over here and bite one of the reporters. A big enough mess is about to happen."

"When I left the house he was sleeping on the couch. He seems to be happy with me." Joy opened the screen door, walked out onto the front porch and headed across the parking lot in the direction of her house on Willoughby Creek two hundred yards away.

Mack returned his attention toward Rat who was attempting to slide out the front door behind Joy. "Rat! You keep your mouth shut. You've seen nothing. Do you understand?"

"What if somebody asks me about the dummy I towed out to the inlet last night? What should I tell 'em if they ask me?"

"The two guys that saw you were probably as drunk as skunks and I seriously doubt that they remember anything about it. Get the boathouse washed out and yourself out of sight as fast as you can. I don't want you around when the media shows up. You only have about fifteen minutes!"

"Aye, aye sir! I understand completely. I shall gladly wash down the boathouse and disappear afterward. Aye, aye sir." Rat saluted Mack with his right hand, dashed out the front door and headed for the storage shed to drag out the clumsy pressure washer and bottles of bleach.

"Tina. Do you think you can get your uncle to shut Elmo up?"

"I'll give him a call. He's over on his ranch in Indiantown with that young intern that's been clerking for him this summer. I've got his ranch telephone number on my cell phone directory. He can call one of his buddies over here and get a gag order issued immediately. What are you going to do when Elmo finishes his media blitz?"

"I'm not sure. It depends on what he's told them and what questions they ask. I don't have any idea who the guy is that washed up on the beach. I was out of town visiting a sick cousin for the last five days and don't know anything."

"I agree. You didn't get back to the marina until about noon yesterday. Then you and I went up to Fort Pierce to rummage around some antique shops. Afterward we had a romantic dinner at Mangrove Mattie's and spent the evening at the Tiki Hut at the Fort Pierce City Marina. I don't know how you could possibly know anything about what happened at the marina while you were gone. I've been here since Friday afternoon and I didn't see anything unusual."

Mack heard the 'whir' of helicopter rotor blades and dashed onto the front porch. A Channel 12 News chopper hovered over the marina parking lot. Dust and pea gravel sucked up from the grass carpet by the powerful suction of the rotor blades flew in all directions. Mack glanced back into the cottage at the television set. A close up view of the marina cottage and Mack on the front porch was on the screen.

The announcer onboard the helicopter spoke into his headset. *"Folks this is Port Sewall Marina and that looks like Mack McCray himself on the front porch. Apparently the body on the beach is indeed someone else. This is a private marina and is owned by Ms. Tina McShay an assistant state's attorney in the West Palm Beach office. She specializes in felony cases. The marina has been in her family for more than fifty years. She uses the marina to store her personal sailboat and those of her friends. Mack McCray moved to Stuart from Chicago in March of this year and he's the marina manager. Perhaps we can persuade Mr. McCray or Miss McShay to come out and speak to us after we land."*

"Tina. I have to keep them from landing that helicopter. Do you have any suggestions?"

"Do you have a shotgun? We can shoot the bastards down and claim self defense!"

"Or insanity! I don't think shooting them down is the right thing to do when we're the focus of their investigative reporting. I'll run out and park my truck in the middle of the parking lot and that'll keep them from landing. Can you get your Beamer off that telephone pole and put it in the middle of the parking lot?"

"No! There's not enough time! While you're getting rid of the chopper I'll call my uncle and ask him to do something to get these people out of here. After you chase off the helicopter block off the entrance to the driveway with your truck to keep the rest of them out."

"They can still get in here by boat. Can you activate the electronic gate that separates North Lake from Willoughby Creek? That'll keep the boaters out."

"I'll run downstairs and trip the gate after I call my uncle."

Mack ran out into the parking lot and frantically waved his arms in an attempt to wave off the helicopter. The alert cameramen aboard the helicopter zoomed in on Mack. His upper torso, arms and face appeared on television sets all over Martin, St. Lucie and Palm Beach Counties.

The excited announcer began his spiel. *"That's Mack McCray waving at us from the marina parking lot. It's obvious that it wasn't his body that washed up on Jensen Beach this morning."*

Mack raced across the parking lot, jumped in his pickup truck, started the engine and backed into the center of the parking lot. He almost nicked the landing gear of the helicopter that hovered seven feet above the parking lot. The shocked helicopter pilot gunned the engine and took off in an accelerated vertical climb that threw the reporter onto the floor of the helicopter.

"That'll give him a headache to remember me by in the morning," Mack chuckled.

If the hit man was watching television he was now aware that he missed his mark Saturday morning. If he was in St. Lucie, Martin or Palm Beach counties and slept in this morning he would still have the opportunity to learn of his miscalculation on the late-night news. His target was still very much alive.

Chapter
16

Mack brought his blue pickup truck to a quick stop just as Deputy Elmo's green and white patrol car, blue lights ablaze and siren whining, screamed into the Port Sewell Marina parking lot. Several media satellite trucks enveloped in a billowing dust cloud followed close behind.

Mack slammed the pickup into gear and raced across the parking lot behind Elmo's patrol car and blocked off the entrance from Old St. Lucie Boulevard. The driver of the first satellite truck slammed on his brakes and the truck immediately behind him slammed into his rear. The resultant chain reaction crash extended for almost one hundred feet down the dusty road. The driver of the first truck jumped out and began to raise hell with the driver behind him. Down the line the action went. Each driver expressed his opinion to the other about his stupidity.

Mack jumped out of his truck and sprinted to Elmo's car.

Elmo opened the driver's side door and showed Mack the roll of plastic yellow crime scene tape in his left hand. He grinned like an opossum in a sewer pipe and tipped his cowboy hat in greeting. "Mack how'd I do with them television people? I just can't cover this up any more. I've gotta' come clean because I'm an officer of the law. I can't lie for you even though you're my friend." Elmo slid out of the patrol car.

"Elmo! What the hell did you think you were doing over there? You ran your big mouth like an open fire hydrant and tried to act like a big shot. Every time you opened your mouth you dug yourself in deeper. Why did you tell those media people that it looked like a homicide to you? Those reporters were already three blocks down the road ahead of you every time you opened your mouth to put your foot into it!" Mack put his hands on his hips and glared at Elmo.

"I did what I had to do." Elmo seemed shocked and surprised that Mack had jumped into his mess kit with both feet. "I can't cover this up."

The first two media trucks extended their satellite transmitter towers skyward and two young male television reporters approached Mack with live microphones in hand. Their respective camera operators followed them in unison.

"The first reporter to arrive, a tall, thin blonde, was evidently a recent graduate of television broadcasting school. "Mr. McCray can you explain why someone who looks like you washed up dead on Jensen Beach this morning with six bullet holes in his back?" The grim-faced reporter extended the microphone toward Mack's face. Mack pushed it away with his left hand.

"I don't know who washed up on Jensen Beach morning. I was out of town the past several days and got back about noon yesterday. I'm certain that Deputy Elmo meant well but got a little confused in the heat of the moment. The investigation is under the jurisdiction of the Martin County Sheriff's Department crime scene detectives and I suggest that you direct your questions to them. Perhaps you jumped to a conclusion that may not be correct. Maybe the guy fell off a boat last night and drowned."

"Deputy Elmo said it was a homicide. What do you say about that?" The reporter shoved his silver microphone toward Mack's face.

"If you don't get that microphone out of my face and those cameramen off the marina's property there might be a crime scene right here in the parking lot. I don't think that you or your producer wants that to happen." Mack turned to face Elmo.

Elmo attempted to respond. "Mack this is the biggest thing that's happen in Martin County in the last fifteen years. Those reporters saw the bullet holes in that guy's back and they know what's going on. Why don't you just tell them what you know?"

"Are you out of your mind? I don't have any idea who shot that guy any more than you do and there's no sense in causing a scene here. Why don't you just play dumb and leave? I think you can do that without much practice." Mack nodded toward Elmo's patrol car. "Just get in your car and drive away and lead that band of reporters with you. Try to keep your mouth shut before you create a problem we can't possibly handle." Mack opened the patrol car door and gestured to Elmo to get inside.

"I can't leave! This is a homicide crime scene and you know it."

"Mr. McCray!" Shouted a young male reporter as he dashed towards the cottage. "Who's that grubby looking guy over there by the stairs with the bleach bottles in his hand?" The reporter pointed toward the cottage. Rat cowered against the east corner of the front porch. The pressure washer was in his right hand and three empty bleach bottles were strung on the fingers of his left hand.

"Excuse me sir," called out the young reporter in Rat's direction. "Who are you? Can you explain what you are doing with a pressure washer and bleach bottles? I'd like to talk to you. Would you come over here for just a minute please?" The reporter gestured for Rat to come in his direction.

Rat attempted to step back down the stairs, slipped and slid face down toward the boathouse. When he reached the bottom of the stairs he saw three boats racing on full plane through North Lake from Willoughby Creek. The boats were filled with reporters and headed toward the boathouse. Rat slipped into the dark shadow behind the staircase and cowered in the corner.

The reporter turned his attention back toward Mack. "Mr. McCray can you explain who that guy is? Why was he holding three bleach bottles and a pressure washer? Is there something going on downstairs in the boathouse that we should know about?"

"You might as well tell him what's going on," Elmo offered meekly. "He'll find out sooner or later. It'll look better for you if you come clean here and now."

"Okay boys. You're onto me and I might as well tell you what's going on. Follow me over to the cottage," Mack responded and motioned for the reporters and cameramen to follow him. When he reached the stairs Mack cupped his hands around his mouth and directed his comments toward the reporters standing on the boat dock. "Gather around the bottom of the stairs and I'll introduce you to the man with the pressure washer and the bleach bottles. Mack gestured for the reporters to walk toward the wooden stairs, held his right hand up and motioned for them to stop ten feet away from the first step. "I strongly recommend that you keep your distance from him and don't get close to the boathouse. You will be shocked when I explain what's going on."

The reporters in the parking lot and their cameramen formed a half circle around Mack and looked in the direction of the dock and boathouse below.

"Make sure you have your camera focused and your sound systems operational before I begin. I don't want to go over this twice." Mack paused for effect as the cameramen adjusted the sound levels and focus of their video cameras. "This might be disturbing for many of your viewers."

"The man you saw at the head of the stairs is called Rat. He lives on a sailboat moored in the St. Lucie River opposite Shepherd's Park. I called him over here this morning to decontaminate the boathouse. Rat spent several years in Southeast Asia when he served in the military and contracted Laotian Hemorrhagic Fever. Obviously it didn't kill him, but he may be a carrier of the fatal disease. Although it's very contagious Rat can't catch it because he already had it and survived." Mack paused as the reporters scrambled for position in front of him. "Hopefully because of his work this morning we contained an outbreak of the disease here."

A young reporter shoved his microphone into Mack's face as his grimacing cameraman adjusted his camera's depth of field. "Mr. McCray please explain in detail what Laotian Hemorrhagic

Fever is and what makes you think there could be an outbreak in this area?"

"Young man that's a very good question. Laotian Hemorrhagic Fever is a form of Ebola. Are you certain that you want your viewers to hear the details?"

"Of course. The public has a right to know the facts."

"Very well. The first symptom consists of vomiting red and black vomit. The vomit reeks of a very repulsive smell. Bleeding from the orifices is a very distinctive sign and the bleeding will go on continually internally as well as through the orifices. The virus is unstoppable. Once it's in the body it immediately starts dissolving the internal organs as well as the skin from the inside. As the virus travels towards the brain, personalities fade and no facial expression will be visible on the hosts' face. The side effects usually start about ten days after infection and after that you have about six days of pure misery to live then you die."

"Is it always fatal? You said that your friend Rat had it and survived."

"There have been several cases where people have survived but it's only a one out of ten chance that you will live. Any other relative questions?"

"What makes you think that there could be an outbreak of Laotian Hemorrhagic Fever here?"

"Rat may be a carrier of the disease. That's why he's hiding under the stairs."

"Can we catch it from him?"

"Maybe, if you get close enough to him and a female flea jumps on you and bites you. I'd keep my distance if I were you."

"Aren't you worried?"

"It's to late for me to worry about something like that."

"Why?"

"I may have already contracted the disease or may also be a carrier. Last week I spent three days visiting my cousin who's in the hospital in Tallahassee. The doctors were unable to diagnose what's wrong with him. When I left late Friday afternoon to return to Stuart the doctors concluded he had contracted Laotian Hemorrhagic Fever. His blood platelets had dissolved and when I left the hospital he was barely clinging to life. When I left they weren't expecting him to last the afternoon."

"Have you heard what happened to him?"

"He died about fifteen minutes after I left the hospital. They called here yesterday afternoon and told me to go to the hospital tomorrow for some blood tests. That's why Deputy Elmo came racing over here from Jensen Beach. I called the Sheriff's Department yesterday and asked them to send a deputy over to put up yellow quarantine tape to keep the public out. Elmo's late."

The young reporter took two steps back from Mack. "Mr. McCray do you think that Laotian Hemorrhagic Fever may spread from Rat, or yourself to the rest of the population in this area." He shoved the microphone in Mack's direction and did his best to maintain his distance."

"When I returned home about noon yesterday I noticed several turkey buzzards perched on top of the boathouse and in the Australian pines around the parking lot. Buzzards have a very keen sense of smell and they can actually sense an outbreak of a fatal disease before anyone becomes infected or dies."

"What does this have to do with Laotian Hemorrhagic Fever?"

"The boathouse was filled with bluebottle flies and they can also be a carrier of the disease. The scientists aren't certain whether Laotian Hemorrhagic Fever is transmitted through the air or whether a person must be bitten by a flea or a bluebottle fly in order to be contaminated."

"So what's your point? You didn't answer my question."

"Hold your horses. I'm getting to the point. Rat returned from a road kill collecting expedition Friday night and left two opossums and a raccoon in the boathouse while he went fishing over by Trickle's Island. He fell asleep and forgot about what he left in the boathouse until about eleven Saturday morning when Ms. McShay's screaming woke him up."

"Why was Ms. McShay screaming?"

"When she exited her sailboat, she sleeps onboard when she's in town, she detected a strong odor coming from the boathouse. Being female and naturally curious she opened the door and saw the dead opossums and raccoon. Then she screamed. You would have too! They reeked!"

"Then what happened?"

"Rat drove his kayak over here from Trickle's Island to see what was going on. When he got here he saw the turkey buzzards and smelled the odor coming from the boathouse."

"What did he do with the opossums and raccoon? Did he eat them?"

"No. They were beyond saving. When I got here I drove over to the fish house, filled up a couple of twenty-five quart coolers with chipped ice and iced them down. He towed them out to the inlet after dark and let them go on the outgoing tide."

"Why the pressure washer and bottles of bleach?"

"He washed out the boathouse with a water hose and detergent, but it wasn't very effective. So he came over here this morning after buying some bleach at Wal-Mart to do it again."

"Mr. McCray when we were at Jensen Beach this morning I noticed several turkey buzzards perched in some Australian pines next to the beach. There were also blue and greenbottle flies on the body. Is there a possibility that the man found dead on Jensen Beach this morning was contaminated with Laotian Hemorrhagic Fever?" The obviously agitated young reporter shoved the microphone into Mack's face.

"Like I told you before, the scientists aren't certain if Laotian Hemorrhagic Fever can be transmitted through the air or whether you must be bitten by a flea or a fly. Turkey buzzards are a definite sign that a fatal disease is in the area. Look up on the roof of the cottage. Several turkey buzzards are sitting on the roof and several more are in the Australian pines. The disease could be carried in their feces or vomit. I suggest that you don't get very close to them."

At that instant, almost as if on cue, Napoleon the Alpha male of the buzzard clan from the Palm City Bridge clan, defecated a massive dropping. It circled lazily through the air as it drifted downward from the tall Australian pine tree. The blob of fecal matter was caught by a warm gust of air and disbursed over the area. It slowly drifted downward over the crowd of nervous reporters. They bolted like frightened rabbits chased by a pack of hungry coyotes.

The reporters and cameramen huddled on the dock next to the boathouse leaped into their boats and took off on full plane out of North Lake toward Willoughby Creek and the St. Lucie River. Their counterparts ran across the marina parking lot, jumped into their vehicles and made a dash onto Old St. Lucie Boulevard and headed in the direction of Martin Memorial Hospital.

"You scared the hell out of them poor boys," offered Elmo. "Are you sure that you don't have that Laotian Hemorrhagic Fever stuff?"

"Rat's embarrassed to talk about it. If I were you I'd check myself into the hospital and get checked out. You may have caught it already. Did you spend any time in the boathouse with him after we talked yesterday afternoon?"

"No. I left just like you told me to do. I got my boat and went looking for Ralph. You think that guy might've died from the fever rather than the bullet holes in his back?" Elmo offered.

"It's obvious what he died from. If the six bullet holes in his back didn't kill him then the one behind his right ear certainly did," Mack responded. "Rather than stringing crime scene tape around the marina can you call someone in the medical unit and have them put the entire marina complex under quarantine. I suggest that you stay away from here too."

"That's a good idea," Elmo blurted out. "I'm sure glad you told about this fever thing. I don't want to get sick and die. Can I still call you to see how you're doing?"

"Of course you can."

Elmo turned toward his patrol car just as Tina emerged from inside the cottage onto the front porch. She tactfully tried to get his attention.

"Deputy Elmo! Get your fat butt over here! Someone wants to talk you on the telephone!" Tina shouted in Elmo's direction and held her cell phone out toward him. "I suggest that you get over here right now and take this call!"

Dutifully Elmo loped over to the porch, took the telephone out of Tina's hand and placed it to his right ear. "Deputy Elmo here. How may I help you?" His face turned beet red as he heard the instructions coming through the plastic earpiece of the cell phone. He offered little response. "Yes sir. I understand sir. I will sir. You can count on me sir. We'll keep all reporters away from the area. I understand completely sir. Goodbye sir."

Elmo sheepishly handed the cell telephone back to Tina. "That was a Martin County judge. He told me to forget anything I saw or heard here. There's a top-secret Federal investigation going on and for me to keep my nose out of it and to keep my mouth shut. You can be assured that I will. Nobody will hear any more from me about it. I didn't see anything in the boathouse."

"You told those reporters there was a homicide when you were on television on Jensen Beach this morning." Mack spat out between clenched teeth. "How will you explain that?"

"Like I told them they have to direct their questions to a Martin County Sheriff's detective unit. I won't have anything more or do with it. You can count on me."

"Get your butt out of here and start looking for Ralph before you get yourself into more trouble."

Elmo eagerly complied and drove off in his patrol car toward Sailfish Marina. He left his boat there last night when he returned from looking for Ralph. He searched for Ralph all the way up the North Fork to Rivergate Park in Port. St. Lucie. He even went down the South Fork to the St. Lucie Lock. Maybe he would have better luck today.

Rat slithered up the wooden stairs and peeked over the top step at Mack and Tina. "Pssst. Mack. Can I come up now? Do I really have that Laotian Fever stuff? Should I stay down here?"

"Rat! Get your furry butt up here. We need to talk. We've got problems."

"Yes sir. I'm on the way." Rat cleared the top step and bounced onto the porch. "What about that fever stuff? I'm worried. I didn't know that I caught it when I was in Laos. I was sick, but nobody ever told me what it was. How'd you know?"

"I didn't," Mack replied. A broad grin spread across his face. "I made the whole thing up. It sounded better and better as I went along so I just kept rolling with it."

"You scared the hell out of me," Rat countered. 'Where did you come up with all those fancy scientific-sounding names for stuff and the symptoms? They were nasty."

"I don't really know. I must've seen a television documentary about it. They'll all get on the Internet and check it out. If I was wrong they'll be back. If I was right they won't."

"They won't be back," Tina chimed in with a grin. "You were one-hundred per cent correct."

"How do you know?"

"I was listening to your diatribe through the screen door. I tried a case last year in Atlanta where a medical researcher swiped some Hemorrhagic Fever bugs from the Center for Disease Control and tried to blame it on another lab guy."

"Where did he hide it?" Mack asked.

"In his refrigerator freezer next to his favorite ice cream. He liked butter brickle. A lab technician testified that the temperature in the freezer was not low enough to keep the Hemorrhagic Fever bugs inert and they migrated into the ice cream. "

"How'd you get him to fess up?"

"We doctored up his meals to give him the vomiting symptoms and he thought he was going to die. He told us where he had stashed the culture and we snatched it. It was next to the ice cream container. Case closed and the good guys won." Tina smiled. "Just like you just did."

"Thanks for the compliment. Rat did you get the boathouse washed down?"

"It's all done. I was bringing up the empty bleach bottles and the pressure washer when those television guys showed up. The boathouse smells like bleach and the flies are all gone. I think that you owe Napoleon a thank you."

"Napoleon? Wasn't he a short French guy with a big ego and a funny hat who got his ass kicked by the British at Waterloo?"

"Nope. This is a different Napoleon. Look up there in that Australian pine tree." Rat pointed toward a tree that fanned directly over the boat dock. "There he is. Ain't he pretty?"

"What?" Mack responded. "All I see up there is a mangy old turkey buzzard. That's the one that took a dump over the reporters and scared them off."

"That's why you owe him a thank you. That's old Napoleon himself. He's my buddy."

"A turkey buzzard's your buddy? Why?"

"Well he's not always my buddy. Some days we argue over things and I have to chase him off with my gaff. He has to understand that I get first dibs on the fresh stuff. But he saved your butt."

"I suppose you're right. He did chase the reporters off. How can I pay him back?"

"Just leave a fish out for him once in awhile on that spit of land that separates North Lake from the river. He'll settle for catfish or black drum. He ain't particular when it comes to fish."

"Consider it a done deal. Napoleon I owe you buddy," Mack waved his right arm in the direction of the disinterested turkey buzzard. "See you around."

The turkey buzzard let out a loud 'squawk' as he sailed out of its perch toward Mack and released another load of foul smelling airborne fecal material. The giant blob spun in the air like a black and white miniature pizza as it sailed toward earth. Rat quickly ducked under the porch, Tina slipped inside the front door and Mack was left to survive on his own. Hopelessly mesmerized by the spinning blob he helplessly raised his right arm over his face as a defensive gesture just as the spinning putrid missile hit its mark. Napoleon's inertial guidance system was accurate and he seldom missed his target!

"Rat!" Mack sputtered. "Take your feathered buddy and go somewhere! Go anywhere at all." Mack pointed toward Rat's green rubber kayak that silently bobbed at the end of the boat dock. "Just get out of here!"

"Okay. I'm leaving. When should I come back?"

"The thirty-fourth of August would be just fine."

"There's no such date. August only has thirty-one days in it"

"I'll call you when I need you for something."

"I don't have a telephone on my boat."

"I'll call you. Let's leave it at that."

Completely dejected at Mack's comments Rat slunk down the dock toward his kayak, started the ancient engine and headed for Willoughby Creek. He didn't wave or look back.

Tina realized that Mack didn't mean to hurt Rat's feelings and tried to make small talk. "I'm really worried about Ralph. I hope that Elmo finds him soon."

"Me too. He might need help."

"Why?"

"His note to Joy said that he was going fishing in the Keys but his truck was in the driveway. If he went to the Keys he would've loaded his boat on the trailer and towed it down."

"Why couldn't he just drive the boat down there? It's a straight shot down the Intracoastal, a run through Hawk Channel and he's there! I've done it a dozen times."

"Because he has a commercial fishing boat and it's as slow as a snail. It'd take him three days to get there and three days to get back."

"Why don't you take your boat out and look for him? You know where he likes to hang out."

"I can't. It's not here. I put it in the shop for a bottom job before I left for Biloxi."

"Biloxi, Mississippi? You told me you were in Tallahassee comforting a sick cousin."

"Oops. It was a slip of the tongue. I meant Tallahassee."

"You certainly did, but you weren't in Tallahassee. I just checked with Tallahassee Memorial Hospital and there was no patient there by the name of McCray!"

"He was my cousin on my mother's side. His last name was Halfast not McCray."

"Try again buster. I just checked with all of the hotels within twenty miles of Tallahassee and you weren't registered in any of them."

"I stayed at my cousin's house."

"Where's that?"

"On Doomar Drive. It's a residential street between Miccosukee and Centerville Roads."

"Why were you checked into a Motel 6 on I-10 west of Lake City last Monday night and again Friday night?"

"It's a long drive up there. I left here late Monday night and it was almost midnight when I reached I-10. I didn't want to wake his mother up in the middle of the night."

"He lived with his mother?"

"No. She lived with him. Are you satisfied now?"

"No! Why'd you say Biloxi if you meant Tallahassee? There's a big difference."

"I guess I was thinking about Biloxi because my cousin and I were stationed there together. It was a slip of the tongue. My mind wandered off when I was thinking about Ralph."

"I'll bet. Do you suppose that Ralph has a girl on the side and just took off for a few days? Maybe he was in Biloxi with you?"

"No! He wasn't."

"So! You were in Biloxi?"

"No! I meant that he doesn't have a girl on the side and he wasn't with me in Tallahassee."

"I think your nose is going to begin growing if you continue."

"Why do you say that?"

"I don't believe you for a minute. That's why. It'll take some doing, but I'll find out where you were all week. You'd better not have some slinky broad on the side."

"Why?"

"Just because. I don't owe you an explanation. It's almost ten o'clock. Let's go have brunch at Indian River Plantation and try to forget all of this. Afterward I'm going back to West Palm. I've got a felony bond hearing in the morning and I want to review the sleaze bag's file."

"Sounds good! Are you buying?"

"No! You are. You owe me big time for the favor that my uncle did for you. He called Elmo."

"Elmo said that he was called by a Martin County judge! Your uncle's in West Palm Beach."

"What makes you think that I only have one uncle? I'm his favorite niece. Let's go."

After a leisurely brunch at Indian River Plantation Mack and Tina returned to Port Sewall Marina at 1:37 P.M. True to her word Tina packed her bags and assigned Mack to retrieve her Beamer from atop the telephone pole. He attached a chain to the Beamer's rear axle and pulled it off backward with his truck. There was no obvious damage except to Tina's pride.

Mack was downstairs checking out the boathouse when she left for West Palm Beach. She didn't offer a 'goodbye' or acknowledge his efforts. He didn't much care at this point. His plate was full. He decided to curl up with the book on treasure hunting that he bought at the Blake Library book signing before he left for Biloxi. Or, was it Tallahassee? Mack wasn't sure about anything any more and he was certain that Tina would find out where he was! Then what?

Chapter 17

It was 4:47 Sunday afternoon. Mack was napping in the recliner and the treasure hunting book was open and across his chest. The black and white cat was curled up in his lap like it was his private property for his afternoon siesta. Deputy Elmo screamed into the marina parking lot in his patrol car, slammed on the brakes and the car came to a screeching stop inches in front of the porch. The noise obviously didn't bother Mack, or the cat, as neither one of them moved. The cat's ears twitched briefly in recognition that he heard something. But, it wasn't important enough for him to get out of his comfortable nest.

Elmo leaped out of the patrol car, ran up onto the front steps and burst through the screen door and stopped at Mack's side. He grabbed Mack by the shoulders and shook him furiously as he attempted to spit out some intelligible words.

"Mack! You have to wake up!" Elmo continued to shake Mack shoulders. "I found Ralph's boat. He's in trouble. Wake up Mack! Ralph needs our help! Wake up!"

Mack jerked upward, shook his head in disbelief over what he thought he had heard. Elmo's flushed face came into focus and Mack saw a look of in terror in his eyes. The color had drained from his face and he appeared to be in shock.

"Where'd you find Ralph's boat?" Mack asked as he attempted to stand up. The cat napping in his lap prevented him from moving. "Was there any sign of Ralph in it?"

"His boat's tied up under that low bridge between the north end of the Archipelago and that small island directly across from Bird Island. It was anchored under the bridge and tied up with a couple of ropes on each end. You wouldn't ever be able to see it from the air."

"What did you do with it? Did you leave it there or did you tow it back here to the marina?"

"I left it there. It's a crime scene and can't be moved. I stretched yellow crime scene tape around the entrance to the Archipelago and between the channel markers. That'll keep curious people away."

"That was certainly a good idea. It'll draw everybody's attention to the fact something happened in there. When we get there everybody in Martin County with a boat will wonder who got killed in the Archipelago." Mack stood up, dusted the cat hair off his lap and placed the treasure hunting book face down on the coffee table. "Let's go over there and take a look around. Ralph must be close by. Maybe he hid the boat so his wife wouldn't know where he was."

"Let's not take my patrol boat. It'll draw attention to us in the Archipelago. If we take your boat the onlookers will think we're going in there to go fishing."

"There are a couple of small problems with that idea. First of all, you already strung yellow crime scene tape up all around the entrance to the Archipelago. People will think it really strange if a private boat goes through the crime scene tape. Second, my boat's not here. I asked Ralph to take it over to Manatee Marine for a bottom job when I left town the first of the week. I intend to pick it up tomorrow. I can't get it today because the yard's closed on Sunday."

"Okay. We'll take my boat. Let's get going!"

"Where's your boat? You drove up here in your patrol car!"

"I left it at the Sandsprit Park boat ramp. I didn't want to call attention to the fact that I was coming over here. Let's go. Get in the car. We can be there in five minutes and be on our way."

"That was certainly a good idea. People saw you pull your boat into the ramp and blow out of there in your patrol car. Now they're wondering where you went and why you left there so fast. How are you going to explain that you and I are taking off together in your patrol boat?"

"I don't have to explain anything to anybody much less a bunch of civilians! Let's get going!"

When Elmo and Mack arrived at Sandsprit Park a crowd of interested spectators had gathered around Elmo's Martin County Sheriff's patrol boat. Elmo had left the blue lights flashing and the pair of super-charged outboard motors running in the idle position. At least a dozen people stood at the end of the boat ramp looking down at the empty patrol boat and trying to figure out what was happening. Elmo swung into an open parking space, slammed the gearshift lever into 'Park' and opened the door.

"Okay Mack. Let's get going. I gotta' shoo those people way from there." Elmo slipped out of the car and took off in a fast trot toward his moored patrol boat and the crowd of spectators.

"Okay folks. There's nothing to look at. Get away from my boat. I've got to check something out offshore."

The crowd obediently scattered in all directions as Elmo trotted down the dock. He leaped feet first into the catamaran with a resultant loud 'thunk'. Mack was amazed that Elmo didn't go through the fiberglass bottom. Mack slowly sauntered out onto the dock and eased his way into the boat. "Elmo I've got the stern line off the cleat. When I throw off the bow line you can put it in reverse." Mack leaned forward and gracefully slipped the braided eye splice off the stainless steel dock cleat. He carefully coiled the lines in a Flemish pattern and placed them on the deck.

When Elmo and Mack arrived at the entrance to the Archipelago a crowd of several dozen floating curious spectators, attracted by the multiple bands of yellow plastic crime tape Elmo had strung up across the channel and between the channel markers, lined the Intracoastal Waterway.

"I'm going to get those people out of our way. Put your fingers over your ears because I'm going to hit the siren." Elmo flipped up a stainless-steel toggle switch mounted in the dash that operated the blue lights mounted in a Federal bar on the hard top and pressed in the red plastic push button that activated the siren. The ear splitting scream got the attention of everyone within a nautical mile and the crowd of boats blocking the channel entrance split in all directions like a school frightened mullet fleeing a marauding barracuda.

"I guess I got their attention. Hold tight while I slip into the channel. We'll come around the inside of the lagoon and slip up on the backside of the bridge and Ralph's boat."

"Let's go around the outside of the island and come in by Bird Island so the people in those boats won't have any idea where we're really going." Mack pointed toward the narrow channel that followed the concrete seawall around the one-acre island.

"We might not have enough water to get this boat through there. It draws thirty-four inches and that channel only runs three feet deep at the highest tide."

"The tide's at a high stand right now and is just beginning to ebb. We don't have much choice because you stretched yellow crime scene tape across the channel entrance. In order to get through that way you have to take the tape down and that'll allow that herd of boats to come right down the channel behind us. I'll stand up in the bow and keep a visual lookout to be sure that you don't go aground." Mack walked to the bow of the boat, peered into the murky water and signaled with his right hand for Elmo go straight ahead. *"Elmo doesn't need to know that I can't see down there any better than he can,"* Mack thought to himself.

When the boat reached the tiny one-lane bridge separating the island from the main part of the Archipelago the tide had stated to ebb and the current was picking up. Ralph's boat was wedged under the concrete superstructure of the bridge. Mack signaled for Elmo to pull alongside of the bridge, drew his index finger across his throat and pointed at the flashing blue lights as an indication that he should turn them off. Elmo obliged.

Mack sized up the situation. Ralph's anchor line led over the bow of the boat and entered the water at a forty-five degree angle. A length of braided yellow polyethylene line led to two bridge supports and held the boat's bow and stern in position.

The top of the windshield scraped the bottom of the bridge. It was obvious the tide had started to go down based on the height of the wetness on the concrete bridge abutments.

"Elmo pull in stern first alongside the bridge and I'll cut the line holding the stern of Ralph's boat to the bridge. The bow will stay in position and the stern will swing under the bridge. Then I'll attach your towline to the front cleat. After that I'll cut the front line."

"What about the anchor line?"

"It's not very deep here. The anchor should pull right out. If it doesn't I'll cut the line."

Elmo expertly swung the boat's stern toward the bridge. Mack leaned over the stern, passed the loop of the eye splice in Elmo's double braided nylon towline under the bow cleat of Ralph's boat and snugly pulled it back over the arms. He snipped off the line securing the stern to the bridge and the boat swung toward the Archipelago. Mack secured the patrol boat's towline to a cleat mounted on the stern quarter and cut the remaining yellow polyethylene line securing Ralph's boat to the bridge. "Elmo go slow ahead let's see if we can pull it out from under the bridge without causing any more damage."

Elmo obliged. Ralph's boat slowly inched ahead, popped free of the bridge and the anchor line pulled loose from the sandy bottom Elmo turned around and faced Mack. "Good job! We'll tow it back to Sandsprit Park and tie it up. The crime scene investigators will want to go through it from bow to stern."

"Crime scene investigators? What makes you think Ralph committed a crime? I think he's hiding out from his wife. He must have a hot sweetie in the Archipelago."

"Take a close look in the bottom of the boat. I'll hold us in position while you look."

"Okay," Mack replied. "I think you're wrong about Ralph." Mack used the towline to pull Ralph's boat alongside and peered inside. What he saw shocked him. "Elmo we're not going to Sandsprit Park! We can't risk someone seeing this."

"Where should we tow it? How about Nurse O'Dell's dock?"

"That won't work. She's on safari in South Africa gathering Bushman poison samples for her collection. Besides it's visible from the river."

"Where else can we take it?"

"We're going to tow Ralph's boat back to Port Sewall Marina and stash it in the boathouse. Nobody except us knows that Ralph's missing. There's no sense in stirring up the media. You did enough of that this morning. Pull up alongside the seawall and I'm going to climb in. It'll look like my boat ran out of gas and you're towing me back."

"What about the yellow crime scene tape I strung around the channel markers? What am I gonna' tell the people when we go through there?"

"Tell them some kids swiped a roll of crime scene tape out of your boat and pulled a prank. Order somebody to pull it down and throw it in the trash when they get back to the dock."

"They're going to see you and they'll know that this isn't your boat. Then what?"

"Use the speaker mounted on the hardtop to give them instructions and don't slow down. I'll pull my hat down and keep my head turned away so nobody sees my face."

"Somebody might write down the commercial registration number on the side of the boat and try to determine who owns it."

"That's not important to these people. There're just interested rubberneckers."

Elmo towed Ralph's boat around the island and entered the channel leading to the Intracoastal Waterway. He flipped on his blue lights and blew the siren to clear a path between the recreational boats hovering around the entrance the channel. When he got within fifty feet of the crowd he keyed his microphone and spoke into it, "Attention boat captains. Please disperse immediately! You're a hazard to navigation. You two guys in the Grady-White rip down that yellow tape, take it back to the dock and throw it in the trash. No crime occurred here. Some kids swiped a roll of yellow crime scene tape out of my boat last night and pulled this prank. The only thing going on is this commercial fisherman who ran out of gas. I'm towing him back to the marina. Thank you for your cooperation." Elmo replaced the microphone on the stainless-steel clip mounted to the dash.

"Mack how was that?" Elmo didn't realize that Mack couldn't hear a word he said over the sound of the purring twin outboard motors.

"Deputy Elmo! That was a great interview you did on Channel Twelve this morning," yelled out a drunk in a Sea Ray. "Think they'll catch the guy who killed Mack?"

Elmo waved at the drunk to acknowledge that he heard the question and didn't respond.

When Mack and Elmo arrived at Sewall's Point Marina Mack cranked up the outboard motor and pulled Ralph's boat inside the boathouse. Once inside he pushed the 'down' control button and the sliding garage door slipped down into place.

Elmo docked his boat, got out and walked into the boathouse to meet Mack. He wrinkled up his nose and looked toward the ceiling. "This place smells like bleach! Now that we found Ralph's boat I have to report him as a missing person. I have to go over to see Joy for some details for the missing person report."

"Elmo we've been over those things before and you really screwed up this morning. Nobody except us knows that Ralph's missing and we know that he went to the Keys to do some fishing. Some kids must have towed his boat away from the dock and stuck it under the bridge as a joke."

"How did Ralph go to the Keys without a boat? His truck's sitting in the driveway."

"I'm sure he found a way. I'm going to go through this boat with a fine-toothed comb and see what I can find."

"Okay. I'll go over tell Joy that we found Ralph's boat. I need to get some information for the missing person report. Maybe she has a good photo of him that I can borrow."

"Don't you tell Joy anything until we know more about what may have happened to Ralph. She thinks he went fishing and will be back on Friday. That's good enough for me."

"But he's a missing person. I have to file a report."

"Who said he's missing? Not his wife. Joy said Ralph went fishing in the Keys and she has a note in his own handwriting to prove it. You would look pretty darn silly wouldn't you?"

"I guess so. But what about those things you saw in the bottom of Ralph's boat? Don't they prove foul play?'

"I don't know what you're talking about. I didn't see any boat. Did you?"

"Of course I did. It's right there," Elmo stammered and pointed at the boat in the boathouse slip. There it is."

"I don't see anything. Tina thinks that you've been working too much and are having serious delusions. Do you think that you're seeing things?"

"No. I see everything that I'm supposed to see. My eyes work just fine. I don't have a vision problem. I can see in the dark better than a cat."

"I'm not talking about what you see with your eyes. I'm talking about what you see with your mind and sometimes a person's mind can play tricks on them. Your mind thinks it sees a boat here, but there's no boat here. It's like yesterday afternoon when your mind thought it saw a dead body in the boathouse. It was really some ripe road kill that Rat forgot to pick up."

"But I did see a dead body in here yesterday! It washed up on the beach this morning."

"What did the judge tell you when he spoke to you this morning?"

"He told me there was a top secret Federal investigation going on and for me to keep my nose out of it and my mouth shut! I'm not supposed to be here either."

"Then what are you doing here?"

"I towed Ralph's boat back for you."

"What boat? I don't see any boat?" Do you see a boat?"

"Yes! It's right there. Oops! I forgot. There isn't any boat here, you're not here and I'm not here either. So if I'm not here I'm leaving."

"That's a good idea. Any idea where you're going?"

"Nope! Do you have any ideas?"

"Why don't you check out all of the hotels in town and see if you can get a line on those two surveyors that were working around Hell's Gate and Sewall's Point?"

"Why?"

"Because you're not here and you have to be somewhere."

"What should I do if I find them?"

"Don't do anything. Just come back here and tell me where they're staying. I might want to have a talk with them later tonight. Remember to stay away from Joy!"

"I can't come back here. The judge told me to stay away."

"Then call me on the telephone."

"Okay," Elmo stammered under his breath. "I'm going now. If anyone asks I wasn't here."

"I never saw hide nor hair of you since this morning." Mack flipped his hand toward the boathouse door as a signal for Elmo to take his leave.

After Elmo was out of eyesight and well down the river Mack closed and locked the boathouse door. Fortunately Rat had replaced the broken hasp that afternoon after he pressure cleaned the boathouse.

"I need to take some pictures and bag some evidence before he comes back and gets nosey. And I know he will," Mack thought to himself as he headed for the stairway leading up to the cottage. The sun was going down and he paused to glance at his watch. It read 7:43.

Chapter 18

Mack paused and made a quick check of the shadowy area under the staircase to be certain there wasn't an unwanted visitor lurking there. He recalled the evening before when the red dot of a laser sight paused momentarily on his forehead. Tonight the stairwell was clear. Mack bounded up the stairs to the cottage porch and heard the telephone ringing as he rounded the corner. He jerked open the screen door, made it to the telephone in five giant strides and jerked the handset off the switch hook.

"Mack here."

"I've been trying to get in touch with you for the last couple of hours and no one bothered to answer the telephone. Where the hell have you been?"

"Tina! After you left I sat down in the recliner and fell asleep. Elmo stopped by about five o'clock, woke me up and asked me to go for a boat ride with him. I got back fifteen minutes ago and was downstairs locking up the boathouse. That's why I didn't hear the telephone."

"Why? He's supposed to be looking for Ralph's boat."

"He found it. It was wedged under the little bridge south of Bird Island that leads to one of the islands in the Archipelago. After we got it loose we towed it back here to the marina."

"Was there any sign of Ralph?"

"No. The boat was securely tied up under the bridge. Someone didn't want anyone to find it."

"I'm afraid that I've got some bad news for you. You might even think it's good news."

"Is this the old I have good news and I have bad news routine? And which do I want first?"

"No it's not! Are you sitting down and do you think you can handle it?"

"No. I'm standing up, leaning on the kitchen counter and talking to you on the telephone. I think I can handle anything at this point."

"The body's disappeared! It didn't show up at the coroner's office, isn't in any of the funeral homes in St. Lucie or Martin County and it's not in any hospital morgue."

"Are you talking about the guy they found washed up on the beach this morning?"

"Of course. That's the only body that I know about. Is there another one?"

"No. There are no other bodies and I'm confused. The television news spot showed two guys coming down the stairs with a gurney, wrapping the body up in a blanket and carting it up the stairs to a waiting van. They had to be from a local funeral home or the coroner's office.

"I have some more news for you. My uncle, the judge in Indiantown, called me because he saw the news broadcast and wanted to be certain that his butt was covered. He told me to find out where the body was and to get a copy of the autopsy report. The bottom line is that there isn't any body and no autopsy report. It's like the whole thing never happened."

"That's what I told Elmo. It ever happened and there wasn't any dead body. I suppose that with the way my luck is going it'll turn up again in the boathouse tomorrow morning."

"I certainly hope not. Did you find any trace of Ralph?"

"No. The boat was tied up under the bridge and we had to work like hell to get it out. The outboard motor runs fine and there isn't any damage that I can see."

"Did you find anything in the boat?"

"There were only three things of any significance."

"What three things?"

"A white rubber boot for the left foot, a three-foot long wooden surveyor's stake with an orange plastic ribbon tied on top of it and a gold coin about the size of a silver dollar."

"That's a strange combination. Weren't some surveyors working around Hell's Gate and Sewall's Point the other day?"

"That's right. But two things really bothered me."

"What two things?"

"There's blood on the boot and the surveyor's stake. It's like someone stabbed a vampire."

"It doesn't sound good, but it could be fish blood. Tell me more about the gold coin."

"It's about the size of a silver dollar. Is there any pirate treasure buried in this area?"

"There was only one documented active pirate in this area. Don Carlos Gilbert. Gilbert's Bar is named after him because his crew lured ships onto it and pillaged them after they went aground. He got caught, was taken back to England and hung. There's always a possibility because his headquarters was on Sewall's Point in the area called High Point. Maybe Don Carlos buried something up there."

"Is there anywhere else you can think of where this coin could have come from? The treasure hunter at the Blake Library last weekend talked about the 1715 Spanish Plate Fleet that went aground and broke up between Stuart and Sebastian in a big hurricane. Could this coin be connected to the those wrecks?"

"I don't think so. Treasure hunters have worked those wrecks since the early 1960s. Maybe somebody left that coin as a sign like the Lone Ranger leaves a silver bullet. 'Hi ho Silver away!' I think the coin is a trinket from a local gift shop. Imitation gold coins sell for about a buck each. Wait a minute! I bet it I know where it came from."

"Where?"

"Stuart's 'Dancin' in the Street' was Friday night. There was a replica pirate ship float in the parade and a bunch of teen-aged pirates on it. They tossed beads and fake coins to the crowd as they cruised down Osceola Street. Just like they do at Mardi Gras in New Orleans. I'll bet that some smart-ass kids threw coins off the bridges as boats passed under them. Ralph might have been passing under a bridge and gotten 'donked' in the head with a fake gold coin."

"That could be it. I'm going to the Blake Library tomorrow and I'll ask around downtown."

"Just be careful and watch yourself tonight."

"I will. Elmo is out checking the hotels to see if those two surveyors are still in town. He's going to call me and let me know what he finds out. Before I turn in I'm going to take a look around."

"Suit yourself. I'm going to turn in early. I'll give you a call tomorrow and you can fill me in then. Lock the front door to the cottage and activate the automatic burglar alarm system."

"Yes ma'am. I will."

"Goodnight. Sleep tight."

'Click.' The telephone went dead and the monotonous dial tone droned in Mack's ear.

Something soft rubbed hard against the inside of Mack's left calf and he jumped half out of his skin. When he looked down he saw the softly purring black and white cat. Apparently the conversation woke the cat up from his nap in the wicker hamper and he expected Mack to immediately feed him dinner.

"Okay Kitty. I'll fix you some dinner. After that I've got to check around the marina and lock things up for the night. We might have some unwelcome company later."

After Mack fed the cat he decided to take quick look around the marina before it got dark. It was 8:17 and would be completely dark by 8:30. He gently pulled open the top kitchen drawer, removed the .25 caliber semi-automatic pistol and stuck it in his waistband. He turned off the lights in the cottage so that his silhouette would not show up to anyone on the outside.

He slipped through the front door, placed his back toward the front of the cottage and paused to allow his eyes to become used to the dim light. The heavy night air was intensely silent. Usually this time of the evening the frogs and crickets were croaking at the top of their lungs in an attempt to attract a mate. Mack heard a shuffling sound from the direction of the boathouse. He froze and listened intently. There was nothing but the eerie silence of nothing.

The rude telephone interrupted the silence with its incessant, obnoxious screaming. Mack spun around and slipped back into the dark cottage. The coffee table caught him directly in the shins, just below the knees, and sent him sailing ass over teakettle into the kitchenette. He did a flip and landed on his back on the kitchenette floor in front of the refrigerator.

"What the hell?" He shook his head and attempted to regain his bearings. A small amount of light from the Manatee Pocket managed to sneak through the glass doors leading to the back deck. Mack crawled along the floor to the counter toward the screaming wall telephone, raised up just high enough to reach the handset and jerked. The lightweight plasterboard plastic screw anchors pulled out and the telephone flew off the wall toward his head.

"Holy crap!" Mack muttered through clenched teeth and ducked as the telephone flew overhead. When it reached the end of the curly cord it bounced back like a little red ball on the end of a paddleboard rubber tether. Mack ducked just in time. The telephone missed his head, smashed into the kitchen counter and split in half. The plastic front cover flew off and sailed in the direction of the living area. The main body of the instrument slid to the floor. Mack placed the miraculously intact handset to his ear.

"Tina! Is this you again?"

"No. It's Elmo. What's going on? I heard a lot of crashing and banging before you answered."

"Nothing important. The phone fell on the floor."

"Oh. I checked out all of the hotels in town for those surveyor guys like you asked me to do."

"What'd you find out? Where are they?"

"They were staying at Ho Jo's and checked out late Friday afternoon"

"Did they leave a forwarding address?"

"Nope and they paid in cash so there's no charge slip to check out."

"Did the desk clerk tell you anything about them?"

"They told her they were land surveyors. They were checking and marking the location of the Spanish Land Grant markers on Sewall's Point for an archeologist."

"Anything else?"

"Yes. Because they checked out late Friday afternoon the maids had already gone home and hadn't cleaned their room."

"So?"

"She let me in to take a look around."

"And?"

"And what?"

"And what did you find? Why do I feel like I'm playing charades here?"

"It can't be charades because you have to be able to see the other person and figure out what their gestures mean. We're talking. That's different."

"Oh. I'm sorry. I didn't realize that you watched television. What did you find in their room?"

"Of course I watch television. I love 'Jeopardy' and 'Wheel of Fortune.' You can learn a lot of things if you pay attention. I even take notes."

"I'll bet you do. What did you find in their room?"

"A couple dozen empty beer cans, one dirty black sock and a pair of jockey underwear with tractor tracks up the rear wide enough to land a commercial jet. They should've burned them."

"No maps, charts, notes or books?"

"Nope. Do you want me to stop back over there tonight?"

"That's not necessary. I'm fine. Didn't the judge tell you to stay away from here?"

"Yep. He sure did. Did you hear that guy's body disappeared? Several reporters went up to the coroner's office to review the autopsy report and the body wasn't there. They're raising pure hell and want an investigation. They think there's a cover up. Some of them were talking about coming over to the marina tomorrow to interview you."

"Nope. I was with you. How could I watch any news? How do you know about it?"

"They had the television on in the hotel lobby when I was there. Are you sure you don't want me to stop by tonight?"

"I'm sure. In the last fifteen minutes I've been harassed by Tina and fed the cat. I was on my way to check the boathouse and lock things up when you called. I'm fine. Call me tomorrow."

"Okay. What time do you want me to call you? I'll be up by six o'clock."

"Try about noon. I'm planning on sleeping in tomorrow. It's been a rough day."

"Okay. I'll call you in the morning. We still have to find Ralph."

"Why do you say we still have to find Ralph? Do you have a mouse in your pocket?"

"What do you mean by that?"

"Are there two of you looking for Ralph?"

"Sure. You and me make two."

"I'm not looking. His wife didn't report him missing. She said he went fishing in the Keys."

"But we found his boat and there was blood on his boot and that sharp stick."

"We don't know if he took his boat to the Keys or if he went with someone else. That's probably fish blood. Some smart-ass kids probably took off with his boat and hid it under the bridge as a joke."

"What about the gold coin?"

"That's a fake. It's made of gold foil wrapped over a piece of candy. They were tossing them off a float Friday night at Dancin' in the Street."

"How did you know that?"

"Know what?"

"About Dancin' in the Street. I thought you were in Tallahassee Friday visiting a sick cousin."

"I was. You know when I got back here. Tina told me about it when she called a few minutes ago. Is there anything else you want to know?"

"Sure. Who was that body in the boathouse?"

"There's no body in the boathouse."

"There was a body. I saw it!"

"We've been down this road before and you need to get some sleep. You've been working too many hours. Good night Elmo." Mack hung up the telephone before Elmo could respond.

"What am I going to do with him?" Mack whispered under his breath. *"He's impossible to deal with."*

Mack shoved the broken telephone into a corner and crawled toward the front door. *"No sense in providing someone with a nice silhouette,"* he muttered to himself. *"I still have to check the boathouse. I swear I heard a noise down there earlier."* He looked at his watch. It read 8:47. There was no moon and it was very dark outside.

Still on his hands and knees when he reached the front door Mack slowly pushed it open and slipped onto the front porch. He turned left and crawled toward the west side of the cottage so he could look down at the boathouse and floating boat docks below. He heard a 'rustling' from the direction of the storage shed and paused at the corner. A knee struck him in the small of the back and drove him into the ground as a thin wire garrote slipped over his head. Mack gasped for breath and desperately attempted to dig his fingers under the taut wire to relieve the pressure.

Just before he lost consciousness he felt hot breath on the back of his neck and a deep male voice whispered in his right ear.

"I figured if I waited long enough you'd come out of your hole. Sleep tight."

Chapter 19

It was 8:14 Monday morning when Mack awoke from his nightmare of the night before. He rubbed his throat and felt a deep depression that ran across his neck slightly above his larynx. A wet tongue splashed across his face and he opened his eyes. His Brittany spaniel pup 'Rocky' was on the bed alongside him, his tail wagging a mile a minute and looking deep into Mack's eyes as if to say, "Good morning boss. Are we going out for our morning walk today?"

Mack blinked his eyes and attempted get his bearings. He realized that he was in his own bed in the marina cottage and had no recollection of how he got there. The last thing he remembered was the searing feeling across his throat and the sharp knee in the middle of his back. He closed his eyes and recalled the hot breath in his right ear and deep raspy voice that said, *"I figured if I waited long enough you'd come out of your hole. Sleep tight."*

Mack shuddered, patted the dog on the head and shooed him off the bed. The dog ran out of the bedroom toward the living area. With his eyes still half closed Mack staggered into the living area. Elmo and Rat sat at the kitchenette table drinking coffee. Joy stood at the stove whipping up a pan of scrambled eggs and bacon.

"How's our boy doing this morning?" Asked Elmo. "That's a pretty nasty welt that you got on your neck last night. You're lucky that I pulled in the marina parking lot when I did. You almost broke your silly neck on the clothesline stretched across the porch."

Mack attempted to speak but only a slight squeak came out of his throat.

"You'd better sit down, have a cup of coffee and some breakfast," quipped Joy with a toss of her head. "If it hadn't been for Rat and Elmo coming by last night you would've laid out on that porch and been dead before daylight. A herd of those nasty saltwater mosquitoes can drain the blood out of a horse in a couple of hours. Why did you have a clothesline stretched across the porch anyway?" Joy returned to stirring the scrambled eggs. She realized she had asked a question that had no good answer.

Mack painfully shuffled over to the kitchenette table and sat down directly opposite Elmo with Rat on his right side. He pointed at the groove in his neck with his right index finger and managed to squeak out a question, "What happened to me last night? How did I get back in the house?" Mack squeaked through his painful voice box.

"When I pulled into the marina parking lot last night about ten o'clock Rat was huddled beside you and trying to turn you over. He thought you broke your neck on the clothesline. I called the paramedics. When they got here I told them that you hit the clothesline and they put a neck collar on you. After they were certain your neck wasn't broken they lugged you in the cottage, put you in bed and gave you a strong sedative to make you sleep all night."

"When I let your dog out this morning to pee he took off like a bolt of lightning toward here. When I got here Elmo was asleep in his patrol car and Rat was curled up into a little ball on the front porch with the cat." Joy offered as she sidled toward the table with a pan of steaming hot scrambled eggs and bacon. "I woke Elmo up and asked him what was going on. He explained to me how you'd run on out the porch and hit your neck on a clothesline. I don't recall a clothesline being on the porch, but Elmo assured me that there was one there and he took it down after your accident." Joy dished out equal portions of scrambled eggs and crisp bacon to Mack, Rat and Elmo. Rat and Elmo dug in immediately as Mack continued to rub his sore throat.

"Elmo looked for Ralph's boat until well after dark last night and didn't find a trace of it anywhere. I'm certain he took it to the Keys with him. I wish that boy had left me a number for me to get hold of him on while he's down there. He's starting to worry me," stated Joy as she rinsed off the frying pan in the sink. "Now that I've fed you boys I'm going back to the house and wait for him to give me a call. He's been gone long enough that he should be checking in to let me know that he's all right. If I can do anything else for you boys just give me a call." Joy dried her hands off on a dishtowel, patted the dog on the head and slipped silently out the front door without a look backwards.

"Mack I decided not to tell her that we found Ralph's boat last night," Elmo blurted out. "Some kids must've stolen his boat and tried to hide it under that bridge where nobody could find it. I'll give him until tomorrow to check-in with Joy. If he doesn't check-in by late Tuesday afternoon I'll have to file a missing person report and get a posse out looking for him."

Mack placed his hand against his throat to relieve the throbbing pain and attempted to speak without straining his larynx, "Do you guys have any idea of what happened to me last night? I went out on the porch to check on a noise I heard coming from the boathouse and heard some scratching in the storage shed. That's the last thing I remember."

Rat looked up from his plate of steaming scrambled eggs and offered a response, "I was down alongside the boathouse the first time you came out. I wanted to talk to you about some of the things that happened yesterday. I came up the stairs when you went back inside to answer the telephone the second time and I was standing next to the storage shed when you came out."

"That was you I heard making noise by the storage shed?" Mack asked.

"Yep. It was me. I'd seen some guy sneaking around earlier when you and Elmo left to pick up Ralph's boat. I went up to the storage shed to see if anything had been swiped. I saw you come out the front door and get down on your hands and knees like an animal."

"I didn't know who was out there and didn't want him to get a shot of me by silhouetting me against the windows. Why didn't you warn me about the clothesline?"

"There wasn't any clothesline. When you reached the end of the porch a big guy hiding in the shadows around the corner put his knee in the middle of your back and shoved you down. I figured he was up to no good. I grabbed a cement block from the side of the storage shed, ran up behind him and put it down real hard on the back of his head."

"Rat!" Elmo's fork paused between his plate and his mouth. "Did you kill the guy?"

"Did you see a body when you drove in here last night?" Rat glibly responded as he smiled and pushed down his greasy, unkempt black beard.

"No! All I saw when I pulled in was you leaning over Mack and trying to pull him toward the front door. I didn't look around to see if there was a dead body laying there."

"What did you do with the guy?" Asked Mack in a painfully squeaky voice.

"I rolled him over the side of the hill into the water beside the boathouse. He floated pretty good I knew there wouldn't be any problem with him staying put unless there were some big bull sharks in the lagoon. It was more important to pay attention to you because you were laying unconscious on the porch with a wire noose around your neck."

"What wire noose around his neck?" Elmo asked. The fork filled with scrambled eggs was poised between his mouth and the plate. "You told me that he ran into a clothes line that was strung up between the corner of the cottage and a pillar on the porch."

"Because that's what I told Joy you told me when she showed up. It won't do her a bit of good if she knows that someone tried to strangle Mack with a piece of plastic-coated wire cable."

"Rat did you stick that guy's body in the boathouse? I sure as hell don't need that kind of mess here again especially if those reporters came back around," Mack interjected.

"You don't have to worry none."

"Why's that?" Elmo asked between munching a mouthful of scrambled eggs and bacon.

"I towed him offshore and let him float off with the outgoing side. He's long gone by now. I don't think he's going to wash up on Jensen Beach. I let him go just as the tide started running out so he had a good six-hour head start. Plus I towed him all the way out to the red sea buoy."

"When I asked you to tow the other guy out you stopped at the mouth of the inlet. How did you get your kayak all way out there to the red sea buoy this time?" Mack asked.

"I didn't use my kayak. I used Ralph's boat. I checked the gas tank to be certain it was full, lashed the guy up to a towline and off we went."

"Wasn't the guy floating?" Mack squeakily inquired. "Did anybody see you?" .

"I got two concrete blocks from the storage shed. I tied one around his neck and one around his ankles. They pulled him in about two feet down under the surface. Nobody saw nothin'."

Mack gingerly massaged his sore neck. "Both of you stick with a story that I ran into a clothesline. We don't need for Tina, Joy or the media people to know that someone tried to 'zap' me. Maybe this nightmare is finally over."

"Mack you do realize that I have to file a report on this incident, don't you?" Elmo asserted as he looked Mack directly in the eyes." I can't hide evidence of a crime two days in a row."

"Elmo there's no body here and if there's no body there's nothing to file a report on," Mack responded with a grim look on his face. "Rat do you see a dead body around here anywhere?"

"No. I don't see anything. There wasn't no body here last night there wasn't no body in the boathouse Saturday," Rat responded with a wide toothless grin. "Elmo must be working too hard. He's having hallucinations and seeing things that aren't there."

"Rat did you do something with that guy's body Saturday?" Elmo inquired as he shoveled the last scrap of scrambled eggs and bacon into his mouth. "Did you swipe the body?"

"Of course not! What guy's body?"

"The body's missing," Elmo responded.

"What do you mean the body's missing? I saw them load it up on a gurney and haul it off in a van," Mack squeaked. "They couldn't have taken it very far. Did you check the funeral homes, hospital morgues and coroners office?"

"The sheriff's department checked them. The media people saw a body on the beach yesterday. They want to know where it went and nobody can provide them with an answer."

"Rat what did the guy that you smacked last night look like?" Asked Mack.

"He was about six feet tall and weighed well over two-hundred pounds. He was a white guy, had a mustache and dressed fairly well. I can't recall any more than that. It was dark."

"How do you know he dressed fairly well?" Elmo snidely commented. "Your idea of the latest fashion is whatever's in the dumpster."

"I have to find out who this guy was so I can eliminate some prospects," Mack interjected.

"Don't you have an easy way to identify him?" Rat responded."

"What do you mean?"

"Didn't you say that they cut off the other guy's fingertips to get fingerprints to run through a scanner so they could identify him through a computer database?" Rat offered.

"That's what I suspect, plus they didn't want anyone here to be able to identify him. What does that have to do with the guy you smacked over the head last night?"

"I saved his fingertips in a glass jar in the refrigerator. I dumped a little white vinegar in the jar with them to keep 'em preserved," Rat gleefully responded.

"My God Rat! You put the guy's fingertips in a glass jar and put them in the refrigerator?" Elmo shouted. "What if Joy had seen them? She would've gone nuts!"

"I put the jar on the bottom shelf and pushed it way in the back. She was only interested in pulling out some eggs and bacon for our breakfast this morning."

"The fingerprints might be a help," Mack glumly responded. "I would've preferred to take a sample of his sweat and run pheromone tests through a database. It's more accurate than fingerprints. Most of these guys don't have their fingerprints on file."

"How do you collect sweat for this testing?" Rat asked. "Can you take it off the clothes?"

"Yes if the someone has sweat profusely. But unfortunately you towed the guy outside the inlet and let him go last night."

"I saved his jacket, shirt, underwear, pants, socks and shoes for swapping at the flea market. I've got 'em all in a gunnysack in the boathouse. If you think you can use 'em for sweat testing you can have 'em," Rat responded with a toothless grin through his bushy black beard.

"I only want his tee shirt. You didn't try it on did you?"

"Nope. It's too big for me. I'll go down to the boathouse and get it for ya'."

"Use gloves when you pick it up. I don't want it contaminated with your pheromones."

"You didn't explain what a pheromone is."

"It's a form of amino acid found in the sweat glands of mammals. Some women's pheromones attract you to them and vice versa."

"Do you mean we smell each other like dogs do?"

"The process is similar but far less embarrassing and traumatic. There are three basic types of pheromones. Primer pheromones and they may or may not be smelled by the nose as an odor. Releasers are what most people think of when they hear the word pheromone. A releaser is a chemical signal that elicits a response such as sexual attraction. The third is the 'signaling' pheromone. It is made up of chemicals that elicit a behavioral response. Among mammals, each individual, including humans, has a unique odor-print that is, in part genetically determined by individual genes. Odor-prints enable mothers to recognize their own baby on the day of its birth and for newborns to recognize their mother by scent alone."

"Is that why animals smell their babies and reject those they don't recognize?"

"That's correct. You should never handle a baby animal, or bird, that you find alone in the woods. Your human pheromones are so strong that they mask the baby's scent from its mother and they will reject it."

"What does a pheromone smell like?"

"You don't actually smell a pheromone like you do an odor. It is detected by specialized structure in the nose called the vomeronasal, or Jacobson organ."

"Where did you learn all of this complicated stuff?"

"I'm not sure as to exactly where and this is the first time I've ever used it in conversation."

"If we can't actually smell pheromones what good are they anyway?"

"They have lots of uses. Perfume manufacturers put pheromones in women's perfumes to attract men. Aftershave manufacturers put male pheromones in their products to attract women."

"Do you mean that women are attracted to us by what they smell in our sweat?"

"Basically yes, but more of what they sense. Also, some pheromones act as repellents. If you haven't been able to get a date for awhile you might want to consider taking a hot bath to get rid of the negative pheromones."

"How can you use pheromones to find out who that guy is?"

"It's simple. The technology is based on the human nose. It uses six hundred and fifty types of receptors found in cells high up in the nasal passages somewhere between our eyebrows. Each receptor in our nose responds to a subtle characteristic of a molecule that carries odor."

"We can smell molecules?"

"Essentially. However, each receptor actually responds to a subtle characteristic of a molecule that carries odor, its particular shape or degree of oiliness, rather than the molecule itself."

"How are you going to test the tee shirt?"

"I'll cut off a piece from under the armpit and insert it in the receptor tube. The sweat will be broken down into its individual elements and electronically analyzed through Surface Acoustic Wave (SAW) chemical sensor technology. Then I'll run the output through my laptop data base."

"What kind of data base?"

"For almost thirty years hospitals have collected swabs of all newborn babies' sweat and blood samples for DNA identification. Anyone who has served in the military has a sample of their sweat and blood on file in a National data bank. The day will come when electronic 'sniffers' will be used to 'sniff' the bad guys out of a crowd of people or a police lineup."

"Anyone can tell where Rat is by following the smell. That's for sure," Elmo chipped in.

"Elmo we're not talking about body odor," Mack replied. "We're talking about pheromones. You don't consciously realize that you smell them. They're just there! You feel them."

"I feel Rat for sure. I know he's here."

"That's because you smell his body odor. I do too. Are you attracted to him sexually?"

"Hell no!"

"His male pheromones have no effect on you. But somewhere out there is a female who will sniff him out because she's attracted to his unique pheromones."

"Another Rat? There could actually be a female human Rat?"

"Might be. You never know who might be living in the next dumpster around the corner."

"Come on Elmo give me a break," chimed in Rat. "I've got a mother who loves me and I used to be married to a wonderful woman."

"Used to be? What happened?" Did she get a good whiff of your pheromones?"

"No. She ran away with her lesbian hairdresser. They're very happy and living in Key West."

"Okay boys," Mack interjected. "This isn't getting us anywhere. We have to identify the guy Rat smacked with the concrete block, find Ralph and keep the media away from here."

"I'm going down to the boathouse and get the guy's tee shirt," Rat stated as he rose from the table and headed for the front door. "I'll be back in a minute."

"Hope you aren't attracted by his pheromones and start rolling around in his clothes," Elmo threw in as Rat went out the door. Rat chose to ignore Elmo's snide comment.

"Elmo you have to stop picking on Rat. He has feelings and he saved my life last night."

"Glad to see you're getting your voice back. I put your telephone back together this morning and stuck it back on the wall. You pulled those little plastic screw anchors right smack out of the plasterboard. I reinstalled it with quarter-inch lag bolts and it'll never come off the wall again."

"Thanks Elmo. Are you going out looking for Ralph after you leave here?"

"Nope. I've been here all night. I'm going home to catch up on a few 'honey-do' projects and catch some solid sleep. I go back on shift at three o'clock this afternoon. I'll keep my eyes open and give you a call if I find anything. What're you going to do today?"

"I'm going by the Blake Library to do a little research. I need to learn a little about surveying, pirates and that Spanish Treasure fleet that wrecked along here in a hurricane in the 1700's."

"You mean what they called the Plate Fleet? It wrecked here in 1715. It's spread all the way from Stuart to Sebastian and they haven't found all of the ships yet. One of them supposedly tried to make it through the St. Lucie Inlet, but they never found out what happened to it."

"Yes. That's what I'm looking for. I'm certain that they must have a lot of information about it at the library. What do you know about the Spanish Land Grants?"

"My grandpa worked as a land surveyor back in the early 1940's. The surveyor's used the Spanish Land Grant markers as reference points for most everything they did. A lot of the old markers still exist over there on Sewall's Point. They're covered up by weeds, but you can find them if you know what you're looking for and where to look. You might have to use a metal detector. They're made out of concrete and have a piece of metal rebar inside."

"Have you ever seen one yourself?"

"Of course. I used to tag around with my grandpa during the summers when I wasn't in school. I used to hold up the tripod for him when he was shooting a line."

"What do they look like?"

"What? The tripod? It has three legs."

"No! Not the tripod! The Spanish Land Grant markers."

"Oh. They're made out of concrete, about six by six inches and the top is beveled off at an angle. They may stick up six inches or so out of the ground. Don't stub your toe on one."

"Are there any of them on Sewall's Point or around Hell's Gate?"

"Of course. That's where the Hanson and Gomez Tracts begin. Anytime there's a re-mapping done the surveyor's use the Spanish Land Grant markers as benchmarks for their measurements."

Rat bounded through the front door dangling a soiled tee shirt in his right hand. "This thing really smells," he gasped. "I'll bet that you can get a ton of pheromones out of this sucker!"

"I don't need a ton of pheromones out of it. Bring it over here and I'll cut the armpit sections out of it and then you can have it."

"I don't want it. It came off a dead guy."

"It's fresher than most of the things you pick up along the road," Elmo jibbed.

"Elmo! Don't start in on him. Go find that glass jar in the refrigerator and take it out."

"Why?"

"Because I want you to take some fingerprints and run them through for identification."

"I'm not a fingerprint technician. I don't know how to do it," Elmo stammered.

"It's not difficult. There's a box of surgical gloves under the sink. I use them so I won't get dishpan hands. Take out a pair, put them on and wear them when you take the fingertips out of the glass jar. Rinse the fingertips off in fresh water and dry them off with paper towels. I'll dig out an ink pad and some blank white paper."

"Don't you have blank fingerprint cards here? I thought you were prepared for anything."

"Of course! Every fishing guide keeps several sets of blank fingerprints cards around."

"I was just joking. We can use regular paper. I'll look for some in the desk drawer."

"That's not necessary. There's a package of blank FBI fingerprint cards inside the bread box."

"What! You have blank FBI fingerprint cards? How'd you get them?"

"I told you before. Every fishing guide keeps several sets of blank fingerprint cards around the house. You never know when you're going to need them in an emergency like this."

"I thought you were just fooling with me about having blank fingerprint cards."

"I am. There's some heavy white paper in the center desk drawer." Mack smiled and snipped away the armpit area of the tee shirt and dropped it into a clear plastic bag for later analysis.

"If you two guys are done pokin' at each other and don't mind I'm leavin'. I've got things to do this afternoon and I don't want to be here if the reporters show up again," Rat stammered as he headed for the front door. Come and get me if you find Ralph. I'll alert all the boys to keep their eyes open," Rat shouted over his shoulder as he headed out the door toward the boathouse and his waiting green rubber war surplus kayak.

"See ya' Rat," Mack shouted back.

"Watch out for your pheromones," yelled Elmo. "I hear they're real attractive to female rats!"

"Elmo was that crack really necessary?"

"Not really, but he didn't hear me anyway. He was already out the door. I wonder if the Sheriff's Department uses pheromone detectors? Can you show me how yours works so I can tell them about it?"

"No and no," Mack replied sternly.

"What do you mean no and no?"

"The sheriff's department does not have pheromone detectors. It is a specialized technology and available only to a few governmental agencies. I doubt the sheriff's department has even heard about them. And you cannot see how mine works. It is very complex and requires very stringent environmental conditions to work properly. Now is not the right time for analysis."

"Why isn't this the right time?"

"It requires a full moon and maximum low tide. Right now we have a new moon and the tide's coming in. I'll have to wait a few days before I can test these samples. I'll call you when I'm ready and if you're free you can come over and watch. How're you making out with those fingerprints?"

"I've got all of them done except the right thumb. But we have a big problem."

"What big problem?"

"When Rat cut off the guy's fingertips he didn't keep the right and left hand separated. All ten of them are in the same jar. Plus, I can't tell which finger is which."

"That's okay. We'll just scan the two thumbprints through the database and see what happens. I'm not expecting to find a match anyway."

"Do you want me to take the prints down to the Sheriff's office and ask the detectives to do it for you? I'm sure they'll do it if I ask them to."

"No thanks. That'll create far to many questions that I don't want to answer. I'll have Tina do it through her office in West Palm Beach. No one will dare ask her anything."

"Okay. Have it your way. The prints are all done. What do you want me to do with the fingertips and the jar?"

"Dump them in the sink and turn on the garbage disposal. Rinse out the jar and turn it upside down on the counter. I might want to keep something in there. Maybe I'll whip up some homemade salsa this afternoon. You like my salsa don't you?"

"Yuk! I'll pass. I'm going home to get started on my 'honey do' projects. I'll check in with you after I come back on duty at three o'clock." Elmo removed the rubber surgical gloves, tossed them into the garbage can under the kitchen sink and headed for the front door. "I'll let you know what turns up on Ralph," he shouted over his shoulder from the front porch.

"See ya' later gator," Mack acknowledged with a wave and wondered why he said it. He attended Florida State University the friendly rival of the University of Florida.

The obnoxious green wall telephone hanging over the kitchen counter stammered out a weak announcement that someone was calling. It was obvious by the pitiful ring that the instrument's ringer had been severely damaged by Mack's earlier attack.

He glanced at his watch as he removed the handset from the switch hook. It was 8:53 A.M.

"Hello. Mack here."

"Mack. It's me Tina. I'm just going into court and had an urge to call you. Are you okay?"

"I'm fine. Feeling your pheromones this morning?"

"Pheromones? What are you taking about? Did you get hit on the head or something?"

"It was more like a noose around a cattle rustler's neck at a necktie party at the old oak tree."

"You're talking gibberish and not making any sense. What's wrong with your voice? You sound like you've been sucking on helium gas?"

"My throat's kinda' bothering me. I'll be okay after I've had some coffee."

"You mean that you're still in bed?"

"No. I've been up for a while visiting with Elmo and Rat. Joy stopped by and fixed breakfast for us."

"Why would she do that? Does she know that you found Ralph's boat and have it in the boathouse?"

"It's a long story. When do you have to be in court? It's after nine o'clock."

'What! I have to run. I'll call you later!"

'Click.' The phone went dead and the dial tone hummed in his ear. It was somehow soothing.

Mack replaced the handset on the switch hook and turned to admire the two haphazard fingerprint cards on the kitchen counter. *"Elmo did a pretty good job with what he had to work with,"* Mack muttered to himself. *"It sure would be nice if I knew which thumb print was the right and which one was the left."*

The sickly telephone chattered again.

"Now what did she forget?" Mack thought aloud. He removed the handset and placed it to his ear. "Hello Tina. What did you forget to ask me?"

"This isn't Tina," boomed the deep baritone male voice. "It isn't CNN either!"

Mack shook his head in disbelief and stammered out a squeaky response. 'What do you want? I thought you were watching out for me. I almost got killed last night."

"I was there. I was in the hedge behind the storage shed. I had been watching the guy for almost an hour and was waiting for him to make a move on you. Your smelly friend kept getting in the way. Every time I was ready to touch a round off he stepped in front of me."

"Why didn't you whack him when he tried to strangle me?"

"I just told you! Your odoriferous friend kept getting in the way. The only clear shot I had was when he dropped the concrete block on the guy's head. But by then it was all over."

"Am I in the clear now?"

"No. That wasn't the guy we're looking for. He's still out there somewhere."

"Who was this guy? He wasn't carrying any identification."

"We don't know. Someone dropped him off in a car with no license plate."

"What the hell's going on?"

"We're not sure, but there's one thing for certain."

"What's that?"

"Someone's still out there looking to nail you. I'll be watching your back."

"Do you know what happened to the body that was in the boathouse?"

"Certainly. Your odoriferous friend towed it out the inlet, let it go and it washed up on the beach yesterday morning. A poor move. You should have stayed around and supervised the job."

"That's not what I mean! What happened to the body after it washed up on the beach?"

"I was watching it on television just like you were. A couple of guys in white long sleeved shirts put the body on a gurney and loaded it into van."

"But the body never showed up at the coroner's office."

"Of course not. Did you really expect it to show up there? You know better than that."

"What do you mean?"

"He was one of ours and so were the two guys with the gurney. We lost him and now we've got him back. That's the end of the story. Watch yourself. This isn't over by a long shot."

'Click.' The telephone went dead and the monotonous dial tone hummed in Mack's ear. He replaced the handset on the switch hook, walked into the living area and stared out at the marina parking lot. He had a lot of loose ends to check on today and wasn't sure where to start.

Chapter 20

It was almost 9:30 A.M. by the time Mack got himself ready to head for the Blake Library. He planned on doing some research on the local pirate Don Carlos Gilbert and the Spanish Treasure Fleet that floundered in a hurricane and sank along the Treasure Coast in 1715.

Someone had tried to take his life and he didn't know when he would try again. Mack patted the dog on the head and scratched him behind the ears on his way out the front door. The dog was not a man-killing monster, but his shrill bark would deter most people who would try to break into the marina. Little did they know that the dog would probably pounce on their chest, hold them down and lick them half to death. He closed the front door and activated the alarm system by turning the bent nail above the doorframe up into a vertical position.

Mack drove north on Old Port St. Lucie Boulevard, turned left onto East Ocean Boulevard and pulled into the Blake Library parking lot at 9:52 A.M. A line of anxious patrons was already formed at the entrance door. He parked the blue pickup truck and headed for the main door.

A smiling middle-aged librarian unlocked the door, opened it wide and greeted all the waiting patrons with a broad smile. Mack entered and headed for the reference desk manned by a woman in her mid-twenties and another who appeared to be middle aged. The older woman was explaining the operation of the library's computer bank to an aged feisty male patron who could no doubt remember the introduction of the horseless carriage.

Mack approached the young woman and asked her to assist him in finding some books dealing with the local pirate Don Pedro Gilbert and the 1715 Spanish Plate Fleet. She directed him to the local section. He gathered several books in his arms and returned to one of the reference department desks to do his homework.

Several minutes later the middle-aged reference librarian paused beside his desk and tapped Mack lightly on the shoulder. "I found a book that may help you. It is very rare and contains the original map of the 1715 Plate Fleet shipwrecks drawn by Bernard Romans in 1765." She smiled and continued, "It was published in 1924 and cannot be taken out of the library."

Mack made several pages of notes on a yellow pad, returned the books to their shelves, thanked the librarians for their assistance and returned to the parking lot for his truck. It was 12:47 P.M. He was surprised at how much time he had spent in the library. He decided to stop at Burger King and have lunch before proceeding to the nursing home for another meeting with Lorna Belle. He anticipated that she had the answers to a lot of unanswered questions.

Mack pulled into the nursing home parking lot at 1:17 P.M. and easily found his way to Lorna Belle's room. Her roommate had passed away earlier that morning. She sat alone and stared out the window from the comfort of a blue wing-backed chair. Mack eased into the darkened room and closed the door behind him so they could talk confidentially.

"Lorna Belle I was here to see you a couple of weeks ago and now my life is in turmoil. Last week I met your sister Hattie Lou in Biloxi and your granddaughter Polly Jo. Your sister told me her life story and yours. She said that you and your daughter had a parting of the ways and a major difference of opinion over her choice of a husband."

"That's true. She married a slime ball, bottom feeding, ambulance chasing lawyer who claims he's connected to some mafia people in Boston. I don't like him and never did trust him. I know for a fact that he doesn't like me either. Polly Jo ran away from home so she wouldn't have to put up with his crap."

"Did you tell me the truth when I visited you a couple of weeks ago?"

"Of course I did!"

"Your sister's story is different from what you told me."

"What do you mean her story is different than mine?"

"She told me a couple of stories and I don't know which one to believe. The first one was that she ran away from home in Helena, Montana when she was fourteen and went on the road to dance in bars. The second story was that both of you grew up on a cotton farm north of Biloxi, Mississippi and your parents were sharecroppers. Which story is true?"

"That woman is mentally disturbed and has been for years. I doubt that she remembers where she was born or where she grew up. Yes. Our parents were tenant sharecroppers on a cotton farm north of Biloxi. We were so poor that my mother used old newspapers for wallpaper. It's also true that she ran away from home when she was fourteen. Hattie Lou's's two years older than me and always rebelled against authority."

"Where'd she run away to?"

"She took off to Helena, Montana with a Greek Ferris Wheel operator in a traveling gypsy carnival. I didn't see her again until she wound up in New Orleans several years later. It was a quirk of fate that we wound up dancing together at the 'Five-hundred Club' in New Orleans. I didn't know she was there when I went in for a tryout."

"Why did she leave the carnival?"

"She caught her Greek boyfriend porking a Navaho Indian squaw behind the ticket booth in Albuquerque after her last show."

"Why did you wind up in Stuart and she's in Biloxi running a bar with your name on it?"

"I met a man who was stationed at Keesler Air Force Base. I got pregnant and when he was discharged in nineteen forty-seven

I moved to Florida with him. His parents didn't like me. His momma knew I was pregnant because I had started to show, but he didn't care about what they thought. We rented a room at the Speedy Inn on Speedy Point. He opened a bait shop at the north end of the Roosevelt Bridge and was stabbed to death by a couple of punks in forty-eight."

"Where's Speedy Point? I thought I knew most of the places around here. That's a new one."

"It's not called Speedy Point anymore. Now it's called Britt Point after the Britt flower farms that used to be along the river all the way up to where North River Shores is now."

"How did you survive after your husband died?"

"I had a baby and had to find a way support myself. I sure as hell wasn't going back to Biloxi! The people who owned the Sand Club on Hutchinson Island felt sorry for me and gave me a job cleaning rooms and waiting on tables. They gave us a spare room in the back of the place to sleep in and took ten bucks a month out of my pay for it. Hattie Lou sent me a few bucks every now and then to keep me and my daughter from starving."

"Frank Holmes, the black man I told you to go see in the nursing home, was the maintenance man at the club. He cut the grass, painted and did odd jobs around the place. He and his wife lived in a little wooden shanty up on Tick Ridge in Jensen Beach. He rode a red Western Flyer bicycle back and forth across the old swinging bridge everyday. Back in those days it wasn't safe for a black man to talk to a white girl and we got together in back of the hotel every once in awhile to smoke a cigarette and talk about how one day we would make it big."

"Did you and Frank have an affair while you were working together?"

"No! He's fifteen years older than me! He was just a friend when I needed one the most."

"Was he married?"

"Yes. His wife Thelma Lou worked at home laundering people's clothes. He didn't need to mess his life up like I did mine."

"Is she still living?"

"The last I heard she was still living in the old house up on Tick Ridge and doing just fine."

"Did they have any children?"

"Only one daughter. Marvette. I never saw her again after her high school graduation. Nineteen fifty-seven I think it was. She went away to a private college somewhere up north."

"Your daughter's living in Boston and your granddaughter Polly Jo's in Biloxi with your sister. What year was Polly Jo's mother born?"

"Nineteen forty-seven. I was twenty-two years old. I raised her in the back room of the Sand Club. The welfare people tried to take her away from me several times. But, the people who owned the Sand Club stood up for me and told them they would watch out for both of us."

"She's forty-eight. Polly Jo is about twenty?"

"She'll be twenty on October sixteenth. After graduating from that fancy college in New York my daughter decided to go to law school. She didn't get married until she was thirty-one because she wanted to have a career. Polly Jo was born when she was twenty-eight. She's illegitimate."

"That explains why you're estranged from your daughter. Did you encourage Polly Jo to run away from home and live with your sister in Biloxi?"

"My daughter's husband is a no good slime ball. He molested Polly Jo and my daughter wouldn't believe a word that Polly Jo said about it. Polly Jo had no alternative except run away from home. She's safe from that bastard now."

"Polly Jo was only sixteen when she ran away from home and was still a minor at the time. Your daughter could have forced her to come back home."

"The two of them didn't give a damn about whether she came home or not. It was better for both of them if she was gone and out of their hair."

"When we first met you told me that when you were working at the Sand Club a hurricane came through in nineteen forty-nine. At that time your daughter would've been two years old. You said that you and Frank ran out on the beach during the eye of the hurricane, saw that thirty feet of sand was gone and the hull of a wooden ship was showing. But you stopped there. Was there more to the story?"

"Yes. A lot more and I didn't tell you because I didn't know at the time if I could trust you. I can't trust my daughter and her slime ball husband. And I'm not sure how far I can I trust my sister. I have something important that I've saved all these years for Polly Jo and I want you to give it to her. Will you do that for me?

"I don't know if I'll ever see her again. I don't have any plans to go back to Biloxi."

"Don't worry. Polly Jo knows that I have something special for her and she'll find you when the time comes. Open the top drawer of that dresser over there against the far wall, pull out the little wooden box that's inside and bring it over here." Lorna Belle pointed at the bird's-eye maple dresser with her trembling left hand. The top was pock'marked with white circles.

Mack slowly pulled the drawer open. Nestled inside was a beautiful wooden chest perhaps ten inches long, six inches wide and four inches deep. When he lifted it out it seemed light and he wondered why she would keep an empty wooden box in a dresser drawer. He handed the box to Lorna Belle. Her frail hands couldn't hold it and she allowed it to fall into her lap.

She cradled it gently like it was a newborn baby, gently stroked the polished wood with her gnarled fingers and smiled as she softly broke her silence. "Mr. McCray what's inside this box has no importance to anyone except me and Frank. Do you remember I told you about the big hurricane that blew through here in nineteen forty-nine? I still remember the date. It was August twenty-sixth. Frank and I went out on the beach and found an old wooden ship."

"Of course I remember. We just talked about it a few minutes ago."

"During the lull of the eye Frank ran back to the club and dragged out an axe, a steel crowbar, a shovel and lugged them down to the beach in a wheelbarrow. He started whacking at the wooden deck of the old ship and you won't believe what he found inside."

"What did he find?"

"He broke through the wooden deck in less than a minute and fell directly into the hold of the ship. It was packed slap full of wooden boxes."

"What did he do with them?"

"He busted one open with the axe and gold coins flew out all over the place. It was apparently one of the Spanish treasure ships that wrecked on the beach in seventeen fifteen."

"What! It was a real treasure ship? A Spanish galleon?"

"Yep. I'd never seen anybody as excited as he was that day. He danced, jumped around and threw coins all over the place. Then he realized that we only had about twenty minutes before the eye of the hurricane would pass through and the wind would pick up again."

"What did you do?"

"Me and Hattie Lou jumped right in there with him. We dragged out nine boxes full of gold coins and stacked them up alongside an Australian pine tree. They were real heavy. Frank loaded them in the wheelbarrow and ran back and forth to the storage shed behind the Sand Club until he had them all there. He almost got his ass blown away when he was trying to get the last box back. It broke open and gold coins spilled out all over the beach."

"What did you do with the spilled coins?"

"My sister scooped up as many as she could before the wind blew her half away. Most of them are still there because the sand covered them up when the backside of the hurricane came through. I stuck a coin in a cleft on the south side of an Australian pine tree to mark the spot. The tree's still there, but the top's broken off and now the cleft's about twenty feet up on the trunk"

"What did you do with the nine boxes of gold coins?"

"Frank left them in the shed and threw a canvas tarp over them. We all agreed that we wouldn't say anything to anybody."

"Did you go back to the beach after the hurricane passed and look for more treasure?"

"Yes. But the ship was gone. The hurricane covered the ship over again with sand. It felt like a dream. But I knew it wasn't because I found the cleft in the tree where I stuck the coin. I couldn't get it out because it was in to far and I left it there. All three of us joined hands and danced around that tree like kids until we realized that a black man and two white women shouldn't be seen together."

"Where's the tree at?"

"Have you been across the Jensen Beach Bridge?"

"Yes. Many times."

"Do you know where the public beach is right across Ocean Drive?"

"Of course. Why?"

"The tree is on the left when you come across Ocean Drive."

"Did you tell anybody about the ship?"

"We agreed not to tell anybody. No one would ever believe us and if they did there'd be a bunch of treasure hunters down on the beach and our lives wouldn't be worth a plugged nickel."

"What did you do with the nine boxes of gold coins?"

"Frank left them in the storage shed for a while. It was a safe place because no one ever went back there except him. The white people who ran the place were afraid of Lulu."

"Who's Lulu?"

"She was the old mama opossum that lived under the workbench."

"Didn't anybody see Frank hauling the boxes of coins back to the storage shed?"

"Nope. The club was closed down for the summer."

"Why did you stay there if a hurricane was coming?"

"My daughter and me were living in the back room of the club. We couldn't leave."

"Why didn't you go to Frank's house? It would've been safer because it wasn't on the beach."

"Do you really think Frank could haul me and my daughter over to Jensen Beach on his Western Flyer bicycle? I hardly think so. His house was solid concrete block on a slab. He felt his family was safe and wouldn't leave us by ourselves. He looked out for us."

"What did you and Frank do with the coins?"

"That's what I'm about to tell you if you'll just shut up for a minute." Lorna Belle placed an arthritis twisted thumb on each

side of the lid and slowly pushed upward. The ancient mirror on
the inside of the lid lit up her face like a pot of gold at the end of
the rainbow. She smiled like a child inside a giant candy store
with a gift certificate.

She reached into the polished cedar box and lifted out a
wooden picture frame approximately six inches tall and four
inches wide. The frame held a faded brown piece of paper. She
cradled it in her twisted hands and silently mouthed the words
typed on the brown paper. After she finished reading she laid the
wooden frame down on her chest as a giant tear slowly ran down
her right cheek."

"What's that? It looks like a faded picture."

"It's a list of rules for the guests to follow when they stayed at
the Sand Club. We had them posted in every room." She reached
into the box and groped around like a raccoon fishing for mussels
along a riverbank until she felt what she was looking for. She
slowly removed a folded green brochure, held it against the side
of her face and smiled. "This is the only one of these left in the
world."

"What is it?"

"It's a Sand Club brochure. No one remembers that it was ever
there except for a few of us old timers. This is my proof that I
was there." She opened the brochure and held it up in front of her
so Mack could read the faded green lettering. It read, *'The Sand
Club of Jensen Beach'* and below it was a photograph of a
building on the beach close to the ocean. Lorna Belle allowed the
green brochure to fall onto her chest, her eyes closed and her
head fell back against the padded headrest. Mack was afraid that
she had died.

"Lorna Belle!" Mack trembled as he lightly shook her right
arm. "Are you okay?"

Her wrinkled eyelids flickered. When she opened them there
was a happy sparkle where there had been a shallow dullness
moments before.

"I took out the things which are important to me. Now I want
you to reach in the box and pull out something for you. I hope
they're still there. This place is full of thieves! They'll steal
anything that's not tied down. I sleep with my false teeth in my

mouth so they won't steal them." She tilted the box toward Mack so he could view the interior. It was lined with gold fabric woven into an intricate design. Nestled in the center of the fabric were two gold coins the size of a silver dollar.

"What are those?"

"These are the last of the coins Frank and I removed from the treasure ship in nineteen forty-nine. I want you to have them. I don't know what the gold in them is worth and they are worth considerable more as collectors' items. If you sell them you'll have to report the sale to the State of Florida and they'll take twenty-five percent right off the top."

"Thank you, but keep your coins." Mack gently closed the lid of the wooden chest and pushed it in her direction. "You might need them yourself someday."

She snapped straight up in her chair and glared at him with eyes that could've melted steel. "I just shared my lifelong secrets with you because I don't know how much time I have left on this pitiful earth. Put those coins in your pocket and don't tell anybody that you ever saw them!"

"But I don't feel right about it."

"I don't give a rat's ass how you feel about it. I want you to have them." She pushed the wooden chest toward Mack. "I trust you. That's why I'm giving you this box, the Sand Club brochure and picture frame. I drew a map on a piece of paper bag and stuck it in the back of this picture frame. It's been there all these years. When I found out that they were going to tear down the place in nineteen fifty-one I went back to that room and removed this frame. I even printed '1951' on the back. She slowly turned over the small frame. The treasure map's behind this piece of cardboard and held in place by these four little rusty nails."

Lorna Belle attempted to bend up one of the rusty nails with her thumbnail and it snapped like a toothpick. "I screwed that up good! Those nails have been in there since forty-nine so I guess they deserve to break. I'm not going to pull the map out because you know where it is."

"What do you expect me to do?"

"I expect you to give it to Polly Jo along with this box and explain everything to her. One day she may want to find that ship and I want her to know that I didn't make up the story. If you want to check my story out run out to Jensen Beach where the Sand Club used to be. The Australian pine tree is on the northeast corner of Ocean Drive."

"It's been a long time. Maybe it's gone."

"It's still there! I was out there the weekend before my daughter came down here and stuck me in this place. The top's broken off but you can still see the cleft about twenty feet up." The old woman sighed. "You won't see much except the parking lot and a concession stand. The ship's under thirty feet of sand about fifty yards south of where the Sand Club used to be."

"The ship's buried under sand and there's no way she can get to it."

"When I see Polly Jo I'll tell her where to find it."

"What did you and Frank do with the gold coins? Treasure is subject to tax and confiscation as historical artifacts by the State of Florida."

"Frank borrowed an old rusty pickup truck, hauled those treasure chests up to his shanty on Tick Ridge and buried them in the backyard. A couple times a month he'd put a naphtha white gas burner under an old cast iron pot and melt the coins down ten at a time. He poured the gold into a mold he dug in the sand and made ingots about six inches long. Each one weighed nine ounces and the gold was ninety-two percent pure. He brought them to me and I sold them to jewelry stores for two hundred bucks each. They snatched them up because the price was about half the market value. They melted the ingots down and made trinkets out of them like dolphins, seahorses, sailfish or whatever. They paid me in cash and we split it fifty-fifty."

"Did you report the income for tax purposes?"

"Taxes? Since when do you have to pay taxes on cash? Buried treasure is finders keepers!"

"Of course you have to report it! You could've gone to jail if you had gotten caught."

"Let's not worry about the small stuff. I didn't and that was a long time ago."

"How much did you make from selling the gold?" Today it's worth almost $400 an ounce."

"We didn't keep any records, but the three of us dragged nine boxes full of gold coins out of that ship in about twenty minutes. This little chest came from the captain's cabin."

"What did you do with your share of the money?"

"I didn't need it. That fall I met an old rich guy at the Sand Club. He asked me to take care of his house out on Sewall's Point because his wife had recently passed away. We got married six months later and he died of a heart attack in the bathtub two months afterward. He was a bootlegger and used the basement in the house to stash the booze."

"What did Frank do after you got married?"

"For years he kept on melting the gold into ingots and bringing them by the house. I hired him as a groundskeeper so it wouldn't look suspicious. We made out real well selling the gold. He sent his daughter to private school in New York and I sent my daughter to private school in Boston. He hurt his back digging a hole in nineteen sixty-five and couldn't work anymore."

"Did Frank and his wife stay in their house on Tick Ridge?"

"Yes. He made a few improvements to the house over the years. He was afraid of doing too much for fear his neighbors would get suspicious and start asking questions about where he got the money. I think he buried the money in the back yard."

"I don't know what to say. You've trusted me with your life story."

"So? I can't trust my daughter and her slime ball husband. He's a bottom-feeding accident chasing lawyer and I'm pretty sure he was behind her jerking me out of my trailer and throwing me in here. And I don't trust my sister any farther than I can throw her fat ass. I don't know much about my granddaughter Polly Jo. She might be just as rotten as my daughter and my sister. I think I can trust you because you're running Port Sewall Marina. Tina's a darn good judge of character. I knew her parents very well."

"You knew her parents? It's a long way from Jensen Beach down to Port Salerno."

"I cleaned the marina cottages for them on the weekends when things were slow at the Sand Club. I'm sure Tina wouldn't recognize me. It was long time ago and I looked much different then. I baby-sat her often and probably changed her soiled diapers a thousand times. I was very pleased to see her go to law school and make something of herself."

"How did you know I'm at Port Sewall Marina?"

"I saw you on television yesterday morning when those reporters were flying that helicopter around everybody at the marina. You ran out into the parking lot, jumped in your truck tried to run over the helicopter. It was a riot! I laughed so hard I almost wet my diaper. Those fools thought you'd been killed and washed up on Jensen Beach. That must've scared the hell out of those Baptists! When I saw Tina walk out on the porch I knew you two were together. If you're with Tina I know I can trust you because I trust her."

There was a 'tap' on the door and a soft voice called out, "Miss Lorna Belle may I come in?"

The door cracked open and a young girl, perhaps twenty years old, peeked her rosy-cheeked face in the doorway. She held a clipboard in her left hand and a pen was poised in her right hand. "I know it's a little bit early, but we're short-handed in the kitchen and I'm taking advance dinner orders. I left a menu on your nightstand earlier. Did you have a chance to look at it yet?"

"I glanced at it but I didn't see anything I wanted."

"What would you like? Perhaps we can make it special for you?"

"How about something I haven't had for years?"

"Certainly," the young girl responded and clicked her pen tip. "What would you like?"

"How about some sex? I didn't see sex on the menu and I haven't had any for a long time."

"Miss Lorna Belle you're always joking with me," the young girl responded as her face turned beet red. "Now be serious for just a minute. What would you like for dinner?"

"If sex isn't on the menu? Then bring me some manatee chops with a side order of coleslaw."

"Manatee chops? What's that?"

"Young lady how long have you lived in south Florida?"

"About two months. My parents moved here from Flint, Michigan."

"Manatee is always a special order this time of year. Just tell the cook who it's for and he'll take care of it. I used to baby-sit him and change his diapers." Lorna Belle grinned and shooed the girl to the door with a backward motion of her right hand. "Guess that'll keep her out of my hair for awhile," Lorna Belle directed her comment at Mack. "Rufus will whip up a couple of pork chops for me and that girl won't know any difference. It takes Yankees a while to learn."

"Lorna Belle you'll have her confused for a month. She believed you!"

"That's good! Now is there anything else you want from me?"

"No. I don't think so."

"Then there's something I want you to do for me."

"What's that?"

"Did you see that old woman sitting in the wheelchair in the lobby when you came in?"

"Yes. She was there the last time I was here."

"I want you to stop and give her a big hug on the way out."

"Why? I don't know her."

"She's waiting for her son to pick her up and take her home. She gets dressed up as best she can every morning and sits out there waiting for him."

"Does he?"

"No. He only came by to see her once since she was admitted. Will you do it for me?"

"Yes. But what if she wants to leave with me?"

"The nurses know how to handle it. They'll be watching. Did you stop by to see Frank like I told you to do when I saw you the last time?"

"No. They wouldn't let me see him. The administrator said Frank has dementia and the family doesn't want anyone to see him because he babbles about lost treasure. Now I know why."

"He might be babbling but he doesn't have dementia. Try to get in and see him again."

"I have one more question for you before I leave."

"What's that?"

"If you married a rich guy and moved into a big house on Sewall's Point why were you living in Stuart's Trailer Town?"

"Do you remember that I told you my daughter's husband was a slime ball and a bottom feeding lawyer?"

"Yes."

"It's their winter home and I just can't talk about how they got it. It hurts too much."

"Yes ma'am. I think I understand," Mack muttered in response as he gathered up the wooden box. He glanced at his watch. It read 3:27 P.M. He'd spent two hours with Lorna Belle and had more unanswered questions than before. "I'll be back to see you again real soon."

She nodded her head in acknowledgment and looked away.

Mack headed for the door and wondered what he would say to the patient woman waiting in the lobby for her son to arrive and take her home.

Chapter 21

The elderly woman patiently waited in the lobby in her wheelchair for her son to arrive and take her home watched Mack carefully as he walked toward her. She reached out and grabbed his arm as he walked past. He paused, reached over and gave her a gentle hug.

She hung on to him with arms of steel and murmured, "I knew that you would come back to get me someday." She rested her forehead on his forearm and wept.

Mack furtively looked toward the nurses' station. He hoped they understood that he was not her son and she had placed him in a very embarrassing situation. The nurses seemed to enjoy his torment and the elation of the desperate woman in the wheelchair. After what seemed a lifetime to Mack one of the nurses approached Mack and whispered into his ear.

"She thinks you're her son, but she also thinks that every man who walks in and out of here is her son. Please don't feel bad about excusing yourself and just pulling away from her. Just tell her goodbye and that'll you stop again tomorrow. It doesn't matter because she won't remember it anyway."

"Does her son come to visit her?"

"Only one time since she's been here."

"Why?"

"He was killed in a car wreck on his way home the first time he came. She doesn't know it."

Mack gently pulled away from the elderly woman's grip and looked her in the eye." I'm very sorry, but I have to leave now. I'll try to come by tomorrow and see you again," Mack whispered into her ear. He callously turned and walked away toward the front door.

The elderly woman turned toward the nurse and said loudly, "That's my son. That's my son. He's coming back to pick me up tomorrow and take me home. That's my son."

The tears in Mack's eyes blurred his vision as he exited into the bright sunlight of the parking lot. He drove down East Ocean Boulevard toward Palm Beach Road in anticipation that he might be able to see Frank Holmes and check some of Lorna Belle's story. The last time he was firmly turned down and this time he was going to be more insistent. For all he knew Lorna Belle was as loony as a gooney bird and living in her own fantasy world. However, she seemed certain of what she did and what she saw. The little wooden cedar chest and two gold Spanish coins backed up her story.

Mack turned onto Palm Beach Road, went down about a quarter-mile and turned into the nursing home parking lot. It was 4:07 Monday afternoon and the parking lot was practically empty. He pulled into a space that offered some meager shade given by a pair of palm trees, slipped out of the truck and headed toward the front door. He took a deep breath before he opened the front door. He anticipated going through the same gauntlet that he had experienced just minutes earlier and didn't think his psyche could take the pressure. Fortunately for him the entranceway and lobby were free of patrons. Mack strode briskly toward the front desk. The same snooty receptionist was at her position as she was a couple weeks earlier. He walked up to the desk and rang the tiny chrome-plated bell to get her attention. She did her best to ignore him until she finally realized that he wasn't going to go away.

"May I help you?" She asked as she continued to shuffle through some papers on her desk.

"I'm here to see Mr. Frank Holmes," Mack stated authoritatively.

"You tried to see him a week or so ago. At that time Mr. Smith plainly told you that you could not see Mr. Holmes under orders of his family," she snippily responded with a sly smile.

"Yes. You're right. I just came from visiting an old friend of his in another nursing home. She asked me to stop by and let him know that she's doing fine." Mack managed a smile.

"Our rules haven't changed in two weeks. We're not allowed to provide any information to non-family members nor are we permitted to allow visitors unless they have written permission on file from a family member and you don't. I'm very sorry. Have a good day." She returned to shuffling the pile of paper on her desk.

Mack thought briefly about asking to see the facility administrator to plead his case, but realized that his position wouldn't change from the previous visit. Not wishing to burn any bridges Mack turned toward the young receptionist smiled and offered a glib but courteous response. "Young lady, thank you so very much for being so understanding. I thoroughly understand your position and I respect it. Have a good day and a good evening."

Mack turned, headed toward the front door and paused when he heard the soft swishing of rubber soles to his left. He turned and was surprised to see the same young black woman he met at the lobby desk during his first visit. As he stood there in shock she smiled.

"Hello. Aren't you the writer that was in here before and Mr. Smith wouldn't let you see the man you were looking for?" She asked with a smile as she crossed her arms over her ample chest. Her starched white uniform accentuated the curves of her upper body and she knew it.

"Yes I'm afraid it was me alright. I wanted to verify a couple of things for a book I'm writing about this area. The administrator told me that I couldn't see the guy under orders of the family. I thought I'd try one more time and that little shrew threw me out again. So I'll be on my way."

"I could smuggle you back to see him, but I'd get fired if I got caught."

"When we met last time you told me you worked for the State of Florida and filed a job application here that they lost possibly because you're black. How did you get hired?"

"I filled out another application on the spot. They called me the following Monday. Told me there was an open position and I took it. I can't tell you any more except to say that my job is to check on interview and employment practices."

"I wish you luck in your new job and I hope you find what you're are looking for. By the way we weren't properly introduced. My name is Mack McCray."

"My friends call me TM," she responded with a smile. "I don't really care for my given name so I use the first initial of my first and middle names. It's worked just fine all my life."

"What do the T and M stand for?" Mack asked. "I'll bet you have a very pretty name."

"I don't discuss them because I don't like them. Call me TM and we'll get along fine."

"Okay TM."

"Maybe I'll see you again under different circumstances. Have a good day." She turned on her heel and headed down the hallway.

Mack turned and headed toward the front door. It was 4:27. He still had time to go to Jensen Beach and check out the Australian pine tree where Lorna Belle claimed she stashed a gold coin to mark the spot where they had spilled the treasure chest.

Mack drove the faded blue pickup truck across the Stuart Causeway, swung around the curve at the Elliott Museum and headed north. Several gigantic mansions blocked the traveler's view of the Atlantic Ocean. Unwanted population growth and congestion were coming soon.

Mack passed Jensen Beach Park and the sign pointing toward the Jensen Beach Causeway. He slowed down and turned right into the swimming area parking lot and noticed a stand of three Australian pine trees on the northeast corner of Ocean Drive. He swung into the parking area and noted there were no Australian pines along the beach side of the parking area. They were cut down under Martin County's plan for the removal of exotic non-native species. The three lonely straggled Australian pine trees stood as silent sentinels as to what may have happened there forty-six years earlier.

Mack pulled into an empty parking place, turned off the truck's ignition, slipped from behind the wheel and walked toward the copse of three trees. They reminded him of three deserted mongrel puppies in an animal shelter. He stood back and scanned the three trees. The trunk of the middle tree was snapped off roughly twenty feet above the ground. About a foot below the break was a vertical cleft perhaps six inches long and it appeared to be partially open.

"I haven't climbed a tree in at least thirty years and I'm probably going to look like a fool when I do it. I don't think that I believe her but I have to know. Here goes nothing but my pride."

Mack walked over to the middle tree, wrapped his arms and legs around the trunk and began to climb upward using broken limbs for hand and footrests where he could. When he reached the cleft he was disappointed. It was almost completely sealed over by tree bark. He took out his pocketknife and carved away at the scar tissue. He was surprised to hear a light 'clink' when the knife blade struck something solid and obviously metallic. He cut away the excess bark and a flash of gold burst out from behind the darkened wood.

"This must be the tree and that has to be the coin she stuck in there in nineteen forty-nine. I'm going to dig that sucker out and see if it matches the two coins in my pocket."

He forgot the aching in his arms and chiseled away at the tree bark and surrounding wood with the short blade of his pocketknife. Chips of dislodged wood settled on the front of his shirt and in his hair. He felt the tension and pressure building up in his left arm as he maintained his firm grip on the tree trunk. Both of his legs were numb because of the lack of blood circulation. He enlarged the hole until he could reach in with his thumb and index finger and was about to pry the gold coin out when he heard a loud voice hollering from just below him.

"Mack! What are you doing up there? Dispatch received a call that some nut was trying to cut down an Australian pine tree with a pocketknife," Deputy Elmo bellowed. "They sent me out here to arrest you. Put that knife away and get your butt down here right now."

A crowd of spectators gathered around the base of the tree looked up at Mack with their cupped hands around their eyes to shade them from the afternoon sun.

"I'm almost done I'll be down in just a minute," Mack responded as he whittled away at the remaining sliver of bark holding the coin captive. "I have to get something out of this hole."

"Get your butt down here right now or I'm going to charge you with the destruction of public property and place you under arrest."

Mack reached into the cleft, grasped the embedded coin between his right thumb and forefinger, twisted, pulled and finally released it from its tomb and slipped it into his shirt pocket.

"Okay Elmo. I'm coming down. I didn't find anything up here anyway. Cover your eyes because pieces of loose tree bark might follow me down."

Mack could hear the snickering of the crowd below him as he slid down the tree. Several buttons on the front of this shirt got caught on snags and pulled off. When he reached the bottom of the tree Mack casually brushed off the loose pieces of bark hanging from his pants and shirt before walking over to Deputy Elmo.

Elmo motioned for Mack to come alongside and whispered in his ear," Mack I had to make a scene about this because the lady who called in the complaint is standing by her car. I have to make this look good so I want you to go along with me and follow my lead."

"It sounds kind of stupid to me. I wasn't doing anything illegal by climbing that tree. It's almost dead and the top half is broken off."

"Mack that woman is very politically connected in Martin County. She called the sheriff on his private number and told him that you were destroying the tree. My sergeant ordered me to arrest you, bring you back to the county jail and charge you with the wanton destruction of public property. I have to make this look good."

"You can't arrest me for the destruction of public property. Australian pines are considered to be an non-native species and should've been cut down by the county anyway," Mack pleaded.

"Mack don't try to confuse me with the facts. Come over here to the side of my patrol car and put your hands on the hood so I can search you for concealed weapons."

"Are you out of your mind? You can't arrest me for something that isn't a crime."

"I don't care at this point if climbing that tree was a crime or not. I was told to arrest you and drag your ass back to jail because of that woman's complaint. And I'm going to do it!"

"Come on Elmo. Be serious!"

"I am being serious. Put your hands behind your back so I can get these cuffs on you. She might be satisfied just to see me shoving you in the back of my patrol car and driving away. Just go along with me. I'll drive across the Jensen Beach Causeway and double back here. If she's gone I'll take off the cuffs, you can take off back to the marina and we'll talk about it later. I'll issue you a Summons to appear in Court over the charge and you can explain it to the judge."

"What if she's not gone? What if she's still here? Then what'll you do?"

"We'll cross that bridge when we come to it. Put your hands behind your back before I pepper spray you and try to look worried. She's watching you and she's on her cell phone. I think she's talking to the sheriff. I may have to Mace you to make it look good."

"I am worried. Elmo stop looking at her."

"Okay the cuff's are on. Just slide into the patrol car nice and easy. Watch your head."

Mack complied with Elmo's request and tried to appear worried. After Elmo strapped Mack's seat belt in place he closed the car door and sidled over to the woman on the cell phone.

"Ma'am did you call the sheriff's department about the man in the tree? I have him in custody and would like to take a statement from you if you don't mind."

"I didn't call anyone about him. I just pulled over here to watch because I wondered what he was doing up there."

"Aren't you on the phone with the Martin County Sheriff's Department dispatcher?"

"Goodness no! I'm talking to my bookie in New York City. I won a bundle on the trotting ponies yesterday."

"Ma'am betting on horse races through a bookie is against the law."

"It's none of your business and New York is out of your jurisdiction. So get lost buster."

"But ma'am you admitted you're involved in an illegal act and I may have to take you in."

"Over your dead body! I'm a resident of New York not this county and you can't touch me."

"Ma'am please turn around and place your hands behind your back."

"No!"

Deputy Elmo pepper-sprayed the feisty woman, threw her down onto the gravel parking lot and cuffed her. He dragged her, kicking and screaming to his patrol car, opened the back door and gestured with a nod of his head to Mack. "Get out. I need the room."

"I can't get out. You strapped me in with the seat belt and shoulder harness."

"Hang on and I'll unclip them. I've got my hands full with this hotshot bookie from New York. She's been giving me a lot of guff and I had to Mace her once already. She's going down."

"You stupid bastard! I'm not a bookie. I told you that I was talking to my bookie in New York. Let me go!" The spry, yet securely handcuffed woman smacked Elmo in the right shin with the pointed toe of her high heel shoe. "That'll teach you to mess with a New Yorker!"

Elmo reacted by throwing her to the ground and held her down with his foot in her back.

"Lean over here and I'll get those cuffs off of you. Then get the hell out of here. I'll stop by the marina later and fill you in on what went down. I've got a wild ass felon here."

Elmo removed Mack's handcuffs and he headed for his truck. Several onlookers, who were obviously irate New Yorkers, jeered at Elmo and gave Mack a 'thumbs up' as he drove out of the parking lot. He turned south and headed toward the Stuart Causeway. It was 5:53 P.M. and Mack decided to stop by the Blake Library and do some research on hurricanes, shipwrecks and Spanish coins.The library parking lot was full and Mack took a space in the Martin County Administration Building lot next door. He walked toward the research desk and a cute young librarian smiled at him as he approached her.

"Yes sir. How may I help you?" She offered with a friendly smile. Mack realized that she had no doubt answered her share of dumb questions during the day but was still willing to help.

"Good evening young lady. I do need some help and I don't know where to begin."

"That's why I'm here sir. How may I help you?"

"How do you pronounce your name? It appears to be French."

"That's correct. My mother was born in France and she named me *Mon Ami*. That's French for 'my friend'. I just use the *Ami* part."

"Very nice and very apt. I need the price of gold for the years of nineteen forty-nine through nineteen sixty-five and on today's open market."

"Did you find a pot of gold at the end of the rainbow?"

"Maybe. I also need some information on the Spanish treasure fleet that sank here in seventeen fifteen."

"That's a popular topic. A lot of people check out those books. I'll show you where they are," she replied as she rose from her chair.

"That's okay. I know where they are. Can you finds out three more things for me?"

"I'll try. What are they?"

"How much does a gold doubloon weigh and what is the percentage of gold purity?"

"Okay. That should be easy. What's next?"

"How many gold doubloons were packed in a wooden treasure chest."

"I'll check some ship manifests. What else?"

"What is the current market value of a gold doubloon?"

"That should be easy. Anything else?"

"I may think of something else as I go along. Do you have a nautical chart of this area?"

"Yes sir. It's posted on that wall," she gleefully answered with a broad smile and pointed toward the far side of the room. "It's the coastline from Jupiter to Vero Beach. Anything else?"

"Not right now thank you," Mack replied as he turned and headed for the chart. He paused in mid-stride and turned to face the young librarian. I know what I forgot to ask you."

"What's that sir?"

"Did a major hurricane pass through this area in August of nineteen forty-nine?"

"That should be easy. We have a book on Florida hurricanes. I'll look it up for you."

"Thank you."

Mack carefully studied the nautical chart and made a note of the latitude of the Jensen Beach Causeway and the location of the now gone Sand Club. It was 27 degrees 15 minutes north. He gathered several books in his arms and headed toward a table where he could spread them out and make some notes. Just as he sat down the young librarian rushed to his side.

"Sir. I think I found everything you asked me to find," she bubbled out with innocent enthusiasm. She placed several sheets of white paper on the table, pointed at the top one and read aloud. "The doubloon was also called *doblon de a ocho* meaning doubloon of eight, because it was worth eight gold escudos. It weighed about twenty-seven grams or slightly less than one ounce. I got that out of the World Book 2003 Encyclopedia."

She pushed the top sheet of paper to the side and pointed to the second one. "Here it is again. *'The largest gold coin was the eight escudo piece which was the same weight as the silver peso, about 0.9 troy ounces or twenty-seven grams and was ninety-two percent gold.'* That's on page twenty of 'The Spanish Treasure Fleets' by Timothy R. Walton."

The number of coins per chest was a little tougher. The only thing I could find was reported finds from that fleet.

'Half buried in the sand was a blackish-brown wooden packing box just under two feet long, eleven inches wide and nine inches deep. Part of the top, one side and an end were missing, but the original contents were still there - three large clumps of silver coins solidly corroded together. The state's documentary research revealed that the chest contained 3,000 troy ounces of silver in three 1,000-ounce bags. The 250 pounds was in four- and eight- real coins. At fifteen coins to a pound there were about 3,750 of them in this conglomerate.' That came from *Florida's Golden Galleons: The Search for the 1715 Spanish Treasure Fleet* by Robert F. Burgess, page one thirty-nine.

'There were 1,300 cedar chests loaded aboard the *Capitana of the Flota* of 1715. Each chest contained three bags of gunnysack-type material, with 1,000 pesos of 4-real and 8-real coins in each bag.' That also comes from *Florida's Golden Galleons: The Search for the 1715 Spanish Treasure Fleet* by Robert F. Burgess. It's from an unnumbered illustration next to page one seventeen."

"Thank you. You have been a considerable help."

"Do you know yet which ship this may be?"

"I'm sorry. What ship are you asking about?"

"The ship that you found. Which ship is it? There are several that haven't been found yet."

"What makes you think I found a treasure ship? I'm doing some research for a book."

"The gold coin sticking out of your shirt pocket gives it away. Were you climbing trees today? You have tree bark all over the front of your shirt."

"It's a long story. I was trying to get a cat out of tree and this isn't a gold coin. It's chocolate candy covered by gold foil. I got it at Dancin' in the Streets Friday night and forgot to take it out of my pocket."

"I got the gold prices for you. That was easy." She grinned from ear to ear and handed Mack two sheets of paper. "It's all right here. The price of gold was between $35 and $40 an ounce from nineteen forty-nine to nineteen seventy-three when it jumped to $63.84 on the open market. It hit a high of $594.90 in nineteen eighty and closed at $386.75 today. How much gold do you think you found?"

"I haven't found any. I'm just doing research for a book."

"They didn't give away foil wrapped coins at 'Dancin' in the Streets'. That one's real."

"What makes you think it's real?"

"It's irregular in shape. Foil wrapped chocolate coins are perfect circles. A genuine gold doubloon is worth $3,500 to $5,000 on the open market to a collector. Come on tell me how you got it. I won't tell anybody. I promise."

"Okay. I'll tell you but you won't believe me."

"Try me."

"An old lady in a nursing home told me she found a gold coin on the beach in nineteen forty-nine right after a hurricane and stuck it in a tree to keep it safe. She told me where it was. I went over to Jensen Beach today, climbed the tree and got it out for her. I'm going to go by the nursing home tomorrow and give it to her. I just wanted to get some information about the coin so I could fill her in on its possible origin and value."

"You really know how to tell stories don't you?"

"What do you mean?"

"I never heard anything so dumb in my life. You made it up."

"I told you that you wouldn't believe me."

"I have to go back to the research desk. There might be a serious person in the library that needs my help. Leave the books on the table and I'll put them back for you." She spun on her heel, flounced her skirt and headed for the safety and sanctity of her desk.

Mack scratched some figures on the back of one of the sheets of paper and thought, *"Let's see. She said that they pulled nine chests out of the ship and each chest most likely held 3000 doubloons. That's 27,000 coins and each one weighed nine tenths of an ounce. That's 24,300 ounces of gold at a purity rate of ninety-two percent and equals 22,356 ounces of pure twenty-four carat gold. At a market value of forty bucks an ounce it was worth $894,240 in 1949. They melted down ten coins to form a nine-ounce ingot and she sold it for $200. That's $22.22 an* *ounce. If she sold all 22,356 ounces at that price she pulled in $496,800 tax-free. But she couldn't dump that much gold at once and had to spread it over several years. If she spread it over ten years the market price was still relatively low and she might have gotten away with it.*

At today's market price of $386.75 an ounce the gold in the nine chests would be worth – let's see 22,356 times $386.75 is $8,646,183! Wow! If she had just one chest of those coins today at a price of $3,500 each that would be $10,500,000! There's some big money here and something isn't right about her story. Why was she living in a trailer? What happened to the money?"

On his way out Mack paused at the reference desk, thanked the young librarian for her help and headed for the front door. Then he paused and returned to the reference desk. "You forgot about the hurricane didn't you?"

"No sir. I was waiting for you to ask about it. I have all the information right here."

"What did you find out?"

"A hurricane with winds in excess of one hundred-sixty miles an hour came through Martin County on August twenty sixth, nineteen forty-nine. The winds at the Jupiter Lighthouse were recorded at one hundred fifty-five miles per hour just before the wind instrument blew away. I remember my grandmother talking about how much of the beach sand washed away."

"Thank you. That confirms my suspicions."

The clock on the library wall read 7:48. Mack headed for the parking lot, his pickup truck and Port Sewall Marina. He had a lot of thinking to do, a lot more questions to ask Lorna Belle and he had to find a way to get in to see Frank Holmes. No wonder the old man babbled about buried pirate treasure. He knows where it is!

When Mack pulled into the Port Sewall Marina driveway he saw Joy sitting on the front step. She stood up, waved something at him and was jubilantly talking in his direction. But he couldn't hear a word she was saying. Joy ran up to the driver's side, jerked open the door and waved a picture postcard in Mack's face. The enthusiastic words spilled out of her mouth, "Ralph's okay! I got this postcard from him today! He's in Marathon and he's having a good time. He should be back Friday."

"Hold it just a minute," Mack offered and pulled the postcard out of his face. "Let me take a look at that." He held the postcard at arm's length and almost needed longer arms. It was a normal tourist postcard with the photo of a sun-baked female wearing a black string bikini lolling on a pink beach towel. The backside read, 'I'm having a great time in Marathon. Wish you were here.' There was a hand written scrawled note in black ink. "Joy, I'm fishing here in Marathon. Should be back Friday afternoon.' It was signed 'Ralph' with an upside down smiley face. Mack flipped the postcard over several times and looked at Joy. "It looks like Ralph's just fine and will be back Friday. Go home and get a good night's sleep. You've been worrying too much."

"See I told you he was okay. Elmo couldn't find his boat because he took it with him."

"You're right Joy. Everything's okay," Mack responded and tried to smile. "Can I hold onto the postcard so I can show it to Elmo tomorrow? This'll make him feel better too."

"Of course you can. I let your dog out a little while ago. I fed him and the cat about five-thirty. Did you have dinner yet?"

"I'm just fine. I caught a bite on the way back here from the library."

"Did you find what you were looking for today?"

"Everything and more. It's eight forty-seven and I'm pooped. I'll see you tomorrow."

"Tina called about an hour ago. She'll call you back about nine o'clock. I'll see you tomorrow." Joy turned and began striding toward her home on Willoughby Creek. There was a lilt in her step. She was obviously happy. She had heard from Ralph.

"If she only knew," Mack muttered to himself as he headed for the front door. "If she only knew and I wish that I didn't."

Chapter 22

It was 8:38 A.M. Tuesday morning. Mack nursed a hot cup of instant coffee as he scanned a nautical chart of the St. Lucie Inlet and Indian River. He was interested in the beach area on the east end of the Jensen Beach causeway. A book he read the evening before carried a quote attributed to the captain of the *Urca de Lima* an ill-fated ship in the 1715 Spanish Plate Fleet. *"My ship is at Palmar de Ayz in 27 degrees, 15 minutes latitude."* This position placed the ship opposite the Jensen Beach Causeway on the Atlantic Ocean side. The *Urca* managed to anchor in sixteen feet of water, but the next evening another storm passed through and the *Urca* promptly sank on the spot.

The obnoxious green wall-mounted telephone jarred Mack back to reality. He dove across the dinette table and answered it on the third ring.

"Hello."

"Are you okay?"

"Tina. Good morning. I'm fine. Why?"

"I called you last night and Joy answered. She told me you were out running around town and she didn't know when you'd come back to the marina."

"I got back a little before nine o'clock. She said that you were going to call me about nine, but the phone never rang."

"I got tied up and forgot about it. Did you miss me?"

"No. What do you know about a place over on Jensen Beach called the Sand Club?"

"Not much. I was five or six years old when the place was torn down. A hot dog stand took its place. I had a babysitter who worked at the Sand Club as a maid. She cleaned cottages at the marina for my parents on weekends."

"Can you remember her name?"

"Lorna Belle! Her name was Lorna Belle! She had a daughter a few years older than me. She used to bring her daughter over to the marina to play with me while she was cleaning cottages."

"Do you remember her last name?"

"Mobley. Her name was Lorna Belle Mobley. Why?"

"It was just a natural reaction. What do you remember about the Sand Club?"

"Nothing I was a kid when it was torn down in the fifties. My parents went there to party."

"Why did they tear it down?"

"It was destroyed in a hurricane. Why are you interested in the Sand Club?"

"I was reading a book about Martin County and it mentioned the Sand Club on Jensen Beach. It sounded interesting."

"There's nothing there now except a county park and the public beach."

"I know. I saw it." It's a nice place."

"Do you remember a hurricane that passed through here in August of nineteen forty-nine?"

"Of course I don't. I was two years old. That's a dumb question."

"It's not as dumb as you think. Did you ever hear anybody talk about how much of the beach was washed away by the hurricane?"

"No. That's another dumb question. The beach is just fine now."

"What do you know about Lorna Belle's husband?"

"He was murdered at his bait shop. After that she worked at the Sand Club and lived in a back room with her daughter."

"Where was the bait shop?'

"At the north end of the old Roosevelt Bridge."

"What was that area called?"

"We called it Lighthouse Point because the Lighthouse Restaurant was there. A two-rut path led down beside the bridge around to the point where the St. Lucie River forks to the north. When I was a teenager we used to water ski there."

"What was Lorna Belle's daughter's name?"

"Johanna. We called her Jo. Her middle name was Pollyanna and she hated it."

"Did you keep track of her?"

"No. She went off to a private college, Boston I think, after high school."

"If her mother was a maid how could she afford to send her to a private college?"

"She married some old rich guy and moved into a big house on Sewall's Point. He died and left her a bundle. He was a well-known local bootlegger and had a tunnel dug from the Indian River to his basement. That's where he stored his illegal hooch. When I was a kid I used to paddle a canoe over to Sewall's Point. Jo and I'd play in the basement."

"How about the tunnel?"

"It was boarded up and padlocked. Miss Lorna Belle told us she'd paddle our butts good if she caught us trying to get in the tunnel."

"How about from the river side?"

"The entrance was about twenty feet up the cliff and we couldn't get up there. A couple of boys tried to get up there once on a dare. One of them fell off and got hurt real bad on the rocks."

"How long did Lorna Belle live on Sewall's Point?"

"She moved in there when I was a kid and moved away in the middle sixties. I graduated from Florida State in 1969. When I came home for the summer before entering law school she was gone. I never heard from Jo after she left for college."

"Where did she go?"

"Who? Jo or Lorna Belle?"

"Her mother. Lorna Belle"

"The rumor was that she got mixed up with a black guy from Tick Ridge and had to get out of town. She came back several years later and moved into Trailer Town on Martin Luther King Boulevard. I saw her every once in awhile. Why does this local history interest you?"

"I met her and she asked about you."

"Where?"

"She's in a nursing home in Palm City off of Loop Road. Her daughter put her in there after she fell down, broke her hip and couldn't move. If the trailer park manager's wife hadn't found her she would've died on the floor."

"Trailer Town used to be run by John Thomas. I went to high school with him."

"He's still there."

"Maybe I'll stop by the nursing home and see Lorna Belle when I get up to Stuart on Friday."

"That's a good idea. She's in room one twenty-six. I'm sure she'd love to see you and talk about old times."

"Mack. I have to go. It's almost nine o'clock and I've got a hearing in five minutes. See ya'."

The telephone went dead in Mack's hand and the buzzing dial tone rang in his ear. He was left with a lot of answers and even more unanswered questions.

"I have to find a coin dealer and get these gold coins checked out." He thought. *"That old lady might be putting me on about finding a wreck on the beach. It doesn't seem reasonable that they dragged out nine boxes of coins during the twenty-minute eye of a passing hurricane. Those boxes had to weigh about one hundred and fifty pounds each. But adrenalin does strange things to people under stress. I guess it's possible."*

"Hey Mack! Are you up?" Elmo's shrill voice echoed from the direction of the front porch. Elmo didn't bother to knock and simply entered the cottage. "I was just over to see Joy. She told me that she got a card from Ralph yesterday and that you have it."

"It's over on the dinette table," Mack responded over his shoulder on his way down the short hallway leading to the bathroom. "Let me know what you think."

"What do you mean what I think?"

Mack didn't hear Elmo's response over the 'tinkle' in the toilet bowl. He returned to the kitchenette and a puzzled Deputy Elmo.

"What do you mean what do I think?" Elmo asked. "Are you talking about the broad in the bikini? She looks just fine to me. I'd give her and eight on a scale of ten."

"No. What do you think about the postcard?"

"Do you see anything unusual about it?"

"Nope. It's from Marathon. Ralph wrote a nice note to Joy saying that he'd be back Friday."

"Look at the postmark."

"It's postmarked. So what?"

"Postmarked from where?"

"West Palm Beach. So what?"

"Marathon's in the Keys. Wouldn't you expect a postmark from Miami or Key West?"

"I suppose so. Maybe somebody dropped it in a mailbox in West Palm for him. Or, maybe it got on the wrong mail truck before it was postmarked."

"Maybe and maybe not. It just doesn't seem right to me Elmo."

"Mack I wouldn't worry about it. Ralph's note said that he'd be home Friday and that's that."

"What if Ralph didn't write the note or mail the postcard?"

"Why do you want to make this so complicated? He said he'd be home Friday afternoon."

"Elmo take a close look at the hand-written note. Do you see the upside down smiley face?"

"Sure. It looks cute. I kinda' like it that way."

"The note Joy found Saturday also had an upside down smiley face on it. I don't like it. The American flag flown upside down is a distress signal. Maybe Ralph's asking for help."

"If Ralph's in trouble and needs help why would someone let him mail a postcard?"

"That's a good point. But how do you explain the bloody boot, surveyor's stake and gold coin in his boat?"

"I can't."

"Me either. That's why I'm worried. I'm going downtown this morning to find a coin dealer and try to get these coins identified."

"Coins? I thought you only found one coin in Ralph's boat."

"I'm sorry. I meant coin. I guess my mind wandered because I'm thinking about Ralph. What are you going to do today?"

"I'm going home to catch some sleep. I got called in last night because of a boat accident."

"Do you know anything about shipwrecks or pirate's around this area?"

"There's always nuts digging up the beach looking for treasure in the middle of the night. I caught a guy with a bulldozer up on Jensen Beach opposite the causeway a couple of years ago about three o'clock in the morning. He'd dug a trench almost one hundred yards long and ten feet deep. He claimed there was a treasure ship buried right in front of the lifeguard station."

"Where'd he get an idea like that?"

"He'd read a book about sunken Spanish treasure ships and claimed that one of the missing treasure galleons from the seventeen-fifteen Plate Fleet had sunk there. He was serious about it."

"Sounds like a nut case to me. What happened to him? Did he find any treasure?"

"When I showed up to arrest him he took off up the beach in that bulldozer for the St. Lucie County line. He made it because I wasn't about to step in front of the bulldozer."

"Why didn't you radio the St. Lucie County Sheriff's Department for assistance?"

"I did. They laughed and told me to go home and sleep it off. The last time I saw him he was headed for Walton Rocks."

"Do you think there's any treasure buried around here?"

"If there ever was it was found a long time ago. Treasure hunters have been working the area from the St. Lucie Inlet to Sebastian since the early nineteen-sixties. Somebody finds something once in awhile that they report, but it's not very often. I'm going home." Elmo turned and headed for the front door. "I'll stop by tomorrow."

"I'll give you a call if anything happens around here," Mack responded and turned his attention back to the nautical chart on the dinette table.

"There's an answer here somewhere," Mack pondered aloud. *"But where is it? I've got to talk to Lorna Belle again and get some straight answers. She knows more than she's telling me." He rose and headed for the front door. "But first I have to get these coins checked out."*

"Exactly where did you find these coins?" The wimpy jeweler's tone of voice was insistent. "They're Spanish doubloons and they may be from the same cob."

"I found them on the beach yesterday afternoon just before dark. I saw something shining along the dune line, kicked the sand and these coins popped out. Are they important?"

"They certainly are," the jeweler responded authoritatively. "According to the date on them they're from the 1715 Spanish Plate Fleet that got caught in a hurricane and wrecked along the Treasure Coast. Exactly where on the beach did you find them? It's important because several of the wrecked ships have yet to be found."

"I found them just north of the Holiday Inn on Jensen Beach," Mack quickly responded. "How do you know they're from the 1715 fleet and what do you mean by cob?"

"The mint mark clearly indicates that they were stamped in 1715. The Spaniards poured the melted gold into long sand molds that formed rods of gold from which they cut each coin. The long rod was called a cob. Just think of a corncob. The raw slice of gold cob was placed between two metal dies, manually stamped on each side, weighed and trimmed along the side to the correct weight of 27.4680 grams or .9 oz. That's why each coin is a little different from the other even if they're cut from the same cob. And they're not perfectly round."

"I see."

"I'll give you twenty-five hundred dollars cash for each coin," offered the jeweler as he closely eyed a coin with his loupe. "That's ten thousand bucks cash money. No taxes either."

"The closing price of gold yesterday was three hundred eighty-six dollars and change."

"The coins are ninety-two percent gold or twenty-two carat. The market price of gold is based on twenty-four carat. The gold in each coin is worth ninety-two percent of the market price. Take or leave it. I don't have time to dicker with you. I see coins like this every day of the week."

"I think that I'll forgo your offer and keep them as souvenirs."

"This coin appears to have traces of tree bark on it," responded the jeweler. "Are you certain that you found it buried in the sand and not under a tree?" He asked as he looked up at Mack.

"I might have gotten some traces of tree bark in it when I rubbed it on the side of an Australian pine tree to see if it was really gold."

"This other coin appears to have traces of red paint or perhaps blood on it," quipped the frustrated wimpy jeweler who felt the traces of a huge profit slipping through his fingers. "Do you have an explanation for that as well?"

"Yes. I cut my finger on a sliver of glass from a pop bottle that was under the sand alongside that coin. I thought that I rubbed it off on my pants."

"My offer of twenty-five hundred bucks cash for each coin is still on the table. I promise that I won't tell a soul where you found them because there's a twenty-five percent State of Florida treasure-trove tax on recovered treasure."

"I don't mean to contradict you, but it's my understanding that under the United States common law of treasure-trove the tax only applies to treasure found on a state's submerged land. I found these coins in a sand dune far above the high water mark even at a spring tide. So they're not taxable as treasure. I'll consider your generous offer, but first I want to do a little more research before I put them on the market. It's my understanding that they're worth considerably more that their raw gold value to a collector. I've heard a figure as high as five thousand dollars per doubloon. That's double your offer and a good profit for you."

"Yes sir. It's indeed possible that you might be able to find a collector willing to spend that much for a coin. First you have to find the collector," offered the jeweler with a smug smile. "I know several local collectors and they prefer to remain anonymous for obvious reasons."

"Thanks for your input," Mack responded as he slipped the four coins into his pants pocket. "I'll get back with you in a day or so if I'm interested in your offer."

"Don't forget that you stopped to see me first," pleaded the wimpy jeweler. "I'll expect to see you in a couple of days. You won't find anyone else willing to make you the same offer."

Mack drove down Colorado Avenue toward Kanner Highway. He planned to take Martin Downs Boulevard west to Route 76A, called 'Loop Road' by long-time Martin County residents, to see Lorna Belle at the nursing home in Palm City.

As Mack drove he wondered to himself, *"If that wimp was willing to offer me twenty-five hundred bucks cash for each coin I doubt that he'd melt it down and sell it on the open gold market for three-fifty dollars an ounce. That'd only give him a profit of about five hundred bucks a coin. He must know a collector who'd give him a lot more in cash. I have a suspicion that he's done that before. Maybe that's where Lorna Belle fenced her raw gold all those years?"*

Mack parked his truck in the nursing home gravel parking lot and headed for the front door. He had the full intention of confronting Lorna Belle. *"That sweet old lady knows a lot more than she shared with me. She gave me just enough information to tickle my imagination and whet my appetite. She wanted me to come back. I'll bet she's sitting in her chair and giggling in anticipation of throwing out a little more bait just to see if I'll take it hook line and sinker. But I'm on to her now. I'll play her like a carp this time."*

The front door was securely locked. A white scrap of paper taped to the window carried an ominous message, 'Because of new state regulations all visitors must check in at the registration desk and be cleared before proceeding to a guest's room. Signed, 'The Management.'

Mack pushed in the white plastic button. A buzzer sounded from inside followed by a 'click' of the door lock. Mack turned the doorknob to the right, pulled the door open and walked inside. A wooden gate, the type usually used to keep rampaging toddlers in check, stretched across the hallway. An enormous black man clad in a white orderly's uniform, obviously the gatekeeper, stood on the other side of the gate. The frown on his face clearly indicated that he was not thrilled to be there. He'd rather be changing diapers or emptying bedpans.

Before Mack could say a word the gatekeeper initiated what was obviously meant to be a one-sided conversation. "Whom are you here to see and how are you related to them."

"I'm here to see Lorna Belle Mobley," Mack responded. "I'm not related to her. I'm just a friend and I was here yesterday."

"I'm sorry sir, but I cannot allow you in to see Miss Mobley," the black orderly responded as he folded his steer-hock arms across his massive chest.

"Why not? I was here yesterday to see her and we had a great time," Mack responded sharply. "What happened between yesterday and today?"

"Direct orders from her daughter."

"What do you mean direct orders from her daughter," Mack snapped back in defiance. "Her daughter's in Boston and hasn't been here to see her for months."

"Her daughter came in this morning and left direct orders that no one is permitted to see Miss Mobley without written authorization. Miss Mobley is not to be disturbed and cannot have any visitors. Apparently she took seriously ill after you left yesterday. Apparently you got her all stirred up over something."

"What?"

"I was told that no one is allowed to see her under any circumstances."

"I have to see her! I need to check some of the things she told me yesterday!"

"Sir if you continue in this manner I'll be forced to call security. They'll turn you over to the Martin County Sheriff's Department and you'll be charged with trespassing."

"This is ridiculous! Somebody is trying to isolate her! She may be in danger!"

"Sir you aren't the only one who wanted to see Miss Mobley today," the attendant offered. "There was a young lady here this morning who claimed that Miss Mobley was her grandmother and I wasn't allowed to let her see Miss Mobley either."

"What was her name?"

"I didn't ask."

"Whom can I talk to about this travesty? This isn't right!"

"You have to get clearance from her daughter."

"Did she happen to say where she's staying? I'll go see her."

"She lives on Sewall's Point."

"What! She lives here? Since when?"

"She grew up here."

"Do you have her phone number?"

"Yes, but I can't give it to you."

"Then I'll look it up in the phone book!"

"What's her daughter's last name?"

"I can't give that information to you either"

"This is a big set up. They're trying to keep her from talking!"

"Sir are you going to leave willingly or do you want me to call security?"

"I'm leaving." Mack spun on his heel and went out the door allowing it to 'slam' behind him. He was furious and knew there was nothing he could do about it.

"I'll go by Trailer Town. That cowboy manager has to know how to get in contact with Lorna Belle's daughter," he muttered. *"He called to tell her that Lorna Belle fell down and broke her hip. I'll slip him twenty bucks and he'll squeal like a pig. I can play him like a fiddle."*

Mack pulled into Trailer Town and Lorna Belle's trailer was gone! John Thomas, the Trailer Town resident manager, walked in front of Mack's truck and held up his open hand as a signal for him to stop. Mack obliged, rolled down his window and leaned out so the manager could hear him.

"What's going on?" Mack bellowed over the roar of the backhoe furiously digging a pit where Lorna Belle's trailer had stood. "Where's Lorna Belle's trailer? Why's that guy digging a hole?"

"I don't know what you're talking about," the manager responded through his cupped hands. "We're digging a hole for a new septic tank because we don't have city sewers in here yet."

"What happened to the trailer that was parked there a couple of weeks ago?"

"The people who bought it towed it off to a migrant camp in Indiantown on Saturday."

"Who bought it? How can I get a hold of them? Do you have their phone number?"

"Even if I wanted to I can't give that information to you. It's between the buyer and the seller. I was just the broker."

"Was Lorna Belle's daughter the seller?"

"Who?"

"Lorna Belle Mobley's daughter! Was she the seller?"

"I'm afraid I don't know who you're talking about. Even if I knew I couldn't say one way or the other. That's proprietary information."

Mack reached into his pants pocket, pulled out a wad of cash and tossed a twenty-dollar bill at the manager. "Here! This is for twenty bucks worth of information."

"I don't know who you're talking about. I don't know any Lorna Belle Mobley," the manager responded as he handed the crumpled bill back to Mack. "Please leave the premises immediately or I will call the police and have you cited for trespassing on private property."

"When I was here a couple of weeks ago you knew who and where she was. You told me!"

"You've mistaken me for someone else. I've never seen you before."

"I was here last week! You told me that Lorna Belle broke her hip and laid helpless in her trailer for three days until your wife found her."

"I told you that? I don't think so. I don't know anyone named Lorna Belle."

"You told me that she was in a nursing home in Palm City."

"No I didn't. I don't know who this Lorna Belle Mobley person is and even if I did I wouldn't tell a stranger. Please leave before I call the police and have you arrested for trespassing."

"I don't know what kind of scam or con game you're trying to play here but I don't like it."

"I don't care what you don't like. Git!"

Mack obliged and backed out of the muddy, rut-filled driveway while talking to himself. *"What the heck is going on here? I can't get in to see Lorna Belle and this clown claims that he doesn't know who she is yet he told me where to find her."* He backed the truck onto Old Dixie Highway, straightened out the wheels and turned left onto Martin Luther King Boulevard and headed for Palm Beach Road. *"I have to talk to Frank Holmes. He's the key to the whole puzzle and I don't give a rat's ass what that administrator says. I'll talk TM into getting me in to see him. She'll do it."*

Mack glanced at his watch. It read 12:27. *"Crap! It'll be lunchtime at the nursing home and I won't be able to get in to see him until the trays have been picked up. I think I'll pull into Luna's for a fast bite. I could use some garlic knots and a big slab of their home-made lasagna."*

Because every meal is individually prepared to order lunch was slower than Mack would have liked. He left the waitress a five-dollar tip and apologized for being in a hurry. He realized that she couldn't possibly have any idea of the tremendous pressure he was under. It was 1:23 P.M. when he left the restaurant and headed for Palm Beach Road. Frank Holmes and Lorna Belle were on his mind. Something ill was blowing in the wind and Mack didn't like the smell.

The snotty nursing home receptionist tried to ignore Mack but his strumming fingernails beat out an urgent tattoo on the plastic countertop.

"Yes sir. How may I help you?" She asked without looking away from her computer screen. "You still can't see Mr. Holmes."

"I'm not here to see Mr. Holmes. I'm here to see that black woman who was here yesterday. She was wearing a nurse's uniform and goes by the initials TM. I need to talk to her about something very important."

"She's not here any longer. She quit yesterday. I guess she didn't like us."

"What! Where does she live? How can I reach her?"

"I can't give out that information. It's proprietary. Have a good day."

"You can't tell me where she lives or how to reach her?"

"That's correct. Was English comprehension a difficult course for you?"

"No it wasn't! I understand completely. Where's your boss? I want to talk to him!"

"He's at a management workshop in West Palm Beach and won't be back in the office until Friday morning," the feisty receptionist responded without looking away from her computer screen. "Have a nice day sir."

Mack spun on his heel without offering a response and headed for the front door. It was a five-minute drive down East Ocean Boulevard, across the Evans Crary Bridge to Sewall's Point Road. Mack decided to shoot craps, drive up and down the residential streets and look for a car with a Massachusetts license plate. He had nothing to lose and might get lucky.

After twenty minutes of fruitless searching Mack spotted two women dressed in white shorts and flip-flops walking their dogs on the west side of Sewall's Point Road just north of the intersection with Mandalay Road. A shorthaired blonde held onto the leash of a hyperactive Jack Russell Terrier and a pony-tailed brunette strained to restrain a feisty Schnauzer.

Mack pulled alongside the strolling pair, rolled down the passenger side window of his blue pickup truck and addressed the brunette. "Excuse me. Do you know of anyone who lives on Sewall's Point that's from Boston?"

The pair enjoyed the attention. The blonde stepped in front of her companion and responded, "Is that the best pickup line you could come up with? Why didn't you try something a little more original? This isn't Port Salerno!" She winked and lightly elbowed her companion in the ribs.

"It's not a pickup line. I'm looking for a woman from Boston who also has a home on Sewall's Point," Mack asserted. "Her mother's in a nursing home out in Palm City and I need to talk to her about something important."

"Do you want to talk to the mother or the daughter?" The blonde replied. "I've heard some guys are into older women. Did you need the daughter's permission to date her mother?" Both women broke into giggle fits.

"I need to talk to the daughter about her mother. It's important!"

The women gained their composure and resumed walking. The dogs were thoroughly confused because they thought they were going for a ride in the truck. Mack pulled back onto Sewell's Point Road and waved his hand in thanks.

"Those two broads are nuts," Mack muttered to himself. He glanced in the rearview mirror. The blonde was talking on her cell phone. *"She's probably calling her shrink to tell him that her self esteem has been restored because a guy tried to pick her up while she was walking her dog."*

When Mack swung around the tip of Sewell's Point Road and headed north a Sewall's Point Police cruiser blocked the road in front of him. When he braked to a stop a second police cruiser pulled in behind him with its roof-mounted red and blue lights flashing.

"What the hell do they want?" Mack mumbled under his breath. *"I sure as hell wasn't speeding. Maybe they don't like pickup trucks."*

The two young officers were very polite and Mack realized that a sure sign of middle age was when police officers began to look like high school students. One adolescent-looking officer approached Mack's truck from the driver's side and the other from the passenger's side. He anticipated their questions, pulled out his wallet and removed his driver's license for inspection.

"We stopped you is because we received a complaint that you harassed two women walking alongside Sewall's Point Road."

"I didn't harass them. I just asked them if they knew anyone in Sewell's Point from Boston."

"That is not an appropriate question to ask one of our residents and we don't take that type of behavior lightly. It might be appropriate in Port Salerno but not on Sewall's Point. Please follow us to the police station."

"What? I didn't break any law! This is stupid! I want to speak to your supervisor."

"Chief Brown wants to talk to you also and he's waiting for you at the police station. Please follow us."

Chapter
23

Mack felt that the two young Sewall's Point police officers thought they were Nazi storm troopers the way they grabbed him by each arm and directed him into the police station. When the trio approached the police chief's desk the mustachioed chief grinned from ear to ear and leaned forward to be certain that Mack could hear what he had to say. His blue and white plastic nametag read 'Chief B. J. Brown'.

"So you're the guy that likes to pick up strange women walking their dogs on Sewall's Point Road are you? That type of activity just doesn't play well here. One of those gals pitched a bitch fit to the mayor on her cell phone after you pulled away."

Mack shook his head from side to side in disbelief.

The irate police chief shook his finger in Mack's face and continued his diatribe, "The mayor wants us to arrest you and throw you in jail, but I can't find a specific statute that covers trying to pick up women. However, Sewall's Point residents take their privacy seriously. Do you clearly understand the message that I'm trying to give you?"

"I didn't do anything wrong and I didn't attempt to pick up them up," Mack answered authoritatively. "Maybe they're disappointed that I didn't and their egos are bruised."

The chief's face turned red and he slammed his fist on the desk. "I don't think you realize who the women are that you offended. I suggest that you get back in your truck and get yourself back across the Evans Crary Bridge before you make me mad." The chief leaned back in his chair and folded his arms across his barrel chest.

"I didn't attempt to pick up those women. I asked them if they knew someone from Boston who lived on Sewall's Point. I'm trying to get in contact with a woman whose mother is in a nursing home off Loop Road in Palm City."

The unconvinced chief leaned forward in his chair, folded his hands on the desk in front of him and looked Mack in the eye. "What's the name of the person you're looking for?"

"Lorna Belle Mobley. Her daughter is from Boston and she lives on Sewall's Point."

"The chief straightened up in his chair and addressed Mack with a wide smile, "You don't mean the Lorna Belle Mobley that worked as a maid at the Sand Club on Jensen Beach?"

"Yes. She's the same one. Lorna Belle and her daughter lived in a spare room in the back of the Sand Club. In nineteen fifty she married some rich guy, an old bootlegger, who lived on Sewall's Point. Before she married him she spent some time as a live-in housekeeper. The guy died a few months after they got married."

"From what I remember about Lorna Belle I'm sure the old guy died with a big smile on his face," the chief replied with a broad grin. "She was quite the looker. She worked in a New Orleans strip club before she found her way over here. A few years after the old guy died she lost the house and moved back to New Orleans. The last I heard she was living in a trailer in a trailer park off of Martin Luther King Boulevard."

"That's right. She was until a few weeks ago. She fell down and broke her hip. She laid there helpless in her trailer for three days before the trailer park manager's wife found her and got her some medical attention."

"I went to high school with the guy that runs that trailer park. If I remember right his name is John Thomas. He thinks he's a cowboy and dresses up in cowboy clothes when he's out cutting the grass in the trailer park. I think he also works as a hunting guide in a private lodge out toward Yee Haw Junction."

"That's right. I spoke to him a couple of weeks ago when I was trying to locate Lorna Belle. He told me that Lorna Belle's daughter checked her into a nursing home on Loop Road in Palm City. I went by there today and I wasn't allowed to see her because her daughter had advised the nursing home that no one was to see Lorna Bell unless they had written permission from her daughter. I stopped by the trailer park today and John Thomas claimed he'd never seen me before and hadn't told me anything. Lorna Belle's trailer was gone and a backhoe was digging up the lot for a new septic tank."

"Lorna Belle and her daughter Jo didn't get along very well. I went to high school with Jo and I remember the day when she was sent off to a fancy college in Boston. She never came back to Stuart. But I can't imagine why Jo would put her mother in a nursing home. Certainly it's not because she doesn't have enough money to take care of her mother and the old house on Sewall's Point Road is large enough for two families."

"Do you know anything about the big hurricane that went through here in nineteen forty-nine?"

"I was only five years old. My father used to talk about how thirty feet of sand was washed completely off Jensen Beach. After the storm went through he picked up several silver and gold coins that had washed up on the beach."

"Do you know Tina Louise McShay?"

"Of course I know Tina. I want to high school with her. I used to do some part-time work there fixing boats for her dad. She's a big shot lawyer down in West Palm Beach. She comes back to Stuart on weekends to spend time on her sailboat."

"My name is Mack McCray. Tina hired me as Port Sewall Marina manager a few months ago."

"Boys go back out on road patrol and try to find some serious law breakers." The chief directed the two young officers away with a wave of his hand in the direction of the front door. "I'll personally take care of Mr. McCray and see that he gets a proper lecture on how to behave when he comes over here." The chief redirected his attention toward Mack.

"If you work for Tina I doubt that you were trying to pick up those women. However, I'm going to give you a 'no trespass' warning and I strongly suggest that you avoid loitering in Sewall's Point. Do you understand where I'm coming from?"

"Of course I understand. I was not trying to pick those women up. I'm not that desperate. I just asked them for directions."

"Let's just leave it at that. It's time for you to get on your way and get back to Port Sewall Marina. Try to keep out of trouble here on Sewall's Point," the police chief responded with a wink. "I've decided not to write up a 'no trespass' citation."

"Can you give me the address of Lorna Belle's daughter's house before I leave?"

"Don't push your luck. I can't tell you where anyone lives on Sewall's Point," the chief responded as he frowned. "Some very high profile people live out here and they want their privacy protected. The best I can tell you is to drive down to the end of Sewall's Point Road and take a gander at the houses at the end of the Road. I can't give you an address because it would be inappropriate. If I remember right Lorna Belle's old house is on top of a high bluff that overlooks the Indian River and St. Lucie inlet." The chief pushed back from his desk and stood up. "Mr. McCray I think you should get on your way. I sincerely hope for your sake that I don't see you in here again."

"You won't see me in here again I can assure you of that. Thank you for your hospitality and consideration." As Mack reached out to shake the police chief's hand he turned away and began to walk toward his office. Mack withdrew his hand, turned and walked out the front door of the police station toward his waiting truck. The wall clock read 3:49.

Still smarting from his lecture and the embarrassment of being stopped by the two young cops Mack turned south on Sewall's Point Road. He kept one eye on the rearview mirror.

"I hope the chief told those two kids to keep off my butt while I'm driving down here," Mack muttered to himself. *"He's the one who told me where to find Lorna Belle's old house."*

Mack reached the end of Sewall's Point Road and noted that there were several houses along the bluff. He had no idea which house was Lorna Belle's. All the way up Sewall's Point Road

Mack carefully watched the rearview mirror. He expected the two young cops to pull him over for speeding. At the intersection with East Ocean Boulevard Mack turned right toward the Stuart Causeway.

"I might as well ride up to Jensen Beach and take a look at Tick Ridge. I couldn't find a Frank Holmes in the Jensen Beach telephone book, but maybe there's a name on the mailbox," he mumbled to himself.

Mack slowed down when he reached Jensen Beach Causeway Park, smiled as he passed the three Australian pine trees on his right and turned left onto Jensen Beach Causeway. He briefly thought about stopping at the Snook Nook to chat with the local fishing guides for a few minutes and put the thought away. It was more important to go to Tick Ridge and attempt to find Frank Holmes's house. He went west on Jensen Beach Boulevard and turned right three blocks past the intersection with Skyline Drive.

Mack spent 45 minutes slowly driving up and down the streets of the Tick Ridge development and didn't find 'Holmes' on any mailbox. Completely discouraged he drove west on Jensen Beach Boulevard toward U.S. 1. It was almost five o'clock. Mack stopped at the Park Avenue Barbecue Grill and devoured a plate of baby back ribs, French fries and a couple of cold beers before returning to Port Sewall Marina.

He pulled into the marina parking lot at 6:27 P.M. and before he could get out of the truck a Martin County Sheriff's Patrol Car pulled up behind him. As Mack exited the truck Deputy Elmo simultaneously exited his patrol car and walked up to Mack with a big grin on his face.

"I hear you had a good time on Sewall's Point with Chief Brown this afternoon," Elmo blurted out. "You're lucky those boys didn't toss you in jail and throw the key away."

"How'd you know that?" Mack asked as he leaned against the hood of his pickup truck. "I didn't tell anybody."

"You didn't have to tell anybody," Elmo gleefully responded. "We all have frequency scanners and we monitor each other's dispatch channels. I heard the boys talking back and forth before they stopped you. I knew it was you because of the description of the blue pickup truck. You've got the only blue Ford F-150 equipped with a camper shell in Martin County."

"Why didn't you call them on the radio and tell them I'm a friend of yours?"

"That wouldn't have done any good because those two kids are rookies. They've only been on the force a couple weeks and they're real 'gung ho'. I knew that BJ wouldn't do anything except give you warning and send you on your way. He's a good old boy."

"You know him?"

"I went to high school with him."

"I called him before the boys got you to the police station and told him who you are. I gave him a call a few minutes ago and he told me that he got a good chuckle over the whole thing."

"Thanks a lot for being my friend and helping me out."

"He told me that there's nothing to worry about. Apparently the mayor's wife and her sister told a different story than you did. But it's all taken care of now. Don't worry."

"What do you know about Chief B. J. Brown?"

"I've known him for over thirty years. He's a pretty good guy. He can't tolerate the Yankees that come down here from up north and think they know everything. But, he tries to be civil to them. He's my brother-in-law. He's my wife's brother. His family's lived in Martin County for five generations."

"Thanks."

"I understand that you're looking for Lorna Belle Mobley's old place. I went to high school with Jo Mobley and I remember where she lived. She's a couple of years older than me. Tina used to sneak out in her canoe and paddle over to Sewall's Point to play with her. It drove her parents nuts because a lot of big bull sharks hang around over there."

"Tina told me about her pal Jo this morning. What did you do constructive today?"

"After I saw you this morning I went home and did most of the 'honey do' projects on my list. I was supposed to come back on duty at three o'clock and got called in early. My sergeant called me about noon and ordered me to investigate an abandoned house trailer that was dumped behind a plant nursery in Palm City."

"Why'd he call you if you were off duty?"

"I live in Palm City and the house trailer was dumped about two miles from my house. A good friend of mine owns the nursery and he's really pissed over it."

"Why would someone dump a trailer behind a plant nursery?"

"I don't know yet, but it looks suspicious. There wasn't much left except the floor, wheels and axles. Whoever tore it apart ripped it from top to bottom with a power saw. There were pieces of aluminum spread all over the back lot of the nursery. I called in a flat bed truck to carry it all to the Martin County landfill. There wasn't shred of identification left on the trailer."

"I think I know who it belongs to and I have a pretty good idea who dumped it out there."

"How would you know anything about somebody dumping a house trailer in Palm City?"

"I think it belonged to Lorna Belle Mobley. According to John Thomas the manager of Trailer Town he sold her trailer to someone who was going to tow it out to Indiantown and park it in a migrant labor camp."

"How do you know John Thomas?"

"I met him two weeks ago when I was trying to find Lorna Belle Mobley. He told me that she was in a nursing home in Palm City and I spent some time with her yesterday afternoon. When I went back today they wouldn't let me to see her under orders of her daughter. I went back to the trailer park today and asked Thomas how to get hold of her daughter and the silly bastard claimed that he'd never seen me before."

"He's always been a shady character. Did he tell you how to contact Lorna Belle's daughter?"

"No. He told me that it's proprietary information. The other strange thing about it is that a backhoe was digging up her trailer lot. Thomas told me they were digging a hole for a new septic tank because the trailer park doesn't have access to city sewers."

"That's probably true. The trailer park doesn't have city sewer service and it was grand fathered because it's been there for so long. I'll stop by there tomorrow and have a little chat with him."

"Let me know what you find out. I still have to find a way to contact Lorna Belle's daughter, I need to get back in that nursing home and see her."

"Be very careful about dealing with Lorna Belle's daughter."

"Why? She doesn't know who I am."

"When she moved to Boston she got in with a bad crowd."

"What do you mean a bad crowd? She's a lawyer and from what I understand so is her husband."

"There's lawyers and then there's lawyers. From what I hear he's on the shady side."

'That's pretty well what Lorna belle had to say about him. If I remember correctly she profiled him as a bottom-feeding scumbag or something close. She doesn't like him very much."

"I never met the guy so I don't know. I have to go back to the office and file my report about the trailer. Have you heard any more about Ralph?"

"What more is there to hear? The postcard that Joy got today said to expect him Friday."

"Okay. I keep wondering about the bloody boot and that bloody surveyor's stake we found in his boat. Did you check out that gold coin?'

"Yep. It was gold foil over a piece of chocolate candy. They were tossing them off the pirate float at 'Dancing' in the Streets' Friday night. I ate it."

"How about the boot and surveyor's stake?"

"I don't know. I suspect some drunk kids took off with Ralph's boat Friday night after 'Dancin' in the Streets' and hid it under the bridge. That's why the coin was in there. Maybe one of the kids fell on the stick, got it stuck in his leg and bled all over the boot. That's my guess."

"Then how did he get to Marathon? His truck's still parked in the driveway at the house."

"I don't know. Maybe he hitchhiked, took a bus or rode with someone else. I guess we'll know Friday when he gets back. All we can do is wait until he shows up."

"What if he doesn't show up Friday? Are you going to tell Joy that we found his boat?"

"No. You and I are making a quick trip to Marathon if he doesn't show up."

"Did you ever get any identification on the dead guy in the boathouse?"

"What dead guy in what boathouse? Elmo you have a short memory."

"I forgot. What about the guy who tried to strangle you? Rat hit him over the head with a concrete block Sunday night?"

"Don't know yet. I'll let you know what comes back."

"Do you think there's still somebody out there trying to whack you?"

"I don't think so. If there is there isn't much I can do about it until they try it. If you don't hear from me tomorrow you'll know."

"I'll stop by in the morning. I'm leaving. I have to get that report about the house trailer filed tonight." Elmo turned, walked back to his patrol car and pulled out of the parking lot.

After Elmo left the marina seemed empty. The sun was going down fast and Mack glanced at his watch. It read 7:36. He had spent more than an hour rapping with Elmo and didn't know much more than he did before Elmo pulled in the parking lot earlier with the big grin on his face.

"Mack! I'm glad you're back," Joy's shrill voice rang over the silence as she walked toward the marina. "I came over and fed your dog about five o'clock. I took him home with me because I didn't know when you'd be home. Was that okay? Do you want me to bring him back now?"

"That's great," Mack responded. "Keep him at your house because I'm leaving early in the morning and I don't know when I'll be back. If Ralph calls tell him I said hello."

Joy waved in acknowledgment, turned and walked down Old St. Lucie Boulevard toward Willoughby Creek. She felt secure with Mack's dog at her house and the dog also seemed comfortable with the arrangement. He got fed well, special treats and lots of ear scratching.

Mack stepped onto the front porch and noticed that the front door was ajar. He specifically remembered securely closing the door when he left that morning.

"Who the hell's been here?" He thought to himself. *"Do I have another unwelcome visitor?"*

Mack probed his waistband for the security of the Beretta semi-automatic pistol. It wasn't there! He had left it in the kitchen drawer under the green dishcloth that morning. He looked around for something to use as a weapon and spotted a rusty tire iron beside the storage shed. Before he could take a step toward the storage shed and the tire iron a sultry female voice oozed from behind the front door.

"Mr. McCray. It's me. You don't have you be afraid of little old me. I'm just a girl."

"What the hell!" Mack instinctively leaped off the porch toward his truck.

"It's okay. You know me," oozed the soft voice in a sultry 'come hither' tone.

"Who the hell are you and what are you doing in my place?"

The front door opened and a tall, long legged brunette with shoulder length hair stepped into the shadow of the porch. Mack couldn't make out the facial features in the shadows.

"It's Polly Jo. I've come to visit you," oozed the sultry voice. "Please don't be mad at me."

"Polly Jo from Biloxi?" Mack asked as he strode toward the porch. "Why are you here?"

"I came to visit my nana and you."

"Your nana?"

"You know her. Her name's Lorna Belle Mobley. She's in a nursing home in Palm City and they wouldn't let me see her this morning even though I came all the way from Mississippi."

Mack strode over to the front porch and leaned against the railing as he tried to figure out the situation. "Polly Jo! How did you find me? What do you expect me to do?"

"Do you remember the night I walked you back to your hotel in Biloxi? We had a nice conversation on the way over there."

"Of course. But what does that have to do with your being here?"

"After we got to your hotel you had a couple of drinks, told me your real name and where you were from. It was easy to find you. Didn't you smell my White Diamonds perfume the next morning when you woke up? You got real lucky and you don't remember what you said?"

"I don't remember us having any such conversation. Did you slip something into my drink?"

"No. My aunt did when you were in the bar. It's an animal tranquilizer called Ketamine Hydrochloride and it affects short-term memory. Teenagers call it Special K."

"I should have known you were up to something. What else did I tell you?"

"Nothing of any real importance. You didn't give away any National secrets. My aunt told me that I could trust you if I needed help. That's why I'm here. I need help."

"Now we've established how you found me. How did you get here?"

"I took a bus. When I got here Monday afternoon I called a friend of mine who works in a strip joint north of the Roosevelt Bridge. She picked me up at the bus station and I spent last night at her place. This morning she took me to the trailer park where my nana lived and the slime ball manager told me that she's in a nursing home in Palm City. She drove me out there and a real mean black guy said that no one could get in to see my nana."

"I know how you feel. I was out there this morning and I couldn't see her either."

"My girlfriend's boyfriend won't let me spend the night at her place tonight. So she brought me here. Can you take me in for a couple of days? I don't want my mother to know I'm here."

"I only have one bedroom and one bed."

"That's okay. We'll make it do somehow even if we have to sleep in shifts."

"Why don't you and your mother get along?"

"The bastard she married tried to rape me when I was twelve. I told her about it and she didn't believe me. He kept after me and after me. I didn't have any choice and ran away to my grandaunt's place in Biloxi. I don't like him. He's a sneaky slime ball."

"Does your mother know you're here?"

"No! And I don't want her to know I'm here either. I'm worried about what's happening to my nana and I want to help her. Will you help me help my nana?"

"I'm not in a position to help her. I don't know if she's in any trouble and it's legally none of my business. Your mother placed her into the nursing home and decided that no one is to talk to her unless they have her permission. Do you have any idea why she did that?"

"Did you know that the man that my mother married is not my biological father?"

"No. How do you know that?"

"My nana told me. That's why she and my mother don't get along. My mother had an affair with a commercial fisherman in Gloucester, Massachusetts. She didn't tell my nana that she was pregnant until after I was born and she brought me home. My mother was still in college at the time and wanted my nana to take care of me until she graduated from law school. My nana kicked my mother out of the house and told her not to ever come back."

"How did your mother survive?"

"My nana sent her money for living expenses, plus she had a scholarship for law school."

"What do you expect me to do while you're here?"

"I was hoping that you'd let me stay here until I get a chance to get in the nursing home and see my nana. My aunt told me she has a present for me. That's why I'm here."

"Yesterday your nana gave me that wooden box on the kitchen table and a picture frame to give to you. She also told me she has secret for you, but she didn't tell me what it is."

"I have to see my nana so she can tell me what the secret is. Some mean woman called here about an hour ago. Her name was Tina and she chewed my butt! She called me a cheap no good 'slitch' and told me to get my ass out of her place. Do you know who she is?"

"I know exactly who she is and she can be very mean. She owns this marina and this cottage. Sometimes she even thinks she owns me. I'll find a way to work around the situation. Have you had anything to eat?"

"Yes. While I was waiting for you on the porch a nice lady stopped by about five-thirty. I told her that we were good friends. Her name is Joy. She invited me in and fixed me some scrambled eggs and bacon. I tried to explain to her that we're just friends and she put her finger to her lips and told me to be quiet."

"Now I understand."

"Now you understand what?"

"Why Joy is keeping my dog at her house and why she didn't walk into the driveway."

"What are you going to do now?"

"That's not important. Did you bring some clothes with you?"

"Yes. My suitcase is in the bedroom. If you want I'll sleep out here on the floor. ."

"It's okay. Leave your stuff in the bedroom. Just toss me out a pillow and a blanket. I'll sleep in one of these chairs. They're recliners and they fold back like a bed. I'll sleep like a baby."

"Are you sure? You can sleep with me. I owe you and I'm really very good in bed."

"Thanks but no thanks. I'm in enough trouble as it is. Did Tina say when she'd call back?"

"No and before she hung up she called me a 'slitch'. What does 'slitch' mean?"

"I don't know but I've got a feeling that we'll find out very soon."

Chapter 24

The obnoxious telephone rang while Polly Jo was in the bedroom unpacking her suitcase. Mack had a good idea who was calling. Joy had forewarned him. Mack wasn't quite sure what he had to explain or how he was going to explain it. Obviously Tina was going to require answers to her questions. He allowed the telephone to ring eight times before he lifted the handset from the cradle and placed it next to his ear. He tried to appear nonchalant just in case Polly Jo was watching.

"Hello. Mack here."

"Don't play games with me," shrieked a shrill female voice on the other end of the telephone line. "I know you've got some 'slitch' there from Biloxi, Mississippi. I know you were in Biloxi because I tracked you down to the Beau Rivage hotel. You weren't in Tallahassee visiting a sick cousin. I want an explanation and I want it now!"

"You shouldn't be so concerned about where I've been. Why are you so concerned about the young lady and what's a 'slitch'?"

"It means 'slutty bitch' and she's no lady! She's a sneaky 'slitch' and she snuck in there this afternoon. When I called this afternoon she answered the telephone in that sweet syrupy southern accent of hers. She thought it was you on the other end of the phone. I called her because Joy called and told me she was there."

"Before you start ranting and raving you should know who she is and why she's here."

"What difference does it make who she is and why she's there? I want her out of my marina and I want her out tonight!"

"Hold your horses and let me explain. Do you remember the story you told me about your friend Jo who lived on Sewall's Point?"

"Of course I remember. Why?"

"The girl took a bus from Biloxi to Stuart yesterday and she's Jo's daughter. Her name is Polly Jo and she came here to see her grandmother Lorna Belle in the nursing home."

"How do you know she's Jo's daughter?"

"Because she told me so and I believe her. She told me her whole story and why she and her mother haven't talked to each other for years. She ran away from home to her aunt's place in Biloxi because Jo's husband tried to rape her when she was only twelve years old."

"What does that have to do with her being at the marina?"

"She got here yesterday and spent the night with a friend."

"Why isn't she at her friend's house tonight?"

"Her girlfriend's boyfriend said she could only stay there for one night."

"Where was she today before she showed up at the marina? Joy told she me fixed her some scrambled eggs and bacon. The girl hadn't eaten all day."

"This morning she went over to the trailer park to see that slime ball John Thomas and find out where her grandmother was. He told her that Lorna Belle was in a nursing home in Palm City. Her girlfriend drove her over to Palm City and the guard at the front door wouldn't let her in to see her grandmother. Apparently Jo is in town and pulling the strings."

"What makes you think so?"

I also tried to see Lorna Belle this morning and I was told that no one is allowed to see her under direct orders of her daughter."

"So what's she doing at the marina?"

"She scared to death of Jo's husband. He isn't her father."

"What!"

"Jo had an affair with a commercial fisherman in Gloucester Massachusetts while she was in college and got herself pregnant. She came back to Stuart and tried to leave her baby with Lorna Belle. She threw her out and told her not to come back."

"Why's she there with you?"

"She's scared to death of Jo's husband. If Jo's in town her husband must be here too. I stopped at the trailer park today. Lorna Belle's trailer is gone and the lot's being dug up with a backhoe. John Thomas told me the hole is for a new septic tank. Elmo came by the marina and told me that he found the trailer in Palm City off of Highway 714. It had been ripped apart by power tools. Somebody is searching very hard for something and they think Lorna Belle has it."

"What do you think it is?"

"I'd rather not say over the telephone."

"Why is she at the marina?"

"She can't stay with her mother on Sewall's Point and she can't stay at her grandmother's because the trailer's gone. There's no other place she can stay and be safe. She's going to sleep in the bedroom. I'm going to drag out a pillow and blanket and sack out in a recliners."

"Send her over to Joy's and let her spend the night there!"

"I'll don't think it's fair to inconvenience Joy with my problem. I'll be fine."

"I don't think so. I talked to Joy before I called you. She said it's perfectly fine if the girl stays with her. She and Ralph have a spare bedroom and at this point Joy can use the company."

"If that's what you it's just fine with me. Should I walk her over to Joy's place or is Joy coming over here to get her?"

"Look out on the front porch. Joy's out there waiting for her."

Mack looked over his right shoulder. Joy was standing outside the screen door. She waved at him and smiled. Mack signaled for Joy to come in and went back to his conversation.

"Joy just walked in the door and she's going to take Polly Jo back to her house with her. So that solves all the problems."

"I don't think it solves all the problems. If Lorna Belle's trailer disappeared and Thomas is digging up her yard with a backhoe something's strange is going on. I wish I could come up there tomorrow and help you out, but I can't. I'll be tied up with this court case until Friday."

"That's just fine. Don't worry about it. I'm going to run by the library in the morning and do some research into the Spanish treasure fleet that sank along the coast in seventeen fifteen. I also want to see what I can find about any possible pirate activity in the area. Can you recall which house on Sewall's Point Jo lived in when she was a child?"

"I can take you right to it, but I can't get up there until this trial is over. Maybe Friday afternoon I can come up and show you. Doesn't Elmo know where it is?"

"He remembers where she lived. Maybe I can talk him into it. I'd go back out there myself except I got pulled over by the Sewall's Point Police today and they gave me a no trespass warning. If they catch me over there again they'll toss me in jail and throw away the key. Can you find those tunnels where you and Jo used to play when you were kids?"

"Sure! I can point them out to you. They were closed up and we weren't allowed to play in them. I'm scared to death of snakes and the whole slope's covered with them. Have you heard anything more about Ralph?"

"Joy got a postcard from him today. The note said he was having a good time down Marathon and will be back Friday."

"Don't give me that crap! You know exactly what I'm talking about! Joy told me about the postcard and I know better. You've got Ralph's boat stashed in the boathouse and something is going on. I'd like to know what it is."

"So would I. If Ralph's not back here by Friday afternoon me and Elmo are taking off to the Keys to find him."

"Okay. You just be sure that girl's out of the cottage and over at Joy's house tonight. Besides someone is still out there looking to whack you over the head and dump your butt in the inlet. I don't want her to be there if it happens tonight."

"Yes ma'am. Have it your way."

"I'll check back with you in the morning."

'Click.' The raucous buzz in his ear told Mack that the conversation had ended. He hung the handset on the switch hook and turned around. Joy was standing in the living room.

"I told Tina there's no problem with that girl. But, she insisted that I come over here and drag her over to my house. It wasn't my idea. It was hers. I hope you don't mind."

"Certainly I don't mind. I need a good night's sleep after everything that's gone on around here for the past couple of days. Hang on and I'll call her.

"Polly Jo! Joy's here and she's going to take you over to her house for the night."

Polly Jo stormed out of the bedroom and paused in the hallway with her hands on her hips. She looked into Mack's face with fire in her eyes. "Why do I have to leave? I figured you could stay up and talk all night about old times."

"Because Tina McShay, my boss, owns this marina. She prefers that you stay at Joy's house tonight. Joy's husband's out-of-town and she can use the company."

"What do you expect me to do tomorrow?"

"You can hang around the Joy's house or come over here to play with the dolphins."

"What dolphins? Do you mean dolphins like Flipper? Can I swim with them?"

"Yes. Real dolphins. Their names are *Puka* and *Kea*. They're from Hawaii and they hang around the lagoon. They might even invite you to go swimming with them if you're real nice."

"I'll be nice. Joy! Wait for me! I gotta' grab my suitcase."

Joy left for her house with Polly Jo in tow and Mack's dog beside them. Mack picked up the library book about the Spanish Plate Fleet that went aground on the Treasure Coast in a fierce hurricane in 1715. He had a lot of homework to do and not much time to do it.

Chapter 25

Mack awoke to the wonderful aroma of sizzling bacon and hot coffee. He turned over on his left shoulder so he could read the nightstand clock. It was 8:23 A.M. He rolled out of bed, pulled on his shorts, threw on a shirt and padded barefoot down the short hallway into the kitchenette. Joy and Polly Jo were cooking breakfast.

"Mornin' sleepy head! It's about time you rolled out of the sack. We thought you were going to sleep all day," Joy bubbled. "Polly Jo and I stayed up all night jabbering away about you."

"What are you talking about?"

"Joy didn't know that you were in Biloxi and that you know my grandmother," Polly Jo enthusiastically chimed in her two cents worth of revealing trivia. "We had a good time talking about you. She told me everything and she explained why Miss Tina's so jealous of me. I promised Joy that I'd behave while I'm here. I don't want to cross Miss Tina. No sir!"

"What the hell's going on?" Mack stammered. "Have I died and gone to hell already?"

"You're just fine," Joy responded with a giggle. "Zip up the front of them shorts before you show off something you shouldn't and sit down. We've whipped up a batch of scrambled eggs and bacon for breakfast."

Before Mack could sit down at the table he heard a rap on the front door, turned toward the front door and made out the shadowy image of a woman through the screen door. He quickly strode across the living area toward the front porch. As he got closer to the door he recognized the woman as the black nurse from the nursing home. He shook his head and mumbled to himself. *"What the hell is she doing here?"* He motioned for her to move out of the direct line of sight with a nod of his head, opened the screen door and slipped out onto the porch.

"TM! What're you doing here?"

"I stopped at the nursing home yesterday afternoon to pick up my check and the receptionist said that you were looking for me."

"How did you know how to find me?"

"It wasn't hard. You gave me your business card the day we met. Did she tell you that I quit?"

"Yes. She said that you gave no reason as to why you quit. I asked her how to get in touch with you and she wouldn't tell me."

"She didn't know how because I didn't give them a correct name or a street address when I applied for the job. I gave them a Post Office Box number and fake name. I was there to do an undercover investigation of the facilities. Plus, my grandfather is a resident there and I didn't want them to find out."

"Your grandfather's a resident at the nursing home?"

"Yes. He's the man you tried to see the day I met you. His name is Frank Holmes."

"Why didn't you tell me? I've been trying to see him for couple of weeks."

"It would've blown my cover."

"Why did you quit on such short notice?"

"I wanted to defer any suspicions about me. Normally an investigator spends several weeks working in a facility. But I got the information I needed the first day."

"Why did you come here?"

"Don't you remember? I told you I might want to write a book some day."

"I don't know how to write a book."

"You sounded very convincing at the nursing home. The administrator believed you."

"I was there to verify something someone told me and I made up the book writing part."

"You went looking for my grandfather's house up on Tick Ridge yesterday afternoon."

"How do you know that?"

"You drove your blue pickup truck past my grandfather's house three times."

"How do you know I drive a blue pickup truck?"

"That wasn't very hard. It's sitting outside and I was looking out the window when you left the nursing home Monday."

"If you saw me why didn't you come out and say something?"

"I didn't want you to know where he lives."

"Why are you here? Is there something you want from me?"

"Do you recall the nursing home administrator telling you that my grandfather can't have any visitors because he has dementia and babbles about buried pirate treasure?"

"Of course. But your grandfather isn't imagining. I think he really knows where it is."

"That's why I'm here. I want you to see what I found at my grandfather's house and tell me what it means." She motioned for Mack to follow her into the parking lot, pushed the remote button and the trunk lid of her silver BMW sedan flew open.

Mack cautiously followed along behind her. He was unsure of what might be in the car trunk.

She reached inside the trunk and lifted out a wooden box stained with black mold. "This old box is two feet long, eleven inches wide and nine inches deep. I measured it this morning. " She strained to hold it up. "Those are odd dimensions. Do you have any idea what was stored in it?"

"No I don't. Why do you ask?"

"There're several of them stacked up in the shed behind my grandfather's house. They're held together with forged handmade nails so they must be very old." She pointed into the recess of the car trunk. "What's that?"

"That's a melting pot," Mack replied.

"What's it used for?"

"Plumbers use them to melt down lead for pipe repairs. Telephone company cable splicers also use them to melt down lead to make their lead splicing sleeves watertight. Why?"

"It was in my grandfather's shed along with a naphtha burner. I also found this." She reached into the trunk and pulled out a flat cast iron cooking pan lined with rigid molded sand. The sand contained six horizontal indentations the length and width of a fat cigar. "This is obviously a mold and I found traces of gold along the edges. Maybe my grandfather robbed a bank and melted down the gold in it? My grandmother always suspected he was up to something back there, but he never talked about it."

"The mold's made of green sand mixed with clay to make it rigid. It was dusted with resin before the gold was poured to keep it from sticking to the sand. Your grandfather was melting down gold, but it wasn't stolen. I have some suspicions, but I have some more checking to do."

"What do you have to check out?"

"I'd rather not say until I know for certain. When're you leaving town?"

"I'm not. I moved to Stuart to provide care for my grandfather. I want to move him out of the nursing home and back into his own home on Tick Ridge, but the nursing home won't release him until his bill is paid in full."

"What do you mean?"

"The nursing home charges two thousands dollars a month for his care and my grandmother is two months behind. I hoped that you would know something about these molds and what he did with the gold. I suppose I was looking for a pot of gold at the end of the rainbow, but there's no rainbow. There's only rain and I don't see it clearing up for us any time soon."

"Your grandfather melted down gold for years and sold it. I don't how much there was, or if there's any left, or where he must have stashed it."

"How do you know all of that?"

"Trust me. I know. Take your grandmother to the nursing home after three o'clock this afternoon. Your grandfather's bill will be paid in full and they will release him to her."

"What? That's nonsense! You certainly aren't in a position to pay four thousand dollars in back fees for my grandfather's care! You don't know anything about us."

"His fees are going to be paid by an old friend who wants to do something for him."

"Why?"

"She would call it an overdue payment for services in kind."

"Who is she?"

"It's a story that goes back to nineteen forty-nine. Your grandfather worked as a maintenance man at the Sand Club on Jensen Beach and a big hurricane hit this area. He remained at the hotel during the hurricane to protect a young woman that worked there as a maid and her daughter. He didn't go home because he knew your grandmother would be safe in their house on Tick Ridge. Your grandfather and this young woman formed a lifetime relationship. At this point in their lives each one of them owes the other something very intangible."

"Who is she? Was my grandfather having an affair with her?"

"No. He wasn't having an affair with her. They were, and still are, just good friends. She's in a nursing home in Palm City and has come into some serious problems the last few weeks. Her granddaughter Polly Jo is inside. Why don't you come in and meet her? Maybe you could help her grandmother out?"

"I don't want to get involved." TM slammed the trunk lid closed and turned toward her car. "It's none of my business."

"It certainly is your business. Her grandmother is going to bail your grandfather out of the nursing home this afternoon and she needs your help."

"What! Why should she do that? If she's in a nursing home she needs the money herself."

"Don't worry about it. It's all settled. What do your mother and father know about your grandfather's activities in the gold black market?"

"I don't know. My mother never mentioned her parents or where she came from. She said that her parents died in a house fire when she was in college and she never went home afterward. When I asked her about it she always told me that she didn't want to talk about it."

"Then why are you here? You must have found out something?"

"My parents were killed in a head-on collision with an eighteen wheeler on the Pennsylvania Turnpike in February. I found the family records when I cleaned out their safe deposit box. I came back here because I wanted to know the truth about my roots. It's important to me."

"What's your real name? It can't be just the letters TM?"

"I was named after my grandmother and my mother. My grandmother's name is Thelma and my mother's name is Marvette. My mother always called me 'TM' and that's what I went by."

"Your mother might have known Polly Jo's mother, but Lorna Belle certainly remembers her. Lorna Belle told me that your mother went away to college somewhere up north right after high school graduation and she never saw her again. The pieces are starting to fit together."

"Who's Lorna Belle and who's Polly Jo? What pieces? You have me thoroughly confused."

"Lorna Belle is the woman that your grandfather protected during the hurricane. She's going to cover his nursing home fees and she wants to see him very much. Polly Jo's her granddaughter. She arrived here yesterday from Biloxi, Mississippi and she's inside."

"Mack! Breakfast's getting cold," Joy's voice drifted through the screen door. She opened the door, stuck her head out onto the porch and motioned for Mack and Thelma Marvette to come inside, "Invite her in Mack. There's plenty to eat and lots of fresh hot coffee."

"No thank you," Thelma Marvette replied. "I don't eat breakfast and I've had two cups of coffee already."

"Another cup won't hurt you. Besides a gentleman shouldn't keep a lady standing outside."

"Come on in," Mack responded in Thelma Marvette's direction. "We have lots more to discuss. We need to make some plans."

"What plans?"

"Just some plans. Come on in before Joy hits me over the head with a broom for being rude."

"Okay. I'll come in for one cup of coffee, but I can only stay for a few minutes. I have a lot of things to do today."

"Don't we all?" Mack responded with a grin and winked at her as he took her elbow.

Once Thelma Marvette and Mack were seated at the kitchenette table Joy spoke up. "Mack hasn't introduced us yet, but I'm Joy and this is Polly Jo. She's from Biloxi, Mississippi."

"My name is Thelma Marvette and my friends call me 'TM' for short. I'm pleased to meet both of you. Thank you for inviting me."

"You're most welcome," Joy cheerfully responded with a wide smile. "Any friend of Mack's is a friend of ours. What brings you to Port Sewall Marina so early in the morning? Did Mack do something bad?"

"No. I just stopped to show him a couple of things in my car trunk."

"I didn't do anything," Mack mumbled under his breath, shook his head and idly stirred his coffee. The coffee was black and didn't need stirring. "This isn't starting out to be a good day."

"Do you have some old fishing tackle in your trunk? Mack knows a lot about that kind of stuff. He's a fishing guide."

"It wasn't fishing tackle," Mack gruffly responded. "Just let it go. It's not important."

"It was a few old things I found in my grandfather's work shed. It's just 'man junk' and I wondered if Mack knew what they were. I'll probably throw them in the trash when I get home."

"What kind of things? Maybe you can sell them at the flea market? I have a booth there."

"It's not the type of stuff that people buy at flea markets," Mack interjected. " It's just crap!"

"That's exactly what people go to flea markets for. They like to prowl around old junk and look for what they consider to be treasure. She might be able to make a few bucks on it. That is if she needs the money."

"I don't need the money and if you don't mind I'd rather not discuss it any further."

"Okay. I get the message. TM what type of work do you do?"

"I inspect nursing homes for the State of Florida."

"My nana's in a nursing home and they won't let me in to see her," Polly Jo piped in between mouthfuls of scrambled eggs. "Can you help me get in to see my nana?"

"Maybe. Why wouldn't they let you in to see her? Did they give you an explanation?"

"Nope," Polly Jo replied as she gnawed on a strip of crisp bacon. "They said that it was because of my mother's orders. Nobody gets in to see my nana without her written permission."

"If she's your nana then you should be allowed to visit her. You're a family member. Did you ask your mother about it?"

"Me and my mother don't talk. I haven't seen or talked to her since I ran away from home. We don't like each other very much. Her husband tried to rape me when I was twelve and she didn't believe me when I told her about it. So I ran away."

"Where do you live? Are you over eighteen years old?"

"I'll be twenty on October sixteenth. I live with my nana's sister and go to Tulane."

"That sounds exciting. Do you have a scholarship or is your family paying for your college?"

"Neither one. I'm paying for it myself. I have a job."

"Good for you. What do you do? Do you work in the college bookstore?"

"Naw. I'm a stripper at my grand aunt's club. I work bachelor and stag parties on the side."

"What!"

"TM don't get excited," Mack interjected. "It's a very strange set of circumstances and I'll explain it to you later when you have more time."

"I have all morning. This sounds very interesting. I always wanted to be a stripper."

"She told me all about it last night," Joy chirped in with a smile. "She's been hooking too."

"Okay ladies and I use that term relatively," Mack tersely interjected. "I asked TM to come in because she has several things in common with Polly Jo's nana and might be able to help her."

"What kind of things?" Joy asked. "They aren't the same age."

"TM's grandfather protected Lorna Belle and Polly Jo's mother during a hurricane in nineteen forty-nine. They worked together at the Sand Club on Jensen Beach. She was a maid and he was the maintenance man. He stayed with them during the hurricane. TM's grandmother rode the storm out all by herself in their little concrete block house on Tick Ridge in Jensen Beach."

"Wow!" Polly Jo exclaimed. "My aunt was there too! Did you ever meet my nana?"

"I'm afraid not. My mother went away to college up north after she graduated from high school and she never brought me back here to see my grandparents."

"Why didn't she bring you back to see your nana? That's mean. Why didn't she?"

"It's a very long story. Maybe some day we'll have a chance to talk about it. But, first we have to see what we can do about getting you in to see your nana and I think I can help."

"How can you help her?" Joy quipped. "Her mother doesn't want anyone to see Lorna Belle."

TM reached into her purse, withdrew a black wallet and flipped it open. "Do you see this gold badge with the State of Florida seal in the center of it?"

"Yes. It's pretty," Joy responded with a frown. "Are you a cop?"

"No I'm not a police officer. I'm a State of Florida nursing home inspector and I can get in to see Lorna Belle. When the nursing home people see this badge they know that I can close them down if they don't cooperate with me. I'll go over to Palm City right after I leave here and review your nana's file."

"TM can you get my nana out of the nursing home?"

"No I can't get her out, but I can certainly get in to see her. I'll pull her file, make copies of the relevant material and then I'll interview her in her room."

"What if they suspect something?" Mack asked. "Won't interviewing her look suspicious?"

"I'll pull several files, make notes, copy a few pages and interview several residents. The nursing home staff will think it's a random selection. It's normal procedure in an audit."

"What will you do with the information?"

"I'll come back here and go over it with you. Will you be here about two-thirty?"

"I don't think so. I have a lot of things to do yet this morning and this afternoon. Besides at two-thirty you should be on your way to pick up your grandfather from the nursing home."

"Your grandfather's in a nursing home too?" Polly Jo inquired as she set her empty orange juice glass on the table. "Is he in the same place as my nana? Maybe they can see each other?"

"No. He's in a different place, but it would be nice if they could see each other some day." TM rose from the table. "I'd better get on my way. I have to stop at my grandmother's house and pick up a few things before I leave for the nursing home."

Mack rose simultaneously and pulled back her chair. "I'll walk you to your car."

"Thank you."

"We'll do the dishes and get things straightened up in the kitchen." Joy offered. "It was nice meeting you TM. I hope we'll see you again soon."

"I certainly hope so," TM responded. "Bye Polly Jo. I'll do what I can for your nana."

"Thank you. Please tell her that I'm here and that I tried to get in to see her yesterday."

"I will."

Mack guided Thelma Marvette to the front door. Once they were outside and beside her car, far out of Joy and Polly Jo's earshot, Mack opened the conversation.

"We have to be very careful with what we say in front of Polly Jo. I'm not certain what she does and doesn't know about her grandmother. Something strange is going on around here."

"What exactly do you mean?"

"Her mother lives in Boston and also has a home on Sewall's Point. I think it may be Lorna Belle's old house, but I'm not sure about that either. She cut Lorna Belle off from everyone, including her own granddaughter, put her in a nursing home, sold her trailer and had the trailer lot dug up with a backhoe. The dismantled trailer was found behind a plant nursery in Palm City. It was ripped to shreds and it appeared that someone was looking for something."

"What do you think they were looking for?"

"What was your grandfather melting down in the back yard?"

"It appears to have been gold. What does that have to do with Polly Jo's grandmother?"

"Do you recall I told you that your grandfather protected Polly Jo's mother and her grandmother during the big hurricane in nineteen forty-nine?"

"Of course! I don't have Alzheimer's yet."

"When an eye of a hurricane is passing through there's about twenty minutes of calm until the backside comes through. During the eye your grandfather and Polly Jo's grandmother walked down to the beach and found the remains of a Spanish treasure ship that was uncovered during the storm. They found the captain's cabin and the gold cache below it. Your grandfather took an axe to the wooden hull and broke it open. They removed nine boxes of gold doubloons and never told anyone about it. There were three thousand doubloons in each box. Each one contained almost an ounce of ninety-two percent pure gold – that equates to twenty-two carat."

"Those old moldy wooden boxes I found in the storage shed are treasure chests?"

"That's correct. Your grandfather melted down the doubloons into nine-ounce ingots and Lorna Belle sold them to jewelers for cash. They made a lot of money."

"Where is it? My grandmother's broke!"

"I don't know. That's why I was trying to see your grandfather. I think he's the only one who knows. Lorna Belle told me that he hid the boxes in the storage shed behind his house, melted down the doubloons, brought the ingots to her and she sold them."

"That's why he had the green sand molds and a naphtha burner!"

"That's correct. I suspect that Lorna Belle's daughter put her in the nursing home to get her out of the way, pretended to sell her trailer and ripped it apart to find the gold. It wasn't there and someone is still looking for it. That's why I told you to be careful with what you say in front of Polly Jo. I don't know which side she's on."

"I didn't see any full boxes in the shed. But I didn't look under the old canvas tarp."

"Be careful when you lift up the tarp. Lulu might be there."

"Who's that?"

"That's the name your grandfather gave to a female opossum who lived under the tarp."

"That was a long time ago. Opossums don't live forty years."

"Are you certain? I'm not. I've seen some really old opossums. Are you an opossum expert?"

"Of course not! It's just common sense. Animals have shorter life spans than humans."

"Seeing as how your mind is already made up about opossums I won't bring up elephants and tortoises. How did your grandfather wind up in a nursing home?"

"After his stroke my grandmother tried to take care of him. When it reached the point that she couldn't physically take care of him any longer she had to put him in the nursing home."

"When was that?"

"It will be a year next month. They had some money saved up and that's what she used. When I found out after my mother's death that I had grandparents I flew down and went to see her. I gave her ten thousand dollars to help with his care. It's all gone."

"Does your grandmother know about the gold?"

"She doesn't believe it. The doctor told her he has dementia because he rants about buried treasure to anyone who will listen to him. And he gets furious when people laugh at him."

"He should! He's the only one who knows where the gold is."

"What are you going to do?"

"I'm going to the library to do some research on pirates and buried treasure. Then I'm going downtown to see a man who likes gold. After that I'll run by the nursing home and bail your grandfather out. Send someone else with your grandmother to pick him up. Don't go yourself because someone on the staff might see you. I have a feeling that someone there has already determined that your grandfather's babblings are not fantasies."

"I don't know anyone with a car. I'll send her in a cab."

"No. That's not a good idea. It'll cause suspicion."

"How about Joy? I'll bet she'll take me."

"No. She has to stay here and keep an eye on Polly Jo for me. I have to be certain that Polly Jo stays put while I'm gone. She could mess up everything if she gets loose."

"Then who else?"

"How about a Martin County Sheriff's Deputy? I know Elmo very well. He'll do it for me."

"What? Send a cop? That might not go over very well in my grandfather's neighborhood."

"That's about the only choice we have. I'm not worried about how it goes over. Besides if a Sheriff's deputy comes in with her there won't be any question that he'll be released."

"Why don't you have him meet us at a neutral location and pick up my grandmother? He can take her to the nursing home and bring her and my grandfather back. How about the Blake Library parking lot? It's a public place and not very far from the nursing home."

"That's an excellent idea. Be at the back of the Blake Library at three o'clock and park in a fifteen-minute space. Watch for a Martin County Sheriff's car to arrive and flag him down."

"How will I know if he's Elmo? How do I recognize him?"

"You'll know that it's Elmo. There's only one. They broke the mold after they made him."

"Okay. When will I see you again?"

"After you get your grandfather home and buttoned down give me a call. The marina number is on the business card. Wait! Better yet. Call me on my cell phone." Mack pulled a marina business card out of his shirt pocket, jotted a number on the back and handed her the card.

"Why can't I call you at the marina number?"

"There are to many sets of eyes and ears here."

"Okay. I'll call you about five o'clock," Thelma Marvette got in her car and drove off.

Mack realized that time was slipping away. He had a lot of things to do and not much time to do them in. He glanced at his watch. It read 10:07. He still had to shave and shower before he could head for the library. Plus, he had to brief Joy and Polly Jo on what to expect and how to behave before he left. There were many loose ends any of which could cause a big snag in the chain of events that he had to orchestrate today. He turned and headed for the cottage.

"How am I going to keep Polly Jo from leaving the marina?" He mumbled to himself as he stepped onto the front porch. *"The dolphins! She can spend the day playing with Puka and Kea."*

Joy was waiting for him when he entered the cottage. "You really like her don't you?" Joy smiled and dug him in the ribs with her left elbow. "She's cute and I think she likes you too."

"What are you talking about?"

"She really likes you a lot. I can tell by the sparkle in her eyes."

"Joy I met her a couple of weeks ago when I stopped at a nursing home to see her grandfather. I'm going to help her get him out of the nursing home and she's going to help Polly Jo get in to see her grandmother. That's it. No more discussion. I have to take a shower and get cleaned up."

"Where're you going? Are you going to meet TM somewhere for a romp on the beach?"

"No! Polly Jo. Come over here please. I want to talk to you about what you can do while I'm at the library."

"Can I go stay over at Joy's house? We get along just great! Your dog's still over there and he likes me."

"I suppose as long as you don't get in Joy's way. I'm sure that she has a lot of things to do today. Don't you Joy?"

"As a matter of fact I don't have much of anything to do with Ralph being gone all week. I've cleaned the house from top to bottom, washed the clothes and even cut the grass. She's welcome to come over. What time do you expect to be back? We'll have dinner ready for you."

"I should be back about five or five-thirty if all goes well. If she gets bored take her down to the lagoon and let her swim with Puka and Kea. They'd like that."

"Do you mean I can swim with wild dolphins? Do they bite?"

"Yes as long as you don't leave North Lake and they don't bite."

"Yippee! I get to swim with real dolphins! Yippee!"

"What do you want me to tell Tina if she calls?" Joy inquired with a sly smirk. "Should I tell her that you have a new female friend?"

"Tell her anything you want! We're not married and she's not my keeper."

"But she's still your boss and she owns this place. You should keep her informed."

"Thank you for reminding me," Mack replied with a wave of his hand as he strode toward the bathroom. "Tell her that I eloped with TM and we're going to honeymoon in Barbados."

"What should I do with this wooden box and picture frame that you gave me?" Polly Jo asked as she waved the cedar box over her head in a spinning motion. "It's cute, but it's empty."

"I don't care what you do with it. Your grandmother asked me to give it to you. It's not empty. Inside there's a little wooden frame and a brochure from where she used to work."

"It looks like a little treasure chest. Do you suppose it had treasure in it like gold coins, pearls, diamonds and fancy jewelry?"

"To your grandmother it's a treasure chest. That's all she has left in the world and she gave her treasure to you. Take very good care of it because it is very old."

"How old is it? Is it older than my grandmother? She's pretty old."

"Yes. It's a lot older than your grandmother and possibly very valuable. At least to her."

Mack left the marina at 10:47 A.M. and sped north on Old St. Lucie Boulevard toward East Ocean Boulevard and the Blake Library. He some important research to do.

Chapter 26

When he reached East Ocean Boulevard Mack turned left and headed west toward Monterey Road and the Blake library. He was momentarily held up at the traffic light and when he finally swung into a parking place it was 11:13 A.M. It seemed strange that on a Wednesday morning almost all of the library parking spaces were filled. Mack passed the book-reading ivy-covered, bookworm statue, entered the double doors, turned to his left and headed for the research desk. A tall, attractive brunette woman, perhaps in her mid-twenties, sat behind the desk.

Mack approached the desk and posed a question. "Excuse me young lady. The other day I checked out several books about the Spanish treasure fleet that went aground here in a hurricane in seventeen fifteen. I still have them, but I need a little more information. Perhaps you could help me?"

"Yes sir. I'll try my best. My name is Johanna. What exactly are you looking for?" Her lithe fingers poised over the computer keyboard. She was ready to look when he gave her the go-ahead. Her fingers quivered in anticipation of the first key word that came out of his mouth.

"I'm looking for pirates that operated in this area in the early seventeen hundreds and perhaps buried treasure here. Do you know about any of them right off the top of your head?"

"The most famous pirate in this area was Don Pedro Gilbert. He was here in the early eighteen hundreds. There's a coral reef offshore of the House of Refuge called Gilbert's Bar and it was named after him. At night his crew would stand along the rocks in front of The House of Refuge and signal passing ships with a small fire on the beach. That's a signal used by stranded sailors to signal a ship. The ship would come close to investigate and go aground on Gilbert's Shoal. The pirates would row out to the ship in their longboats, slaughter the crew and pillage the ship. No one knows if Don Pedro Gilbert buried any treasure here, but his headquarters was in the High Point section of Sewall's Point. He often anchored his ships around the Two Cent Hill in an area the pirates called the Bleech Yard.   The freshwater killed the barnacles attached to the ship's bottom and they fell off thus increasing the speed of the ship. The pirates washed their ship's sails in the clean river water and spread them out on the sand hill to dry. That's why that sand hill was called the Bleech Yard."

"I know about Don Pedro Gilbert. He was hung in Boston in eighteen thirty-four. There weren't any Spanish treasure ships passing through here when he was active. I'm looking for pirates who were here much earlier than that. In the seventeen hundreds Spanish treasure ships en route to Spain first stopped at Havana, Cuba for supplies and repairs. From there they sailed north, along the east coast of Florida, picked up the Westerly Trade Winds north of Jacksonville and sailed across the Atlantic Ocean to Spain. I'm looking for pirates who may have plundered some of the Spanish treasure ships and needed a place to temporarily stash their ill-gotten bounty. Johanna do you have any ideas?"

"Don Pedro Gilbert is the only local pirate I ever heard about. Would you mind waiting a few minutes while I check our reference system? Most people who come in the library asking about treasure are interested in the 1715 Spanish Plate Fleet that went aground here in a hurricane."

"Take your time I'm doing research for a book I may write in the future."

"Oh. You're an author?"

""Not yet. I have aspirations, but I have to do my research."

"Hey! I found somebody you might be interested in. Captain Henry Jennings was an English pirate who lurked here and the Bahamas in the early seventeen hundreds. It says that Jennings raided the Spanish salvager's ships as they left the Treasure Coast and headed back to Cuba with their salvaged treasure. The Spanish treasure salvers and their Indian helpers were lightly armed and unable to fend off the fierce English pirates."

"That's sounds exactly like the guy I'm looking for. Does it say where he headquartered?"

"From what I can see here Jennings spent quite a bit of time along the Treasure Coast preying on the Spanish salvage fleet. According to this source he established a home base in Nassau where he easily eluded the Spanish Navy. Several other pirate captains joined Jennings in Nassau because they liked the closeness to the eastbound Spanish shipping lanes that transported gold and silver from South America to Spain. Captain Jennings retired to Bermuda and apparently did very well for himself along the Treasure Coast."

"Did he bury any of his ill-gotten loot in this area?

"It doesn't indicate that he buried any treasure. It just says that he preyed on the Spanish treasure fleets as they passed through here and kept his headquarters in Nassau. I suppose if he had more treasure onboard his ship than he could easily handle it would be easy to bury it somewhere along the coast. He could always come back and get it if he had a map. Is there anything else I can help you find?"

"No thank you Johanna. You found all the information that I need at this time. If you don't mind would you please print out the page you're reading for my research files?"

"No problem sir. I'll push this button and it'll come out of that printer right over there. Here it is." She pulled a single sheet of white paper out of the inkjet printer and handed it across the counter to Mack. He nodded a 'thank you' and headed toward the front door. It was 11:48 A.M.

"Lorna Belle might have told me a little white lie about where she and her pal Frank found those gold doubloons. It seems to me that the Spaniards would find it relatively easy to salvage the gold from the aft section of a galleon that washed up

on the beach. " Mack muttered under his breath as he went out the door. *"There's no doubt in my mind that she and Frank found some gold coins. He melted them down into ingots and she sold them for cash somewhere in the area. The coins must be from the 1715 Spanish Plate Fleet because they're dated 1714. Perhaps they did find the captain's quarters and the gold horded below the poop deck after the hurricane. Or, perhaps they found gold buried by the pirate captain Henry Jennings who buried it to keep it away from the Spaniards while he plundered their treasure ships."*

Mack turned right out of the library onto Monterey Road, turned left onto East Ocean Boulevard and headed for downtown. The jewelry shop was on Osceola Avenue. He pulled into an empty parking place in front of the Arcade Building at 12:03.

The tiny silver bell mounted over the jewelry store door chimed out a crisp greeting as Mack entered. The proprietor looked up from his workbench and pushed the brass-trimmed loupe above his highbrow so he could use both eyes to see who came into the store.

"Good morning sir," the jeweler cheerily offered. "I had a feeling that I would see you again." The jeweler ended his sarcastic greeting with a smirk and folded his arms across his chest. "What can I do for you this fine morning?"

Mack strode across the room, stopped at the glass-topped display counter, pulled two gold doubloons out of his pant's pocket and held them at arm's length toward the smirking jeweler. "I had second thoughts about selling you these coins. I now realize that you made me a fair offer."

"What you're telling me," the smirking jeweler responded, "is that you checked around and found that you can't dispose of them by yourself. My offer stands at twenty-five hundred each."

"I remember your offer. I also realize that you will make between five hundred and a thousand dollars profit on each coin, but that's okay. You're in business to make a profit."

"I don't have enough cash on hand to buy very many of them right now. In the future give me at least one day's advance notice as to how many you going to bring in so I have time to get down to the bank and have cash on hand."

"I have two of them with me today." Mack placed the coins on a black felt display panel on the countertop. "I'd like the money in one hundred dollar bills. I have some bills to pay today."

"The smirking jeweler approached the display counter and reached out to remove the two coins from the display panel. Mack reached out with his right hand, placed it under the jeweler's hand and blocked him from touching the coins. "If you don't mind I'd like to see the cash in advance." Mack smiled and gently guided the jeweler's hand away from the coins.

"Absolutely no problem sir. Please wait while I go back to the safe and determine if I have enough cash on hand to make the purchase. Do you want a receipt?"

"No thanks. I don't need a receipt. It leaves a paper trail. You should know that. Hurry if you don't mind. I have a lot of things to do today and I don't have much time."

"I understand sir. Wait just a minute. I'll be right back." The jeweler slipped around the door into another room. Apparently he had a 'special' safe hidden somewhere else in the building because Mack could plainly see a large safe right behind the jeweler's worktable.

After several minutes the jeweler returned carrying a bulky legal-size brown envelope in his right hand. He smiled and placed the envelope on top of the glass display case. "In this envelope is five thousand dollars in one hundred dollars bills just as you requested. Would like to count it?" The jeweler smiled and pushed the envelope across the counter in Mack's direction.

"I don't have to count it. I know where you live. If you find that these coins are not up to the quality that you expect let me know and I'll replace them."

"What do you mean you'll replace them?" The apparently stunned jeweler inquired. "Are you telling me that you have more of them?"

"I have a few and I'd prefer to do business with just one person. You could be that person if you can keep your mouth shut and come up with enough cash." Mack clasped the envelope under his arm and headed for the door. "It was nice doing business with you."

The shocked jeweler started to respond, but Mack was out the door before the words formed in his brain could get to his mouth. He settled for muttering to himself, *"That dumb bastard knows what he has and I think he has a lot more of them. I'd better give my cousin a call and tell him that he was here."* The jeweler reached for the telephone and dialed a number.

Mack swung around Confusion Corner and headed down East Ocean Boulevard. It was 12:34. *"That little slime ball knows a lot more about these coins and where they came from than what he let on. His eyes really lit up when he saw them. He knows exactly where they came from and I have a gut feeling that he processed a lot of them through his store over the years. I'll even wager that he even bought quite a few nine ounce gold ingots shaped like cigars."*

Mack pulled into the nursing home parking lot at 12:49 P.M. stuffed the envelope under his arm and headed for the front door. He smiled when he imagined what the snotty receptionist would say when he piled $4000 in $100 bills on the counter in front of her. Apparently she saw him coming and had alerted the nursing home administrator because he was standing at the reception desk when Mack walked through the door. The administrator smiled and stepped forward toward Mack with his right hand extended for a handshake.

"Mr. McCray. It's nice to see you again. However I still cannot allow you see Mr. Holmes and I explained why when you were here before. Is there something else I can do for today?" The balding, bloated, middle-aged man looked stupid with his right hand extended in midair.

"I'm not here to see Mr. Holmes. I'm here to pay his bill," Mack emphatically stated. "I want this to be an anonymous gift. His wife only needs to know that the bill was paid in full and she doesn't need to know by whom. Do you think you can keep this little secret just between us?"

"Yes sir Mr. McCray. We can keep this transaction confidential. No one needs to know how his bill was paid. Are you planning to pay for his future stay as well?" The smiling administrator asked and nodded toward the brown envelope under Mack's arm.

"No. He won't be here next month. His wife is coming by about three o'clock this afternoon with a Martin County Sheriff's Deputy to pick him up. I assume that you'll have no problem releasing him to his wife. Or, will you?"

"It's very unusual for someone to anonymously pay a resident's bill and ask for them to be released. I suppose it's okay because Mrs. Holmes is the responsible party and she registered him into our facility. Step up to the counter Mr. McCray. Sheila will locate Mr. Holmes's statement and determine the current balance. He nodded at the frowning receptionist and motioned to Mack to join him with a wave of his hand. Mack obliged and stepped in front of the counter.

"Here it is," the receptionist offered as she opened a manila file folder. "The current balance is four thousand, two-hundred sixty-seven dollars and thirty-four cents. Do you think that you can handle that amount?" She smiled, closed the folder and placed her folded hands over it.

Mack turned toward the grinning administrator. Please inform your employee to mark the invoice paid in full and account closed." Mack glibly responded as he pulled the brown envelope from under his arm, turned it upside down and spilled the five stacks of rubber band wrapped $100 bills onto the counter.

"I'm going to pay Mr. Holmes' bill in one hundred dollar bills. Here are four stacks of one-thousand dollars each," Mack said sarcastically and smiled as he pushed the four stacks of crisp $100 bills toward the administrator. "And three single one hundred dollar bills to cover the two-hundred sixty-seven dollars and thirty-four cents."

"It's certainly okay with us Mr. McCray," the administrator crisply responded. "Sheila will write you out a receipt. I will inform the orderly to give Mr. Holmes a bath and pack up his clothes and personal items. You may advise Mrs. Holmes that he'll be ready to go at three o'clock. Mr. McCray did I hear you correctly that a Martin County Sheriff's Deputy will be accompanying Mrs. Holmes? Is that really necessary?"

"You heard correctly. Mrs. Holmes is unable to drive. Do you have a problem with it?"

"I don't see any problem at all sir." The administrator reached for the four piles of $100 bills.

Mack placed his hand over the bills. "I assume that you'll maintain the confidentiality of my gift?" Mack inquired. "And mark the invoice paid in full?"

"Yes sir. Our records indicate that Mr. Holmes' bill was paid in full by an anonymous donor."

Mack removed his hand from the stacks of $100 bills and gently pushed them toward the administrator's outstretched hand. The receptionist handed Mack a receipt stamped 'paid in full.'

"Thank you Mr. McCray. It was nice doing business with you. Maybe we'll see you again?"

"I don't think so. What happened to the black woman, TM I believe, that worked here?"

"It was unfortunate. She had her own ideas as to how things should be run around here and didn't accept that she was just an employee. She thought she was a manager or something! People who move down here from up north want to do things here the way they did them where they came from. She was a perfect case of northern mentality and just didn't fit in with everyone else. We couldn't change the way we do things just to suit her."

"Did you fire her?"

"Oh no! We couldn't do that! She just up and quit with no notice. She walked out yesterday afternoon after causing a very bad scene here at the front counter with Sheila. Unfortunately I didn't get an opportunity to give her an exit interview, but Sheila filled me in about what happened and wrote a detailed report. I put it in the girl's file in case we get audited by the state or sued for racial discrimination."

"What happened? She seemed to be a nice person."

"I can't discuss our employees with you. That's confidential information."

"I understand," Mack softly responded with a frown as he stuffed the remaining stack of $100 bills into the brown envelope. "Thank you for your confidentiality." Mack didn't wait for a reply, and headed for the front door.

"That was easier than I thought it'd be. Without a doubt that fat bastard will tell everyone in town that I paid Frank Holmes'

bill," Mack thought to himself on the way out to the parking lot. *"He has no idea where the money came from, but as small as this town is I'm certain that he'll do his best to find out."*

It was 1:23 P.M. and Mack was hungry. *"Luna's sounds real good for lunch. It's past one o'clock and most of the lunch customers should be finishing up and going back to work. Some hot buttered garlic knots and homemade ravioli will hit the spot. I've still got lots of time before I have to get over to Palm City to see Lorna Belle,"* Mack thought as he drove down East Ocean Boulevard toward downtown Stuart.

He pulled into an empty parking space in front of the Lyric Theater just as a large group was leaving Luna's. *"Looks like it should be easy to get a table,"* he mumbled as he stuffed the brown envelope under the truck seat. Mack paused inside the doorway to allow his eyes to become used to the dim light inside the restaurant. When he could see he realized he shouldn't have stopped there for lunch!

"Mr. McCray! How nice to see you again so soon," chimed out the jeweler from a booth in the back of the restaurant next to the soft drink cooler. "We just got here and have room at our table. Why don't you join us for lunch? I'll treat!"

Shocked at the unexpected outburst Mack stood in awe and didn't know how to respond. The little slime ball was waving at him from a booth next to the cold drink cooler in the rear of the restaurant. Mack waved back and nodded in acknowledgement. *"That slime ball is the last person that I wanted to see again much less eat lunch with,"* Mack thought to himself as he maneuvered his way through the diner-filled tables toward the back booth.

The jeweler stood up when Mack reached the booth and waved him toward a seat. "Mr. McCray I'm so glad that you could join us. This is my cousin Vinny from Boston. He's in town for a few days. Vinny this is the guy I was telling you about."

"Pleased to meet you Vinny," Mack responded as he slid into the booth. "Exactly what did he tell you about me?"

"He was just telling me that he bought some gold Spanish coins from you today."

"He did?" Mack looked the nervous jeweler in the eye as he spoke. "I thought we agreed to keep our little transaction between ourselves?"

"Vinny's my cousin. He isn't going to say anything to anybody. He's safe!"

"I don't care who he is. We had an agreement." Mack slid out of the booth and stood up. "It's very unfortunate for you because now I have to find someone else to do business with."

"Hold on for just a minute," the jeweler pleaded as he grabbed Mack's wrist.

"Why should I? We had an agreement and you violated it!"

"Sit down and we'll talk about it. Vinny knows a lot of people in New York in the gold and jewelry business. He can move a lot of stuff with no questions asked. What do you say?"

"Not interested," Mack sharply responded as he brushed the man's hand away and turned to leave. "You had your chance and you blew it." Mack walked away toward the door.

"Mr. McCray! Come back and we'll talk about it some more," the jeweler pleaded in vain.

Mack went outside, ordered two slices of pepperoni pizza and a big glass of sweet ice tea from the 'take out' window and left. *"I'll stop over at Shepherd's Park and share my pizza with the squirrels. I won't get any arguments out of them,"* he mumbled to himself as he swung the blue pickup truck down West Ocean Boulevard. *"They might steal a crumb or two of my pizza, but at least I can see them doing it and they won't take it out of my pocket."*

Mack pulled into the nursing home on Loop Road at 3:17 P.M. He removed five $100 bills from the brown envelope, stuck them in his shirt pocket and shoved the envelope under the seat. *"I have a bad feeling about this,"* he thought to himself. *"But I've also got a feeling that the ugly bastard blocking the door might let me in to see Lorna Belle if he has a couple of these green bad boys in the palm of his hand."*

Mack swung open the front door and the huge black orderly was waiting for him. He stood in the entranceway with his massive arms folded across his barrel chest and a frown on his face. He reminded Mack of a black 'Mr. Clean'.

The orderly glared at Mack and stated his challenge. "You cannot see Miss Mobley under orders of her daughter. You caused some big problems for her the last time and it's my job to keep you out." The orderly took a giant step forward toward Mack, unfolded his arms and placed his hands on his hips. It was body language for a challenge and obviously meant, "I dare you!"

Mack responded with a smile, reached into his shirt pocket and removed the wad of five $100 dollar bills. He peeled off the top $100 bill, held it at arm's length in front of him, opened his fingers and watched it gracefully glide to the tiled floor. He peeled off a second $100 bill and repeated his performance. This time the bill landed on top of the orderly's shoe and the giant of a man stood in silent amazement. He didn't know what to do or how to respond. Mack smiled, removed a third $100 bill, held at the big man's eye level and slowly released it from his fingertips. The crisp bill fluttered lazily from side to side and joined its companion on the big man's shoe tip.

"If you bend over to clean up that mess I just might be able to slide by you and drop by Room 126 to see Miss Lorna Belle Mobley for just a minute. What do you think?"

The stunned orderly didn't know what to say and simply stared at Mack with large eyes the size of saucers. Clear drool rolled out the side of his mouth and ran down his cheek.

"Sir I can't let you in to see Miss Mobley, but I just might have to use the bathroom for just a minute. That is if you don't mind. Would you mind waiting here while I'm gone?" He bent over, picked up the three $100 bills and stuffed them into his pants pocket.

"I don't mind at all," Mack responded with a smile. "Take your time. I'll wait right here for you to come back." Mack was pleased with himself. He'd dropped only three of the $100 bills and was prepared to drop all five of them if that's what it took. "I'll be standing right here when you get back. I promise. You trust me don't you?"

"Yes sir I trust you to wait right here. I'll be gone from here for at least fifteen minutes because the bathroom's all the way down that hall." The big man nodded toward the opposite hallway from Lorna Belle's room, smiled and turned to go down the hallway.

"I'll be standing right here with a smile on my face when you get back. Take your time."

After the orderly turned the corner Mack dashed up the short entranceway hallway, turned left and headed for Lorna Belle's room. The hallway was empty and Room 126 was the second to the last room at the far end of the hall.

The interior of the room was dark just as it was on his first visit and the wingback chair faced the window. Lorna Belle was slight of build and Mack didn't expect to be able to see her from behind the chair. Not wishing to startle her if she was asleep he softly called out, "Lorna Belle. Are you awake?" There was no response. Mack softly slipped up alongside the chair half expecting to find Lorna Belle fast asleep, but the chair was empty. He glanced toward the bed and it was neatly made. He pulled open the top dresser drawer and it was empty! A look around indicated that the room was strangely empty as if no one lived there. *"What the hell!"* Mack exclaimed under his breath. *"Where'd she go?"*

He half ran and half walked down the hallway to the nurse's station. It was manned by a bored, middle-aged, fake blonde female nurse watching television. "Can I help you sir?" She managed to squeak out without taking her eyes off the television screen.

"I'm here to see Lorna Belle Mobley. She's supposed to be in room one twenty-six, but she isn't there. Did she change rooms?"

"Naw," the fake blonde responded without missing a word of television dialogue. "Her daughter checked her out about an hour ago."

"Checked her out! Where did she take her? I need to talk with her. It's very important!"

"Sorry. I don't have that information and even if I did I couldn't give it to you."

Mack turned away and ran down the hall toward the entranceway *"That white-jacketed monster must know something. They had to take her out the front door. It's the only way out of here,"* he muttered under his breath.

Mack turned the corner and stopped short. The orderly wasn't there! *"That bastard! He knew Lorna Belle wasn't here. He took me for three hundred bucks!"* Mack stammered. *"They knew I'd come back looking for her and they put her away where I'll never find her!"*

Mack ran out the front door of the nursing home, jumped into his truck and headed for Port Sewall Marina. *"If they know that I'm looking for Lorna Belle they know that I'm getting close to the answer. My God! Polly Jo's at the marina! If they got to Lorna Belle they'll go after Polly Jo and Frank Holmes next."*

It was 4:27 P.M. when Mack turned off Indian Street onto Old St. Lucie Boulevard for a straight shot to Port Sewall Marina. He rounded the curve at Whiticar's Boat Yard and headed for the marina driveway. He didn't anticipate trouble, but trouble was waiting for him. A Martin County Sheriff Deputy's patrol car was in the marina parking lot. Polly Jo, Joy, TM and Elmo sat in a somber row on the front porch. Joy was crying and Polly Jo cradled her head in her lap. A fierce scowl framed TM's face and Elmo stared at his feet.

However, the dog was happy to see Mack. His stubby tail wagged furiously as he leaped off the porch to greet him.

Chapter 27

Mack was distraught over losing contact with Lorna Belle and he feared for her safety. There was no telling what her daughter might do to keep her from communicating with him. When Mack drove into the marina parking lot Elmo dashed toward his truck at a trot. Before Mack could get out Elmo came alongside and held the truck door closed with his hands.

"You've got big problems," Elmo whispered with a sorrowful look on his face. "I called your cell phone to warn you, but you didn't answer. I don't know how you're going to handle it, but you've got three very upset women sitting over there on the porch. They know everything."

"What are you talking about?"

"Joy knows about Ralph's boat."

"How could she know about Ralph's boat? I stashed it in the boathouse where nobody could see it."

"You left that teenybopper stripper here all alone while you took off gallivanting around town all day long. She snuck into the boathouse and found Ralph's boat."

"How could she get into the boathouse? I left it padlocked!"

"That wasn't hard. She was swimming in the lagoon with the dolphins and when they swam under the boathouse door she followed them inside."

"How do you know she told Joy about Ralph's boat?"

"Take a look at Joy," Elmo whispered and gestured with a nod toward the porch. "I got here fifteen minutes ago and Joy was sitting there bawling her eyes out. She hasn't moved since I got here. She knows about Ralph. What're we going to do?"

"What do you mean she knows? We don't even know what happened to him!"

"She saw the blood on the white boot and the surveyor's stake. She has a good idea that somebody did something to him and that those postcards she got were faked. What're you going tell her?"

"That depends upon what you told her."

"I told her that I found Ralph's tied up under that little bridge in the Archipelago south of Bird Island the other night and we towed it back here."

"Is that all you told her?"

"I told her that we didn't know who the blood belongs to or what happened to Ralph."

"That's exactly what we know. She has a note from Ralph saying that he went fishing in the Keys. And she got a postcard from him yesterday saying that he was having a good time and will be back Friday. I don't think there's much to worry about."

"She thinks somebody killed him and she thinks that we're covering it up."

"Elmo I should have leveled with you, but Ralph asked me to keep it quiet. Did you notice that my boat isn't in the boathouse?"

"Yes. You told me that Ralph took it over to Billy Bob's Marina for a bottom job."

"That's not exactly true. Ralph took my boat to the Keys because he hurt himself pretty bad the other night. He didn't want Joy to know that he got hurt and thought the best thing to do was to disappear for a couple of days until it healed up. He'll be back Friday. That upside-down smiley face on the postcard is his code to me that he's okay."

"Are you going to tell Joy that Ralph took your boat to the Keys?"

"Now I don't have any choice. She must be reassured that he's okay and will be home Friday. I'll go over and try to make her feel better. Keep quiet and don't say anything."

Elmo backed away from the truck door and held it open as Mack slipped out of the cab. Mack slipped the truck keys into his pocket, pasted a broad smile on his face and strode toward the front porch. "Hello ladies. Why do we all look so blue? It's a nice sunny day and it hasn't rained. What's going on?"

Polly Jo looked up at Mack as she cradled Joy's head in her arms. "You knew all long that something real bad happened to Miss Joy's husband and you hid it from her."

"No I didn't!"

"Yes you did. Admit it! I found his boat in the boathouse. There's blood all over his boot and a long wooden stake. It looks like somebody stabbed a vampire! When I saw it I screamed and called for Miss Joy to come down to the boathouse. She broke the padlock off the boathouse door and got inside with me. She screamed when she saw his boat and his bloody boot. You know that somebody did something bad to him don't you?"

"Nothing serious happened to him. When he was fishing Friday night over by Sewall's Point he slipped in the mud, fell on a surveyor's stake and got stabbed in the thigh. The doctor at the emergency room sewed him up and told him to take it easy for a few days. He's embarrassed about what happened and didn't want anyone to know. He decided to go fishing in the Keys and I loaned him my boat."

Joy looked Mack in the eye and sobbed a couple of times. "If that's true why didn't you tell me right off and save me all this aggravation?"

"Ralph didn't want me to tell you that he got hurt because he knew you would worry about it. That new medication he's taking caused him to black out and he fell on the surveyor's stake. Like he said on the postcard he'll be back Friday. You don't have anything to worry about."

"Are you sure?" Joy sniffed as a giant tear ran down her cheeks.

"He's just fine. Didn't you get a postcard from him telling you he would be home Friday?"

"Yes. When I saw the blood all over his boot and the bloody stake I thought somebody had done something bad to him. I always think the worst about things."

"Ralph's fine and he'll be home Friday. I thought it best to keep his boat inside the boathouse because Elmo blundered across it the other night."

"What do you mean I blundered across it?" Elmo asked. "It was good police work. I found it! You didn't know it was there."

"How do you suppose Ralph got back to the marina if he tied his boat up under the bridge?"

"I never thought about that," Elmo responded with a quizzical look on his face.

"After Ralph got hurt he came over here, showed me how bad the gash was and asked me to help him hide his boat under that little bridge. We didn't expect that anyone would ever find it."

"I found it," Elmo chimed in. "It wasn't hid so good under there. It was easy to spot."

"Elmo shut up!" Mack responded in a gruff tone that meant business.

"I guess that makes sense," Elmo mumbled. "It would've been a long walk home from there."

"Joy why don't you go home and relax? Ralph's just fine and he'll be home Friday."

"Are you sure?" Joy pleaded. "Mack are you really sure?"

"He's just fine and needs to be alone for a few days."

"Okay. I'll go home, have a cup of hot tea and try to relax. Polly Jo, do you want to go home with me? I can use some real good company right now."

"Of course I'll go with you. We have a lot more things to talk about now."

Polly Jo wrapped her arms around Joy and the pair traipsed off toward Joy's house on Willoughby Creek. Mack's dog was torn in his emotions. He quickly decided that he would fare better at Joy's house and took off running down the gravel road behind the two sobbing women.

Elmo shuffled over to Mack and turned his head so that TM couldn't read his lips. "You told her a very big fib. Something's happened to Ralph and you know what it is."

"Sometimes you have to tell people what they want to hear. I don't know where Ralph is any more than you do and it's best for her to think he's fishing in the Keys. What makes you think I made that story up?"

"Ralph disappeared Friday night and you didn't you didn't show up here until about noon on Saturday," Elmo responded with a grin like he had solved the mystery of the ages. "I saw your boat up on a paint rack at Billy Bob's Marina this morning. They finished the bottom job yesterday afternoon and are giving it a couple days to dry. I knew you were telling her a fib the whole time."

"I guess you got me! I suppose that you're the last great detective. Let's keep this between ourselves until we see what happens on Friday. If Ralph shows up he has a lot of explaining to do. But, if he doesn't show up we're going to have to find him ourselves."

"Finding Ralph isn't your only problem."

"Isn't finding Ralph a big enough problem?"

"That black woman on the porch calls herself TM and she's really pissed off at you.

"Why should she be pissed off at me? I bailed her grandfather out of a nursing home and it took more than four grand out of my pocket."

"I'm sure she's grateful, but she chewed my ass out real good when I got here. She said that I was supposed to meet her behind the Blake Library at three o'clock and escort her grandmother over to the nursing home to pick up her grandfather. I didn't know I was supposed to meet her and I wasn't there."

"Crap! I forgot to call you. I'm dead meat! What happened?"

"She waited until a quarter after three and was about to leave when she saw a Martin County Sheriff's patrol car pull into the parking lot of the Martin County Administration Building. She stopped the deputy and asked him if he was me. He listened to her story and called me on the radio. He asked me why I wasn't there and I told him that I didn't know I was supposed to be there. I told him it was okay and he took her grandmother over to the nursing home to pick up her grandfather."

"Do you know the deputy?"

"He's my cousin Hubert. But he didn't tell her that you forgot to call me. When I showed up here she was sitting on the porch snarling like a Bengal tiger in heat. She chewed my ass and didn't give me time to explain that you never called me."

"What did you do?"

"After she calmed down I told her that you didn't call me, but I don't think she believes me."

"I'll take it from here. It's my fault. I'll tell her that I forgot to call you and she can chew my ass. I'll take the blame"

"Good! I got off-duty at four o'clock. I have to go home and start on my 'honey do' projects. I'm really concerned about Ralph. Give me a call if you hear anything."

"I will." Mack gave Elmo a wave as he pulled away in his patrol car. "Thanks for stopping by and watching the girls for me." Mack deliberately spoke loud enough so that TM would hear him. After Elmo pulled out of the parking lot Mack walked up to the porch and sat down beside her. "How'd you make out with your grandfather?"

"My grandfather's home resting and my grandmother's in Seventh Heaven. Thank you for paying his bill. However, you need to do a better job of keeping track of your obligations. When you make a commitment I suggest that you do a better job of follow through."

"You're correct. I got tied up and forgot to call Elmo. It was my responsibility to call him and I apologize."

"That's okay. My grandfather's home and that's all that matters. But, you have a major problem with Miss Lorna Belle."

"I know. When I got to the nursing home she was gone. Her daughter had checked her out."

"That's not much of surprise considering what I learned after I left here."

"What do you mean?"

"I went to my grandmother's house before going to the nursing home. I wanted to check out the wooden boxes behind my grandfather's shed."

"How many did you find?"

"There are four whole boxes and one that's smashed. Lulu the opossum wasn't hiding under the tarp, but there was one very nasty raccoon under the workbench."

"What time did you arrive at the nursing home?"

"Eleven o'clock. I introduced myself to the administrator and asked to see a listing of the home residents. I chose six files at random for interviews including Lorna Belle's and he allowed me to interview her in her room without supervision."

"What did you find out?"

"Her daughter was there earlier that morning and told her that she knows about the gold she found on some treasure ship about fifty years ago. She also told her that they trashed her trailer and dug up the lot, but didn't find any gold."

"That explains why the backhoe was there the other day."

"What do you mean?"

"When I stopped at the trailer park her trailer was gone and a backhoe was digging up the lot where her trailer used to stand. The manager told me they were digging a hole for a septic tank."

"What's the manager's name?"

"John Thomas."

"He's the guy! He's the snitch she told me about!"

"What guy? What snitch?"

"Lorna Belle suspects that her daughter paid Thomas to keep an eye on her. That's why his wife found her laying on the trailer floor. She was snooping around. Her daughter threatened to move Lorna Belle into a state home for indigents if she doesn't tell her where the gold is hidden. Lorna Belle told her that she doesn't know what she's talking about."

"I've done a lot of checking the last couple of days. Between your grandfather and Lorna Belle there's a lot of gold from a Spanish treasure ship unaccounted for."

"What Spanish treasure ship?"

"Lorna Belle and your grandfather found part of a Spanish treasure galleon on the beach in nineteen forty-nine after a hurricane went through here. According to her they carried off nine boxes of gold doubloons and hid them in a storage shed. Your grandfather took them home in a pickup truck and melted the coins down into ingots. Lorna Belle sold the ingots to jewelry stores and they split the proceeds. That's how your grandfather could afford to send your mother to a private college up north."

"She told me that she worked her way through college."

"Maybe she did. I wasn't there."

"How much was the gold worth?"

"Back in the fifties the world market-price of gold averaged forty dollars an ounce. Each gold ingot weighed nine ounces and she sold them for two hundred dollars each. I'll guess it would be close to thirty million in today's market. I don't know how many of the gold coins your grandfather melted down and Lorna Belle converted into cash. They pulled nine boxes of gold coins off that ship and you found five boxes behind his shed. Maybe your grandfather buried the other four boxes in his backyard."

"Do you want to dig up the back yard?"

"Not yet anyway and your grandfather isn't going to be much help if he has dementia. You should spend time with him and take notes. You don't know what he might say."

"Should I tell my grandmother about the gold?"

"Don't tell her anything because she'd probably panic. If those people go after her and she knows something about the gold they're apt to do anything to get the information. It's better if she knows nothing. Tell her to pretend she has Alzheimer's and can't remember anything if anyone asks."

"She doesn't have to pretend from what I've seen. I know that my grandfather isn't nuts and I believe Lorna Belle. I have a feeling that whoever is involved in this situation isn't going to give up until they have the gold or the money."

"I agree. Someone's playing for high-stakes. I threw out some bait this afternoon and I'm waiting for a big fish to nibble. I have a feeling that it won't take very long."

"What do you mean you threw out some bait? Did you go fishing today?"

"You might say that I went shark fishing. I had the opportunity to swim with a couple of big ones and they sniffed around me pretty good. If they sense weakness they'll attack."

"What do you mean they'll attack? Attack who?"

"Me. They think Lorna Belle told me where she stashed the gold. I don't think they know your grandfather was involved in the gold operation unless the nursing home administrator told them. We have to be careful and see where it goes from here."

"Why do you keeping saying they? They who? Who besides Lorna Belle's daughter."

"I'm not sure about that either, but someone's tried to kill me twice in the last two days."

"Where does Joy's husband fit into this? She thinks he was killed."

"I think so too."

"Why?"

"Maybe he was in the wrong place at the wrong time or saw something he shouldn't have seen. Elmo found Ralph's boat under a bridge and there was no sign of him. Only a bloody boot and that surveyor's stake."

"Is the story you told Joy about loaning him your boat to go to the Keys to go fishing true?"

"It was a white lie to make her feel better."

"It sounds to me like there's a lot of very bad things going on around here."

"That nursing home administrator and his gal pal Sheila know more about your grandfather's affairs than they're letting on. I made the point of paying his bill in one hundred dollar bills. He suspects where the money came from and I'm sure the word is all over town. Everybody in this town seems to be related to each other."

"What makes you think that paying my grandfather's bill in one hundred dollar bills made him suspicions?"

"That little weasel of a jeweler that bought two gold coins from me is the town crier. I stopped at Luna's for lunch and he was in there with a cousin of his from Boston. Supposedly the guy has connections with gold and jewelry houses in New York City. I think a lot of local people know about the ship your grandfather and Lorna Belle found in nineteen forty-nine and some of them know more than they want to remember."

"What are you going to do?"

"I'm going inside and fix myself something to eat. Then I'm going to pour myself a hefty glass of warm Merlot, sit my butt in a recliner and read the library books that I checked out about lost treasure ships on the Treasure Coast."

"That sounds like a plan!"

"Tomorrow's another day and I have some more checking to do. I don't think anyone harmed Lorna Belle because they need her to find out where the gold is stashed. Keep your grandfather under lock and key because now that he's out of the nursing home he's unprotected. If I need you I'll come up to the house."

"How will you find me? You don't know my grandfather's address."

"I looked up your grandfather's name in the city directory at the library. There's only one Frank Holmes in Jensen Beach. After lunch I drove by the house and your silver Beamer was in the driveway. You didn't remove your New York license plate off the front of your car."

"You got me. It's difficult for New Yorkers to give up their roots. I'll expect to hear from you tomorrow and I'll try to find out what my grandfather knows. But there's a major problem."

"What's that?"

"He had a stroke in the nursing home. His speech is slurred and it's very difficult to understand what he's trying to say. I'll take him back to his tool shed and ask him about those five wooden boxes. Maybe that'll jog his memory and he might be able to point something out."

"That sounds like a good idea. I'll see you tomorrow."

Thelma Marvette drove out of the driveway and gave Mack a wave as she pulled onto Old St. Lucie Boulevard.

Mack turned and entered the cottage. He didn't have much to go on and had to find Lorna Belle before something serious happened to her. The clock on the kitchenette wall read 5:24. The green Sand Club brochure, the little wooden picture frame and the polished cedar box were still on the dinette table where Polly Jo left them earlier that morning.

"Apparently Polly Jo didn't care about those things her grandmother wanted her to have. I suppose that if it's not cash, a check or a money order she doesn't appreciate its value. I'll stash them away under the kitchen counter for safekeeping. If she asks about them I'll tell her where they are," Mack muttered to himself. *"If she doesn't want them I'll keep them myself. They'll make excellent conversation pieces."*

Chapter
28

It's 5:17 A.M. Thursday and Mack dozed comfortably in the big green recliner where he fell asleep the night before. The book about the 1715 Spanish Plate Fleet lay open across his chest. Vivid images of bloodthirsty, swashbuckling pirates and gold doubloons hidden in beachside grottos danced in his head. Glittering gold pieces dashed through his sleeping brain and a broad smile crossed his face as he imagined himself as a dashing pirate. His dreams of wealth and adventure came to abrupt halt when a light 'rap' sounded on the screen door.

"Mack. Wake up," whispered the raspy voice from the front porch. "I know where Ralph is. Wake up," Rat's raspy voice scratched out from under his scraggly black beard. Mack didn't respond. Rat opened the screen door, entered the cottage, slunk up alongside Mack and shook his right shoulder. "Mack you gotta' wake up," Rat rasped through his rotten front teeth. "I saw Ralph over at Sewall's Point last night. I think he's in trouble and we gotta' help him," Rat sputtered as he feverishly shook Mack's shoulder.

"Huh? What do you mean you saw Ralph?" Mack responded through a white haze that enveloped his foggy brain. "What're you talking about?" He attempted to sit up and fell back against the cushioned chair back. He shook his head and attempted to bring Rat's bearded face into focus. His eyes and brain were cluttered over with a thick milky haze."

"I saw Ralph over at Sewall's Point last night and I think he's in trouble." Rat shook Mack's shoulder ferociously. "Mack wake up!"

"Okay. Okay. Take it easy on the shoulder." Mack shook his head and the milky haze slid away into the darkness. He shook his head. "What do you mean you saw Ralph?" Mack sat up straight, snapped the library book shut and tossed it onto the coffee table. "Ralph's down in the Keys fishing. There's no way you could see him on Sewall's Point."

"I'm telling you that I saw Ralph last night! I was cat snapper fishing on the little island south of Sewall's Point where the post office used to be when I saw a raccoon running along the shore. He had something wrong with his right rear leg and couldn't run very fast. I figured that I could run him down and club him with my gaff. I ran my kayak up on shore and started chasing him."

"Did you catch him?"

"No. It ran into a hole about twenty feet up on the southeast side of the bluff. It was too dark for me to try crawling around after him and there's really big snakes up there."

"What does a raccoon have to do with Ralph?"

"When I was climbing up the bluff I heard a couple guys talking to the right and below me. I swung around to that side so I could see. It was Ralph and some guy that I never saw before. The other guy went up some wooden steps and disappeared. Ralph starting walking along the beach like he was looking for something. I hollered down at him and he looked up at me. When he saw me he covered his face with his hands and took off running up the same steps the other guy went up a few minutes before."

"What makes you so certain the guy was Ralph?"

"I've known Ralph for years and I know him when I see him. I don't understand why he ran away after I yelled at him."

"It wasn't Ralph and you probably scared the poor guy half out of his wits. What would you do if a bearded guy hiding in the bushes hollered at you? It was dark and maybe you had a little bit to much Aqua Velva and Sterno to drink before you went cat snapper fishing."

"It wasn't dark because the moon was out and I didn't have anything to drink. I'm sure it was Ralph. Why don't you go over there with me and look for yourself?"

"It's only quarter after five in the morning and anybody with any common sense is still in bed. What time was it when you think Ralph over there?"

"About eleven o'clock last night."

"If you saw him at eleven o'clock why did you wait until five o'clock this morning to come over and wake me up?"

"The tide was runnin' just right and the cat snapper's were biting good. The tide went slack about four o'clock and they stopped biting. By the time I got them iced down it was almost five. Besides I figured he'd probably gone to bed. Why do you suppose Ralph's hiding out over on Sewall's Point? Are he and Joy having problems? Does he have a girl friend over there?"

"What makes you think that he's hiding out over there?"

"I figured you knew where he was and was keeping it quiet. I saw something real strange when I got to the top of the bluff."

"What do you mean by strange?"

"When I looked over the top of the bluff I saw some people watching a backhoe dig a hole in their backyard. I thought that was pretty strange."

"They were digging a hole with a backhoe at eleven o'clock at night? That doesn't make any sense."

"It was a backhoe and they were definitely digging a hole. The guy I saw with Ralph was directing the backhoe operator with a flashlight and Ralph was watching him."

"It was probably a septic tank company digging up the septic tank to pump it out. When a septic tank plugs up and the toilets backup you don't have much choice except to call a septic tank service to clean it out right then."

"Two women were standing around the hole watching the guy work. One woman looked to be in her late forties and the other one had to be at least seventy."

"How do you know she was at least seventy?"

"She had white hair and couldn't stand up straight. The younger woman kept shaking her arm and yelling at her. I couldn't make out what she was saying because of the noise from the backhoe."

"She was yelling at her?" Mack sat up in the recliner and shook his head.

"Yes. She was shaking her arm, yelling and pointing at the hole like it was the old lady's fault the septic tank plugged up."

"How long did you hang around?"

"When the marsh mosquitoes started to bite I headed back down the bluff. I figured they were digging up the septic tank and the old lady was the only one who knew where it was. But when the younger broad slapped her I knew there was something wrong and it was none of my business. I backed down the bluff to my kayak and went back to cat snapper fishing."

"You should've come over and gotten me when you saw what was happening."

"Why? Do you get your kicks watching people dig up old septic tanks in the middle of the night?" Rat grinned from ear to ear.

"No! Septic tanks aren't my cup of tea, but this might have something to do with some of the things that have happened around here the past several days."

"Like what?"

"Ralph's been missing since Friday night and Elmo found his boat stashed under that little bridge in the Archipelago south of Bird Island. There was a bloody left boot and a bloody surveyor's stake in the boat. Something real bad may have happened to him. Joy received two postcards allegedly from Ralph saying he is in Marathon fishing, but I don't think so."

"Does Elmo have any ideas about what happened to Ralph?"

"Only Elmo knows what Elmo thinks about anything. I told him to keep his mouth shut about finding Ralph's boat."

"What did Elmo do with Ralph's boat?"

"We towed in over here and stuck it inside the boathouse. There's lots of room because my boat isn't there. Ralph took it over to Billy Bob's Marina for a bottom job when I went out of town last week. Joy found his boat in the boathouse yesterday afternoon and she's upset because Elmo and I didn't tell her what was going on. I told her that Ralph hurt himself on that bloody surveyor's stake, didn't want her to see it and went to the Keys to recuperate. I told her that he took my boat and he'll be back on Friday."

"Is that true?"

"The part about Ralph taking my boat in for a bottom job is, but my boat is setting up on stands in the boatyard. I don't know where he is or what's happened him. I have some suspicions and none of them are pretty."

"Why do you think he was watching the guy dig up a septic tank last night?"

"It wasn't Ralph. It was somebody else who looks like him."

"What makes you so sure it wasn't Ralph?"

"If it was Ralph there was no reason for him to run away when you called him."

"Who do you think it was?"

"Do you remember the manila folder that Elmo found in the Trans Am Saturday morning?"

"Of course. So what about it?"

"There was a bio and photo of everyone I know except for you. Next to Ralph's photo there was a notation indicating that he may have to be neutralized. I think that's what's happened."

"What do you mean neutralized?"

"It means to render someone ineffective or get them out of the way. I think somebody whacked Ralph and substituted a body double in his place."

"Why would they do that?"

"Someone was sent here to neutralize me and I suspect that it's Ralph's double. He whacked the guy in the boathouse Saturday morning, but he didn't realize that it wasn't me."

"Who was the guy I clobbered on the front porch Sunday night?"

"I don't know, but I have a feeling that there's still someone out there looking to get me. Whoever killed that guy figured that he did his job, but when he saw the news reports and my face on live television he knew he screwed up."

"Are you going to tell Elmo that I saw Ralph last night?"

"No. Don't say a word to him about this."

"Why not?"

"If he gets involved he'll screw everything up. Do you know which house it was?"

"I think so."

"How about if we jump in my truck, run over to Sewall's Point and you point it out? The backhoe might still be there."

"Okay, but it's only a little past five-thirty and it's still dark. I gotta' run over to the fish house in the Manatee Pocket, drop off my cat snappers and run my kayak back to Shepherd's Park. You can meet me there in about an hour. It'll be daylight then and we'll be able to see."

"The fish house opens at six o'clock and the sun comes up about six-thirty. I'd like to get this nailed down as soon as I can. Why don't you run down to the Manatee Pocket in your kayak, drop your cat snappers off at the fish house and run back up here? I'll leave the boathouse door open so you can slip your kayak inside. I don't want anyone, especially Elmo, to know that you've been here. Then we'll jump in my truck, run over to Sewall's Point and you can point out the house for me."

"It'll take me fifteen minutes to run down to the Pocket and fifteen minutes to get back here. How about if I leave my kayak at the fish house and we meet at the Queen Conch for breakfast? It's a block up the road from the fish house."

"That's the best idea you've had this morning. I'll jump in the shower and meet you at the Queen Conch in thirty minutes."

"Roger." Rat slithered out the front door, down the wooden steps to the boathouse and his waiting rubber kayak.

Mack rose from the recliner, ambled through the kitchenette onto the back deck and watched Rat idle though North Lake toward Willoughby Creek. Rat provided a key bit of information that might help solve the mystery of Ralph's disappearance and help him to locate Lorna Belle. Mack turned and walked back into the cottage. Thoughts swirled around in his head like dust devils on a summer day.

"Somebody whacked Ralph, put a body double in his place and is mailing Joy postcards from West Palm Beach to make it

look like he's in the Keys. I've got a gut-feeling that Lorna Belle's daughter and her husband were doing a little yard work last night with that backhoe and it had nothing to do with pumping out a septic tank. If Lorna Belle buried gold in the backyard and they find it there'll be no reason to keep her around. That slimy jeweler knows exactly where those gold doubloons came from because he fenced them for Lorna Belle for years. His supply ran dry when she went into the nursing home. Word travels fast in this town and I think the pieces came together for whomever's been searching for Frank and Lorna Belle's treasure trove of Spanish gold doubloons."

He sat down in the recliner, picked up the book he had tossed on the coffee table a few minutes earlier and thought aloud. *"It looks to me like there may be two sources of the doubloons in Lorna Belle and Frank's treasure trove. I don't believe her story about finding the captain's quarters of a Spanish treasure galleon and chests of gold doubloons on the beach after that hurricane. If a ship washed up on the beach in 1715 the Spanish salvage crew would've seen it quite easily, unless it was too far south from where they were doing their searching. Anyone traveling the area over the years would readily see a ship washed up on the beach.*

I suspect that the pirate Henry Jennings had a lot to do with Lorna Belle's secret. According to this book Jennings operated between the St. Lucie Inlet and Nassau during that same period. He made his fortune pillaging the Spanish salvage crews working between Sebastian and Fort Pierce and raided the Spanish salvage boats headed back to Cuba as they passed the St. Lucie Inlet. Jennings did something with the gold and other treasure he took from the salvage crews. What did he do with it? It would've been dangerous to take it to Nassau because there were other pirate bands there!

I have a feeling that Jennings stashed his excess treasure around here. If I were Jennings I'd look for a high point of land that I could use as an observation platform to watch for the Spanish salvage ships as they slowly made they way down the coast towards Cuba. If I were him I'd stash my treasure where someone would least expect it to be - like under my headquarters. The cave Rat found on the bluff might lead to Jennings's ill-gotten loot. I have a feeling that there's more gold involved in Lorna Belle's story than what she says they found on the beach and stashed in the storage shed behind the Sand Club in nineteen forty-nine."

Mack slammed the book closed, slid it under the recliner so it wouldn't be visible to people entering the cottage and headed for the bathroom. He wanted to look presentable when he introduced himself to Lorna Belle's daughter and her husband in their fancy Sewall's Point home.

Chapter 29

Mack turned off Old Dixie Highway into a parking space beside the Queen Conch. Two Martin County Sheriff's patrol cars and a Martin County arson investigator's car were parked in front of the restaurant. When Mack entered Deputy Elmo hailed him from a table in the rear of the restaurant. "Mack! Come over and join us." Elmo gestured in Mack's direction with his hand.

"I can't. I'm meeting Rat for breakfast and it looks like you're tied up," Mack responded as he slid into a chair behind an open table. *"I hope Elmo doesn't come over and start asking questions when Rat shows up,"* Mack thought to himself.

Elmo got out of his chair, came alongside Mack's table, squatted on his haunches and looked him in the eye. "There's something real strange going on around here and I think that you know more about it than what you let on. Do you know any of those guys sitting with me?"

"The only one I recognize is Mel Mangini. He's the detective that worked on Bear's case a couple of months ago."

"He's assigned to crime scene investigation and was with me investigating an arson fire at Stuart Trailer Town early this morning. The head of the Martin County Fire Marshal's arson division is also with us."

"So? What do your breakfast buddies have to do with me?"

"Were you at Stuart Trailer Town recently?

"I was there a couple of days ago to see the manager. Why?"

"The fire that we investigated at three o'clock this morning was at Stuart Trailer Town. John Thomas and his wife burned to death in their trailer. The fire was intentionally set. It was arson!"

"What makes you think it was arson?"

"There were five plastic milk jugs spread around the trailer and they had been filled with gasoline. The fire was set directly under the bedroom of the trailer and the front door was locked with a padlock. No one could get out."

"Was anyone inside the trailer?"

"The John Thomas, the trailer park manager, and his wife were inside. It was their trailer."

"Couldn't they break a window and get out?"

"Thomas tried to get out the bay window directly in the front of the trailer. We found his body draped half out of the window and a bullet hole in the middle of his forehead."

"What about his wife?"

"She was much worse off. She hid inside the bathroom and couldn't get out because the window's too small. She roasted to death. It was a nasty scene and we're very upset about it. We pulled in here a half hour ago to have breakfast and compare notes. Do you have any idea who would want to bump off John Thomas and his wife? There has to be a motive."

"No. When I was over there the other day he didn't want to talk to me."

"Why not?"

"I'm certain that the torn up trailer you found in Palm City was Lorna Belle's. When I got to the trailer park her trailer was gone and a backhoe was digging a hole for a new septic tank according to Thomas. But, I've got other suspicions."

"What other suspicions?"

"I have a feeling that Thomas was involved in some kind of activity involving Lorna Belle and her daughter, but I haven't been able to put my finger on it."

"Do you have any information that you'd like to share with the arson investigators? You might have the lead they need to solve this thing."

"I don't have anything concrete at this point. I have a feeling that isn't the only fire that you're going to see around here in the next few days. Here comes Rat." Mack pointed out the window and waved to Rat as he slogged his way up the gentle hill from the fish house. "Elmo go back there and sit with your buddies. Rat's bashful around strangers."

"It's unusual for you to be here so early in the morning especially with Rat," Elmo offered with a frown. "Why don't you tell me what's going on?"

"There's nothing going on. Rat stopped by the marina a little while ago with a cooler full of cat snappers. He's having problems with the outboard motor on his kayak and he asked me to meet him down here after he sold his cat snappers. We're going to load his kayak in my truck and I'm going to take him back to Shepherd's Park so he can work on his motor."

"Mornin' Elmo," rang out Rat's raspy voice as he slid behind the table. "What brings you in here this fine morning?"

"I asked Mack the same question. He told me that you're having outboard motor problems."

"My motor's working just fine," Rat offered with a crushed look on his bearded face. "Mack why'd you say that?"

"When you stopped by the marina you told me that your motor was missing. I offered to load your kayak in my truck and take you to Shepherd's Park." Mack blurted out and simultaneously kicked Rat's shin under the table. "Did your motor straighten itself out when you ran down to the fish house? Maybe the plugs were fouled?"

"Oh that? I forgot. It's missing a little and I gotta' feeling it's from dirty gas. You don't have to take me back to Shepherd's Park. The mechanic at the fish house is going to drain the carburetor and run some fresh fuel through it while I'm having breakfast. It'll be okay."

"I'm glad that I got to see both of you here together this morning because we may have a slight problem," Elmo offered with frown.

"What kind of a problem?" Mack asked. "I don't need any more problems."

"Were you at Sewall's Point about eleven o'clock last night?"

"No. After everybody left the marina yesterday afternoon I fixed myself something to eat and spent the evening reading a book. I fell asleep in my chair and Rat woke me up about five o'clock this morning to show off the mess of cat snappers he caught last night."

"How about you Rat?" Elmo asked with a serious look on his face. "Were you sneaking around Sewall's Point last night and peeping though bathroom windows?"

"Me peep through windows? I was cat snapper fishing last night by the little island south of Sewall's Point where the Stuart Post Office was years ago. I got done about five o'clock and stopped by Mack's place to show off the mess of cat snappers I caught. He was sleeping in that old recliner and snoring like a country hog. I figured it was time for him to get up. So, I woke him up and we agreed to meet here for breakfast after I sold my cat snappers at the fish house."

"Why are you asking Rat about Sewall's Point? He doesn't have any business over there."

"Chief B. J. Brown called me last night and told me that an influential property owner phoned in a complaint. She reported that a scruffy-looking bum with a black beard was lurking around her backyard and peering at her through the bushes while a backhoe was digging up her septic tank. The guy scared the hell out of her and two other people. Two police officers spent a couple of hours beating through the bushes and they didn't find anybody. Rat's the only guy I know that meets that description. Were you in her bushes last night?"

"Of course not! I already told you I was fishing for cat snappers. How could I get all the way from down there up to the top of Sewall's Point? The whole place is full of big snakes and they come out of their holes at night."

"Stay away from there because they have an 'All Points Bulletin' out for you." Elmo nodded at Mack "That goes for you too. My brother-in-law told me to remind you that if they catch you sneaking around over there they're going to throw your butt in jail and throw away the key. I won't be able to help you get out of it."

"Tell him that Rat wasn't sneaking around over there or peeking in people's windows. I learned my lesson the other day when those two young cops pulled me over and harassed me. The two broads walking their dogs got their rocks off when I pulled alongside and asked them for directions. They phoned in a report to the cops because I didn't ask them to get in the truck."

"Based on what he told me I don't think that's the whole story. Just remember that I warned both of you to stay away from Sewall's Point!" Elmo stood up, turned and walked back to the table to join his companions.

"We can't go over to Sewall's Point today," Rat softly hissed between his rotten front teeth. "If the cops catch us they'll put us in jail and throw away the key. Why don't you just forget about it?"

"I can't. Last night the trailer park manager and his wife were murdered. I think somebody killed them to keep them from talking to me. I don't have a choice. I have to go over there. The murder of the trailer park manager and his wife isn't where this thing is going to end by any stretch of the imagination."

"What thing are you talking about? Does this thing have anything to do with Ralph?"

"Maybe. Somebody wants me out of the way and they're not going to stop until they succeed. They saw you last night and they know that we know each other. Now you're also in danger. Maybe you're next."

"What do you mean I'm in danger and maybe I'm next? Next for what?"

"Those people you saw last night were trying to dig up buried chests of gold with that backhoe. I've got to find out which house it is and verify it with Tina. If it's the one I think it is she might know how to get inside."

"Why do you want to get in there?"

"Because if the old lady you saw last night is who I think she is her life isn't worth a plug nickel if they found the gold. It's a long story. Here comes Mary with our breakfast. Let's hurry up, eat breakfast and get out of here before Elmo drags a couple his friends over and starts asking questions that I don't want to answer."

The duo gobbled down their meal without hesitation and Mack left three singles on the table for a tip. When he walked over to the counter to pay the bill Elmo met him at the cash register. "I know that without a doubt the two of you are going over to Sewall's Point today. Be careful. I can't help you if you get picked up for trespassing. My brother-in-law made that very clear. Do you understand?"

"I understand. What're your plans?"

"I have to go to the office and file a report on the arson fire. Then I'm going home to sack out. I'm come back on duty at three o'clock. Do you want me to stop by the marina then?"

"That's a good idea, but come in your boat. Your patrol car attracts too much attention. If Joy sees you she'll come running over to find out if you know any more about Ralph."

"Do you know anything more about Ralph?"

"I don't know any more than you do. I have a feeling that Ralph's in very serious trouble. Don't tell anyone that I was at Trailer Town the other day talking to the manager. I don't want to become involved in an arson and murder investigation."

"You might be a material witness!" Elmo exclaimed loud enough for his companions sitting at the back table to hear him. "You can't duck out of being a material witness!"

"I can only be a material witness if someone knows I was there. I haven't told anyone and there aren't any witnesses."

"You told me just a few minutes ago that you were there."

"No I didn't! You made it up."

"I didn't make it up! You told me that you were there the other day, talked to John Thomas and that Lorna Belle's trailer lot was being dug up by a backhoe for a septic tank."

"I don't remember telling you any such thing and I certainly couldn't support it in a court of law. What is it about what I didn't say that you don't you understand?"

"I understand. You weren't there, you don't know anything and neither do I." Elmo turned, walked away and joined his companions."

Mack tugged on Rat's arm as he walked out of the Queen Conch and steered him toward his truck. "Get in the truck. We have to get over to Sewall's Point and find that house."

"You heard what Elmo said! If we get caught over there those cops will throw us in jail and we might never see the light of day again. There's nothing wrong with my outboard motor and I can find my way back to Shepherd's Park," Rat sputtered and turned toward the fish house.

Mack pulled Rat toward him and looked him in the eye. "You don't have any choice because you're as deep in this mess as I am. Those people know who you are and you might be the next spontaneous fire on their list. How would you like a fire on your sailboat in the middle of the night?" Mack squeezed upper Rat's arm.

"Nobody's going to burn my sailboat. People are watching it for me."

"The people we're dealing with will find a way to do anything. You're simply another set of eyes and ears that can get in their way. They'll find a way to get rid of you and it won't be pretty. I can guarantee it. Get your flea-bitten butt in my truck and let's get over to Sewall's Point." Mack released Rat's arm and turned toward his truck.

Rat paused momentarily as if he was mulling over the concept of being burned alive in the cabin of his fiberglass sailboat. He turned toward Mack and responded. "You're not giving me any choice in the matter. I guess my kayak will be okay at the fish house for a couple of hours. I'll go with you if you promise to bring me back here afterward." Rat started to make his way into the passenger's side of the blue pickup.

"No problem. I'll bring you back to the fish house when we're done."

"What're you going to do if we get caught over there?" Rat paused. "They'll throw me in jail and I'll never get out."

"Nothing's going to happen to us. Elmo was pulling your leg. The police chief is Elmo's brother-in-law. If we get in trouble I'm sure he'll help us out."

"Didn't Elmo specifically tell you that he wouldn't be able to help us out?"

"Stop worrying about it. Nothing's going to happen," Mack responded as he made a sharp right turn off of Old Dixie Highway onto Indian Street and headed east.

"Are you going back to the marina?"

"No. Joy might see me and ask questions. I prefer that she not know what's going on. I'm going up Old St. Lucie Boulevard to East Ocean Boulevard. I'll make a right and go across the Evans Crary Bridge to Sewall's Point."

Mack crossed the Evans Crary Bridge and swung south on Sewall's Point Road. The speed limit sign read thirty-five miles an hour and his truck's speedometer read thirty-four. He saw no sense in tempting fate by going over the speed limit. Mack slowed down to a crawl at the curve marking the end of Sewall's Point Road and poked Rat in the ribs with his elbow.

"Keep your eyes open and try to spot that backhoe in one of these backyards."

"If they were digging a septic tank they should be done and gone by now."

"They weren't looking for a septic tank. Keep your mouth shut and your eyes open."

Mack turned right on the curve at High Point and glimpsed flashing red and blue lights in his rearview mirror accompanied by the 'growl' of a police car siren. A second Sewall's Point police car, also with its red and blue lights flashing, blocked the road. The young police officer leaned across the hood of the police cruiser with his drawn revolver pointed directly at Mack.

"We've got a slight problem. Hunker down and keep your mouth shut," Mack whispered. "Those are the same cops who pulled me over the other day. Be quiet! Here he comes."

The young police officer approached the rear of Mack's truck with his revolver drawn and a matte black container of red pepper spray in his left hand. He cautiously approached the driver's side window and stopped three feet behind the cab.

"Driver! Put the truck into park, turn off the engine and set the parking brake. Roll down the window and stick your hands up where I can see them. Passenger you do the same."

"Yes sir," Mack politely responded in a loud voice to be certain the young officer heard him. He shoved the gearshift lever into park, turned off the ignition, pressed down hard on the parking brake pedal with his left foot and held his hands above his head.

"Driver! Reach down, remove the ignition key and throw it out the window."

Mack complied and tossed his key ring onto the shoulder on the far side of the road.

"Driver! Open your door, exit the vehicle with your back toward me and slowly walk backward toward my voice. Passenger! Keep your hands where I can see them and don't make any sudden moves."

Mack exited the truck, walked three steps backward and paused. He anticipated that the police officer had additional instructions for him.

"Driver! Drop down on your knees, clasp your fingers together and place your hands over your head. Passenger! You stay in the vehicle!"

Mack dropped to his knees, interlaced his fingers and placed his hands on top of his head. The officer's boot hit him squarely between the shoulder blades and the forcible blow thrust him face forward onto the asphalt. Momentarily stunned by the blow he instantly felt warm blood cascading through his nostrils into the split in his lower lip.

"Put your arms behind your back and don't move," barked out the young officer. Mack complied and felt him snap the handcuffs on his wrists. "Stay in that position while I take care of your grubby-looking passenger."

"Passenger! Exit the vehicle, put your hands in the air and walk backward toward my voice."

Rat dutifully complied.

"Passenger! Stop! Drop to your knees, clasp your fingers together and put your hands on top of your head."

"Yes sir," rasped Rat through his broken front teeth. "Don't shoot me."

The officer followed the same procedure as he did with Mack including the kick between the shoulder blades. However, Rat was more fortunate because his thick beard cushioned the impact on the asphalt and he didn't suffer any facial damage. The officer jerked Rat over and looked directly into his eyes. "I know you're the guy who was sneaking around in the bushes last night and scared the hell out of those people. I spent two hours:

crawling through those bushes looking for you and I'm real glad that I found you this morning. I don't know your name, but I can tell just by looking at you that you should spend some quality time in our jail to clean yourself up. Don't say a word and stand up. My partner will put you in his car and escort you to jail."

"Yes sir," Rat softly mumbled, "I understand sir."

The officer turned his attention back to Mack who sat upright on the asphalt. Blood ran out of his nostrils and down his face onto the front of his shirt. His swollen and severely cracked lower lip looked like a slice of red meat protruding above his chin. He didn't speak.

"Stand up! I'm going to put you in my patrol car and transport you to jail. You were warned not to come back here. You must have a severe hearing problem. Perhaps a stay in our jail will improve your hearing and help you to understand our rules."

"Yes sir," Mack mumbled through his swollen lip. "May I make a telephone call once we get to the police station?"

"You're not entitled to any telephone calls until you're placed under arrest," the beaming officer responded with a grin. "You're not under arrest at this time. I'm simply restraining you to protect both of us while I escort you to the station. If the chief determines that you should be placed under arrest you'll be permitted to make one telephone call after you've been processed."

"Anyone detained by law-enforcement is allowed to make one telephone call!"

"That's not the way I understand it sir," the officer responded. "Please watch your head as you get into my car. I don't want to get blood all over the window. It was washed this morning and it can't be washed again until the end of my shift."

The two-mile ride to the police station was the longest ride Mack had ever experienced in his life. He was about to learn a lesson he would remember for a long time to come.

Chapter
30

The highly irritated police chief looked across his desk at
Mack and shook his head from side to side to indicate his disgust
that he failed to heed his clear warning of two days earlier.

"Mr. McCray I definitely recall that during a similar meeting
on Tuesday I strongly advised you to stay away from this area.
Do you have a short memory span or are you just stupid?" The
rough-hewn chief tapped his desktop with the eraser end of a
yellow wooden pencil. "Mr. McCray I'm patiently waiting for
your explanation."

"BJ I can explain our reason for being over here this
morning," Mack muttered between pauses to lick the blood from
his lower lip. His severely swollen lip made it extremely difficult
to properly pronounce his words although he attempted to
enunciate each one clearly. "I have a hunch that someone on
Sewall's Point is in dire danger and her life may be in jeopardy."

"Mr. McCray address me as Chief Brown! I never invited you
to refer to me as BJ! The only thing that I see in jeopardy here is
your skinny ass and that of that vagrant bum you had in your
truck with you. I'm certain he's the guy my boys spent two hours
looking for last night."

"Chief Brown I can assure you that my friend was nowhere
near that woman's bushes last night. He was with me at Port

Sewall Marina all night. We sat around, played chess and swapped a few stories."

"I can't imagine for a minute that this bum has the slightest idea how to play chess and I'm somewhat surprised he can even talk. He smells so bad that I find it difficult to be in the same room with him."

"Are we under arrest?"

"Not yet. You're simply being restrained while I review the evidence against you before I make my decision whether you will be placed under arrest. I'm permitted to hold you for twenty-four hours without placing you under arrest," responded the burley chief with a knowing smirk. *"Check mate!"* The chief thought to himself. *"I've got this Yankee smart ass good."*

"I want to call my attorney!"

"Under Florida law once you've been placed under arrest we have to make a telephone available to you within twenty-four hours. Then you can call your attorney or anyone else who suits your fancy. That twenty-four hour clock begins once you are placed under arrest. Until then you are only being held for observation."

"Observation for what?"

"I haven't decided. My deputies indicated that you were driving erratically and have a fixation with women who walk their dogs. We have to run you through various databases to find out if you are a child molester or have any outstanding warrants. We'll have an answer shortly."

"Place me under arrest or release me. You don't have any grounds to hold me."

"Mr. McCray you've tried my patience to the limit. Boys take Mr. McCray back to the booking room for photographs and fingerprints. Then give him a new set of our clothes and toss him into a holding cell for observation. We'll pull him out tomorrow morning, put him up in front of a judge on a First Appearance and see what he has to say for himself."

"Then you have officially placed me under arrest?"

"Yes."

"Then I want to make a phone call. You can't deny me that under the law."

"I suppose you're technically correct, but I don't have to allow you to make a telephone call until you have been processed into our system. That'll easily take us an hour or so. But our fingerprint technician doesn't come on duty until eight o'clock and as you can see by the clock on the wall behind me it's only seven twenty-seven. Enjoy yourself while you're waiting. My boys will see to your every need."

"What about my friend? Are you placing him under arrest and charging him for something?"

"We're charging him with vagrancy. We checked his pockets. He has no identification and not even one dollar in cash on him. His looks, smell and totally disagreeable breath make it obvious that he's a vagrant. Mr. Mathers you're under arrest and charged with vagrancy and trespassing." The chief nodded at two additional officers who had taken up their positions behind Rat. "Boys take this filthy bum to the back, clean him up and put him in a holding cell far away from Mr. McCray."

"I didn't do anything!" Rat screamed as the two grinning officers pulled him toward the back of the police station. "Mack! Tell them that I didn't do anything!" He expected a beating.

After the two officers closed the soundproof doors Rat's verbal protests ceased. Mack thought he detected the sound of soft thuds and scuffling on the concrete floor.

Mack decided to play the cards in his hand and see how far he could string out the chief. "Chief Brown I respect your position of authority and your rationale for placing me under arrest. I'll tell my side of the story to the judge when I make my first appearance. Now I want your personal guarantee that I can make a telephone call after I've been processed."

"That's a nice change of attitude. I was getting worried about you and your snotty Yankee attitude. Didn't my brother-in-law Elmo tell you to stay away from Sewell's Point and if you got caught over here there'd be nothing he could do for you?"

"Yes he did. But, I wasn't planning on calling Elmo. He told me this morning that you advised him to tell me to stay away from here. But, I'm not a very good listener and I didn't pay attention. I'm very sorry. Now I apologized so why don't you just let us go? You and your boys got your kicks."

"I'm afraid I can't do that Mr. McCray. You violated our rules and made a general nuisance of yourself. Our residents want their privacy respected and their anonymity maintained. Boys take Mr. McCray to the back. After he's been photographed, fingerprinted, taken a shower and changed clothes allow him to make one telephone call. Mr. McCray you have to make that call collect. I certainly hope you know someone who will accept the charges."

"I hope so too." Mack offered no resistance as he was escorted toward the back of the room and the soundproof doors. He expected a thorough beating to teach him a lesson followed by an immediate release. The chief had no grounds to hold him except trumped up trespassing charges. Mack hoped he had an ace up his sleeve if he could make one telephone call.

Mack hoped the blustery chief was bluffing, but after he was photographed and fingerprinted he realized it wasn't a bluff. He was taken to a back area, ordered to remove his clothing and forced to take a shower. Afterward his street clothing was replaced with jail attire consisting of a blue jumpsuit and fabric slippers and he was thrown into an empty holding cell. He wondered what happened to Rat. Mack expected that the two officers who spent several hours the night before crawling through the bushes looking for Rat were taking their frustrations out on him somewhere else. They wouldn't expect a vagrant to file a complaint. Mack sat down on the concrete bench, folded his arms across his chest, closed his eyes and waited for the vicious scenario to play out. He expected Chief Brown to come in and apologize after he realized he had no grounds to hold him.

A brass key rattled in the steel lock, the heavy steel door swung open and Mack awoke to the harsh voice of Chief Brown. "Mr. McCray you have been processed into our system. Now you may make the one telephone call you're entitled to make. It's eight forty-seven in the morning. I hope that whomever you call is home and that you don't lose your one opportunity."

Mack sat up, attempted to get his bearings and hoped he was having a bad nightmare. When he looked down saw the blue jail jumpsuit he realized that it wasn't a dream.

Chief Brown smiled through the bars of the cell door, made a sweeping gesture with his left arm and smiled as he spoke.

"There's a pay telephone across the hall and you can have all the privacy you desire. You can only make a collect call from that phone and I hope you are on good terms with whomever you're going to call. After you've made your call you'll be put into the general jail population until it's time for your first appearance about nine-thirty this morning when the judge will hear the charges against you. After that, if you're lucky, perhaps you can find someone to post bail for you. If not you will spend some more time with us as our guest."

"Just point me toward the telephone and leave me alone for five minutes. I don't know where you're going with this charade of trumped up charges against me and my friend, but let me assure you that you're not going to get away with it."

"Trumped up charges you say Mr. McCray? I won't get away with it you say? That sounds like a threat. I don't think that you wish to be put on record as threatening an officer of the law. I'm just going to let it go by and pretend that I didn't hear it. That is unless you decide to make it an issue. Get your sorry ass over there and make your one telephone call. I certainly hope you make a good one."

After he made his telephone call Mack was taken to a large rectangular shaped cell holding twenty-four prisoners. He detected an obvious 'pecking order' by the way the prisoners positioned themselves in the chairs in front of the television set. The only other white man in the cell looked to be as mean as the devil himself and wore an orange jumpsuit. His shaven head was decorated with Nazi swastikas and blue lightening bolts. He looked like a human bulldog and had no neck. He arms were festooned with tattoos from his shoulders down to his fingertips. Mack figured he had no choice except to challenge or befriend the cell 'enforcer' at the risk of getting beat to a pulp himself. He knew that his safety would depend on it during the night.

"I hope that big, mean-looking, bald-headed bastard takes a look at my swollen lip and figures that I put up a good fight before they got me handcuffed."

Mack walked directly up to the fierce-looking man lounging against the open cell door and held out his right hand in greeting. The human bulldog ignored his gesture and looked away.

"Excuse me. I stuck my hand out to introduce myself. It appears to me that you are the man in charge around here and I'd like to be on your side. Those cops beat the crap out of me and I'm not in very good shape right now. If you don't mind I'd like to hang out with you until I get my strength back."

The human bulldog seemed taken aback by Mack's direct approach because his external ferocity scared away the other inmates. He snorted, took a deep breath, crossed his massive tattooed arms across his barrel chest and spoke. "I don't care who you are, why you're here or what your problems are. My job is to keep those punks out there in line so the guards don't have to bother with them. To them you're a fresh piece of meat. If they sense a weakness they'll tear you apart and feed your bones to the cockroaches. You can sit right over there if you keep your mouth shut." He nodded toward the toilet. "I'll do what I can to keep them away from you, but I want something from you in return for my protection."

"I don't have anything to give you."

"The guard comes around at eleven-thirty to serve lunch and I want yours. I have to keep my strength up in order to maintain my position of authority in his hellhole. You'd better be real careful when the guard brings lunch around. There're twenty-four seats available around those six tables and when you came in there were already two dozen guys in here."

"What're you trying to tell me?"

"You're odd man out when the dance music stops."

"Odd man out? Does that mean that I don't get to sit down?"

"That's exactly what it means. Each guy has staked out his regular seat around one of the tables and it's marked with a tiny piece of paper. They'll kill you if you take their seat. We aren't allowed to take our seat until each man has his own tray. I want you to take your tray over there," he nodded at the stairway leading to the upper tier of cells. "Sit your butt down on the stairwell and keep your mouth shut. Half of these guys will be nipping at your heels wanting a bite of this, or that, but it's all mine. Remember that! After the guard leaves bring your tray over here and exchange it with mine. My tray will be empty. You'll turn in an empty tray and I get to have your lunch."

"I'm liable to starve to death. What about dinner?"

"It's the same deal, but you can have the desert. It's Jell-O on Thursday night. If you're lucky someone will bail your sorry ass out of here before lights out. You're the fresh meat in here and there's not much I can do to help you after dark."

"They only allowed me one telephone call and the person I called wasn't home. I left a message on their answering machine and I might not get bailed out of here until tomorrow."

"Then you really need my help. The top bunk is empty. Slip up there and I'll do my best to protect you. They won't mess with me. They know better."

There was no mattress on the top bunk. Mack swung up onto the tubular steel framed bunk and tried to ignore the bare steel springs digging into his back. The cell's ceiling and walls were decorated with art-deco style drawings apparently done by Mack's cell companion. He was a neo-Nazi based on the slogans and swastikas on the walls and ceiling of his cell home.

"This guy is a very disturbed puppy," Mack thought to himself. *"Why was this Neanderthal so willing to share his cell and protect me if I'm considered to be fresh meat?"*

The obvious explanation wasn't very palatable from Mack's perspective. Fitfully he dozed off and awoke to squeaking wheels announcing the lunch cart's arrival at the cell doorway.

Mack's cellmate forcefully shook the upper bunk. "Remember what I told you. Pick up your lunch tray, slip over to the stairwell, sit down and keep your mouth shut. I'll signal you with my fork when my tray's empty so you can bring yours over to me. Don't do it while the guard's watching or he'll toss me in solitary for a week. If I lose my strength these guys will tear me apart when I come back here."

"I understand completely. What're you in here for?"

"Why is that important to you?"

"I'd just like to know. I might write a book someday and this would make a good chapter."

"Manslaughter. I beat a guy to death with a tire iron because he was messing with my girlfriend."

"What about your girlfriend?"

"She disappeared. Nobody knows what happen to her."

"Do you know where she went?"

"Maybe and maybe not, but even if I do I'm not telling you. Get ready! Lunch is here."

The prisoners lined up in their invisible, but highly obvious priority order at the cell door for their lunch trays. The orange-clothed enforcer was first in line and Mack took his understood place at the end of the line. When Mack was the third man from the front of the line Chief Brown walked down the hallway, paused in front of the cell door and looked directly at Mack.

"You're a very lucky man Mr. McCray. You're getting out. Step over to the cell door and put your hands behind your back."

"Why?"

"I'm going to put handcuffs and leg shackles on you for my protection. You're still under arrest and a prisoner in this facility until you are processed and released."

Mack decided not to make small talk and keep his mouth shut.

"This is your lucky day."

"Why?"

"Tina McShay called me about five minutes ago. She wants you back out on the street. She's a powerful woman in this county and she could have my ass in a minute if she tried for it."

"When am I getting out?"

"We have to put you through reverse processing and document the correct paperwork trail for your release. It'll take twenty minutes or so give or take. After you've been processed an officer will bring you to my office so we can sit down and discuss this unfortunate incident."

"What about my friend?"

"Tina didn't mention anything about him. What does she have to do with that bum?"

"He does a lot of work around the marina when I need his help. When I left the message on her voice mail I forgot to mention that he was locked up with me. Do you want me to call her and have her call you back?"

"That won't be necessary, but Mr. Mathers had an unfortunate accident in the shower. He slipped on a bar of wet soap and fell down. He's in the infirmary being X-rayed for possible rib fractures. He'll be okay in a few days."

"What you're telling me is that those two punks beat the hell out of him."

"That's a terrible accusation to make against two fine police officers. Your friend slipped on a bar of soap in the shower and fell down. That's the end of the story."

"If he's hurt I'll have you in front of the police board before you can sneeze!"

"Don't threaten me Mr. McCray. I've lived in this county all of my life. Anything you have to say won't pull any weight with anybody. After I release you I suggest that you and your friend get out of here. And don't come back." The burley police chief shoved Mack into an open doorway, turned and walked down the hallway.

"I understand," Mack mumbled under his breath as he entered the room. "I really understand."

"Mr. McCray! Shut your yap, turn to face me and stand at attention with your arms at your sides," bellowed the officer behind the desk. Mack's torment was far from over.

After filling out and signing the required forms Mack was given back his clothing, shoes and personal effects. However, the four $100 bills in his wallet were missing!

"Where's my money!" Mack demanded. "I had four hundred bucks in one hundred dollar bills in my wallet when you clowns picked me up this morning."

"According to the inventory sheet you had a watch and a black leather wallet. The wallet only contained your driver's license, a couple of credit cards and some photos. There was no money in your wallet. It's all spelled out on your charge sheet."

"What charge sheet! I'm being released!"

"You're being released on your own recognizance, but the charges weren't dropped. You're charged with trespassing. It's a misdemeanor. You'll get away with a small fine and court costs. That is unless you come back here and trespass again."

"That's really stupid! I didn't do anything!"

"Take it up with the chief.. He's waiting for you in his office."

The officer led Mack down the hall, through two steel doors and pointed at an open door. "That's the Chief's office. He's waiting for you. Good luck Mr. McCray. You'll need it."

Mack cautiously entered the spacious office and Chief B. J. Brown sat behind a massive oak desk with a frown on his face.

"Mr. McCray! How nice to see you under different circumstances. I trust that we took good care of you. My officers told me that you were very cooperative."

"Cut the crap! Where's my friend?"

"Tina authorized his release and he's being processed for release as we speak. He'll be ready to leave in a few minutes."

"How do you know Tina?"

"This is a small town. I went to high school with Tina and even dated her a few times. But, she was stuck on a football player. Her family had money and she went away to college. I wound up stuck here as a law enforcement officer. But, the town's been good to me. I haven't been shot and can retire in four more years."

"Why are you sticking me with those ridiculous charges?"

"We need the revenue. We try to recover enough revenue in fines to cover our annual operating budget, plus my retirement fund."

"My four hundred bucks went to your retirement fund?

"What four hundred bucks are you talking about?"

"The four hundred bucks that was in my wallet when your goons dragged me in here."

"According to our inventory officer you had a watch, an empty wallet and no money when he booked you this morning."

"He's a liar! He took my four hundred bucks!"

"I just told you what he told me. Do you want to press charges against my officer?"

"No. I suppose not. You'd find a way to charge me with something else stupid."

"That's a poor attitude Mr. McCray and I'm sincerely sorry that you feel that way."

"Mack cool down before you get yourself in deeper," Elmo's voice came from the open doorway. Mack turned to face him. "He's gonna' win no matter what. Just drop it and let's go."

"What do you mean let's go?"

"I called Elmo and asked him to escort you back to Port Salerno so that you don't get into any more trouble over here."

The chief's telephone intercom rang. He took the call, hung up the receiver and turned to face Mack. "Mr. McCray your friend's waiting for you in your truck."

Mack rose to his feet, put the palms of his hands on the chief's desk and leaned into his face. "My friend had better not be seriously hurt or I'll have your ass. That's not a threat. It's a promise." Mack turned on the balls of his feet and headed for the door. "Elmo are you coming? It smells in here."

"Elmo! Come in and sit down," the chief barked. "I have a few things to talk to you about before you leave."

"Mack this shouldn't take very long. Wait for me outside."

"Don't take too long. If you hang around here you might come down with the same attitude problem your brother-in-law seems to have."

"Shut up! You're still in his jurisdiction."

"That's darn good advice Mr. McCray," Chief Brown offered. " Go outside and wait for Elmo and your friend. I need to chat with Elmo for a few minutes about our plans for this weekend. We're having a family picnic on Boy Scout Island."

Mack sauntered out of the police station, made his way down the wooden steps and walked toward his truck. It was parked directly in front of the police station and the passenger's side faced the building. Rat's bandaged head was visible and he appeared to be sleeping. His head was back against the seat and his eyes were closed.

"Rat! Are you okay?" Mack stammered as he leaned forward into the open the truck window.

Rat's eyelids flickered and he cautiously opened his eyes. "I'm okay. I think. But, I've got a real bad headache."

"What happened to you? Did they beat you up?"

"The last thing I remember is that I was in the shower soaping myself up. I woke up in a cell with this diaper on my head and a splitting headache. When they took me in for an X-ray they told me that I slipped on a bar of soap in the shower and hit my head on the tile. A doctor said that I'm okay to leave. There's something odd about the whole thing."

"What's that?"

"I don't remember seeing a bar of soap. There was a liquid soap in a dispenser on the wall."

"Don't worry about it. You have a headache and I'm out four hundred bucks! Tina sprung us out of here and Elmo's in there meeting with that horse's ass of a police chief."

"Why's Elmo here?"

"The police chief's his brother-in-law and he called Elmo to escort us back to Port Salerno."

"Why? Don't you know how to get back?"

"Of course I know how to get back. There's something real strange going on here."

"What do you think it is?"

"I'm not sure, but I have a feeling that Elmo's getting an earful right now. Here he comes."

Elmo and Chief Brown came out the front door of the police station together. "Elmo get your friends back to Port Salerno before they get into some more trouble over here," Chief Brown offered. "I'll call you later and we can finalize our plans for this weekend."

"Okay BJ." Elmo responded walked over to Mack and whispered under his breath. "Get in your truck and get out of here before he changes his mind. He's really pissed off at you. We have to talk."

"Where do you want to go? Back to Port Sewall Marina?"

"No. I didn't have lunch and I'm starved. Did they feed you in there?"

"No. But I almost got fed to the lions. How about the Queen Conch?"

"Nope. There're too many eyes and ears there. Meet me at the 'Taste of Italy' in the Publix Shopping Center on U.S. 1 in Stuart. They have a great lunch buffet. Be careful when you go up Sewall's Point Road and west on East Ocean Boulevard. His jurisdiction goes to the Evans Crary Bridge."

"I understand. What did he talk to you about in there?"

"You don't want to know. You're in enough trouble as it is. Don't make it any worse!"

Chapter 31

During lunch Elmo advised Rat that he towed his kayak back to Port Sewell Marina because the mechanic at the fish house told him that he cleaned out the carburetor. After finishing lunch at the 'Taste of Italy' Rat and Mack returned to Port Sewall Marina so that Rat could pickup his kayak and return to Shepherd's Park. Elmo followed closely behind because he had something gnawing at him that he wanted to talk to Mack about.

After Mack parked the truck at the marina Rat headed for the thirteen wooden steps that led toward the boathouse and his waiting kayak. Mack sat down on the front porch step, motioned for Rat to join him and opened the conversation. "After you've had a chance to rest up come back here about seven o'clock tonight. We still have some important things to do."

"Aye, aye sir. I'll be here at seven. Right now I want to get back to my boat, take a nap and try to shake this headache. I still can't figure out how I slipped on a bar of soap in the shower because the soap dispenser was built into the tile shower wall."

"You'll figure it out," Mack replied and gave Rat a wave of his right hand as he disappeared down the steps toward the boathouse dock.

Elmo pulled into the marina parking lot and parked his patrol car beside Mack's pickup truck. Mack waved and gestured for

Elmo to join him on the porch step. Elmo sidled up the walkway and sat down beside Mack.

"Elmo what did your brother-in-law have to talk about after he threw me out of his office?"

"It's just like he told you. We talked about our plans for a camping trip this weekend at Boy Scout Island. My wife and his wife are sisters and they grew up around here. Camping on Boy Scout Island was a big thing for their family. What do you think he wanted to talk to me about?"

"I had a feeling there was something on his mind that he didn't want me to hear."

"He told me to keep you out of Sewall's Point. He's been police chief for a long time. He's very territorial and does his best to protect the residents' privacy. He's may drop the charges against you because Tina really chewed his ass. He stood her up one night when they were supposed to go to a party together and went snook fishing instead. She never forgave him."

"He stood her up to go snook fishing?" Mack chuckled and smiled. "I can understand that, but he's lucky that she didn't draw and quarter him on the courthouse steps on Monday morning."

"She's not very happy with him. You won't have any problems as long as you stay away from there. Now it's time that you and I had a discussion about why you're really here."

"What do you mean why I'm really here? I came here from Chicago to be a fishing guide and that's exactly what I am. End of story."

"Several of us in local law-enforcement knew there was something different about you when you blew into town a few months ago. The cottage has a lot of electronic surveillance equipment including those big antennas strung right over the parking lot. What're they used for?"

"They're rhombic antennas. They're directional and used for high frequency radio reception. One of them is oriented north to south and the other east to west. I'm an amateur radio operator and I enjoy listening to short wave radio broadcasts from all over the world."

"Come on Mack be serious. There's more to those antennas than you're telling me."

"If I held a mirror in front of your face and asked you to look into it what would you see?"

"I'd see myself."

"What else would you see besides your smiling face?"

"Just me that's all."

"What are you wearing Elmo?"

"My uniform."

"You hit the nail on the head! You're a member of law-enforcement. It isn't necessary for you to know any more about me except that I came here from Chicago and I'm a fishing guide. You can make all the assumptions that you want, but I suggest that you not probe to far. You might not like what you find."

"I think I understand. You aroused my suspicion when you talked using pheromones for identification a few days ago. I ran it by our crime investigation unit and they told me it was only a theory and not used because the science hasn't been solidified."

"That's exactly what I'd say too if someone asked me. Do you suppose there might be a few scientific tools available that local law-enforcement agencies don't know about?"

"I suppose so. Are you going to stay away from Sewall's Point like the chief told you to do?"

"He won't catch me driving down Sewall's Point Road again. I can assure you of that. But, there're some very strange things going on over there."

"What you mean?"

"You grew up here right?"

"Yes. My family is fifth generation here in Martin County."

"Did you ever hear of Lorna Belle Mobley? She also worked as a housekeeper in the Sand Club on Jensen Beach back in the days when you were in grade school. She worked at Port Sewall Marina for Tina's parents and cleaned rooms on the weekends."

"Of course I remember her! She used to baby-sit me when I was a kid. She had a daughter named Jo. After high school Jo went away to college somewhere up north and didn't come again after that. I heard she got pregnant and Lorna Belle wouldn't allow her back in the house."

"Lorna Belle came across some Spanish gold coins from a ship that went aground in seventeen fifteen and lived off selling them since nineteen forty-nine. Her daughter found out about the gold, came down after Lorna Belle broke her hip and committed her to a nursing home off Loop Road in Palm City. I went out there to see her yesterday and she was gone. Her daughter paid the bill and checked her out. They wouldn't tell me where she took her. Rat saw Lorna Belle about eleven o'clock last night in the backyard of a house on Sewall's Point watching a backhoe digging up the yard. But they weren't digging up a septic tank. A younger woman grabbed Lorna Belle's arm, shook it hard and pointed at the hole in the ground like she was supposed to produce something out of it like magic. I suspect the younger woman was her daughter."

"Does Rat know what house it was? I remember where Lorna Belle lived! My mom used to drop me off at her house in the morning on her way to work."

"Yes he does. But here's the strange thing about it. Rat chased a crippled raccoon into a hole in the side of the bluff and heard some voices below him. When he looked down he thought he saw Ralph and hollered at him. The guy ducked, ran up some wooden stairs and disappeared."

"Was it really Ralph?"

"He thinks so, but I don't. I think it was a body double. Something very serious happened to Ralph based on the bloody boot we found in his boat. I've got to get back over there, find out what's happened to Lorna Belle and maybe, just maybe, I'll find out what happened to Ralph."

"My brother-in-law is really pissed off at you. If he catches you over there again he's gonna' put you in jail and I doubt that he'll pay very much attention to what Tina has to say about it."

"He's not going to catch me. I'm not going to be driving."

"What do you mean? The only way you can get down Sewall's Point Road is by car."

"Who said we're going down Sewall's Point Road? There's another way."

"The cops will be waiting for you up there."

"I don't think so. The only way they'll know we're coming is if you tell your brother-in-law."

"I wouldn't do that!"

"He thinks he has us scared half to death. They beat the hell out of Rat in the shower and figure he's too scared to ever come back. There might be a connection between what Rat saw on Sewell's Point last night and what I saw at the trailer park the other day."

"What? You told me that Lorna Belle's trailer was gone and some guy was digging up the trailer lot with a backhoe for a septic tank."

"John Thomas told me they were digging the hole for a septic tank. It was strange because the backhoe operator looked a little like Ralph. I waved at him and the guy didn't even acknowledge that I was there. Maybe he has something to do with the backhoe that Rat saw digging up that backyard last night. I'd sure like to talk to Thomas about it."

"That's not possible. Thomas is in a cooler in the coroner's office along with what was left of his wife."

"Damn! I forgot! What're you doing this afternoon? Did your brother-in-law tell you to watch me and report back to him?"

"No! He didn't. I'm going to do some snooping around of my own. My wife's sister runs that nursing home in Palm City. I'll give her a call and see what she'll tell me."

"If you find out anything call me immediately. What do you know about the nursing home on Palm Beach Road?"

"I don't know anybody over there. The guy that runs the place is from New York. He's been there for about ten years and doesn't have very much to do with the locals in the community."

"What do you know about the guy who runs the jewelry store downtown?"

"I went to high school with him. His great-grandfather started the jewelry store back in the eighteen hundreds. His grandfather ran it until he passed away and then his father ran it. He took it over twenty years ago after his father passed away."

"Do you know him very well?"

"I stop by and say hello once in awhile. I bought my wife's wedding ring there. Why?"

"What would you say if I told you that he bought gold coins from Lorna Belle for years and paid her about half the market value for them?"

"I don't see anything wrong with that. If someone finds a gold coin on the beach it didn't cost anything to find it. Anything he pays them is pure profit for them. He's a businessman and he has to turn a profit in order to pay his bills and keep his doors open."

"Do you know his cousin Vinney?"

"I didn't know he had a cousin. Why?"

"I stopped at Luna's for lunch the other day and the jeweler introduced me to his cousin Vinney from Boston."

"I wouldn't doubt that he has a cousin up there somewhere. Not everybody who was born in Martin County stays here. Some of them move away and move back years later after they realize that they left Paradise. Do you want me to stop by the store and ask him about his cousin?"

"No. I don't want to raise any suspicion. I don't think he's done anything illegal, but he fenced gold coins for Lorna Belle for the past twenty years."

"Mack it's almost two o'clock. I gotta' get back to the house and clean up. I come back on duty at three o'clock. Should I stop by here after dinner and check on you and Rat?"

"No. We won't be here and it's best that you don't know where we're going. I don't want to get you involved because of your brother-in-law."

"Okay. I'll talk to you tomorrow morning. If you get picked up again he's not going to let Tina or me know that you're there. You just might just disappear altogether." Elmo stood up.

"Don't worry. We'll be okay." Mack saluted Elmo as he walked toward his patrol car. After Elmo pulled out of the parking lot Mack turned and entered the cottage. *"Something's going on and I think Elmo knows more than what he's letting on. I'd better do my homework about Spanish Treasure ships and the pirate Henry Jennings,"* he mumbled under his breath.

Before Mack got into the kitchenette there was a soft rapping on the screen door followed by Joy's shrill voice. "Mack! Are you there? I stopped by earlier this morning and you weren't home. Did you find out anything more about Ralph?"

"Joy! Come on in. I'll explain why we put Ralph's boat in the boathouse and didn't tell you. It's unfortunate that you found it before we had an answer for you and I apologize."

Joy entered the cottage and Polly Jo followed behind her. Did you find my nana?" Polly Jo whined. "I'm worried about her."

"We found her. She's staying with your mother on Sewall's Point and Rat saw her in the backyard last night about eleven o'clock. We went over there this morning to check on her and we were arrested by the Sewall's Point Police Department for trespassing. We spent the morning in jail and were ordered to never come over there again."

"What are you going to do about my nana?"

"I don't know. We can't accuse your mother of kidnapping her own mother. I've got a few things to check out this afternoon and tonight. I'm certain that we'll have your nana back home relatively soon. However, it's very important that you stay with Joy and keep her company just in case Ralph comes back from his fishing trip early."

"What makes you so certain that he's on a fishing trip?" Joy wailed. "You found his boat and his boot was covered with blood! And don't forget that bloody wooden stake!"

"I hope there's a logical explanation for the blood on his boot and why his boat was hidden under that little bridge in the Archipelago. Only Ralph has those answers and he'll have to tell us when he comes back tomorrow."

"What if he doesn't come back tomorrow? What if he's dead?" Joy shrieked as she paced around the room. \

"Don't get upset. We don't know where Ralph is, but we have to assume that he went fishing in the Keys like he told you in the note and in the two postcards that you received."

"What if he doesn't show up tomorrow afternoon? Then what're you going to do?"

"Elmo and I are taking off for the Keys Saturday morning. We'll stop at every motel and marina along the way and ask about him."

"I think somebody killed my Ralph."

"Don't get all worked up. If he doesn't show up tomorrow afternoon you can file a missing person report and alert law enforcement personnel all over the state will be looking for him."

"How're you going to get my nana away from my mother?" Polly Jo whined.. "She might hurt her!"

"Why would your mother hurt your nana? She's her mother."

"My mother thinks that my nana found some gold and buried it somewhere. Her husband's a no good rotten bum and he'll do anything to find the gold."

"What makes you think she found some gold? Did she tell you?"

"When I was little girl my mother told me a story about a Spanish treasure ship that washed up on the beach. A young girl found the ship, removed some of the treasure and hid it in a safe place. She told me that my nana told her the same story when she was a little girl."

'What makes you think the story is true and has anything to do with your nana?"

"My nana always carried a gold coin her purse and she told me that when she was gone that it would be mine. I think my mother took it away from my nana."

"Your mother doesn't have the gold coin," Mack responded." Your nana gave two of them to me when I stopped to see her in the nursing home."

"What did you do with them? I want my gold coins!"

"I sold them to get money to pay a nursing home bill for an old friend of your nana's."

"I want my gold coins!" Polly Jo screamed. "You sold my gold coins!"

"Do you remember the little wooden chest and picture frame that I gave you the other day?"

"Yes! So what?"

"Your nana asked me to keep them for you. She knew that you would come here some day and she wanted you to have them. They might be very valuable someday."

"I don't want that stupid wooden box or that silly looking picture frame. You keep them! They're not worth anything. I want my gold coins!"

"Polly Jo! Stop your whining and listen to me! The story your mother told you about the young girl who found a wrecked treasure ship and gold chests on the beach is true. That girl was your nana."

"What did she do with the gold and treasure?"

"That's the mystery that I'm trying to figure out. There was a lot of gold involved and your mother and her husband are here after it. Did your grandmother ever say anything to you about where she stashed the gold?"

"No! I want my gold coins!"

"I'm sorry. I don't have them. I told you that I sold them to help out an old friend of hers."

"Who's the friend?"

"It's the man who dragged the treasure chests off the wrecked ship and hid them for her. They were to heavy for her to handle. They were business partners for many years."

"I want my gold coins!"

Mack recalled the single gold coin he found inside the crevice in the Australian pine tree on Jensen Beach and briefly considered giving it to her. "Polly Jo I know what your nana wanted you to have. Wait here and I'll get it for you." Mack stood up and headed toward the kitchenette and the lower cabinet where he had stashed the polished cedar box.

"It'd better be a gold coin!"

"Polly Jo! Don't be so greedy," Joy blurted out. "Whatever your grandmother gave Mack to give to you must be very important to her and much more valuable than two gold coins."

"I don't care what she gave to him. Those gold coins belonged to me!

When Mack returned to the living area his outstretched hands held the cedar box that contained the Sand Club brochure and the wooden picture frame. "Polly Jo I must be honest with you," Mack spoke in a soft yet authoritative tone. "Your grandmother told me that this box is very valuable and she wanted to have it." Mack extended his arms in Polly Jo's direction. She pushed the box away, turned and headed for the front door.

"You keep the damned box!" Polly Jo screamed as she burst through the screen door onto the front porch. "You should've saved those two gold coins for me!" She shouted over her shoulder as she stepped onto the walkway. She headed down the gravel driveway toward Old St. Lucie Boulevard, paused and turned back toward the cottage. "Joy! Are you coming?"

"I'll be there in just a minute," Joy hollered back. "I want to talk to Mack. Wait for me at the end of the parking lot."

Polly Jo nodded, turned her back to the cottage and stomped heavily in the gravel as she made her way toward Old St. Lucie Boulevard.

"We're going to have a problem with that girl," Joy stated. "She thinks that you took advantage of her grandmother when you took those two gold coins. I don't know what I'm going to do with her, but she can't stay with me much longer because she's driving me nuts."

"I don't know what Lorna Belle meant when she told me that this box is valuable and that I should save it for Polly Jo. From what I can see it's empty and this little picture frame is about to fall apart. I'll stick it back under the kitchen cabinet and hold it for her until she comes around. If she decides that she doesn't want it it's just fine with me. I'll keep it."

"Did you have lunch? I can fix you something before I leave."

"No thanks. I had lunch at 'A Taste of Italy' and I'll warm up some leftovers for dinner."

"Have you heard anymore about Ralph?"

"No. If I knew anything I'd let you know. He wrote in the postcards that he'd be home on Friday and this is only Thursday afternoon. We still have a full day to go."

"Okay. I'll take Polly Jo back to my house and do my best to calm her down. What plans do you have for the rest of today and tomorrow?"

"I have some studying to do this afternoon. I think Polly Jo's grandmother is in extreme danger. Rat's coming by later and we have some investigating to do. If everything pans out the way I expect it to I'll have a pretty good answer as to where Polly Joe's grandmother stashed some gold away in the 1960s."

"Is it okay if I stop by later?"

"No. We'll be out most of the night. Keep Polly Jo away from here because she gets in the way. Do whatever you have to do to keep her occupied and out of my hair."

"What're you going to do with Ralph's boat?"

"I'm going to leave it in the boathouse until he shows up. It's his boat."

"I've got to get going. That girl's standing out there in the driveway and she's getting madder by the minute. I might take her for ride this afternoon and show her around town."

"Keep her away from Sewall's Point. Her grandmother's over there and the last thing I need is for Polly Jo to see her. Take her to the beach and let her spend the afternoon collecting shells."

"That's a good idea. I'll check with you in the morning and find out how you and Rat made out tonight. If you find something out about Ralph call me. Please."

"I don't expect to hear from him until he gets back tomorrow afternoon."

As Joy turned to leave the avocado green telephone mounted on the kitchen wall began clamoring like a spoiled brat whining for it's mother's attention. "I have to catch the phone. I think I know who it is and it's not going to be pretty." Mack gestured toward the front door and turned toward the telephone. It shrieked as if it knew who was calling.

Mack raised the handset up to his ear. "Hello."

"I got your sorry ass out of jail this morning and you're still in a lot of trouble!" Tina's shrill voice rang out from the telephone receiver. "Stay away from Sewall's Point because I can't control BJ. I could've had his ass in a sling over some of the things he's pulled over the years and he knows it. But he's still the chief of police over there. He warned you not to show up over there again or you'll be arrested for trespassing. Do you understand?"

"Yes. I completely understand. Rat and I thank you for bailing us out of jail. But he didn't have any solid grounds to hold us."

"He had all the grounds he needed! He warned you two days before about trespassing over there. There's only one way in and out and you have to go right past by the police station in either case. Stay away from there. I can't help you if you get in trouble again."

"There're still a few things I have to check out. Lorna Belle's over there and she's being held against her will by her daughter. Rat was over there last night about eleven o'clock and saw them digging up the back yard with a backhoe. They were trying to make it look like they were digging up a septic tank, but he didn't see a septic tank company truck in the area."

"Lorna Belle baby-sat BJ years ago. He'd be there in a minute if he thought she was in any trouble. But you and Rat had better keep away from there."

"I understand, but it really bothers me. Did you know that the manager of the trailer park where Lorna Belle kept her trailer was murdered early this morning? His wife burned to death in the bathroom and he was shot between the eyes as he crawled out the front window."

"No, I haven't seen any police reports about it. That's Martin County and the report won't show up in West Palm Beach. What did Elmo have to say about it?"

"I saw him this morning at the Queen Conch and he was having breakfast with some Martin County arson investigators. He said the fire was deliberately set. There were several empty plastic milk jugs close to the trailer that had contained gasoline. The front door of the trailer was bolted shut and padlocked. It was impossible to escape from the inside. It was a double murder."

"I'll make a few phone calls this afternoon if I have time and see what I can find out. It's three o'clock and I'm out of court on a five-minute recess. My assistant's signaling me that it's time to go back into the courtroom. I'll call you this evening. I assume that you'll be around?"

"I might be, but then again I might go snook fishing. The tide's just right."

"If you go fishing take your cell phone so I can reach you. And keep your butt away from Sewall's Point!"

"I'll keep my cell phone on just for you. I'll be fine. I know how to fish all by myself."

"Bull crap!"

'Click.' The dull, monotonous drone of the dial tone buzzed in Mack's ear. Tina had once again ended their one-sided conversation on her terms. He hung up the phone and turned around.

"Mr. McCray. I must talk to you right away," the soft feminine voice echoed through the cottage. Thelma Marvette stood outside the screen door. "I learned something important from my grandfather today. He told me about the gold coins. He's not crazy after all! It's really true!"

"TM! Come on in. We have a lot to talk about. I might just have some news for you too! Let's compare notes."

Thelma Marvette opened the screen door, entered and stood inside the doorway.

"Come on in and sit down here at the kitchen table. I won't bite. I had lunch."

"I'm not worried about you biting me. I owe you an apology and a big thank you."

"Why? You didn't do anything to apologize for and I don't know why you want to thank me."

"You paid my grandfather's bill at the nursing home."

"No I didn't. Lorna Belle paid it. I made the payment for her because she couldn't."

"What do you mean Lorna Belle paid the bill? She doesn't have any money. She lived in a broken down old trailer until she broke her hip and her daughter put her in the nursing home."

"She gave me two gold Spanish doubloons and I sold them. There was more than enough money to pay your grandfather's bill. When you see her in person you can thank her."

"What do you mean when I see her in person? She didn't say anything about it when I saw her in the nursing home yesterday."

"She doesn't know that I sold the coins, but when she finds out she'll be pleased. She thinks a lot of your grandfather. They were business partners for many years."

"What do you mean business partners?"

"Do you remember that your grandmother thought your grandfather was nuts because he kept talking about buried pirate treasure and gold before he had his stroke and could still talk?"

"That's why I'm here. He found some gold coins on the beach years ago and melted them down in that iron pot I showed you."

"That's almost correct. Your grandfather and Lorna Belle found the gold coins together. He melted the coins down and poured the liquid gold into the sand mold you found in his shed to form gold ingots. She sold the ingots to local jewelry stores for cash and they split the money."

"Well, well! That explains what he told me this morning."

"What do you mean he told you? I thought he couldn't talk because of his stroke."

"He can't speak, but he communicates in his own way. He grunts and points at things with his cane. He drew a map for me this morning and I've got it right here in my purse."

"What kind of map?"

"I guess you could call it a buried treasure map." She removed a folded sheet of yellow tablet paper from her purse. "He even wrote out the word 'treasure' and put an 'X' on the map. Look!"

Thelma Marvette smoothed out the folded sheet of paper on the kitchen table and pointed at the crude pencil drawing. The squiggly vertical and horizontal lines appeared to have been drawn by a person who couldn't control the movement of their hands and fingers.

"There's an 'X' right there." She pointed at what appeared to be the tip of Sewall's Point."

"But, there's another 'X' right here and it appears to be right on Jensen Beach," Mack replied as he pointed out the crudely lettered words 'Jensen Beach' and pointed at the second 'X' mark.

"You're right! What does that mean?"

"I think it means that they found treasure in two places, or found it in one place and buried it in the other. I have my suspicions. What did your grandfather tell you?"

"I took him out to the shed this morning and pointed out the five wooden boxes that I told you about. Then I showed him the sand mold, cast iron pot and naphtha burner."

"What did he do?"

"He got very agitated and tried to speak, but nothing intelligible came out. He just drooled all over the front of his shirt. He hobbled over to the concrete wall that separates the back yard from the drainage ditch behind the house and pointed at five openings, spaces I'd suppose you could call them, along the top of the wall. Then he hobbled back over to the storage shed and tapped on the wooden boxes with his cane. What do you supposes that meant?"

"I think he was trying to tell you that he hid the wooden boxes inside the concrete wall. There were five spaces and you found five boxes. What else? Where did he hide the other four boxes?"

"What other four boxes?"

"Lorna Belle told me that they dragged out nine boxes of gold coins out of a wooden shipwreck they found on the beach in nineteen forty-nine. You've accounted for five of them."

"Are you accusing my grandfather of stealing?"

"Of course not! I think he reburied the other four boxes somewhere to keep them safe."

"Why would he do that?"

"Someone else was looking for them. But, there might be only three boxes left."

"What happened to the fourth one?"

"Lorna Belle told me that it broke open on the beach. I assume they left it there and that it got covered up when the backside of the hurricane went through. Maybe that's what the 'X' on Jensen Beach means. When did your grandfather hurt his back?"

"Nineteen sixty-five I think. He was digging a hole for a septic tank and ruptured a disk."

"Where was he digging the hole?"

"In the ground of course. Septic tanks are underground."

"I know that. Was he digging the hole in Jensen Beach?"

"I don't know. I'll ask my grandmother when I get back. What do you want me to do?"

"Nothing. But, don't get your grandfather excited. We're going to need him very soon."

"Need him for what?"

"He's going to lead us to the treasure. If it's still where he buried it in nineteen sixty-five."

'What makes you think he buried any treasure and why in nineteen sixty-five?"

"He drew you a treasure map and he hurt his back digging a hole in nineteen sixty-five. The pieces all fit together, but first I have to shake Lorna Belle loose because she holds the missing piece of the puzzle."

"What do you mean shake her loose? Did you find her? Where is she? Is she safe?"

"Her daughter's holding her in a house on Sewall's Point and is trying to get her to tell her where she and your grandfather buried the gold. I'll know for sure tomorrow."

"Why wait until tomorrow? Can't you find out today? Just drive over to Sewall's Point and look for her. Do you know which house? If you don't go from door to door if you have to."

"If you only knew."

"If I only knew what?"

"It's a very complicated story and we don't have time for it this afternoon. Check back with me tomorrow morning. Why don't you take your grandfather for a ride over to Jensen Beach? He might be able to point something out to you."

"That's a good idea. Maybe we'll drive down Sewall's Point and look for Lorna Belle."

"That's not such a good idea. Stick with the beach idea."

"Why?"

"Trust me. Just take him to the beach and let him walk around. There's a small copse of Australian pine trees on the left when you enter the public beach area. Do me a big favor and direct him over there. I'd be very interested in his reaction."

"Should I bring him back here?"

"No. It's almost four o'clock and I have a lot of things to do before dark. Check back with me tomorrow before noon."

"Okay." Thelma Marvette rose from the table, turned and walked directly to the front door. She paused, turned and looked back at Mack who was still sitting at the table. "I have a feeling that you know a lot more about what's going on than you're telling me."

"You could be right, but then again you might not. We'll see very soon."

After she left Mack glanced at the wall clock. *"It's three fifty-seven. I'd better get to my homework and get ready. I've still got some packing to do before Rat shows up."*

Chapter 32

"Pssst. Mack. It's ten-thirty. It's time for us to get going if we're gonna' do any checking around on Sewall's Point." Rat's raspy voice swirled its way through Mack's auditory canals and settled into his brain's audio receptors.

Mack shook his head opened his eyes and struggled to get his bearings. The book he was reading when he fell asleep slipped from his chest onto his lap.

"Is that a book about treasure hunting?"

"It's about the seventeen fifteen Spanish treasure fleet that ran aground here during a hurricane."

"Why are you reading a book about the treasure fleet?"

"Lorna Belle convinced me that she and Frank Holmes, the black guy from Tick Ridge who worked as the maintenance man at the Sand Club, found the poop deck and captain's cabin from a Spanish treasure galleon. However, the more research I do the more variables I uncover."

"Variables? Like what?"

"A pirate by the name of Henry Jennings hung around the St. Lucie Inlet and sailed back and forth to his headquarters in Nassau. He raided the unarmed Spanish salvage vessels as they made their way down the east coast toward Cuba."

"How does that relate to Lorna Belle?"

"I've established that she had her hands on a lot of gold coins and Frank Holmes was her partner. He melted them down into nine-ounce ingots and she sold them for cash to jewelry stores all over Florida. She said they discovered the poop deck and captain's cabin of a vessel called *Urca De Lima* on Jensen Beach right after the nineteen forty-nine hurricane. But, the more research I do the more I suspect that they found Henry Jennings's stash of gold buried on the beach."

"What does that have to do with anything?"

"It has everything to do with everything. She told me that she and Holmes dragged nine boxes of gold coins from the wreckage. One of the boxes broke open and the coins were scattered every which way. She marked the spot by sticking a gold coin in a cleft in the trunk of an Australian pine tree. When she went back to the spot after the hurricane was over the coins were gone."

"What do you mean everything?"

"That backhoe you saw in the backyard of the house on Sewall's Point wasn't digging up a septic tank. They were looking for the three boxes of gold that Holmes and Lorna Belle buried in the backyard."

"What makes you think there are boxes of gold buried there?"

"Holmes has five empty cedar boxes stashed alongside a storage shed behind his house. They dragged nine boxes of gold off the ship, there're five empty boxes beside his shed and that means there's four boxes unaccounted for. One of the boxes broke open on the beach and that leaves three boxes unaccounted for. In nineteen sixty-five Holmes was supposedly digging a hole for a septic tank in Lorna Belle's backyard on Sewall's Point and injured his back He was never able to work after that, but somehow he and his wife managed to survive. I suspect it was from the proceeds of the gold that Lorna Belle sold. Shortly after Holmes injured his back Lorna Belle sold her house and moved to Mississippi."

"How does all of this fit together?"

"Lorna Belle's daughter and her husband think that Lorna Bell still has some gold stashed away and they're determined to find it. They thought that she had buried it close to her trailer and that's why they dug up the lot with a backhoe. But there was never any gold buried there. They were afraid that the trailer park manager was going to talk and that's why he was killed. He was their eyes and ears, but they couldn't leave any witnesses."

"What does this have to do with us?"

"Lorna Belle's daughter and her husband have Lorna Belle stashed away in the house on Sewall's Point. They'll do whatever it takes to make her tell them where she and Frank stashed those boxes of gold coins. She apparently told them that Holmes dug a hole in the backyard in nineteen sixty-five and buried the gold there. That matches the story that the treasure hunter told me at a book signing at the library a couple of weeks ago. He told me that a woman contracted with him to search her property with ground searching radar because she heard a rumor that a pirate had buried treasure there. He found several caves, but she wouldn't allow him to excavate the area. About six months afterward the backyard was dug up, the house was sold and she moved away. I'm certain that woman was Lorna Belle."

"The people digging up the backyard with the backhoe weren't going to find anything were they?"

"No. They could've dug all the way to China. It isn't there. Lorna Belle's daughter and her husband are apt to force her to talk, but she doesn't know where Holmes buried the boxes."

"Why do you want to go up there?"

"I want to find out what happened to Lorna Belle. Her daughter and her husband pulled off the murder of the trailer park manager and his wife. They might have something to do with the guy who was whacked in the boathouse Saturday morning and the poor slob that you clobbered with that concrete block Sunday night. I got too close and they can't afford to have me around."

"What's in that green Army duffel bag over by the front door? I've got a bag like that stashed away on my sailboat that I brought it back from Nam' and never opened it since."

"A few things that we might need."

"Like what?

"An infrared heat detector, night vision goggles, a flashlight, a metal detector, a steel grapple with 200 feet of one-inch double braided nylon line, a Jacobs ladder, a pheromone detector, and a .22 caliber High Standard laser sighted rifle."

"It's some of the same stuff we carried back in Southeast Asia in the nineteen-sixties."

"There're a couple new things like the pheromone and infrared detectors."

"You told me Saturday that the military tracks pheromones for human identification. Are you looking for somebody particular?"

"No, but I might take a sample if I get close enough. Are you ready to go?"

"Your cat's hanging around the refrigerator and I think he's hungry. Do you want to feed him before we take off?"

"Go over to the refrigerator, pull out a can of cat food and put couple spoons full on a paper plate. Heat it up in the microwave for thirty seconds and you'll make him as happy as a clam. I'll carry my duffel bag down to your kayak and stow it away. Did you fill up your gas tank before you left Shepherd's Park?"

"It could probably use a little bit."

"I've got two five gallon gas cans in the boathouse and I'll top off the tank. I don't want to run out of gas if we have to make a run for it."

Rat fed the cat and made his way downstairs to the boathouse where Mack was already seated in the kayak. Rat cranked up the oil-belching outboard and headed toward Willoughby Creek.

"Rat keep the motor down to idle speed so we don't make very much noise. The tide's starting to run out and we can take a straight shot across the river from Willoughby Creek to the north side of Trickle's Island."

"Aye, aye, sir," Rat mockingly responded and gave Mack a crisp salute. He grinned and swiveled the outboard motor hard to the left to enter the mouth of Willoughby Creek and headed across the St. Lucie River toward Trickle's Island. Rat traveled at idle speed across the grass flats south of Hell's Gate and swung into the outgoing current to clear the submerged Australian pine tree along the northern side of Trickle's Island. He skirted the south side of the oyster bar protecting Sewall's Point and deftly maneuvered between the two small islands that were used by the mail boats in the days when Stuart was called Potsdam. Rat steered the kayak toward the bluff projecting out from the southeast corner of Sewall's Point.

"Pull under those mangroves and we'll tie up here." Mack gestured toward a stand of red mangrove trees. "No one will be able to see the kayak unless they're directly alongside it."

Rat deftly guided the kayak into the shelter of the mangroves.

"That wooden stairway leads straight up the bluff. We'll go up alongside of it just in case they have infrared detectors installed on the steps to warn them that company's coming."

"Aren't you afraid of big snakes at night?"

"No. Snakes are more afraid of you than you are of them. Kick the ground with the toes of your boots and set up a vibration. The snakes will scatter in front of you."

What if there's a snake up there that doesn't scare easily?"

"He'll probably sneak behind you and bite you on the ass. You'll scream, lose your grip, fall all the way down the bluff and land on your back on the sharp rocks below. End of story."

"I see your point," Rat replied as he thumped the toes of his boots into the limestone bluff.

Mack and Rat used tree roots and limestone outcroppings for handholds.

"Rat I'm at the top of the bluff. Crawl up here beside me." Mack gestured with a forward wave of his arm for Rat to pull up alongside him.

The rim of the bluff was edged in several rows of red hibiscus bushes. The two nervous men eased themselves over the top of the bluff and crawled through the hibiscus bushes so they could get a good view of the house. The house was dark and there wasn't a front porch light on.

"I'm going to scan the house with the infrared detector. After I make a scan I'll know what's going on." Mack reached into the duffel bag and pulled out what appeared to be an old-fashioned blunderbuss shotgun. He raised the wooden stock to his shoulder, pointed the barrel at the house and slowly scanned from left to right.

"How does that thing work?" Rat whispered under his breath.

"It detects the heat given off by the human body. You can read the heat through wooden walls unless the exterior walls are very well insulated and prevent the heat from passing through.

"Do you see anything yet?"

"There's nobody inside the house. I've got a gut feeling that they got Lorna Belle to talk, found the gold and took off. We have to get inside the house."

"Why? You said that there's nobody in the house."

"She could be in the basement or even dead. Here's what we're going to do. You crawl around the hibiscus bushes toward the back of the house and I'll go around to the front. When you reach the back door, crawl up on the porch and try to open the door. If it opens whistle three times and I'll come around and meet you. If I get the front door to open I'll whistle three times. That's the signal for you to come around to the front and meet me. Do you understand?"

"I understand completely. Do you want a high pitched or low pitched whistle?"

Mack slapped Rat lightly on the back of his head and smiled. "It doesn't matter. Just whistle three times if you can get in the back door."

"How'll you know it's me whistling at ya'?"

"How many people do you think are dumb enough to be out here whistling in the dark?"

"Just us I suppose. What are you going to do with all that stuff in the duffle bag?"

"I'll leave it here while we check out the house."

Just as Mack crawled onto the front porch he saw the headlights of an approaching car traveling south on Sewall's Point Road. The car slowed, paused and a bright halogen spotlight suddenly lit the night sky and the front porch. Mack was silhouetted against the wall.

"Oh shit!" He muttered under his breath. *"The cops know we're here. I hope that Rat doesn't whistle now."*

"Tweet. Tweet. Tweet." Rang out a shrill, high-pitched whistle from the back of the house. *"Tweet. Tweet. Tweet."* The whistle rang out again. The urgent call carried across the spacious, well-manicured yard to the Sewall's Point Police cruiser. It was a signal for action!

The police cruiser's spotlight immediately flashed to the rear of the house and caught Rat directly in the center of the high-powered Halogen beam. Rat instinctively froze, got his bearings and scrambled on his hands and knees backward toward the safety of the hibiscus hedge. The police cruiser leaped forward, turned into the driveway and raced toward the house as Rat disappeared into the hedge. Mack rolled off the front porch, landed on the manicured grass and crawled on his hands and knees in the direction of where Rat disappeared seconds earlier.

The police cruiser screeched to a stop in front of the three-car garage and was immediately joined by a second one. Two powerful Halogen spotlights slowly picked through the hedge and simultaneously paused at Mack's green duffle bag. Mack couldn't reach the duffle bag and drag it to safety without exposing himself to the spotlights. He elected to slide head first down the steep bluff and hoped that there were no exposed sharp roots lurking in the darkness to rip out his intestines or large snakes blocking his path. He didn't have time to tap the toes of his shoes into the dirt to announce his presence.

Mack slid 'ass over teakettle' down the steep bluff and came to an ungracious stop against the trunk of a Brazilian peppertree. He felt his skull with both hands to be certain that it hadn't split wide-open or turned into mush by the tree trunk. He turned his head toward the top of the bluff and made out the outlines of two police officers silhouetted in the harsh glare of their cruiser spotlights.

"Pssst." A raspy voice rattled from a dark area in the bushes to Mack's right. "It's me Rat. Crawl about twenty feet to your right and you'll find me. I've got your duffel bag. I dragged it down here with me and it broke my fall when I fell into this big hole. Can you see me?"

"No, but I have an idea where your voice is coming from. Give me a minute. I've got to check to see if I broke any of my arms or legs. If I'm still in one piece I'll try to crawl over there."

"Don't make any noise or those two bozos up there might start shooting."

Mack flexed his arms and legs. Fortunately nothing was broken. Confident that he was still in one piece he began a slow crawl across the steep bluff using tree trunks and exposed roots for handles. *"This isn't the time for an armadillo or a snake to pop up,"* Mack thought to himself. *"Those cops know we're down here. They might start throwing rocks down the hill to flush us out and then shoot us like a covey of quail."*

"Keep crawling toward me. You've got fifteen feet to go."

"I don't see you."

"I see you. I'm scrunched up inside a big hole. Keep crawling the way you're going. There's plenty of room in here for both of us and they can't see us from up there."

Mack continued his crawl toward Rat's raspy voice. He reached out for a handhold and felt the firm grip of a hand on his wrist. "What the hell?"

"Take it easy. It's me. Hang on and I'll pull you up. If those guys bring in portable spotlights they'll pick us off like a couple of rats swimming away from a sinking ship." Rat tugged on Mack's wrist and guided him toward the hole in the bluff. Mack slid into the opening and felt something warm squirm under the palm of his hand. "What the hell was that?"

"It's my leg and if you don't mind I'd like you to get your hand off my thigh."

Mack was amazed at the excellent view of Boy Scout Island, Clam Island and Sailfish Point across the Indian River. *"I wonder what it was like in 1715 when Henry Jennings and his band of pirates roamed this area in search of unarmed Spanish treasure salvage vessels,"* he thought.

"Is this a cave?"

"I think so. This is the same hole that lame raccoon ducked into the other night when I chased him up here. The entrance is about four feet wide and four feet high. There's plenty of room for both of us to sit in here. Who do you think dug it?"

"There were a lot of rumrunners here during prohibition. Maybe the local boys used it to stash their illegal booze. I'll pull the flashlight out of the duffle bag and take a look around."

Mack glanced at his watch. It read 11:42 P.M. He maneuvered the duffel bag around so that he could unsnap the metal hasp that kept the top fold in place, felt around inside with his right hand, pulled out the flashlight and flipped it on.

"Rat! This is a cave!" The amazing sight before him caused Mack to drop the flashlight and the cave went dark. "You won't believe what's in here!"

"Is it furry and does it have big teeth? Will it try to eat us?" Rat stepped away from the entrance to assure himself that any animal trapped inside the cave would have an escape route. "There's not much meat on my skinny ass!" Rat muttered as he mentally calculated the distance to the rock-studded shoreline below.

"Take it easy! It's not anything that'll eat you. This place is full of old boxes, boxes and barrels. We may have hit the mother lode! This might be where that pirate Henry Jennings hid his loot." Mack picked up the flashlight and flipped the 'on' and 'off' switch back and forth several times. "The bulb broke when I dropped it. We'll come back in the morning when it's daylight and check this place out. I've got a feeling that we just found what somebody else has been looking for."

"What's that?"

"Treasure!"

"Pirate treasure? Just like in the movies? Did you see any skeletons? Pirates always killed the guys who buried the treasure so they couldn't tell where they hid it. Dead men tell no tales."

"It might be pirate treasure, but I didn't see any skeletons."

"Look!" Rat gurgled and pointed at a nylon rope that dangled over the cave entrance. "Are they coming down after us?"

"Let me take a look." Mack stuck his head out of the cave entrance and looked up toward the top of the bluff. "They're coming down. Do you have a sharp knife on you?"

"I always carry a knife. Never know when I might have to field dress something."

"Give it to me!"

Rat reached into the leather case on his hip and unsheathed what could best be termed as a Mississippi 'frog sticker' with a ten-inch blade. "Will this work?"

"You should have been in Texas defending the Alamo with Davy Crockett! You could skin an elephant with this thing!"

"My grandpa told me that if a man was going to carry a knife he should carry a real knife!"

"Hold it steady," Mack directed as he pulled the nylon rope tight and cleanly sliced it in two. "There. If they get down this far they'll have to swing into the cave or just let go of the rope."

"How are we going to get down?"

"Dump the duffle bag out onto the floor. There's a twenty-foot Jacob's ladder in there that should reach to the bottom of the bluff. We'll tie it off on that tree and climb down."

"Can't they follow us down by using the ladder?"

"No. I'll tie it off with a slipknot and release it from below with a smaller line."

Mack secured the Jacob's ladder to the base of a large Brazilian pepper tree and lowered the duffle bag down the bluff on a light nylon line until it came to rest on the rocky shore.

"Rat climb down the ladder, pick up the duffle bag and toss it in your kayak. I'll be right behind you. I want those guys to see us leaving so they'll stop climbing down their rope. We don't need for them to find our little treasure trove of goodies now do we?"

"Are you going to tell anybody?"

Of course not! Haven't you heard of finders-keepers and losers–weepers?"

"Do you mean that we get to split the treasure?"

"I'm not sure. Someone else might already have a claim on it."

"I'm leaving. That guy climbing down the rope's getting closer." Rat began to climb down the wooden-runged rope ladder toward the shoreline some twenty feet below.

Mack grabbed the rope above the cave entrance and swung it hard to one side. The climber, now halfway down the bluff, began swinging from side to side like a giant clock pendulum.

"That should keep him out of our hair for a few minutes," Mack mumbled to himself as he reached for the top rung of the Jacob's ladder and headed for the bottom of the bluff. When he reached the shoreline he looked around for Rat. He was nowhere to be seen. *"Where could that smelly little guy have gone? He was just here a minute ago."*

"Mr. McCray. How nice to see you this evening," resonated a deep male voice from the shadows twenty feet to Mack's left. "It's unfortunate that you and your friend didn't take the chief's advice when you left his office this afternoon." The Sewall's Point Police officer stepped out of the shadows into the moonlight. We can do this the easy way or we can do it the hard way. It's your choice. Your friend is already in custody."

"What did you do to him?"

"Nothing real serious yet. He was a little belligerent at first, but the Tazer calmed him down real quick. Which way do you want to go?" The officer reached for the Tazer pistol mounted in a holster on his left hip. "The hard way or the easy way?"

"You don't have to use that! I haven't done anything wrong."

"Of course I don't have to use it, but I'd sure like for you to give me a reason to use it! You were warned about trespassing on private property. Turn around, drop to your knees and put your hands behind your back. The chief wants to see you and he's not happy about being called out at this time of night for a couple of trespassing vagrants.

Chapter 33

The two police officers shuttled Mack and Rat up the wooden stairs to the top of the bluff. They placed Rat in one police car and Mack in the other for transport to the police station. Mack was escorted to the chief's office, the handcuffs removed and he was rudely pushed into a wooden chair strategically placed in front of the chief's massive mahogany desk.

"Mr. McCray. What a pleasant surprise," the police chief offered with a sly smirk. "Why did you come back over here? I thought that we arrived at an agreement this morning."

"I had to find out if Lorna Belle was okay."

"She's back at my wife's nursing home in Palm City and she's doing just fine. You screwed up our operation yesterday. We've had them under surveillance all week and were ready to pop them last night when your buddy showed up and they called nine-one-one. But, we got them tonight and they're in custody."

"You got who?"

"Lorna Belle's daughter and her husband. We'd been watching them since last Thursday. They were holding Miss Lorna Belle hostage. What did you do with Ralph?"

"What do you mean what did I do with Ralph? He's my friend. He disappeared last Friday and I've been looking for him. I think he's in trouble."

"You've got that right.

"What do you mean?"

"We picked up a body double of Ralph on a traffic violation on Tuesday. That was the same day my boys picked you up. We watched him like a hawk after that."

"Where is he? I want to ask him a few questions."

"He's not talking to anyone right now."

"Why not?"

"He's dead. He tried to run for it when we raided the house."

"Did you shoot him?"

"Heck no. He fell over the bluff and broke his neck when his head hit a limestone rock on the way down the hill. He was dead when he hit the bottom."

"How did you know he was a body double and not Ralph?"

"He's a third cousin on my mother's side."

"Why didn't you arrest him when you pulled him over for the traffic stop?"

"That would've been real smart wouldn't it? I had no grounds except for a speeding ticket and he'd have taken off like a cat with turpentine on its sandpapered ass if he suspected anything."

"You held me on no grounds!"

"I don't like you. Now how about telling me where you fit into this mess of trouble?"

"What mess of trouble? I didn't do anything."

"Let me refresh your memory. We picked you up twice this week on trespassing charges. The other night your buddy was spotted sneaking around in the hibiscus bushes and tonight we caught both of you sneaking around over there. I figured that you'd be back."

"Why don't you ask Elmo about me?"

"Elmo's not the sharpest pencil in the box. Do you have any idea why a body double of Ralph was holding Miss Lorna Belle against her will and digging up the backyard of her old house with a backhoe the other night?"

"No. Should I?"

"Yes you should and I believe that you do. I know you're after Miss Lorna Belle's gold. We've been watching you and your derelict buddy all week."

"What gold? I was trying to help her."

"How? By stealing her gold coins and selling them?"

"No! I didn't steal her gold coins!"

"Yes you did. You sold two gold coins for twenty-five hundred bucks each and pocketed the cash. You only had four of the one hundred dollar bills on you when we picked you up."

"Who told you that?"

"My cousin. He runs the jewelry store where you sold them. He figured that you'd be back and we fixed him up with five grand in marked one hundred dollar bills."

"I didn't steal them those coins! She gave them to me."

"What did you do with the money my cousin gave you? Five grand is a lot of cash to get rid of in a couple of days. You should've bought a new truck."

"I used it to help an old friend of hers. I paid his nursing home bill."

"Do you mean that crazy old man Frank Holmes?"

"Yes."

"That guy's as nutty as a fruitcake. He thinks he knows where some pirates buried gold and treasure on Jensen Beach."

"Maybe he does."

"What do you mean by that crack?"

"Nothing. But maybe, just maybe, he's not nuts."

"Bull crap! Do you know where Ralph is?"

"No! He left a note for his wife saying that he went fishing in the Keys and would be back tomorrow."

"That's a load of crap. Elmo told me that you disappeared Monday of last week and didn't get back until Saturday. Ralph disappeared Friday night. What'd you do to him?"

"Nothing. He was gone when I got here about noon on Saturday."

"That's exactly my point. Elmo told me that you didn't seem very excited when he told you about finding Ralph's boat under that little bridge in the Archipelago."

"Why should I get excited? I was worried about Ralph."

"What do you know about the trailer park manager that got burned up the other night?"

"Nothing."

"I know better. You stopped over there a couple of times to ask him about Miss Lorna Belle. You wanted to know where she was and he told you."

"How do you know that?"

"He was my wife's cousin."

"Did you shoot him and burn down his trailer?"

"Of course not!"

"You might have to prove it. My wife's family is really pissed off over it."

"How can I prove that I didn't do something?"

"You can't. It's a slam-dunk. The Stuart Police boys want to talk to you about that fire."

"Why? I wasn't there."

"Poor old John Thomas was shot between the eyes with a .25 caliber pistol. It was an old Italian semi-automatic Berretta based on the shell casings found at the crime scene."

"What does that have to do with me?"

"Do you own a .25 caliber Italian Berretta semi-automatic pistol?"

"Yes I do! My grandfather brought it back from Italy after the war as a souvenir."

"The boys at the crime lab are doing ballistics tests on it to determine if it's the same gun that killed John Thomas."

"How'd they get my pistol?"

"They went through your place with a search warrant for probable cause."

"I didn't shoot Thomas."

"Maybe you didn't, but maybe your gun did it all by itself. It might be the same gun that killed that guy who washed up on Jensen Beach Sunday morning. They're checking the body."

"There isn't any body. It disappeared before it got to the coroner's office on Sunday."

"How'd you know that?"

"Somebody told me. I don't remember who it was."

"Another guy disappeared Sunday night."

"So? What does that have to do with me?"

"The Martin County boys watched him all last week. The last time anybody saw him he was riding a black Jet Ski north on the

St. Lucie River toward Hell's Gate. He turned into Willoughby Creek about eight-thirty Sunday night and never came out."

"I don't know anything about that and I didn't see anybody riding a black Jet Ski."

"I didn't suppose you would as busy as you are and everything. Elmo found the Jet Ski on a sand bar in front of Sandsprit Park Monday morning. Didn't he tell you about it?"

"No. Why should he?"

"I figured as close as you are with him that he told you everything."

"What did you do with Lorna Belle?"

"Why are you so worried about her? She's at the nursing home and counting sheep by now."

"Because she told me that she didn't trust her daughter and her husband."

"She doesn't have to worry about them anymore. We have them in custody right back there."

"Why did you arrest them?"

"They threatened to kill Lorna Belle if she didn't tell them where she buried the treasure. She was wearing a wire when her daughter took her out of the nursing home. She told them that she buried it in the backyard. That's why they had a backhoe in there digging the place up."

"Did they find it?"

"Of course not. She was stalling for time and helping us to build a case against them. She ran through that little bit of gold she found years ago. That's why she was living in the trailer park. She was flat broke."

"No she wasn't! She still had two gold coins she gave me."

"They weren't real gold. They were real good fakes. My cousin made 'em and we provided them to her. She didn't know who you were and figured that her daughter sent you."

"She seemed to be serious about everything she told me. You mean it's not true about the treasure ship that she and Frank Holmes found on the beach after the nineteen forty-nine hurricane?"

"Of course not! She was just stringing you along like we told her to do and you took the bait!"

"There was never any gold or treasure? She made it all up?"

"That's right. There were all kinds of rumors about her finding gold after she married that rich guy and moved into that big house on Sewall's Point in the early fifties. He had a cache of gold coins in a big steel chest that was welded to a steel beam in the basement. After he died she peddled them to my cousin's father for several years until they ran out."

"She sure does tell a good story doesn't she?"

"You believed her! How do we get our money back?"

"You'll have to go to the nursing home where I bailed out her friend Frank Holmes and ask them. You got the four hundred bucks that I had left over."

"The bills are marked. We'll find them soon enough."

"Who was the guy that I met in Luna's? Your cousin said that he was his cousin Vinney."

"He is his cousin and his name is Vinney. He's an undercover officer and lives in Palm City."

"Then it was all a big hoax and I got taken in by all of you."

"Yep. We might even get a bonus."

"A bonus for what?"

"We solved a murder and caught the perpetrator."

"Who's that?"

"You. I figure you killed John Thomas and the guy that washed up on Jensen Beach. The way I see it you made the guy on the black Jet Ski disappear as well. We'll know for certain when the ballistics boys are done with their tests on your pistol."

"BJ why don't you turn him loose?" resounded Elmo's stern voice from behind Mack. "You know those ballistics tests didn't match Mack's pistol to the one that killed Thomas." Elmo walked into the chief's office. "You've had them since three o'clock yesterday afternoon."

"Elmo! How nice to see you. How long have you been standing out there in the hall? Mr. McCray and I were having a very enjoyable conversation. Come in and sit down."

"No thanks. How about turning him loose in my custody? You got the people you wanted."

"I was just trying to find out what else he might know about all the things that's been going on around here."

"I told you this afternoon that he was straight. Why don't you just leave him alone?"

"If he's so straight what was he doing sneaking up over the bluff tonight about midnight?"

"I don't know. But I'm sure that he has a good reason. Did you ask him?"

"Of course I asked him. He tried to feed me some crap about being worried about Miss Lorna Belle. I know better. He thought that she still had some of those gold coins and was sniffing around trying to find them. The gold fever got him."

Elmo looked Mack in the eye and spoke softly, "Mack everybody in town knows the story about Lorna Belle, Frank Holmes and the treasure ship. The only thing true about it is the gold coins she found in that steel trunk in the basement of the old house when her husband died. She cashed them in and when they ran out she sold the house and moved to Mississippi."

"Elmo everything she told me checked out and I believed her."

"The old lady took you to the cleaners. You're lucky she didn't ask you for money."

"Okay Elmo you can take him home. Everything's wrapped up and we won't file any charges against him." The police chief turned his attention to Mack. "Mr. McCray you don't have anything to worry about unless you have some of Miss Lorna Belle's gold. Do you?"

"No! How could I? It's all fake. How about my friend? I want him released too!"

"You are a strange man Mr. McCray. Just a few minutes ago I had you convinced that you were being charged in a double homicide, plus a dead body on the beach and a missing person. I had you eating out of my hand and now you demand something? How strange."

"Why don't you cut the crap and let me and Rat go? Do you want me to call Tina again?"

"That won't be necessary. Your friend is being escorted up here as we speak."

"There is one thing that really bothers me."

"What is it? I'll answer it for you if I can."

"How did you know that we were coming back tonight?"

"It was easy. We placed a GPS radio transmitter in your friend's rubber kayak and monitored his travels all day long. My officers were stationed at the base of the bluff. When you reached the top of the bluff they radioed the two police cruisers that were waiting for you. You didn't have a chance. Cutting off the rope didn't accomplish much because my men weren't going to slide down it anyway. They would've taken the stairs. It's much easier. You should try it next time."

"What did you do with his kayak?" Mack demanded. "That's his only transportation."

"I already towed it back to the marina," Elmo responded. "It's tied up on the dock beside the boathouse. Let's go. We'll meet Rat outside." Elmo urgently tugged at Mack's arm.

Mack, Elmo and Rat arrived at Port Sewall Marina in Elmo's patrol car at 1:43 A.M. Elmo didn't bother to turn off the engine because he didn't intend to stay and opened the conversation.

"Mack I suggest that you go to bed. Rat you'd better hightail it back to Shepherd's Park before the police chief changes his mind. Your kayak is tied up beside the boat dock. I topped off the gas tank and pulled out the GPS transmitter. Don't even think about slowing down when you are going up the river. The shoreline of Sewall's Point runs all the way up to the bend."

"I'm going," Rat muttered under his breath. "If you don't hear from me tomorrow you can figure that the *Gestapo* over there got me again." He slipped out of the patrol car and slunk down the stairs toward the boathouse.

"I hope that you learned your lesson. The chief wanted your hide on his wall and was willing to do whatever it took to get it."

"He was bluffing. He didn't have any legitimate reason to hold me and he knew it. I saw right through him from the start. He'd make a lousy poker player."

"He wasn't bluffing. He told me that the ballistics tests indicated that the bullets that killed the trailer park manager came from your gun."

"What!"

"But, that wasn't enough grounds to hold you. Besides Stuart is out of his jurisdiction."

"Tomorrow Mel Mangini, a Martin County Sheriff's Department homicide detective, is coming by the marina to talk to you."

"I didn't shoot that guy in the trailer park!"

"Of course you didn't, but somebody else got hold of your pistol and did it for you."

"Why would anyone do that?"

"Somebody with a motive wanted John Thomas shut up and you out of the way. Any ideas?"

"No!"

"Where were you at two o'clock this morning? I saw you and Rat at the Queen Conch about six o'clock for breakfast. That seemed awfully early in the morning for you."

"Rat stopped by about five-thirty with a load of cat snappers and wanted me to meet him at the fish house because he was having outboard motor trouble. I told you that this morning."

"I guess you did. I told Mel that you couldn't have had anything to do with the fire, but he still has to check out all the leads. Do you really think that Ralph will show up tomorrow like he said in his postcards?"

"No. Check with me tomorrow and I'll let you know if I found out anything else."

"Okay. See you tomorrow," Elmo replied, waved and cruised out of the parking lot.

Dejected and confused Mack headed for the cottage while shaking his head and talking to himself. *"How could that old lady have conned me so completely? Everything that she told me checked out. Something's wrong. I need some answers and I'm going to get them tomorrow."*

Chapter 34

Multiple rays of bright sunlight knifed through the windows on the east side of the cottage and the cat meowed for attention at the front door. Mack had fallen asleep in the green recliner in the early morning hours. The open treasure hunting book lay open on his chest.

Joy and Polly Jo arrived at the front door and Joy didn't knock to announce their presence. She jerked the screen door open and kicked the footrest of the recliner with her right foot to get Mack's attention.

"Mack! Wake up!" Joy yelled. "Where were you all night? I was worried about you!"

Mack heard her words through the fogginess lodged in his brain. He sat up and shook his head in a futile attempt to clear his thought process. He opened his mist-covered eyes and attempted to focus them on his screaming adversary.

"Mack! Get your butt up!" Joy yelled in his ear as she simultaneously shook his shoulder like a pit bull with a rawhide chew bone gripped between its clamped jaws. Where were you all night?"

"I'm getting up," Mack responded through tightly gritted teeth. "Rat and I had a few things to do last night. We got back here about two o'clock this morning. Everything's just fine."

"That's where you're wrong! Ralph is still missing. Why didn't you tell me that you hid his boat in your boathouse?"

"I didn't want to worry you. Wait until this afternoon and see if Ralph comes home like he promised. If he doesn't show up by three o'clock Elmo and I'll go looking for him."

"You know full well that something bad happened to Ralph. He's not ever coming home," Joy stammered as giant tears rolled down her cheeks. "I saw his bloody boot and the bloody stake in his boat. Somebody did something real bad to Ralph."

"Don't get upset." Mack sat up and shook his head. "We don't have all the facts."

"Why are you reading a treasure hunting book? There's no treasure buried around here and everybody in town knows it. You're wasting your time if you think there is."

"You're probably right," Mack replied as he placed the book face down on the coffee table. "People have been looking for treasure around here for years and from what I read most of it has already been found. I couldn't sleep when I got back last night so I poured myself a glass of Merlot and decided to thumb through this book. It's very interesting. A naïve person could get gold fever just by reading it."

"Do you know where my nana is?" Polly Jo inquired as she stared directly into Mack's eyes. "I'm worried about her. My mother may do something bad to her."

"She's safe and back in the nursing home."

"She's back in the nursing home? Nobody told me that she was out of the nursing home! Where did she go? Did my mother snatch her up? Did my mother do something bad to her?"

"It's a long story. But she's safely back in the nursing home and resting comfortably. Perhaps Joy will take you out there this morning to visit her." Mack gave Joy a wink.

"Polly Jo I'd be glad to take you out to Palm City to visit your nana," Joy responded with a wink in Mack's direction. "Mack's going to have his hands full around here this morning."

"Joy you can't miss the nursing home. Take Monterey west, go across the Palm City Bridge, turn right on Route 714 just before the turnpike entrance and go south on Loop Road. It's on the right hand side of the road about two miles down."

"Thank you Mr. McCray," Polly Jo responded with a smile.

"The wooden box your grandmother gave me to give you is under the kitchen counter. Do you want to take it with you?"

"What about my nana's gold coins? Are you going to give me her gold coins?"

"The coins weren't real. They were fakes and had no value."

"You told me that you sold the coins and used the money to pay off some old fart's nursing home bill!" Retorted Polly Jo with her hands solidly planted on her svelte hips. "Why would a jewelry store buy them if they were fake? That must be a real stupid jewelry store owner!"

"The jeweler was in on the scam and he knew that they were fake. Somebody thought that I was trying to steal gold from your grandmother and tried to set me up with the fake coins in a sting operation. They weren't worth anything."

"What happened to the money you got for the coins?" Polly Jo spit out vehemently as she stamped the floor four times with her right foot. "If someone paid you for them you should give the money give to me. Those coins belonged to my grandmother and she needs the money!"

"The money was paid in marked bills and Martin County is entitled to recover the money from the nursing home where I paid your grandmother's friend's bill. Do you want me to get the box for you?"

"I don't want it! You keep it! You already took everything valuable out of it!"

"Polly Jo. I don't have any reason to keep that box. Your grandmother wanted you to have it."

"I don't want it!" Polly Jo venomously spat back. "You can have it! Joy are you ready?"

"Your grandmother wants you to have it. Its yours!"

"Keep it! You need it for your ego," Polly Jo retorted as she brushed past him on her way out the door. "Joy! Are you coming?" She screamed over her right shoulder.

"I'll be right there. Wait for me in the parking lot. I need to talk to Mack for a few minutes."

"What do you want to talk to me about?"

"You know that Ralph's not coming back don't you?"

"I'm expecting him to show up this afternoon."

"How do you expect him to get here? His truck's parked in our driveway and his boat's in your boathouse. Is a Good Fairy going to drop him off in a hollowed out pumpkin carriage?"

"I don't know. We just have to wait and see if he shows up this afternoon. If he doesn't we'll take it from there."

"Ralph told me that if anything ever happened to him that he wanted you to have his boat."

"He'll need his boat after he gets home."

"I don't believe that he's ever coming home and neither do you," Joy sniffed. "I've accepted that my Ralph's gone forever and my life must go on. I'll be okay."

"Don't be so willing to accept that he's gone. Wait until this afternoon."

"Joy! Are you coming?" Polly Jo's voice bellowed from the parking lot. 'We don't have all day!"

"I'm coming. Just hold your damn horses!" Joy turned to face Mack and continued. "I have to take that spoiled brat out to see her nana before she has another hissy fit. She's about to blow a gasket. I'd love to paddle her little pink ass to a bloody pulp with a mangrove switch and teach her some manners."

"You can't do that. She's not your kid."

"I can fantasize about it can't I?" Joy turned to leave and paused at the front door. "Do what you can to find Ralph, but I'll understand if you can't. There's a lot of water out there."

"I will," Mack muttered as Joy stepped off the front porch into the parking lot.

The wall telephone angrily chattered it's tinny greeting and broke the quiet silence. Mack strode across the living area to the kitchenette in three strides and snatched the handset of the chattering monster out of its resting place.

"Hello."

"Hello my ass!" Resounded the shrill female voice from the receiver. "What the hell do you think you're doing over there on Sewall's Point? I've bailed your ass out twice and BJ's losing patience with me!"

"Tina! How nice to hear from you on such a wonderful Friday morning. Isn't it a nice day?"

"What the hell are you talking about? Are you on drugs? You don't realize just how much trouble you're in! Is that cheap Mississippi 'slitch' still there? Listen to me!"

"I'm listening. Did I ever tell you that your voice sounds very sweet early in the morning?"

"Mack! Now you listen to me! You're in big trouble!"

"I can't hear you. There's something wrong with our connection. Are you on your cell phone?"

"No! I'm sitting in my office! I can hear you just fine!"

"I'm sorry. I can't hear you. You're fading in and out. I'm going to hang up so you can call me back. Maybe we'll get a better connection." Mack replaced the receiver on the switch hook, ripped the telephone off the wall and pulled out the connecting cord. *"That should take care of that bad connection."* The telephone on the bedroom nightstand rang and he ignored it.

The crunching of tires in the gravel driveway caught Mack's attention and he turned toward the front door. The silver BMW slammed to a stop, a tall black woman leaped out of the driver's side and raced toward the cottage. "Mr. McCray! Are you there?" She screamed, "Something's happened to my grandfather!" She sobbed as she burst through the screen door.

Mack met her at the door. "TM! What's wrong? What happened to your grandfather?"

"He had a stroke last night!" Sobbing uncontrollably she collapsed into his arms. "He's gone!"

"What!"

"I went in to wake him up for breakfast about eight-thirty this morning. I shook his arm, but he didn't move. I put my hand on his forehead to check his temperature and it was cold! He passed away during the night!"

"How's your grandmother taking it? Is she okay?"

"The paramedics knew it was hopeless, but they went through the motions anyway." She sobbed into Mack's shoulder, paused and looked up. "My grandmother's okay. She was expecting it and had all of the arrangements made in advance."

"How is she going to pay for his funeral?"

"He was a Navy veteran and the VA is taking care of it."

"Is there anything that I can do for her or you?"

"Not at this point. But, after this is all over I want to check out that map he gave me. I know that he was trying to tell me something. I'm certain that he knew where the treasure's buried. Will you help me look for it?"

"Of course, but right now I've got a plate full of problems. Let's get together next week."

"Okay. I'm concerned that my grandfather kept some of the gold for himself and didn't share it with Miss Lorna Belle. If we can find it I want to give her a fair share."

"That sounds like a good idea because she's back in the nursing home in Palm City."

"She's back in the nursing home? What happened?"

"Her daughter was holding her against her will and trying to find where she hid the gold."

"I want see her again and talk to her about what she and my grandfather did with the gold they found on the treasure ship."

"That's a dead end."

"What do you mean?"

"There wasn't any Spanish treasure ship. Lorna Belle found a chest full of gold coins locked up in a steel chest in the basement after her husband died. She didn't want anyone to know about the chest because she'd have to pay taxes on the gold. So she made up the story about the treasure ship so she could share the proceeds with your grandfather."

"How do you know that? Can you explain the five wooden boxes I found behind his shed?"

"It's a long story and I learned about it the hard way. No. I can't explain where they came from. I suspect that they're old carpenter's nail boxes that your grandfather got from a hardware store and stored the coins in before he melted them down."

"How about the two gold coins that Lorna Belle gave you? Doesn't that prove that she had some gold coins?"

"It doesn't prove anything. The coins she gave me were fake."

"What? How could you sell them if they were fakes? You could be arrested!"

"TM it's a long story. I could write a book about it and maybe some day I will. You go take care of your grandmother. I'll fill you in next week when we get together."

"What should I do with the cast iron pot and the sand molds?"

"Maybe you can sell them at an antique store."

"I'll keep them as mementos of my grandfather."

"That's an excellent idea." Mack gently guided her toward the front door. "Call me next week after you have everything straightened out and we'll have lunch."

"Okay," she sniffed. "Thanks for being here and listening to me." She gently bussed him on the cheek, drifted onto the front porch and headed for her BMW. She waved as she drove off.

"We'll never know if he stashed some of the gold away for himself," Mack muttered.

Mack glanced at his watch. It read 9:42. *"I'd better get going. I've got to wash Tina's boat and charge up the battery before she gets here,"* he mumbled to himself.

Before embarking on his morning tasks Mack scrambled three eggs with four strips of bacon, made a pot of coffee and fed the ravenous cat. He made it down to the boathouse dock to work on Tina's boat at a quarter after ten. He spent a few minutes playing with the pair of Atlantic Bottlenose dolphins that he and Tina brought back from Hawaii. Although *Puka* and *Kea* had rejoined their original Indian River family pod they checked in at the marina on Fridays. They knew that their pal Tina showed every Friday afternoon to play with them in North Lake.

At 11:27 Ralph's green pickup truck swung into the marina parking lot at breakneck speed. The driver slammed on the brakes, the brakes locked up, and the truck slid twenty feet before it came to a stop in the loose gravel five feet from the front porch. Joy leaped out of the cab and ran into the cottage screaming. "Mack! They're gone! Mack are you here?"

Mack didn't hear her screams. He was down at the boat dock adjusting the mooring lines on Tina's sailboat. He had given the boat a good wash down in preparation of her arrival that afternoon. Joy caught a glimpse of Mack through the kitchenette window, reversed her course, ran out the front door and headed for the thirteen steps leading to the boathouse dock.

"Mack! They're gone!" Joy screamed as she raced down the treacherous wooden stairway. "They're gone and it's my fault. I'm sorry. I'm really sorry."

Mack dashed to the base of the stairs and caught Joy in his arms just as she slipped off the bottom step and flew forward. "Hold it right there," he offered. He felt a tingle go through his body as her soft form squirmed in his arms. She smelled good. "What's wrong?"

"They're gone! They left! It's all my fault!"

"What're you talking about? Who's gone? Settle down and take a deep breath."

"Polly Jo and Lorna Belle! They're gone and it's my fault!"

"What do you mean they're gone and that's it's your fault? I don't understand."

"They're gone! That sneaky Polly Jo fooled me! I could wring her skinny neck!"

"Slow down. Start at the beginning and speak slowly so I can understand what you're saying."

"Polly Jo had it all planned out! She took Lorna Belle! She's gone!"

"What are you talking about?"

"You asked me to take Polly Jo by the nursing home to see Lorna Belle. Right?"

"Of course. So what? Did you take her out there?"

"Yes I did! And I made a big mistake!"

"What kind of mistake?"

"I left them alone while they visited."

"What's wrong with that? They're family."

"They hatched up a scheme to take off together."

"What? How could they do that? Lorna Belle's not in any condition to take off anywhere."

"At first everything seemed just fine. They finished visiting about ten-thirty and came out into the lobby together. Polly Jo said that Lorna Belle wanted to go for a ride and stop by the trailer park to see an old friend. I asked the nursing home administrator if it was okay and she said it was fine as long as I got her back before five-thirty."

"That sounds fine to me. So, what's the problem?"

"On the way into town Polly Jo asked me to stop at the Greyhound Bus Station on Monterey so she could check out the bus schedule to Mississippi. Lorna Belle went in with her."

"So? What's wrong with that?"

"I waited for almost thirty minutes and they never came back out. Polly Jo took off with her!"

"What makes you think that?"

"I went inside and they weren't there! The station manager told me that Polly Jo bought two one-way tickets to Biloxi and they together left on the eleven o'clock bus! They left me sitting there in the parking lot and got a ten-minute head start. Polly Jo had it all planned!"

"I think that's fine. There's nothing for Lorna Belle here any more. At least in Biloxi she has a place to stay and her sister will take real good care of her. There's nothing to worry about."

"Do you really think so?"

"Yes. It's fine. Don't worry about Lorna Belle. I'll have someone in Biloxi check on her."

"How do you know about her sister? Did you meet her?"

"Yes. I know her almost as well as I know Lorna Belle."

"Oh," Joy uttered as she tapped Mack on the arm. "Lorna Belle asked me to give this to you." She extended her open right hand. A flat lump wrapped in blue tissue paper and tied with a piece of pink crepe ribbon rested in her open palm There was a neatly-tied pink crepe bow on top.

"What is it?" Mack asked as he retrieved the flat lump from Joy's hand.

"She didn't tell me what it was. She asked me to give it to you. She told me that it was a 'lay up' or something like that."

"What?"

"She said that 'lay up' was a French Creole word and that if you have any Cajun friends they would be able to explain it to you. Do you know anyone who speaks Creole?"

"Yes. I have a very good friend from Louisiana who runs pontoon boat nature tours on Lake Okeechobee and also at Harbor Branch. I'll give him a call and ask him."

"What's his name? Ralph and I know a few old Louisiana coon asses in Okeechobee City."

"His name is Harry, but he likes to be called Clip.

"Clip? That's a strange name even for a coon ass. Why does he want to be called Clip?"

"He invented a machine that fits behind a boat and clips off the tops of marsh reeds as it travels down the bayou. It's used to make paths through the swamp for the hunters and fishermen. How did she pronounce that word again?"

"It sounded like 'lay up' and I think it has something to do with basketball."

"A 'lay up' is a basketball shot." Mack carefully untied the pink ribbon, unwrapped it from the flat blob and carefully peeled the blue tissue paper away from the flat object.

"What is it? It looks like a gold coin."

Mack laughed, gripped the coin between his right thumb and forefinger and sailed it across North Lake. It skipped on the surface four times before it lost momentum and sank below the dark surface.

"Why'd you do that? That was a gold coin! It's worth a lot of money to a coin collector."

"It's a fake." Mack spat in the water and turned toward to face Joy. "That crazy old lady wanted to poke fun at me one more time just to remind me that she sucked me in real good."

"I think that was a real coin. She wouldn't have wrapped a fake coin up that securely."

"Oh yes she would. She's a devious old bat and I don't need the grief."

"Why don't you call your Cajun friend in Okeechobee and ask him what that word means?"

"I will," Mack replied as he removed his cell phone from its belt clip and searched the directory for his friend's name. "Here it is. Hang on while I ask him what the word means."

"I don't think that I pronounced it right, but it sounded like 'lay up'."

"Hey Clip! Are you awake," Mack spoke into the cell phone. "I need your help. What is the meaning of a Cajun word that sounds like 'lay up'? Can you spell it for me? Thanks old buddy. I owe you one." Mack clicked the cell phone off and replaced it on his belt clip.

"What'd he say? Did I pronounce it right? What's it mean?"

"You were pretty close. It's pronounced *lan yap* and has a weird spelling."

"How's it spelled? I'll look it up in the dictionary at home."

"It's spelled l-a-g-n-i-a-p-p-e and pronounced *lan yap*."

"What's it mean in English?"

"*Lagniappe* means a small gift or token from a merchant, like a tip, given to a customer as a way of saying thanks for shopping at his store."

"Why did Lorna Belle tell me to tell you that coin was a 'lay up'?"

"I don't know. She's nuts."

"I think she's sweet. Polly Jo's the one who's nuts! The nursing home administrator is also a real sweet woman. Her husband is the Sewall's Point Police Chief and he stopped by to see Lorna Belle while I was there. He said that Lorna Belle baby-sat him when he was little and he gave her four one hundred dollar bills as a present. He said that he won the money in a high stakes poker game and wanted her to have it."

"It was a high stakes poker game alright," Mack muttered under his breath.

"What'd you say? I couldn't understand you."

"I said that I'm a lousy poker player. I can never figure out when someone else is bluffing."

"Oh."

"I don't mean to be rude, but I have a lot of things to do today and it's almost noon. Now that Lorna Belle and Polly Jo are out of my hair I can catch up things here at the marina. I have to cut the grass before Tina gets up here this afternoon."

"What about Ralph?"

"If he doesn't show up by three o'clock Elmo and I'll go looking for him."

"Thanks Mack," Joy gushed as she stood on her tiptoes and gave him a soft kiss on the cheek. "I'm going back to the house and get it cleaned up before Ralph gets here. That Polly Jo was a real pig! What do you want me to do with your dog?"

"Keep him at your place until Ralph gets back. You can use the company."

Joy turned, walked up the thirteen wooden stairs to the cottage porch, stopped at the top and waved a kiss in Mack's direction. He gave her a wave of his arm in response.

"*What am I going to tell her if Ralph doesn't show up this afternoon?*" Mack muttered to himself. "*I know that he's not going to show up and she knows it too.*"

He shook his head as he headed for the closed boathouse door. "*Damn! I still have to find the battery charger and connect it to the battery bank on Tina's sailboat. Maybe I should just hook up the shore power and be done with it.*"

Chapter 35

Mack heard a 'screech' from directly above the boathouse and looked up. An enormous black turkey buzzard stared down at him from the tin roof as if he expected Mack to provide him with his lunch. Mack waved him away and muttered under his breath, *"What the hell is Napoleon doing here on a Friday afternoon? He should be sunning himself on the island south of the Palm City Bridge with the rest of his smelly cohorts."*

Mack opened the boathouse door and slipped inside the darken space. A nasal voice rang out of the darkness, "Don't turn on the light! It's me!

Taken back Mack mumbled out a reply. "Rat! What the hell are you doing in the boathouse? At two o'clock this morning you were on your way back to Shepherd's Park."

"I knew that you wanted to see me today and I didn't feel like risking it by going past Sewall's Point last night. I had a feeling those bastards would be waiting for me at the Evan's Crary Bridge and spent the night in the boathouse. Give me a minute for my eyes to get adjusted before you turn on turn on the lights."

A slithering noise came from the northwest corner of the boathouse and Mack made out a thin dark shape shuffling towards him. "You couldn't have been very comfortable sleeping here."

"I found a couple of life preservers in Ralph's boat. That's all I needed for a pillow. Back in Nam' I spent a lot of nights sleeping on nothing except the ground." Rat shuffled up alongside Mack and tapped him on the forearm. "You're all tensed up. What's going on'?"

"All hell broke loose this morning and I'm not sure where it's going to go from here," Mack responded. "Lorna Belle and her rotten granddaughter took off in a bus for Mississippi this morning. TM's grandfather died last night and she's in a panic about where he might have hidden some gold. Then Tina called and chewed my ass. I told her that her telephone wasn't working and I couldn't make out what she was saying. Then I hung up. I don't need her crap."

"Is your telephone broken?"

"It is now. I broke it when I ripped it off the wall."

"What're your plans for this afternoon? Elmo said that a detective is coming by to talk to you about the guy that got shot in the trailer park. Did you shoot him?"

"No! And I don't intend to wait around here for him to show up. I didn't have anything to do with it and Elmo knows it."

"What're we going to do now?"

"Do you remember when we fell down the bluff and landed in that cave?"

"How could I forget it? The place is full of old chests and barrels. It's probably where the pirates stashed their loot. Let's go for it! I'm ready! My kayak's gassed up and ready to go."

"We don't dare take your kayak over there. The cops will be watching for you. We stand a better chance if we take Ralph's boat. It's less obvious and it can go faster if someone decides to chase us. Where's your kayak?"

"I stashed it alongside the northwest corner of the boathouse where nobody can see it."

"Drag that five gallon gas can over here and top off the gas tank in Ralph's boat. If we have to make a run for it I want that tank full."

"Aye, aye sir. Your wish is my command."

While Rat fueled up the boat Mack removed Ralph's bloody boot and carefully placed it on the boathouse dock along with the

bloody surveyor's stake. After Rat climbed onboard Mack
backed Ralph's boat out of the boathouse into North Lake. When
he was clear of the boathouse he pushed the electronic garage
door opener and the boathouse door slipped down into place.
Mack turned the steering wheel hard left, shoved the shift lever
forward, pointed the boat's bow toward the mouth of Willoughby
Creek and looked at Rat.

"We're going to climb up the bluff to the cave. I want to find
out what's inside those chests and barrels. If we find what I think
is up there we'll never have to work another day in our lives."

"What do you think is there?"

"From what I read I believe it's the illicit booty hidden by
Captain Henry Jennings a pirate that operated here in the early
seventeen hundred's. He preyed on the unarmed Spanish salvage
boats trying to get back to Cuba with the treasure from the 1717
Plate Fleet. There was a lot of treasure on those small boats and
he didn't have enough room to carry it in his ship. He had to
stash it somewhere! He was a greedy bastard and I think he stuck
his treasure in that cave. If it's there then we have another
problem."

"That's just what we need - another problem. What is it?"

"How do we get the treasure out of the cave and down the
bluff without anybody seeing us? Got any ideas?"

"We can roll the barrels down the bluff and pick 'em up at the
bottom."

"Now that's really a bright idea isn't it? The gold and jewels
would spill all over the beach. Come up with something else."

"How about if we lower 'em down the bluff with ropes? Then
we can load 'em in the boat."

"That might work. But, we have to find a way to make
ourselves so obvious that no one will suspect what we're really
doing up there."

"Let's dress up like surveyors! There's dozens of wooden
surveyor's stakes with yellow, red and blue plastic tape wrapped
on the top of them stuck all over Sewall's Point. We can go over
there, pull a bunch of 'em out and pretend we're replanting 'em."

"That's the best idea so far. Hang on. We're coming out of
Willoughby Creek into the St. Lucie River. I want to get the boat

up on plane so we can get across that sand bar between here and Trickle's Island. I'm going to scoot around the north side of Trickle's Island and try to miss the oyster bar on the south side of Sewall's Point. Then I'll slip in behind those two little islands where the Stuart Post Office was years ago. I'll pull up close to the bluff and tuck the boat under the mangroves so nobody can see us from the top of the bluff."

"Did you bring a snake bite kit?"

"Why should I bring a snake bite kit? Poisonous snakes don't come out in the daytime. It's to hot for them. They only come out at night when it cools off. You have nothing to worry about."

"Yeah. Right. If I get bit on the pecker you'll have to suck the poison out."

"Not in this lifetime! If you get bit by a snake there you're going to die."

"Come on Mack. I'd do it for you."

"It's not going to happen to me. Keep your eyes open for Elmo's boat and the cops."

The climb up the bluff was laborious and uneventful. The stubborn duo used pepper tree roots and limestone outcroppings for handholds. When Rat reached the mouth of the cave he paused and looked down the bluff. "It looks a lot different up here than it did last night and it's a long way down. We would've gotten hurt real bad if we'd fallen down there in the dark."

"That's old news. Now it's time to find out what Captain Jennings left us."

"Mack! Look at all the barrels and chests! I'll bet there's a fortune in gold and jewels here. I've always wanted to take a bath in jewels ever since I saw the movie *King Solomon's Mines*."

"You won't be taking a bath in those jewels if I have anything to say about it. It would take a week to clean them off so that a woman could wear them. The smell might never go away."

"Are you saying that I smell bad?"

"It's all relative."

"Relative to what?"

"Whatever you're compared to. It could be a skunk, a dead bear or a three day old salmon."

"That doesn't sound very nice."

"It wasn't meant to sound nice. Pop the lid on that trunk and let's take a look inside."

"What if there's a poisonous snake inside and he bites me?"

"Just pray that he doesn't bite you on the pecker because I'll guarantee that you'll die."

"There's nothing in here except a bunch of old whiskey and rum bottle labels."

"Try another one."

"It's also full of whiskey and rum labels."

"There's no pirate treasure in here. This is where a bootlegger from the Prohibition days kept his stash of generic labels. After he bottled the booze he pasted on whatever label the customer requested. Good old American ingenuity and free enterprise at work."

"How about the barrels?"

"Push on one and tip it over. They might still be full of illegal hooch."

"If they are I get first 'dibs.' My boys are tired of drinking Aqua Velva cut with Sterno."

"You can have all of it if you can figure out how to get it out of here and down to the bottom."

Rat put his skinny shoulder against the closest barrel and pushed. It tipped over and hit the dirt with a hollow 'thud.'

"It's empty," Rat reflected with an empty sigh as he threw his hands upward.

"I figured that much. Wooden stave barrels aren't airtight and the booze evaporated. Let's get out of here and back to the marina before someone sees us." Mack motioned toward the cave entrance with his arm. "I don't want to see that Sewall's Point Police Chief again especially if his boys catch us in here. He made that very clear last night! Let's go."

Rat stuck his head out of the cave entrance and a deep male voice rang out from above. "What's going on down there? Who's in the cave? That place is dangerous and you're trespassing on private property! If you don't get out of there right now I'm calling the cops!"

"They know we're in here! We're going back to jail for keeps this time!"

"Relax. It's not the cops. Let me handle it." Mack stuck his head out of the cave entrance, cupped his hands around his mouth and yelled upward to the man standing on the rim above.

"It's okay. We're land surveyors. We were taking some readings for new topographical maps. We just finished up and we're leaving. Thank you for your concern for our safety."

"Oh. Then it's okay," the voice replied from above. "I thought you were some kids playing in the bootlegger's cave or another crazy treasure hunter. We get a lot of them over here."

"I'll make sure that you receive a copy of the new map when it comes out next month."

"Thanks. Have a good day and be careful going back down. That bluff is real steep in a few places. Keep a good eye out because there's a lot of poisonous snakes in the rocks."

"Thank you. We'll watch our step and where we put our hands." Mack pulled his head back into the cave entrance. "I told you it would be okay."

"Did you hear what he said about the poisonous snakes?"

"Did you hear what I told you will happen if you get bitten? Be careful."

"I heard. Let's get out of here before something bad happens."

"Go ahead. I'm right behind you."

Rat slithered out of the cave and slid head first down the bluff pausing momentarily when he reached a rock outcropping. Poisonous snakes were on his mind.

Mack looked at his watch. It read 2:42 P.M. *"I've got to get back to the marina. Tina might show up at any time and Ralph's due back this afternoon,"* he mumbled to himself.

Ralph's boat was waiting where they left it and there were no cops at the bottom of the bluff to arrest them for trespassing. They piled into the boat and headed for Willoughby Creek and Port Sewall Marina. Mack spotted Elmo on the boat dock when he turned into North Lake from Willoughby Creek. His first inclination was to turn the boat around and head out to sea. But, he idled across North Lake, pulled up to the dock and tossed Elmo the stern line.

"Elmo make a round turn around that cleat, follow it up with a couple of figure eights and a half hitch at the end." Mack made a circling gesture with his hand. "Rat throw the bow line around the other cleat and do the same thing that Elmo's doing."

"Aye, aye sir."

"Mack why do you have Ralph's boat out?" Elmo inquired with a frown.

"I had to make a quick trip and Rat's kayak's to slow."

"Joy was down here earlier, peeked in the boathouse and saw that Ralph's boat was gone. She thought somebody stole it to get rid of the evidence and she called me."

"I didn't steal Ralph's boat and I put his boot and that surveyor's stake on the dock in the boathouse where they'd be safe. Where's Joy now?"

"She's in the cottage crying her eyes out. She thinks that you did something to Ralph."

"That's ridiculous and you know it!"

"Of course I do, but she doesn't. Why were you sneaking around Sewall's Point again?"

"What did you say? I didn't hear you."

"Why were you were sneaking around Sewall's Point again."

"Huh? I still can't hear you. Can you repeat the question? I must have wax in my ears."

"You don't have anything in your ears or between them for that matter. My brother-in-law is really pissed off at you. He figures that you knocked off the trailer park manager and were trying to rip off Lorna Belle Mobley for her gold coins."

"Neither of those things is true. I had nothing to do with the trailer park manager getting whacked although if anyone deserved it he did. I was just trying to help Lorna Belle."

"That's not what he thinks. His wife said that Lorna Belle left town with her niece to get away from you. She's afraid of you."

"Who told her that crap?"

"Lorna Belle's niece told her this morning when Joy took her to the nursing home to visit her. They had a meeting and BJ gave Lorna Belle the four hundred bucks that his men took off of you. It was her money anyway."

"Did Lorna Belle say that she was afraid of me?"

"I don't know. Her niece did all of the talking before they brought Lora Belle into the office."

"That figures. Poison mouth Polly Jo hates everyone except herself."

"Why weren't you here when detective Mel Mangini stopped by? I told you last night that he was coming by today to talk to you about the trailer park manager that was killed."

"I forgot about it and I don't have anything to offer. I only saw the man twice."

"Maybe so, but from what I hear you might be a suspect."

"Why? I didn't do it. What motive would I have to kill him?"

"To shut him up about what he told you about Lorna Belle."

"That's ridiculous!"

"Joy's coming down the steps," Rat offered. "She looks sad."

"Mack don't say anything to her about what I told you. She's upset enough as it is."

"Yes Elmo. I understand. Just pull the ring in the back of my shirt when you want me to open my mouth and you can put the words in all by yourself. Don't let her see your lips move."

"Did you find Ralph?" Joy squeaked out between gasps for breath.

"No. Rat and I took a run over to Sewall's Point and the Archipelago to look for clues."

"Did you find anything?"

"Nope."

"What am I going to do without Ralph?"

'Blaaat! Blaaat! Blaaat!' Three prolonged blasts from a commercial fishing boat's dual stainless steel air horns split the still air like a knife.

"Who's that?" Rat pointed toward the entrance to Willoughby Creek.

"That's Bobo's roller rig boat," Elmo responded. "He was down south fishing for sardines."

'Blaaat! Blaaat! Blaaat!" The resonating air horns announced the proud boat's grand entrance as it turned and slowly made its way into North Lake.

"What does that guy want?" Elmo inquired. "He should be unloading down at the fish house."

"Who's that up on the flying bridge waving his hat?" Mack questioned. "That's not Bobo!"

"It's Ralph! It's Ralph! Joy screamed. "It's my Ralph! He's back. It's Ralph!"

"It is Ralph!" Elmo blurted out. "Why didn't he tell us he was going to the Keys with Bobo?"

"It's Ralph! It's Ralph!" Joy screamed. It's Ralph! It's Ralph!"

"Maybe he forgot," Rat offered. "Or, maybe he didn't know where he was going."

"Ralph knew where he was going," Mack offered. "He wrote Joy in his note that he was going fishing in the Keys. He just forgot to say that he was going with Bobo. A simple oversight."

"That let's you off the hook over Ralph's disappearance last Friday night," Elmo spouted. "I never did think that you had anything to do with it anyway."

"That isn't what you were suggesting five minutes ago. How about the trailer park guy? Am I off the hook for what happened to him too?"

"That's not in my jurisdiction. I only get involved with crimes that happen on the water."

Bobo swung the forrty-five foot boat alongside the dock as neatly as a surgeon removing an appendix. Ralph leaped off the flying bridge onto the dock and Joy caught him with outstretched arms. She attempted to smother his mouth with hers, but he deftly dodged her direct attack.

"Hi guys! Anything interesting happen around here while I was in the Keys with Bobo?"

"Nothing much at all Ralph," Mack responded. "Nothing much at all."

"Me and Bobo were in Marathon fishing for ballyhoo. We caught a couple hundred and sold them to bait shops in Miami and West Palm on the way back up here."

"I'm so glad you're home, "Joy cooed in Ralph's ear. "Let's go home and talk about it."

"Hang on a minute. I've only been gone a week and we're not newly weds anymore. First, I gotta' get caught up on what's happened around here while I was gone."

"Ralph can I see you in the boathouse for a minute?" Mack asked. "I'll fill you in."

"Okay. Joy hold that thought for a minute. I'll be right back. Mack wants to talk to me."

Mack and Ralph walked down the dock together and turned left into the dark boathouse.

"Ralph where the hell have you been? We've all been scared half to death that somebody 'popped' you and dumped your body offshore."

"I was fishing with Bobo in Marathon."

"Don't give me that crap! You don't have any sunburn."

"I wore sunscreen."

"Lift your watch band up."

"Why?"

"I want to know what time it is."

"Look at it your own watch!"

"It doesn't work."

"It sure does! I can read the dial from over here. It shows three forty-five just like mine."

"You and I both know you weren't fishing in the Keys with Bobo. There's no white line under your watchband and there're no round white raccoon marks around your eyes where the skin was protected by sunglasses. You weren't fishing! Where were you?"

"Will you promise me that you won't tell Joy?"

"No! Did you two run off with a couple of strippers like you did a couple of years ago?"

"No. I was in the hospital, but don't let Joy to know about it. She'd worry herself to death."

"What! Why were you in the hospital? Where?"

"In West Palm Beach. I was in the VA Hospital."

"Why?"

"I was fishing over by Bird Island last Friday night. About midnight a bunch of teenagers came by and started throwing rocks at me off that little bridge in the Archipelago. When a rock hit me in the head, I fired up the engine and took after them. They thought it was funny and kept throwing rocks at me. The boat hit the beach at full speed, I flew out and my left leg hit a wooden surveyor's stake. It went through my left thigh all the way to the bone. I was bleeding like a stuck pig!"

"What did you do?"

"I tried calling you for help. You didn't answer your phone."

"I was out of town."

"I called Bobo on my cell phone and he came down and got me. We tied my boat up under that little bridge. I didn't figure I'd be gone long enough for anyone to find it."

"Elmo found it and towed it back here. You forgot your left boot and it was covered with blood. The surveyor's stake was in the boat and it was also covered with blood."

"When Bobo pulled it out of my leg blood shot all over the place. There was so much pain in my leg that I forgot about the boot."

"Why was there a gold foil covered chocolate coin in the bottom of your boat?"

"I thought the kids were throwing rocks at me, but they were throwing those coins. I can't imagine where they got 'em."

"They came off a float that was in the 'Stuart Dancin' in the Streets' parade."

"Oh."

"How did you get that note in the house that said you went fishing in the Keys?"

"Bobo snuck in and left it. Joy sleeps like a zombie and snores like a deaf Iowa hog."

"The two Florida Keys postcards that you sent Joy had West Palm Beach postmarks."

"That's because I was in the VA Hospital in West Palm Beach."

"How did you get there?"

"In Bobo's boat. He dropped me off at the Riviera Beach Marina and I took a cab over."

"How did you get your hands on Florida Keys postcards in West Palm Beach?"

"They sell 'em in the gift shop. So you picked up on that too did you?"

"That wasn't hard. Why the upside down smiley face?"

"I wasn't feeling good I had a big hole in my left thigh."

"Joy said you weren't feeling so hot and that you couldn't remember things."

"Yep. The VA gave me some new heart medication and it didn't get along with me. It made me dizzy and I think that's why I fell down when I was chasing those teenagers."

"Okay. The mystery of your disappearance is solved and your secret's safe with me. Did you ever know a Lorna Belle Mobley?"

"Of course I know her! She baby-sat me when she lived on Sewall's Point. B. J. Brown, he's the Sewell's Point Police Chief, and I used to sneak down the bluff behind her backyard and hide out in an old cave. We played pirate in there for years and she never knew where we were."

"That explains a lot."

"It explains a lot of what?"

"Nothing. It's not important now. Did her house have a basement?"

"Yep. But she didn't like for us to go down there. She said it was haunted by pirate ghosts."

"Did you ever go down there?"

"Does a bear crap in the woods? Of course we did. There was a trap door down there to a tunnel that led into the cave and she didn't know about it. When we heard her hollering for us up on the bluff we'd sneak through the tunnel and come up out of the basement. She thought we'd been down there the whole time."

"Was there anything strange in the basement?"

"There was lots of strange stuff down there? Like what exactly?"

"Did you ever see and old metal chest down there?"

"Oh yeah! There was a solid metal box in a corner. It was welded shut and welded to a steel beam that stuck up out of the concrete floor. We never got to see what was inside."

"Did you ever see a black man hanging around her place?"

"Old Frank Holmes from Tick Ridge in Jensen Beach came over every week to cut her grass and trim the bushes. He did odd jobs around there for years."

"Did you ever see him digging any holes in the backyard?"

"Yeah! One day he was digging a hole for a septic tank when he screamed and jumped out of the hole and ran down the road. I think he hurt his back real bad because he never came back"

"Why'd he run away?"

"He found a human skull. Lorna Belle figured the back yard was an Indian burial ground."

"What happened to the hole?"

"She hired a couple of guys to come over and fill it up."

"Ralph take Joy home. I'll keep your secret and you forget everything you told me."

"Okay. Is there anything else you want to know about? I'm in no big hurry to go home."

"No. But Joy's in a big hurry to get you home. I think she wants to talk to you."

"Okay," Ralph replied with a knowing grin. "Wanna' go snook fishing tomorrow?"

"No thanks. I have a lot of things to catch up on and so do you. Sleep in tomorrow."

"I guess I do too," Ralph replied.

When Mack opened the boathouse door he gestured for Ralph to go out ahead of him. When he stepped out Joy ran across the dock and jumped up into his arms. "I think she missed me," Ralph muttered in Mack's direction.

When Mack came out of the boathouse he saw that Rat and Elmo were engaged in a serious conversation at the end of the dock. He knew he had to break it up before Rat said something that he shouldn't. *"Rat! Keep your mouth shut,"* Mack softly mumbled to himself. He rambled up to the animated duo and hailed them. "Looks like all the excitement's over. Ralph's back and Joy's happy. He's going to pick his boat up in the morning."

"Where was he really?" Elmo asked. "I know he wasn't fishing. He didn't get any sun."

"Promise you won't tell Joy? You too Rat!"

"I promise," Elmo replied.

"Me too," Rat responded. "Come on Mack. Tell us where he was. We won't tell."

"Ralph and Bobo picked up a couple of strippers at that topless bar in Rio. They spent the week tied up in a slip at Riviera Beach Marina. That's why Ralph didn't get any sun."

"She'll kill him if she finds out!" Elmo exclaimed. He's a dead man!"

"She won't find out unless one of you says something to her."

"I won't say anything," Elmo replied with a grin. "My lips are sealed forever."

"Me too," Rat squeaked. "It's almost four thirty and I've got to go. I'll see you tomorrow." Rat slithered around the corner of the boathouse and was gone.

"Mack! Look who's coming down the stairs," Elmo stammered. "It's time for me to go too!"

Mack swiveled his head around just in time to see Tina reach the bottom step. "Elmo hang around for awhile. She doesn't look very happy."

It was too late. Elmo had cast off his lines and was already halfway across North Lake.

"Okay buster. Let's talk about this. What the hell have you been up too? You've got half of Martin County up in arms."

"Tina! I don't know what you mean. I haven't done anything."

"Right! How about getting arrested twice by BJ for trespassing after he warned you not to come back to Sewell's Point?"

"I don't hear very well. I think I have a hearing defect. I should get it checked."

"You hear exactly what you want to hear and there's nothing wrong with your telephone line. It works just fine. I had it checked by the telephone company right after I called you."

"The telephone's broken. Go in the cottage and look for yourself."

"I've already been there. The telephone in the bedroom works just fine. I called it on my cell phone while I was standing beside it. Now what's your excuse?"

"I'm stupid, lazy and inconsiderate?"

"That'll do for now. I've had a rough week. I need a couple of drinks and a good dinner. You're taking me out to dinner and if we hurry we can still make happy hour."

"It's not even five o'clock yet! That's too early for dinner!"

"It's eight o'clock somewhere! Did you wash my boat down and charge up the batteries?"

"Yes."

"Did you fill up the fresh water tank? I want to take a shower."

"It's all set. The water should be hot because I plugged in the shore power about noon."

"I'm going to freshen up and change clothes. You need to take a shower and clean up before you go anywhere! I'll meet you upstairs in twenty minutes. Be ready! I'm starved."

"I'll be ready." Mack turned toward the boathouse. "First I'll pull Ralph's boat into the boathouse." Mack entered the dark boathouse and reached for the electronic door opener control mounted on the wall.

"Mr. McCray! Don't touch the light switch," rang out a deep, resonant male voice from deep in the shadows. It wasn't the voice of CNN!

Chapter 36

Mack recoiled instinctively and stammered out a reply, "How did you get in here?"

"I have an electronic garage door opener just like yours."

"Were you in here when I was talking to Ralph?"

"Of course."

"Why didn't I see you?"

"You didn't turn on the light. I've been waiting for you to come back for almost two hours."

"Who killed the guy in the boathouse Saturday morning?"

"Ask your girlfriend. She balled him all night."

"Who was he?"

"He was a body double. We sent him here as a decoy for you."

"A decoy? Why? I can take care of myself."

"Not this time. There was more than one person involved. But you can relax .We got the last one last night. It's over."

"What do you mean you got the last one? How many guys were after me?"

"Let's just leave it at more than one."

"Why did you drag me to Biloxi and shuttle me to Washington and back?"

"You crossed the wrong people when you started sniffing around for buried treasure. They picked up on you when you stopped at the trailer park to get information on the old lady. They thought you were after her gold. We called you to Biloxi to get you out of here."

"Was the guy who got whacked in the boathouse here because I was looking for treasure?"

"No. Some people in Chicago felt that you were a loose end that needed to be cleaned up. You have some enemies that want to see you gone and you have to be careful."

"Which guy was sent down here from Chicago to whack me?"

"There were three. We got the last one last night."

"Three!"

"Yes three, but they've been taken care of. You're smelly buddy smacked one guy over the head with a concrete block Sunday night and dumped the body offshore."

"Who was he?"

"We don't know. Somebody dropped him off in a black limo with no license plate early Sunday evening. He hung around the north side of the cottage and waited for you get back."

"Why didn't you do something about it before he broke my neck with that wire cable?"

"Your friend smacked him in the head with a concrete block."

"Why didn't you do something first?"

"I couldn't get a clear shot at him because your friend kept getting in the way."

"What do you know about the guy that got whacked in the trailer park Tuesday night?"

"We took care of him."

"What! A crazy police chief wants to pin it on me. He said the guy was shot with my pistol!"

"He's bluffing. Your pistol is in the kitchen drawer where you left it. He didn't have any ballistics test results. He was trying to find out what you knew and he got you to admit that you own a semi-automatic Berretta pistol. The Martin County Sheriff's Department forensics people identified the murder weapon as a Berretta based on the empty cartridge cases left at the scene."

"So, somebody sent a goon down here from Chicago to whack me and somebody else was after me because I knew about the old lady's buried treasure. How do they tie together?"

"Most of it was coincidental. The trailer park manager was the eyes and ears of the old lady's daughter. The first time you stopped at the trailer park he dropped a dime on you right after you left. When they brought in a body double of your friend Ralph we knew they had something planned. But, we didn't know what. That's why we called you back to Biloxi."

"How about the meeting I had with the old lady's sister at Books A Million in Gulfport?"

"That was coincidental. We had no idea that she would show up there. We don't understand how the old lady knew who you were unless her sister called her and told her you were coming."

"What about the young stripper in the bar? She's the old lady's granddaughter!"

"Be happy. You got lucky."

"What am I supposed to do now?"

"Make up with your girlfriend. My job's done."

The garage door slowly slid up. Before Mack's eyes became accustomed to the sunlight a Jet Ski engine cranked up in a dark corner of the boathouse and suddenly it was gone. The garage door slid down and sealed off Mack's view into North Lake. He reached for the control box mounted on the wall and pressed the 'up' button with his thumb. Nothing happened.

"That smart bastard disconnected the electrical power to the control box," Mack mumbled as he strode out of the boathouse and bumped into Tina."

"Where do you think you're going?" Tina shoved Mack away with both hands. "I told you to get upstairs and clean up because we're going out for dinner!"

"I got hung up with a guy in the boathouse."

"Hung up with a guy in the boathouse? I don't see anybody."

"Do you see the guy on the black Jet Ski heading for Willoughby Creek?"

"Of course I do. A guy on a Jet Ski isn't such a big deal."

"He was waiting for me in the boathouse and I spent the last twenty minutes talking to him."

"Why would a guy wait in the boathouse just to talk to you?"

"It's a long story. What do you know about the dead guy you found in the boathouse?"

"Nothing! Get upstairs and get yourself cleaned up. It's already after five o'clock. Happy hour is going to start in a few minutes and I don't intend to be late!

"Fine," Mack responded as he turned toward the stairway leading up to the marina cottage. I'll be ready to go in five minutes."

"This time I'm going with you to be certain that nobody's hiding in the bathroom."

"Where's that little Mississippi slitch that spent all week here with you?"

"She's gone. She and her grandmother left for Mississippi on a bus about noon. Joy dropped them off at the bus terminal."

When Mack and Tina entered the cottage Mack headed for the bathroom as Tina sat down in the recliner. She picked up the open treasure hunting book and casually snapped a quip over her left shoulder just as Mack entered the bathroom. "I understand that you met Lorna Belle. She had a thing going on with a black guy from Tick Ridge for almost fifteen years. She kept it under wraps, but all the locals knew what was going on."

"What!"

"Did she tell you a wild story about finding buried pirate treasure on the beach during a hurricane?"

"She sure did," Mack responded as he walked out of the bathroom toward the living area. "She and the black guy found the poop deck and captain's cabin of a Spanish treasure ship. They whacked it open with an axe and dragged off several boxes of gold coins that they hid in a storage shed behind the Sand Club on Jensen Beach."

"She told that story to a lot of people. It's not true! She made it all up!"

"What!"

"BJ and everybody in town knew she was nuts."

"Where'd she get the gold coins that she peddled around here for years?"

"She married an old guy who stayed overnight at the Sand Club when he got so smashed that he couldn't drive home. He was a treasure hunter in the late 1940's. Rumor had it that he made a major strike in the Keys and didn't tell his financial backers. He kept his gold in a steel chest in his basement that was welded to a steel beam embedded in the concrete floor. After he died Lorna Belle hired a welder to cut the box open. It was filled with gold coins! The black guy melted the coins down with a blowtorch and she peddled the gold to jewelry stores between here and West Palm Beach."

"You knew what she was up to all along?"

"The whole town did. When she ran out of gold she moved to Mississippi and went back to stripping. After she got to old to strip she moved back here and bought a trailer in Trailer Town."

"If you knew all this why didn't you tell that crazy police chief to leave me alone?"

"It was a lot of fun and BJ enjoyed having you as his guest. We go back a long way."

"I heard he went snook fishing when he was supposed to take you to a school dance."

"Who told you that?"

"Elmo."

"Elmo has a big mouth!"

"Are you sure that you don't know anything about the dead guy you found in the boathouse?"

"I already told you that I didn't know anything about him. I was only attracted to him because I was smashed and he looked like you. He was a lousy lay and not worth the effort."

"There's nothing better than the original."

"Did you ever hear of the 'Real McCoy'?"

"I heard the expression, but I have a feeling that you're going to tell me anyway."

"Captain Bill McCoy was a well-known local rumrunner during Prohibition.

"He advertised his rum as being the best available. If it passed his test it was called 'The Real McCoy'. He kept his labels in that cave you and Rat were playing in the other night. That gave BJ quite a laugh. Are you the real Mack McCray?"

"I think I can pass the taste test."

"That's not funny! Get your butt in the bathroom and get cleaned up! It's almost happy hour and I'm ready to go. I had a really bad day."

A few minutes later Mack emerged from the bedroom in a pair of gray slacks, a powder-blue shirt and blue blazer. "Do I look passable?" He asked as he did a pirouette in the hallway.

"You'll do for tonight. At dinner I want you to fill me in on everything you did last week. We have a lot to talk about with your trip to Biloxi and all. I'd like to take off for a few days, go to Biloxi and gamble. I'd like to stay at the Beau Rivage and eat at McElroy's Seafood Restaurant. Would you show me around? I hear there's a cute little cottage on Melody Lane in Bay St. Louis. We could stop in at a quaint little tavern called Lorna Belle's for a nightcap and walk along the beach back to the Beau Rivage. It'll be lots of fun."

Mack shuttered as he shook his head. *"She knows everything,"* he thought to himself.

Tina chose Indian River Plantation Resort for dinner. She dined on whole Maine lobster chased by six *Absolut'* vodka martinis. Mack chose a medium rare cut of prime rib and three brandy Manhattans. He drove Tina's BMW Z3 back to Port Sewall Marina because she couldn't see to drive. He parked it in front of the steps that led down to her boat, but she had other plans for him. It was only 8:43 P.M. He walked around to Tina's side of the car, opened the door and extended his hand toward her. "Ma'am. May I help you out?"

"Are you the real Mack McCray?" She asked with an opossum-eating grin on her face. "I'd like to find out for certain so I can give you the proper stamp of approval."

"Yes I am and I can to prove it."

Tina squeezed his hand and used it to pull herself out of the bucket seat. "Let's go inside and find out." She stood up, passed out and fell across his chest.

"You'll never know," Mack mumbled under his breath.

"Oh yes I will," Tina replied as she stuck her tongue in his ear. "I was checking your reflexes and you passed. Now pick me up in your arms and carry me across the threshold of your castle."

"It's not a castle and it's not mine. It's a cottage over a boathouse and it belongs to you."

"I forgot. Carry me in anyway. I can't walk. I'm plastered."

Once they were in the cottage Mack gently positioned Tina in one of the recliners. "You wait here while I brew up a pot of coffee. If we're going to do this we're going to be sober."

"I don't want to be sober and I don't want any coffee." Tina extended her arms out toward him and cooed, "I just want you." She beckoned him with her fingers.

"First I want you to tell me everything you know about the guy who looked like me."

"Why?" She whined.

"Someone wants to kill me and you might have a clue who it is."

"I don't want you killed." She stuck out her lower lip in a fake pout. "I'll tell you everything."

"Go ahead. I'm listening."

"Come closer so I can whisper in your ear. If somebody's outside waiting to kill you I don't want him to hear what I'm telling you. He might get mad at me."

"Okay." Mack pulled a dinette chair alongside the recliner. "I'm ready."

"I did it."

"You did what?"

"I shot him with the Berretta semi-automatic pistol that you keep in the kitchen drawer."

"Why?"

"I was sleeping right here in this recliner when he showed up about two in the morning. I was half in the bag and I thought he was you. Plus, I was horny and needed to be laid."

"Why did you kill him?"

"That wasn't my original intent. He balled me three times and passed out. That pissed me off. I used Ketamine Hydrochloride spray to keep him quiet while I went through his pockets."

"What did you find?"

"He was carrying your driver's license, social security card and credit cards in his wallet. I think it was your wallet."

"It probably was. I left it here when I went to Mississippi. Was he carrying a gun?"

"Yes. He had a cute *Glock* nine millimeter equipped with a military silencer in his jacket."

"When did you shoot him?"

"I stayed awake all night because he snored like a camel. I woke up about seven o'clock and got dressed. Then I woke him up. After he got dressed I told him that I heard a noise coming from the boathouse and was afraid. His male chivalry came out and he had to save a damsel in distress by slaying the evil dragon. That was his mistake."

"What do you mean his mistake?"

"He took off down the stairs to the boathouse and I followed him down with the Berretta in my pocket. I hung onto his shirttail and whimpered like a scared little girl. He liked that."

"Then what? You popped him?"

"Of course, but I waited until he got inside the boathouse. It was dark inside and he was real cautious. I threw a quarter in the water to distract him and popped him six times in the back."

"That explains it!"

"Explains what?"

"Rat said that you told him the guy was shot with a German or Italian semi-automatic pistol because of the circular holes in his back. You told him that because you did it. Then what?"

"After he fell over I gave him a final shot behind the right ear. He never knew what hit him."

"What happened to his gun?"

"He dropped it in the water when he fell."

"Now it all fits together."

"What do you mean it all fits together?"

"You screamed about eleven o'clock, but he was killed about seven. That's why he was stiff as a board when I got there. He'd been dead for four hours. Why'd you cut off his fingertips?"

"I saw it in a spy movie a few years ago."

"Where'd you get the knife?"

"Your kitchen. Do you want to know which one I used?"

"No thanks. What did you do with his fingertips?"

"I sliced them off over the water and the cat snappers living under the boathouse ate them."

"You knew the whole time that I was me! Even when you were sitting on top of me with the duct tape and bottle of fingernail polish remover ready to torture me. You bitch!"

"I'll take that as a compliment. But I feel really bad about one thing," Tina sniffed.

"You feel bad? Come on give me a break!"

"I do so feel real bad! Do you want to know why?"

"I suppose that you wanted to drive slivers of bamboo under his fingernails and light them?"

"No. *Puka* and *Kea* saw me shoot him and they got very upset. They think I'm a killer."

"They seemed happy the last time I saw them. They know that I'm okay."

"Good. I was worried."

"There is one thing that you should improve in your technique if you're planning on continuing as an assassin."

"What is it? Do you really think that I could do something like this again?"

"You have the taste for it and you only made one mistake."

"I made a mistake? Then why did it take you so long to figure out that I shot him?"

"I had a suspicion from the beginning. His fingertips were sliced off at an angle with a knife. Only an amateur would do that. Next time use a cigar trimmer so you can roll them onto fingerprint cards and make useable prints."

"I never thought of that."

"Everyone thinks he spent the night with you on your sailboat. How did you pull that off?"

"Easy. After I whacked him I got on my boat and went to bed. I needed some sleep. Speaking of sleep I'm bushed. Would you mind if I spent the night up here? I'm a little hesitant to spend the night on my boat alone. After all I am a defenseless woman."

"No problem. Go into the bedroom and make yourself right at home. I want to do some reading before I turn in."

Chapter 37

Weekends often come and go without a whisper. This was such a weekend at Port Sewall Marina.

Tina returned to her condo in West Palm Beach on Sunday afternoon to prepare for a Monday trial. Ralph and Joy didn't leave their love nest and their friends wisely refrained from bothering them. They sent Mack's dog home Saturday morning with a note tied to his collar that read 'Do not disturb'. There was a smiley face on the bottom of the hand-penned note.

Rat enjoyed a fruitful weekend gathering fresh road kill along Interstate 95 in spite of Napoleon's jealous screams. Deputy Elmo spent the weekend at the sandbar north of Clam Island harassing dozens of teenaged boaters out feeling their oats and enjoying too much beer.

Mack put up with Tina's constant barrage of banter about his whereabouts the week before and the Mississippi 'slitch' who appeared at the marina shortly after his return. He offered several clear alibis and denials none of which were acceptable to Tina. He reluctantly agreed to take her to Biloxi and Gulfport, Mississippi for a long weekend if she promised to stop asking questions.

Monday dawned anew with the fresh breath of another day. It was 8:28 A.M. when Mack finished breakfast, fed the dog and the cat, and sat down in the green recliner with a cup of coffee to enjoy a few moments of peace.

"There's nothing that can get me excited today," Mack thought to himself.

At 8:42 Mack slurped down the last sip of lukewarm coffee and replaced the cup on the saucer. *"I've got to do it,"* he said under his breath. He held his hand up palm forward toward his dog and gave him strict instructions. "You stay here and watch the place. I have to make a run over to Jensen Beach." The dog seemed to understand and placed his muzzle between his outstretched front paws. On the way out the front door Mack patted his right front pants pocket. *"It's still there,"* he whispered to himself.

Mack pulled into the Jensen Beach Park parking lot and parked his truck alongside the small copse of three weathered Australian pine trees bordering the main road. He scanned the parking lot with his eyes and didn't see any cars. *"It's a Monday and there's no reason for anyone to be on the beach. I should be out of here in five minutes."* He slipped into the waist high growth and headed for the tree with the broken off top.

It took him less than a minute to shinny the twenty feet to the top. He hung onto the trunk with his left arm and probed his pants pocket with the fingers of his right hand. He grasped the coin tightly between his thumb and index finger and allowed himself one last glimpse of the shiny metal before he stuffed it into the cleft with his thumb. It softly slipped into its original cocoon of tree fiber.

"Lorna Belle would have wanted it this way," Mack chuckled to himself as he slid down the tree trunk to the sandy soil below. *"Like the ghost of a swash buckling treasure burying pirate she'll be back one day to claim it."*

Epilogue

"One writes out of one thing only – one's own experience. Everything depends on how relentlessly one forces from this experience the last drop, sweet or bitter, it can possibly give."

James Baldwin
(1924-1987)

"If you want to check my story out run out to Jensen Beach where the sand Club used to be. The Australian pine tree is on the northwest corner of Ocean Drive. The top's broken off but you can still see the cleft about twenty feet up."

Lorna Belle Mobley speaking to McCray, Chapter 20, p. 226.

PROBLEMS OF PIONEERING

   You are living on an undeveloped island,
"Hutchinson" by name. It is 27 miles long,
extending from Ft. Pierce Inlet, St. Lucie
County, to St. Lucie Inlet, Martin County.
Though it is practically uninhabitated, you
will find it the most beautiful beach in all
of Florida.

   Because of pioneering, we have two BIG
problems:

   1. ELECTRICITY. We make our own. It's
supply is limited and sometimes it stops
entirely. There are candles in your room.
If this happens we beg your forbearance and
hope the delay will not be for long. Because
the motor is noisy, all lights will be cut
at 11:30 P.M.

   2. WATER. The main supply is from an ar-
tesian well, 1300 feet deep. It is slighty
salty and sulphurous, pure, good for you.
Occasionally sulphur flakes, black, which
collects on the pipes, will descend on you.
Just be patient. Keep the water running and
it will disappear. Drinking water carried from
the m inland is in the lounge.

   Sand Flies(tiny "No-See-Ums") with a
wicked bite come on the West wind. Your
screens will be "painted" and these should
never bother you inside.

                              The Management

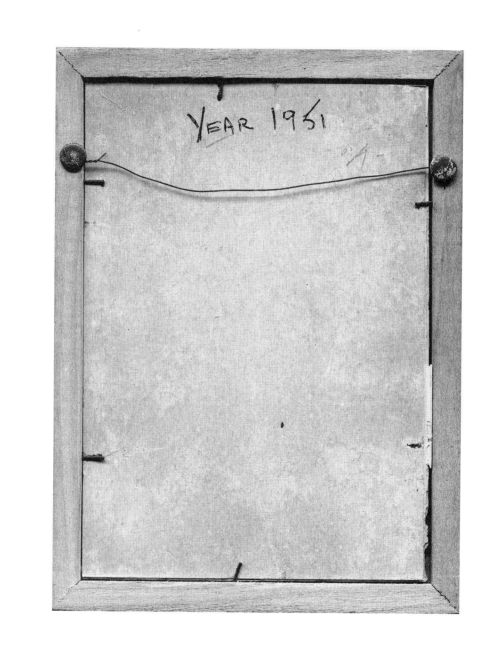

A Typical Bedroom . . .

•

Comfort . . . in Natural Beauty

Accommodations are superb in a
lovely setting of sand and sea . . .
for the ultimate pleasure of your
Florida vacation

Operated by
Mr. AND Mrs. FORREST B. LINDLEY

•

The Club Lounge . . .

The SAND CLUB

A Delightful, Informal
Oceanfront Resort
on the Atlantic

at

JENSEN BEACH, FLORIDA

A quiet, exclusive club, offering a beautiful beach and the finest surf bathing and fishing

The **SAND CLUB**

BOX 648   JENSEN BEACH, FLORIDA

Charming modern accommodations — beautifully furnished bedrooms with individual adjoining baths — in a residential atmosphere on unspoiled Hutchinson's Island.

In its naturally lovely setting of private beach, with miles of open ocean beaches nearby. The Sand Club offers relaxation and recreation close by the sea and Gulf Stream . . .

Bathe or sun bathe, enjoy surf fishing, or just relaxation by sand and surf, sea grapes, spanish bayonets and palms . . .

Easily reached by causeway from mainland. Convenient to churches, schools and shopping centers. One hour drive to Palm Beach, fifteen minutes to Stuart, thirty minutes to Fort Pierce along the beautiful Indian River.

Guests residing at the Club automatically become members.

Inquiries invited for reservations and particulars.

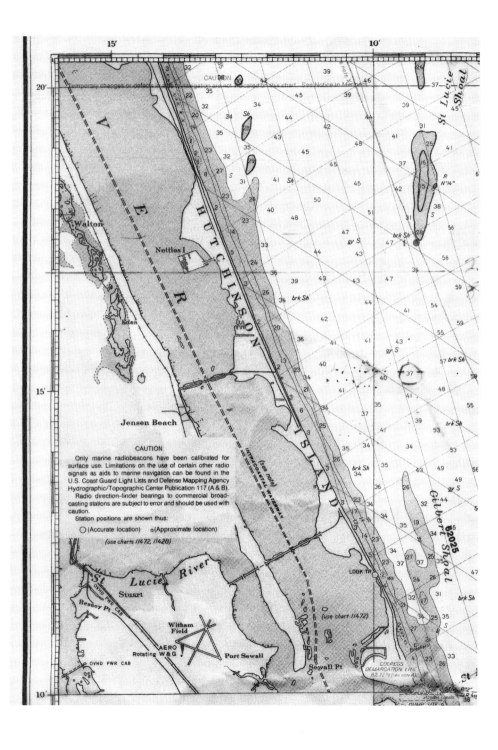

"These are the last of the coins Frank and I removed from the treasure ship in nineteen forty-nine. I want you to have them."

Lorna Belle Mobley to Mack McCray, Chapter 20, page 225.

ACKNOWLEDGEMENTS

How does one go about providing acknowledgment of all those people who provided assistance, input, constructive criticism and encouragement to one foolish enough to take on the formidable task of writing a novel? It couldn't have been done without each and everyone of them and unfortunately I cannot find words adequate to thank them enough.

Many days I looked at a blank computer screen and wondered if I could go on for another day. But, I forced myself to continue so that I would not let them down. Each if them is a driving force behind this humble effort and each of them shares significantly in its completion. However, all errors and omissions are my own responsibility and I refuse to share that credit with them.

The joy I felt when I could turn two pages of the first draft and not find any corrections and/or notations in the margins was nothing less than exhilarating! But those times were rare indeed. Yes my friends and colleagues you were brutal and to the very end and showed no mercy. And for that I thank you one and all.

Paul Mc Vey

Paul McElroy is president of Charter Industry Services, Inc. headquartered in Stuart, Florida. The company specializes in conducting professional maritime training courses. He founded *Charter Industry* a trade journal for professionals in the marine charter industry in 1985. He has extensive writing experience in magazines and newspapers with more than 200 published articles to his credit.

Captain McElroy received his first United States Coast Guard license in 1983 and operated a sport fishing charter business in the Chicago area for several years. He currently holds a Merchant Marine Officer's MASTER - Near Coastal license He served in the United States Air Force, spent a two-year tour in the Far East and specialized in electronics. He speaks Japanese and Spanish.

Mr. McElroy received his Bachelor of Science Degree in Business Administration from Florida State University. Prior to joining the maritime industry he was an executive in the headquarters of a major telecommunications corporation. He lives in south Florida with his wife Michi, is a member of the Mystery Writers of America and the National Association of Maritime Educators.

Contact him at: www.TreasureCoastMysteries.com